SPECIMEN COPY

MEN AND WOMEN

BROWNING

Men and Women

Edited with introduction
and notes by

PAUL TURNER

Lecturer in English Literature
University of Oxford

OXFORD UNIVERSITY PRESS

1972

Oxford University Press, Ely House, London W. 1

GLASGOW NEW YORK TORONTO MELBOURNE WELLINGTON
CAPE TOWN IBADAN NAIROBI DAR ES SALAAM LUSAKA ADDIS ABABA
DELHI BOMBAY CALCUTTA MADRAS KARACHI LAHORE DACCA
KUALA LUMPUR SINGAPORE HONG KONG TOKYO

PRINTED IN GREAT BRITAIN
AT THE UNIVERSITY PRESS, OXFORD
BY VIVIAN RIDLER
PRINTER TO THE UNIVERSITY

PREFACE

THIS edition is intended for use in schools and colleges as well as in universities; the abbreviated references in the Notes are probably more relevant to students at the higher level, where they will assist further research. I have tried to incorporate the most useful findings of modern Browning scholarship. Apart from the addition of line-numbers in some poems, the text is that of 1855.

I should like to express my gratitude to Dr. Park Honan (who tactfully taught me about Browning when I was his supervisor), Mr. George Bull, Mr. D. E. Olleson, Dr. C. M. Perrins, Mr. Hugo Cole, Mr. Jonathan Mayne, and Mr. and Mrs. James Turner for items of information on subjects ranging from Florentine topography to the physiognomy of swans; to the late Miss Grace Hadow (who prepared the 1911 edition) for the use of her indexes; to Miss Margaret Weedon and Miss Eileen Davies for helping me to find books I needed; to Dr. Ronald Hewitt for keeping the editorial apparatus in working order; and to Jane, my wife, for turning it on and supplying motive power.

CONTENTS

Abbreviations	ix
Introduction	xv
Browning's Life	xxix
Contents of Vol. I	3
Text of Vol. I	5
Contents of Vol. II	165
Text of Vol. II	167
Notes	313
Select Bibliography	389
Index of First Lines	391
Index of Titles	393

ABBREVIATIONS

AM   *Atlantic Monthly*.

AV   Authorized Version of the Bible.

AW   E. F. Benson, *As We Were : A Victorian Peep Show*, 1930.

B   Browning.

BA   F. Baldinucci, *Notizie*, 1846 edn.

BBI   *Baylor Browning Interests*, Baylor Univ., Waco, Texas.

BC   *The Browning Collections*, Sotheby's sale-catalogue, 1–8 May 1913.

BE   E. Berdoe, *The Browning Cyclopaedia* (1891), 1964 rpt.

BF   B. W. Fuson, *Browning and his English Predecessors in the Dramatic Monolog*, 1948.

BM   *Burlington Magazine*.

BMA   *Browning's Mind and Art*, ed. C. Tracy, 1968.

BMLA   *Bulletin of the Medical Library Association*.

BP   *Bells and Pomegranates*.

BZ   H. de Balzac, *Œuvres Complètes*, 1927.

C   *Letters of T. Carlyle to J. S. Mill, J. Sterling, and R. Browning*, ed. A. Carlyle, 1924.

CC   L. C. Collins, *Life and Memoirs of J. C. Collins*, 1912.

CH   *Browning: the Critical Heritage*, ed. B. Litzinger and D. Smalley, 1970.

CL   *Comparative Literature*.

CM   *Cornhill Magazine*, New Series.

D   W. C. DeVane, *A Browning Handbook*, 1955 edn.

D2   W. C. DeVane, *PMLA*, xl, 1925, 426–32.

DG   J. H. Miller, *The Disappearance of God*, 1963.

DK   *New Letters of R. Browning*, ed. W. C. DeVane and K. L. Knickerbocker, 1951.

dm.   dramatic monologue.

DRL	*Dramatic Romances and Lyrics*, 1845.
DRN	*De Rerum Natura.*
EB	Elizabeth Barrett Barrett (Elizabeth Barrett Browning).
EBL	E. Blom, *Stepchildren of Music*, 1925.
EBM	Memoir in *The Poems of EB*, Albion Edn., n.d.
EBP	EB, *Poetical Works*, 1889–90.
EG	E. Gibbon, *Decline and Fall of the Roman Empire* (1776–88), 1820 edn.
ELN	*English Language Notes.*
Exp.	*The Explicator.*
FB	F. Bacon, *Works*, ed. J. Spedding, R. L. Ellis, and D. D. Heath, 1857–74.
FH	F. E. Hardy, *Life of T. Hardy 1840–1928*, 1965.
FK	*Letters of EB*, ed. F. G. Kenyon, 1897.
G	R. Salvini, *All the Paintings of Giotto*, tr. P. Colacicchi, 1963.
GC	G. K. Chesterton, *Robert Browning*, 1903.
GD	Sir C. G. Duffy, *My Life in Two Hemispheres*, 1898.
GH	*Men and Women*, ed. G. E. Hadow (1911), 1971 rpt.
GM	W. H. Griffin and H. C. Minchin, *Life of R. Browning*, 1938 edn.
GR	G. M. A. Richter, *The Sculpture and Sculptors of the Greeks*, 1930.
GT	G. Tillotson, *Criticism and the Nineteenth Century*, 1951.
H	Park Honan, *Browning's Characters*, 1961.
HC	R. Holinshed, *Chronicles* (1577), 1808 edn.
HD	H. C. Duffin, *Amphibian : A Reconsideration of B*, 1956.
HM	*R. Browning : Poetry and Prose*, ed. Sir H. Milford (1941), 1966 rpt.
IA	I. Armstrong, *The Major Victorian Poets: Reconsiderations*, 1969.
JA	*Journal of Aesthetics and Art Criticism.*

JE   J. Evelyn, *Diary*, ed. A. Dobson, 1906.

JEGP   *Journal of English and Germanic Philology*.

JK   *Life, Letters and Literary Remains of J. Keats*, ed. R. M. Milnes, 1848.

JW   *R. Browning and Julia Wedgwood*, ed. R. Curle, 1937.

K   *Letters of R. Browning and EB 1845–6*, ed. E. Kintner, 1969.

L   Lucian, *Satirical Sketches*, tr. P. Turner, 1968.

LH   *EB : Letters to her Sister, 1846–1859*, ed. L. Huxley, 1931.

LL   *Learned Lady : Letters from R. Browning to Mrs. T. Fitzgerald*, ed. E. C. McAleer, 1966.

LP   *Literature and Psychology*.

LW   L. Whiting, *The Brownings*, 1911.

M   B. Miller, *R. Browning : A Portrait*, 1952.

MD   M. Dolmetsch, *Personal Recollections of A. Dolmetsch*, 1957.

MG   *Selections from the Poems of R. Browning*, ed. M. G. Glazebrook, 1936.

MH   *The Correspondence of G. M. Hopkins and R. W. Dixon*, ed. C. C. Abbott, 1935.

MI   B. Melchiori, *REL*, vii, 1966, 20–42.

ML   Sir T. Malory, *Le Morte d'Arthur*, Everyman edn., 1935.

MLN   *Modern Language Notes*.

MLQ   *Modern Language Quarterly*.

MLR   *Modern Language Review*.

MLV   *Works of T. Malory*, ed. E. Vinaver, 1967.

MP   *Modern Philology*.

MT   *Musical Times*.

MW   *Men and Women*, 1855.

N   *Nature*.

NA   J. H. Newman, *Apologia pro Vita Sua*, ed. M. J. Svaglic, 1967.

NH   Pliny, *Natural History*, Loeb edn., 1938–63.

NM   J. H. Newman, *Two Essays on Biblical and Ecclesiastical Miracles*, 1873.

NQ   *Notes and Queries.*

O   Mrs. Sutherland Orr, *A Handbook to the Works of R. Browning*, 1919.
OA   *Oxford Companion to Art*, 1970.
OC   *Oxford Dictionary of the Christian Church*, 1957.
OD   Dante, *Tutte le Opere*, ed. E. Moore, 1904.
OED   *Oxford English Dictionary.*
OL   Mrs. Sutherland Orr, *Life and Letters of R. Browning*, 1908.

P   *Parodies: An Anthology*, ed. D. Macdonald, 1964.
PD   P. Drew, *The Poetry of B : A Critical Introduction*, 1970.
PL   Milton, *Paradise Lost.*
PM   E. W. Naylor, *The Poets and Music*, 1928.
PMLA   *Publications of the Modern Language Association of America.*
PN   *MW*, ed. F. B. Pinion, 1967.
PP   J. Bunyan, *The Pilgrim's Progress* (1678), ed. J. B. Wharey, 1960.
PQ   *Philological Quarterly.*
PR   B. Melchiori, *B's Poetry of Reticence*, 1968.
PU   P. B. Shelley, *Prometheus Unbound*, 1820.

R   J. Ruskin, *Works*, ed. E. T. Cook and A. Wedderburn, 1903–12.
RA   *Rassegna d'Arte.*
RB   Robert Browning.
RC   Roman Catholic.
REL   *A Review of English Literature.*
RMI   *Rivista Musicale Italiana.*
RW   W. G. Collingwood, *Life and Work of J. Ruskin*, 1893.

S   A. Symons, *An Introduction to the Study of B*, 1906.
SEL   *Studies in English Literature.*
SH   *Shelley: Poetry and Prose*, ed. A. M. D. Hughes, 1931.
SHT   *Studies in Honour of J. C. Hodges and A. Thaler*, 1961.
SP   *Studies in Philology.*
SR   *Sewanee Review.*

st.	stanza.
T	*Letters of RB*, ed. T. L. Hood, 1933.
TH	T. Heywood, *The Hierarchie of the blessed Angells*, 1635.
TLS	*Times Literary Supplement.*
TP	G. B. Taplin, *Life of EB*, 1957.
TRB	*The Ring and the Book*, Everyman edn., ed. J. Bryson, 1962.
TSL	*Tennessee Studies in Literature.*
TV	E. D. H. Johnson, *The Alien Vision of Victorian Poetry*, 1952.
UTQ	*University of Toronto Quarterly.*
UWR	*University of Windsor Review.*
V	G. Vasari, *The Lives of the Painters, Sculptors and Architects*, Everyman edn., tr. A. B. Hinds, 1963 edn.
V1	G. Vasari, *Vite*, 1550.
V2	G. Vasari, *Vite*, 1568.
VC	*Vestiges of the Natural History of Creation* (1844), 1853 edn.
VN	*Victorian Newsletter.*
VP	*Victorian Poetry.*
VS	*Victorian Studies*
W	*MW*, ed. B. Worsfold, 1904.
WD	M. Ward, *RB and his World: The Private Face (1812–1861)*, 1967.
WP	W. S. Peterson, *Interrogating the Oracle: A History of the London Browning Society*, 1969.
WR	W. O. Raymond, *The Infinite Moment*, 1965.

INTRODUCTION

i

FACED with seventeen volumes of collected works,[1] the newcomer to Browning may well feel baffled, and wonder where to start. The answer is: with *Men and Women* (1855). *Pippa Passes* (1841) is a fascinating but hardly successful experiment. *Dramatis Personae* (1864) contains some fine lyrics and satires, but is overloaded with didacticism. *The Ring and the Book* (1868–9) is perhaps the poet's greatest achievement, but with its sordid subject, complex structure, and enormous length, it can scarcely be recommended as an easy introduction to Browning. *Men and Women*, however, is clearly his best collection of short poems, and best illustrates the character and variety of his powers.

ii

It also represents a critical phase in his personal and literary career. The story of his love for Elizabeth Barrett (a chronic invalid when he first met her), their secret marriage, and elopement to Italy is well known; and even if their relationship was not quite so idyllic as it once seemed,[2] it is hard to read their love-letters, their love-poems to one another, or Browning's account of her last illness and death (1861),[3] without feeling

---

[1] 1888–94 edn. [2] See M, pp. 164–83.
[3] T, pp. 58–63.

moved and impressed. *Men and Women* is the first
important product of this love-affair, reflecting it in
a new understanding of the problems involved in real,
as opposed to imagined, sexual relationships.

A side-effect of the marriage was an increased con-
cern with religion. Browning's mother was an ex-
tremely pious member of the Walworth Congregational
Church. When he was small, she kept him out of mis-
chief (e.g. putting a Brussels lace veil into the fire,
because of the 'pretty blaze' it made) by holding him
on her knees and telling him Bible stories. At this age
he was 'passionately religious'.[1] In adolescence, under
the influence of Voltaire and Shelley, he became for
a while an atheist; and although this phase was over
before he wrote *Pauline* (1833), he remained sufficiently
worldly to make friends with an actor (Macready) and
write several (unsuccessful) plays for the stage (1836–
46). But Elizabeth, a dissenter no less pious than
Robert's mother, encouraged him to forget about the
theatre and, 'having thought so much & deeply on life
& its ends', to teach what he had learnt 'in the
directest & most impressive way, the mask thrown
off however moist with the breath . . . it is not, I be-
lieve, by the dramatic medium, that poets teach most
impressively.'[2] The immediate result of this invitation
to religious didacticism was *Christmas-Eve and Easter-
Day* (1850), and in *Men and Women* the faintly
nauseous 'Guardian-Angel'. Elsewhere in this volume,
happily, the religious concern is dramatically ex-
pressed, e.g. through Karshish, Blougram, or Cleon,
so that even readers allergic to piety can enjoy the

[1] OL, pp. 22–5.
[2] 25 May 1846; K, ii. 732.

realism of the 'mask', and avert their eyes from any didactic 'moisture' that seeps through.

When Robert first wrote to Elizabeth in 1845, he was already thinking of returning to Italy, and her state of health was another reason for going there. Their Italian experiences are constantly reflected in the volume, most effectively, perhaps, in the poems about painters like Fra Lippo Lippi and Andrea del Sarto, whose pictures they saw in Florence. Elizabeth had not much interest in music, but Italy gave Robert many opportunities of indulging his. At Vallombrosa he played the organ that Milton had played two hundred years before; and at Casa Guidi, their home in Florence, a visitor once found him 'playing with all his heart and soul on a grand piano'.[1] He may even have had access to a clavichord, although the instrument shown to Arnold Dolmetsch in Florence as 'Browning's clavichord' turned out to be a square piano.[2] Such active music-making, with some more passive opera-going, gave rise to poems like 'Master Hugues' and 'A Toccata of Galuppi's'.

iii

In Browning's literary fortunes also *Men and Women* marks a turning-point. Before it he had failed, both as a playwright and as a poet. *Sordello* (1840), which was meant to be 'more popular'[3] than *Paracelsus* (1835), was ignored or badly reviewed by the critics, and by 1855 had sold only 157 copies from an edition of 500. *Men and Women* was intended to make the

---

[1] EBM, p. xix.   [2] MD, p. 27.
[3] Preface to *Paracelsus*.

public forget about *Sordello*. It was written as 'a first step towards popularity for me'[1] (Elizabeth's poetry was already popular). 'I hope to be listened to, this time', he wrote (2 April 1854);[2] but once more popularity seemed to have escaped him. 'It is really high time', said the *Saturday Review*, 'that this sort of thing should, if possible, be stopped. Here is another book of madness and mysticism.'[3] *Blackwood's* remarked: 'There is no getting through the confused crowd of Mr. Browning's Men and Women.'[4] Other reviews, including one by George Eliot, were more favourable; but nobody seemed to realize the true value of the poems, except the young Pre-Raphaelites. 'What a magnificent series is *Men and Women*', wrote D. G. Rossetti in a private letter. '. . . The comparative stagnation, even among those I see, and complete torpor elsewhere, which greet this my Elixir of Life, are awful signs of the times to me';[5] and William Morris, in the short-lived *Oxford and Cambridge Magazine*,[6] placed Browning 'high among the poets of all time, and I scarce know whether first, or second, in our own; and it is a bitter thing to see the way in which he is received by almost everybody . . . Yes, I wonder what the critics would have said to *Hamlet, Prince of Denmark*, if it had been first published by Messrs. Chapman and Hall in the year 1855.' Sales were enough to clear expenses, but they soon fell off; and to his publisher Browning expressed his acute disappointment: 'don't take to heart the zoological utterances I have stopped my ears against . . . of late.

[1] GM, p. 189.   [2] DK, p. 77.
[3] CH, p. 158.   [4] *Blackwood's*, lxxix, 1856, 135.
[5] CH, p. 161.   [6] CH, pp. 195–6.

"Whoo-oo-oo-oo" mouths the big monkey—"Whee-ee-ee-ee" squeaks the little monkey and such a dig with the end of my umbrella as I should give the brutes if I couldn't keep my temper, and consider how they miss their nuts and gingerbread!' 'As to my own poems—they must be left to Providence and that fine sense of discrimination which I never cease to meditate upon and admire in the public: they cry out for new things and when you furnish them with what they cried for, "it's *so* new", they grunt.'[1]

Gradually, however, the view of *Men and Women* taken by a very small minority (which included Carlyle and Ruskin) began to spread, and although in *The Ring and the Book* (1868–9) Browning could still address the British Public as 'ye who like me not' (i, 410), they were already beginning to like him a great deal, and by 1873 at least one of them was under medical treatment for a delusion that Browning's voice was the voice of God.[2] In 1881 the Browning Society was founded, to explicate and publicize his work. It organized public Browning recitations, to one of which Society members secured admittance by wearing brown velveteen shooting coats.[3] Soon there were hundreds of Browning societies and clubs in America, and the Philadelphia Public Library announced that Browning was the most widely read of all modern English poets. It has sometimes been thought puzzling that a man of Browning's intelligence and sense of humour should not have objected to all this ridiculous adulation; but he solved the problem quite adequately when he said: 'Object to it ?

[1] DK, pp. 85, 92.   [2] WP, p. 3.
[3] WP, pp. 158–9.

No, I like it! . . . I have waited forty years for it, and
now—I like it!'[1]

iv

The poems in *Men and Women* are mostly dramatic
monologues. This form (for which the nineteenth-
century term was 'monodrama') has been recently
defined as 'a single discourse by one whose presence
is indicated by the poet but who is not the poet
himself'.[2] The discourse normally describes feelings,
thoughts, and events contemporaneous with the speak-
ing of the discourse (or the writing of it, when it takes
the form of a letter) ; and there is often an audience
of one or more people, whose reactions, comments,
replies, or objections are expressed or implied by the
monologue-speaker. Any story that the dramatic
monologue has to tell is usually told indirectly through
quasi-stage-directions inserted into the text of the
speech itself.

The form is extremely ancient. *Idyll* ii of Theocritus
(third century B.C.), spoken by a girl practising witch-
craft to bring back her unfaithful lover, is an early
example of the spoken variety, and the *Heroides*
of Ovid (43 B.C.–A.D. 18), written by mythological
females to their lovers, of the epistolary type. In
English literature the form had been used by at least
200 poets before 1840,[3] most effectively, perhaps,
in Tennyson's 'St Simeon Stylites' (written 1833).
Browning made the form his speciality, taking an
individual line in avoiding traditional monologic
situations (death-beds, betrayed women, exiles, etc.),

[1] WP, p. 178.   [2] H, p. 122.   [3] BF, p. 90.

and shifting the focus 'from melodrama and exploitation of emotion' to 'psychological subtlety'.[1] He developed a brilliant technique for conveying, through natural speech, a whole range of oblique information about the speaker's situation, environment, and audience, and, above all, about his character. Much of this character revelation is made to appear involuntary. The speaker may be trying to defend or justify himself, to project an image of himself that will win his audience's approval; but through his very words and allusions he unconsciously betrays what he is really like. This ingenious technique of apparently unconscious self-revelation, by contradictions between a speaker's intentions and the impression that he actually makes on the reader, may be regarded as a highly sophisticated extension of dramatic irony.

Why did Browning choose to write dramatic monologues? Perhaps because he had too complex a personality to be satisfied with expressing any single view of life.

> I cannot chain my soul: it will not rest
> In its clay prison, this most narrow sphere:
> It has strange impulse, tendency, desire,
> Which nowise I account for nor explain,
> But cannot stifle, being bound to trust
> All feelings equally, to hear all sides . . .
>
> (*Pauline*, 593–8)

Pauline was written

in pursuance of a foolish plan which occupied me mightily for a time, and which had for its object the enabling me to assume & realize I know not how many different

[1] BF, pp. 90–1.

characters; — meanwhile the world was never to guess that 'Brown, Smith, Jones & Robinson' . . . the respective authors of this poem, the other novel, such an opera, such a speech, etc. etc. were no other than one and the same individual.[1]

The dramatic monologue may also have served Browning as a device for freeing his moral judgement from the rigid code of ethics under which he had been brought up; for he often used the form to defend apparently indefensible characters. The theory of this is stated in *Sordello* (iii. 786 ff.):

> . . . ask, moreover, when they prate
> Of evil men past hope, 'Don't each contrive,
> Despite the evil you abuse, to live ? —
> Keeping, each losel, through a maze of lies,
> His own conceit of truth ? to which he hies
> By obscure windings, tortuous, if you will,
> But to himself not inaccessible;
> He sees truth, and his lies are for the crowd
> Who cannot see; some fancied right allowed
> His vilest wrong, empowered the losel [to] clutch
> One pleasure from a multitude of such
> Denied him'.

Browning's first attempt to express the 'conceit of truth', the subjective view of the world which justifies an 'evil' man to himself, was the early dramatic monologue spoken by a murderer, 'Porphyria's Lover' (1836). Another exercise in a somewhat similar style was the prose *Essay* on the literary forger, Chatterton (1842). The climax of such moral acrobatics is reached in the two great monologues of the wife-murderer

---

[1] RB's MS. note in J. S. Mill's copy of *Pauline*; D, p. 41.

Guido in *The Ring and the Book*; but 'Bishop Blougram's Apology' in the present volume probably belongs to the same category. In all these cases Browning, like Shakespeare with Shylock, appears to condemn, even while doing his utmost to defend. Thus the form gave him scope to express his own ambivalence, 'by talking out of both sides of his mouth' simultaneously.[1]

Browning himself insisted that his poems were 'always dramatic in principle, and so many utterances of so many imaginary persons, not mine',[2] and denied in a letter to Ruskin that he ever consciously expressed himself through his characters.[3] In fact he felt some difficulty in expressing himself directly. To Elizabeth he wrote: 'you *do* what I always wanted, hoped to do, and only seem now likely to do for the first time. You speak out, *you*,—I only make men & women speak— give you truth broken into prismatic hues, & fear the pure white light, even if it is in me: but I am going to try . . .'[4]

. . . These scenes and song-scraps *are* such mere and very escapes of my inner power, which lives in me like the light in those crazy Mediterranean phares I have watched at sea, wherein the light is ever revolving in a dark gallery, bright and alive, and only after a weary interval leaps out, for a moment, from the one narrow chink, and then goes on with the blind wall between it and you; and, no doubt, *then*, precisely, does the poor drudge that carries the cresset set himself most busily to trim the wick . . .[5]

[1] R. D. Altick, SEL, iii, 1963, 449.
[2] Preface to *Poetical Works*, 1868.
[3] R, xxxvi, p. xxxv.   [4] 13 Jan. 1845, K, i. 7.
[5] 11 Feb. 1845, K, i. 17–18.

What, then, was the 'blind wall'? Possibly the excessive fear of self-exposure, the 'male prudery' which prevented him from sharing a bedroom with his wife, and had made him, as a small child, edge his way along his bedroom wall 'because he was not fully clothed, and his reflection in the glass could otherwise have been seen through the partly open door'.[1] His first publication, *Pauline*, though part of a scheme for multiple impersonation, was recognized as autobiography by John Stuart Mill, who had been asked to review it; and Browning's embarrassment at this involuntary self-betrayal may have frightened him into adopting the mask of the dramatic monologue from then on.[2] The mask probably served a further strategic purpose when Browning wished to attack contemporary orthodoxy, as in Fra Lippo Lippi's vindication of 'grass', i.e. 'The value and significance of flesh':

> What would men have? Do they like grass or no—
> May they or mayn't they? all I want's the thing
> Settled for ever one way: as it is,
> You tell too many lies and hurt yourself.
> You don't like what you only like too much,
> You do like what, if given you at your word,
> You find abundantly detestable.

Lippi gave Browning a useful alibi for this bold assault on the Victorian attitude to sex.

v

Relations between Browning and the Victorians were never wholly easy. At first they refused to read him, because he was 'obscure' and 'unmusical', by

[1] OL, pp. 24–5; M, pp. 104–8.　　　[2] D, pp. 45–7.

which they meant that they could not understand him, and had no ear for his music (Donne suffered similarly from their intellectual and aesthetic incapacity). When they did understand him, they disapproved of his ideas. Thus the *Quarterly* complained that his 'mode of thought, without being anti-English, constantly bears an indescribable savour of the continent'; and the *Christian Remembrancer* was shocked by the ethics of 'The Statue and the Bust'.[1] Later, perhaps appeased by the subject-matter (religion versus science) which had helped to make Tennyson's *In Memoriam* (1850) their favourite poem, and protected by inadequate understanding from the full impact of Browning's ideas, they decided that he was primarily a religious and ethical teacher, and it was as 'the greatest Christian philosophic poet now living' that he was chiefly discussed by the Browning Society.[2] What they liked best about him was 'his admirable optimism and heartiness, his assurance that apparent failure may be success in the eyes of heaven, his glorification of romantic passion, and above all his Christianity'.[3] Their belief in his 'optimism' presumably survived the massive contradiction of *The Ring and the Book*, by the simple process of ignoring Guido, and concentrating on Pompilia, a heroine apparently constructed on the Little Nell formula.

vi

The modern reader is unlikely to find Browning particularly obscure or unmusical. Our norm in these

[1] WD, p. 248.   [2] WP, pp. 109–11.
[3] WP, p. 110.

matters is now based, not on Tennyson, but on T. S. Eliot and his successors. We expect poetry to be difficult, and we no longer expect it to be 'poetical'. Most of us will be satisfied with Browning's own defence of his 'obscurity', in a letter to Ruskin (10 December 1855):

We don't read poetry the same way, by the same law; it is too clear. I cannot begin writing poetry till my imaginary reader has conceded licences to me which you demur at altogether. I *know* that I don't make out my conception by my language; all poetry being a putting the infinite within the finite. You would have me paint it all plain out, which can't be; but by various artifices I try to make shift with touches and bits of outlines which *succeed* if they bear the conception from me to you. You ought, I think, to keep pace with the thought tripping from ledge to ledge of my 'glaciers', as you call them; not stand poking your alpenstock into the holes, and demonstrating that no foot could have stood there;— suppose it sprang over there? In *prose* you may criticise so—because that is the absolute representation of portions of truth, what chronicling is to history—but in asking for more *ultimates* you must accept less *mediates*, nor expect that a Druid stone-circle will be traced for you with as few breaks to the eye as the North Crescent and South Crescent that go together so cleverly in many a suburb.[1]

This does not mean that Browning's poetry is impressionistic, that there is no 'prose-meaning' to be found in his words. In this volume at least, the 'stone-circle' can be traced with reasonable certainty, even if it sometimes needs a little spadework. As Browning told Carlyle, apropos of *Men and Women*:

[1] RW, p. 200 (R, xxxvi, pp. xxxiv–xxxv).

'I never designed to puzzle people, as some of my critics have supposed. On the other hand, I never pretended to offer such literature as should be a substitute for a cigar or a game of dominoes to an idle man.'[1] In this edition most of the necessary spadework has been done, I hope, in the Notes; for reasons of space, however, these do not normally contain explanations of words which appear in the *Concise Oxford Dictionary*.

So much for the 'difficulty' of Browning's style: what of its positive merits ? The greatest are immediacy, vitality, and freedom from literary convention. His manner was described by Gerard Manley Hopkins as 'a way of talking (and making his people talk) with the air and spirit of a man bouncing up from table with his mouth full of bread and cheese and saying that he meant to stand no blasted nonsense'.[2] This was not meant as a compliment, but it does suggest one admirable feature of Browning's poetry, its capacity not merely to describe, but to embody and present physical experience. 'He wants his words to be thick and substantial, and to carry the solid stuff of reality. He . . . manages, before every other poet, to convey the bump, bump, bump of blood coursing through the veins, the breathless rush of excited bodily life, the vital pulse of the visceral level of existence, the sense of rapid motion.'[3] This is the real justification for the liberties that he takes with syntax; and the result of this aspiration towards the condition of physical sensation is that his *Men and Women* often seem to come almost literally to life—a miracle which

[1] C, p. 299.   [2] MH, p. 74.
[3] DG, pp. 118–21.

Browning was later to call 'mimic creation, galvanism for life', by which the artist

> May so project his surplusage of soul,
> In search of body, so add self to self
> By owning what lay ownerless before . . .
> That, although nothing which had never life
> Shall get life from him, be, not having been,
> Yet, something dead may get to live again . . .[1]

The chief pleasure, then, to be got from these poems is probably the illusion of participating in the resurrection of various quasi-historical characters. There is also the pleasure of admiring Browning's virtuoso performance, the ingenuity of his technique, and the astonishing 'surplusage' of mental activity which spills over into so many original creations.

And what of the great thinker and teacher? Few readers now, perhaps, will find his religious ideas very helpful, though many will sympathize with his disgust at 'religious' sadism. His greatest appeal for our age may be his psychological insight, and his reluctance to make explicit moral judgements. He appears in these poems, not as a sage who can tell us how to live, but as an intelligent, sensitive, and attractive person, who realizes, as few Victorians did, the complexity of life. We shall not, in this century, mistake his voice for the voice of God; but we may not be too deluded if we hear in it the authentic voice of humanity.

[1] TRB, i. 723–9.

BROWNING'S LIFE

1812 (7 May)	Born at Southampton Street, Camberwell, son of Robert Browning and Sarah Anna Wiedemann Browning, daughter of a German and a Scotswoman.
c. 1820–6	Weekly boarder at school in Peckham.
c. 1824	Volume of poems, 'Incondita', sent by parents to publishers without success.
1826	Reads Voltaire and Shelley.
1828 (30 June)	Enrolled at new London University to read Greek, German, Latin, but leaves for home in second term.
1833 (March)	*Pauline* published; reads J. S. Mill's 'not flattering' comments (30 October).
1834 (March–April)	Visits St. Petersburg with Russian consul-general.
1835	*Paracelsus.*
1836	'Johannes Agricola' and 'Porphyria's Lover' published in *Monthly Repository* (January).
1836 (26 May)	Meets Macready, who asks him to write a tragedy.
1837 (May)	*Strafford* published and performed five times at Covent Garden.
1838 (April–July)	First visit to Italy (Venice in June).
1840 (March)	*Sordello* published, and fails.
1841 (April)	*Pippa Passes* published as first of eight pamphlets called *Bells and Pomegranates* (BP).
1842 (March, November)	BP ii, iii (*King Victor and King Charles*, *Dramatic Lyrics*).

1843 (January, February) BP iv, v (*The Return of the Druses,
                          A Blot in the 'Scutcheon*); latter performed
                          three times at Drury Lane, and fails.

1844 (April)   BP vi (*Colombe's Birthday*).

     (August or September–December) Second trip to Italy
                   (Naples and Rome).

1845 (10 January) First letter to EB (born 1806): 'I love your
                  verses with all my heart . . . and I love you
                  too.'

     (20 May)   First meeting with EB at 50 Wimpole St.

     (6 November) BP vii (*Dramatic Romances and Lyrics*).

1846 (13 April)   BP viii (*Luria and A Soul's Tragedy*).

     (12 September) Marries EB secretly at St. Marylebone
                    Church.

     (19 September) Leaves England with his wife and settles
                    at Pisa.

1847 (April)   They move to Florence; (July) visit Vallom-
                   brosa.

1848 (May)   They take unfurnished rooms in Palazzo
                   Guidi (Casa Guidi) and make it their home.

     (July)   Trip to Fano, Ancona, Rimini, Ravenna.

1849 (January)   *Poems* (2 vols.).

     (9 March)   Birth of only son, Robert Wiedemann
                   Barrett Browning (Penini, Pen).

     (18 March)   RB's mother dies.

     (July–October) Trip to Lerici, Bagni di Lucca, Prato
                    Fiorito.

1850 (1 April)   *Christmas-Eve and Easter-Day*.

     (September)   Trip to Siena.

     (November)   EB's *Sonnets from the Portuguese* published.

1851 (2 May)   Leave for Venice (May–June), Paris (July),
                   London (July–November), Paris (October
                   1851–June 1852), London (July–November).
                   Back to Florence by mid-November.

1853 (April)   *Colombe's Birthday* produced seven times at Haymarket Theatre and well reviewed.

(July–September) At Bagni di Lucca.

(November 1853–May 1854) In Rome.

1855 (June–October) In London (13 Dorset St.).

(October–June 1856) In Paris.

(17 November 1855) MW published in 2 vols.

1856 (July–September) In England (London, Ventnor, West Cowes, Taunton). EB's *Aurora Leigh* published (15 November): an enormous success.

(October)   Back to Florence.

1861 (29 June)   EB dies.

(August)   RB leaves Florence with son.

1862 (June)   Settles at 19 Warwick Crescent, London, W.

1863   *Poetical Works* (3 vols.).

1864   *Dramatis Personae.*

1867   Made honorary M.A. of Oxford University, and honorary Fellow of Balliol College.

1868   *Poetical Works* (6 vols.).

1868–9   *The Ring and the Book.*

1869   (Alleged proposal to Lady Ashburton, T, pp. 325–8.)

1871   *Balaustion's Adventure. Prince Hohenstiel-Schwangau.*

1872   *Fifine at the Fair.*

1873   *Red Cotton Night-Cap Country.*

1875   *Aristophanes' Apology. The Inn Album.*

1876   *Pacchiarotto.*

1877   *The Agamemnon of Aeschylus Transcribed* (i.e. literally translated).

1878   *La Saisiaz* and *The Two Poets of Croisic.*

1879   *Dramatic Idyls.*

1880   *Dramatic Idyls Second Series.*

1881   Browning Society founded. RB: 'I had no
            more to do with the founding of it than the
            babe unborn . . . I am quite other than a
            Browningite.'

1883   *Jocoseria.*

1884   *Ferishtah's Fancies.*

1887   *Parleyings with Certain People of Importance
            in their Day.*

1888–9   *Poetical Works* (16 vols.; vol. xvii, 1894).

1889 (12 December) *Asolando* published. Dies at Venice in
            son's home (Palazzo Rezzonico) from bron-
            chitis, having read telegram: 'Reviews in
            all this day's papers most favourable,
            edition nearly exhausted.'

    (31 December) Buried in Poets' Corner, Westminster
            Abbey.

MEN AND WOMEN

BY

ROBERT BROWNING

IN TWO VOLUMES

VOL. I.

LONDON

CHAPMAN AND HALL, 193, PICCADILLY.

1855

CONTENTS

———•———

	Page
LOVE AMONG THE RUINS	5
A LOVERS' QUARREL	9
EVELYN HOPE	16
UP AT A VILLA—DOWN IN THE CITY. (AS DISTINGUISHED BY AN ITALIAN PERSON OF QUALITY.)	19
A WOMAN'S LAST WORD	24
FRA LIPPO LIPPI	26
A TOCCATA OF GALUPPI'S	39
BY THE FIRE-SIDE	43
ANY WIFE TO ANY HUSBAND	54
AN EPISTLE CONTAINING THE STRANGE MEDICAL EXPERIENCE OF KARSHISH, THE ARAB PHYSICIAN . . .	60
MESMERISM	70
A SERENADE AT THE VILLA	76
MY STAR	79

CONTENTS

	Page
INSTANS TYRANNUS	80
A PRETTY WOMAN	83
"CHILDE ROLAND TO THE DARK TOWER CAME."	87
RESPECTABILITY	95
A LIGHT WOMAN	96
THE STATUE AND THE BUST	99
LOVE IN A LIFE	109
LIFE IN A LOVE	110
HOW IT STRIKES A CONTEMPORARY	111
THE LAST RIDE TOGETHER	115
THE PATRIOT.—AN OLD STORY	120
MASTER HUGUES OF SAXE-GOTHA	122
BISHOP BLOUGRAM'S APOLOGY	128
MEMORABILIA	162

MEN AND WOMEN

LOVE AMONG THE RUINS

1.

Where the quiet-coloured end of evening smiles
      Miles and miles
On the solitary pastures where our sheep
      Half-asleep
Tinkle homeward thro' the twilight, stray or stop
      As they crop—

2.

Was the site once of a city great and gay,
      (So they say)
Of our country's very capital, its prince
      Ages since
Held his court in, gathered councils, wielding far
      Peace or war.

3.

Now—the country does not even boast a tree,
　　　　As you see,
To distinguish slopes of verdure, certain rills
　　　　From the hills
Intersect and give a name to, (else they run
　　　　Into one)

4.

Where the domed and daring palace shot its spires
　　　　Up like fires
O'er the hundred-gated circuit of a wall
　　　　Bounding all,
Made of marble, men might march on nor be prest,
　　　　Twelve abreast.

5.

And such plenty and perfection, see, of grass
　　　　Never was !
Such a carpet as, this summer-time, o'erspreads
　　　　And embeds
Every vestige of the city, guessed alone,
　　　　Stock or stone—

6.

Where a multitude of men breathed joy and woe
　　　　Long ago ;
Lust of glory pricked their hearts up, dread of shame
　　　　Struck them tame ;
And that glory and that shame alike, the gold
　　　　Bought and sold.

7.

Now,—the single little turret that remains
    On the plains,
By the caper overrooted, by the gourd
    Overscored,
While the patching houseleek's head of blossom winks
    Through the chinks—

8.

Marks the basement whence a tower in ancient time
    Sprang sublime,
And a burning ring all round, the chariots traced
    As they raced,
And the monarch and his minions and his dames
    Viewed the games.

9.

And I know, while thus the quiet-coloured eve
    Smiles to leave
To their folding, all our many-tinkling fleece
    In such peace,
And the slopes and rills in undistinguished grey
    Melt away—

10.

That a girl with eager eyes and yellow hair
    Waits me there
In the turret, whence the charioteers caught soul
    For the goal,   [dumb
When the king looked, where she looks now, breathless,
    Till I come.

11.

But he looked upon the city, every side,
          Far and wide,
All the mountains topped with temples, all the glades'
          Colonnades,
All the causeys, bridges, aqueducts,—and then,
          All the men !

12.

When I do come, she will speak not, she will stand,
          Either hand
On my shoulder, give her eyes the first embrace
          Of my face,
Ere we rush, ere we extinguish sight and speech
          Each on each.

13.

In one year they sent a million fighters forth
          South and north,
And they built their gods a brazen pillar high
          As the sky,
Yet reserved a thousand chariots in full force—
          Gold, of course.

14.

Oh, heart ! oh, blood that freezes, blood that burns !
          Earth's returns
For whole centuries of folly, noise and sin !
          Shut them in,
With their triumphs and their glories and the rest.
          Love is best !

A LOVERS' QUARREL

———•———

1.

Oh, what a dawn of day!
How the March sun feels like May!
    All is blue again
    After last night's rain,
And the South dries the hawthorn-spray.
    Only, my Love's away!
I'd as lief that the blue were grey.

2.

Runnels, which rillets swell,
Must be dancing down the dell
    With a foamy head
    On the beryl bed
Paven smooth as a hermit's cell;
    Each with a tale to tell,
Could my Love but attend as well.

3.

Dearest, three months ago !
When we lived blocked-up with snow,—
When the wind would edge
In and in his wedge,
In, as far as the point could go—
Not to our ingle, though,
Where we loved each the other so !

4.

Laughs with so little cause !
We devised games out of straws.
We would try and trace
One another's face
In the ash, as an artist draws ;
Free on each other's flaws,
How we chattered like two church daws !

5.

What's in the " Times ? "—a scold
At the emperor deep and cold ;
He has taken a bride
To his gruesome side,
That's as fair as himself is bold :
There they sit ermine-stoled,
And she powders her hair with gold.

6.

Fancy the Pampas' sheen !
Miles and miles of gold and green

Where the sun-flowers blow
In a solid glow,
And to break now and then the screen—
Black neck and eyeballs keen,
Up a wild horse leaps between !

7.

Try, will our table turn ?
Lay your hands there light, and yearn
Till the yearning slips
Thro' the finger tips
In a fire which a few discern,
And a very few feel burn,
And the rest, they may live and learn !

8.

Then we would up and pace,
For a change, about the place,
Each with arm o'er neck.
'Tis our quarter-deck,
We are seamen in woeful case.
Help in the ocean-space !
Or, if no help, we'll embrace.

9.

See, how she looks now, drest
In a sledging-cap and vest.
'Tis a huge fur cloak—
Like a reindeer's yoke
Falls the lappet along the breast :
Sleeves for her arms to rest,
Or to hang, as my Love likes best.

10.

Teach me to flirt a fan
As the Spanish ladies can,
      Or I tint your lip
      With a burnt stick's tip
And you turn into such a man !
      Just the two spots that span
Half the bill of the young male swan.

11.

Dearest, three months ago
When the mesmeriser Snow
      With his hand's first sweep
      Put the earth to sleep,
'Twas a time when the heart could show
      All—how was earth to know,
'Neath the mute hand's to-and-fro !

12.

Dearest, three months ago
When we loved each other so,
      Lived and loved the same
      Till an evening came
When a shaft from the Devil's bow
      Pierced to our ingle-glow,
And the friends were friend and foe !

13.

Not from the heart beneath—
'Twas a bubble born of breath,

Neither sneer nor vaunt,
Nor reproach nor taunt.
See a word, how it severeth !
Oh, power of life and death
In the tongue, as the Preacher saith !

14.

Woman, and will you cast
For a word, quite off at last,
Me, your own, your you,—
Since, as Truth is true,
I was you all the happy past—
Me do you leave aghast
With the memories we amassed ?

15.

Love, if you knew the light
That your soul casts in my sight,
How I look to you
For the pure and true,
And the beauteous and the right,—
Bear with a moment's spite
When a mere mote threats the white !

16.

What of a hasty word ?
Is the fleshly heart not stirred
By a worm's pin-prick
Where its roots are quick ?
See the eye, by a fly's-foot blurred—
Ear, when a straw is heard
Scratch the brain's coat of curd !

17.

Foul be the world or fair,
More or less, how can I care ?
    'Tis the world the same
    For my praise or blame,
And endurance is easy there.
    Wrong in the one thing rare—
Oh, it is hard to bear !

18.

Here's the spring back or close,
When the almond-blossom blows ;
    We shall have the word
    In that minor third
There is none but the cuckoo knows—
    Heaps of the guelder-rose !
I must bear with it, I suppose.

19.

Could but November come,
Were the noisy birds struck dumb
    At the warning slash
    Of his driver's-lash—
I would laugh like the valiant Thumb
    Facing the castle glum
And the giant's fee-faw-fum !

20.

Then, were the world well stript
Of the gear wherein equipped

We can stand apart,
Heart dispense with heart
In the sun, with the flowers unnipped,—
Oh, the world's hangings ripped,
We were both in a bare-walled crypt !

21.

Each in the crypt would cry
" But one freezes here ! and why ?
When a heart as chill
At my own would thrill
Back to life, and its fires out-fly ?
Heart, shall we live or die ?
The rest, . . . settle it by and by ! "

22.

So, she'd efface the score,
And forgive me as before.
Just at twelve o'clock
I shall hear her knock
In the worst of a storm's uproar--
I shall pull her through the door—
I shall have her for evermore !

EVELYN HOPE

1.

BEAUTIFUL Evelyn Hope is dead
  Sit and watch by her side an hour.
That is her book-shelf, this her bed ;
  She plucked that piece of geranium-flower,
Beginning to die too, in the glass.
  Little has yet been changed, I think—
The shutters are shut, no light may pass
  Save two long rays thro' the hinge's chink.

2.

Sixteen years old when she died !
  Perhaps she had scarcely heard my name—
It was not her time to love : beside,
  Her life had many a hope and aim,
Duties enough and little cares,
  And now was quiet, now astir—
Till God's hand beckoned unawares,
  And the sweet white brow is all of her.

3.

Is it too late then, Evelyn Hope ?
  What, your soul was pure and true,
The good stars met in your horoscope,
  Made you of spirit, fire and dew—
And just because I was thrice as old,
  And our paths in the world diverged so wide,
Each was nought to each, must I be told ?
  We were fellow mortals, nought beside ?

4.

No, indeed ! for God above
  Is great to grant, as mighty to make,
And creates the love to reward the love,—
  I claim you still, for my own love's sake !
Delayed it may be for more lives yet,
  Through worlds I shall traverse, not a few—
Much is to learn and much to forget
  Ere the time be come for taking you.

5.

But the time will come,—at last it will,
  When, Evelyn Hope, what meant, I shall say,
In the lower earth, in the years long still,
  That body and soul so pure and gay ?
Why your hair was amber, I shall divine,
  And your mouth of your own geranium's red—
And what you would do with me, in fine,
  In the new life come in the old one's stead.

6.

I have lived, I shall say, so much since then,
 Given up myself so many times,
Gained me the gains of various men,
 Ransacked the ages, spoiled the climes ;
Yet one thing, one, in my soul's full scope,
 Either I missed or itself missed me—
And I want and find you, Evelyn Hope !
 What is the issue ? let us see !

7.

I loved you, Evelyn, all the while ;
 My heart seemed full as it could hold—
There was place and to spare for the frank young smile
 And the red young mouth and the hair's young gold.
So, hush,—I will give you this leaf to keep—
 See, I shut it inside the sweet cold hand.
There, that is our secret ! go to sleep ;
 You will wake, and remember, and understand.

UP AT A VILLA—DOWN IN THE CITY

(AS DISTINGUISHED BY AN ITALIAN PERSON OF QUALITY.)

———

1.

HAD I but plenty of money, money enough and to spare,
The house for me, no doubt, were a house in the city-
    square.
Ah, such a life, such a life, as one leads at the window
    there !

2.

Something to see, by Bacchus, something to hear, at
    least !
There, the whole day long, one's life is a perfect feast ;
While up at a villa one lives, I maintain it, no more than
    a beast.

3.

Well now, look at our villa ! stuck like the horn of
    a bull
Just on a mountain's edge as bare as the creature's skull,
Save a mere shag of a bush with hardly a leaf to pull !
—I scratch my own, sometimes, to see if the hair's turned
    wool.

4.

But the city, oh the city—the square with the houses !
　　　Why ?
They are stone-faced, white as a curd, there's something
　　　to take the eye !
Houses in four straight lines, not a single front awry !
You watch who crosses and gossips, who saunters, who
　　　hurries by :
Green blinds, as a matter of course, to draw when the
　　　sun gets high ;
And the shops with fanciful signs which are painted
　　　properly.

5.

What of a villa ?　Though winter be over in March by
　　　rights,
'Tis May perhaps ere the snow shall have withered well
　　　off the heights :
You've the brown ploughed land before, where the oxen
　　　steam and wheeze,
And the hills over-smoked behind by the faint grey olive
　　　trees.

6.

Is it better in May I ask you ? you've summer all at
　　　once ;
In a day he leaps complete with a few strong April suns !
'Mid the sharp short emerald wheat, scarce risen three
　　　fingers well,

The wild tulip, at end of its tube, blows out its great red
    bell,
Like a thin clear bubble of blood, for the children to pick
    and sell.

7.

Is it ever hot in the square ?   There's a fountain to spout
    and splash !
In the shade it sings and springs ; in the shine such foam-
    bows flash
On the horses with curling fish-tails, that prance and
    paddle and pash
Round the lady atop in the conch—fifty gazers do not
    abash,
Though all that she wears is some weeds round her waist
    in a sort of sash !

8.

All the year long at the villa, nothing's to see though
    you linger,
Except yon cypress that points like Death's lean lifted
    forefinger.
Some think fireflies pretty, when they mix in the corn
    and mingle,
Or thrid the stinking hemp till the stalks of it seem
    a-tingle.
Late August or early September, the stunning cicala is
    shrill,
And the bees keep their tiresome whine round the
    resinous firs on the hill.
Enough of the seasons,—I spare you the months of the
    fever and chill.

9.

Ere opening your eyes in the city, the blessed church-
      bells begin :
No sooner the bells leave off, than the diligence rattles in :
You get the pick of the news, and it costs you never a pin.
By and by there's the travelling doctor gives pills, lets
      blood, draws teeth ;
Or the Pulcinello-trumpet breaks up the market beneath.
At the post-office such a scene-picture—the new play,
      piping hot !
And a notice how, only this morning, three liberal thieves
      were shot.
Above it, behold the archbishop's most fatherly of
      rebukes,
And beneath, with his crown and his lion, some little
      new law of the Duke's !
Or a sonnet with flowery marge, to the Reverend Don
      So-and-so
Who is Dante, Boccaccio, Petrarca, Saint Jerome, and
      Cicero,
" And moreover," (the sonnet goes rhyming,) " the skirts
      of St. Paul has reached,
Having preached us those six Lent-lectures more unc-
      tuous than ever he preached."
Noon strikes,—here sweeps the procession ! our Lady
      borne smiling and smart
With a pink gauze gown all spangles, and seven swords
      stuck in her heart !
Bang, whang, whang, goes the drum, *tootle-te-tootle* the fife ;
No keeping one's haunches still : it's the greatest pleasure
      in life.

10.

But bless you, it's dear—it's dear ! fowls, wine, at double
the rate.

They have clapped a new tax upon salt, and what oil
pays passing the gate

It's a horror to think of.   And so, the villa for me, not
the city !

Beggars can scarcely be choosers—but still—ah, the pity,
the pity !

Look, two and two go the priests, then the monks with
cowls and sandals,

And the penitents dressed in white shirts, a-holding the
yellow candles.

One, he carries a flag up straight, and another a cross
with handles,

And the Duke's guard brings up the rear, for the better
prevention of scandals.

Bang, *whang*, *whang*, goes the drum, *tootle-te-tootle* the
fife.

Oh, a day in the city-square, there is no such pleasure in
life !

A WOMAN'S LAST WORD

1.

LET'S contend no more, Love,
   Strive nor weep—
All be as before, Love,
   —Only sleep !

2.

What so wild as words are ?
   —I and thou
In debate, as birds are,
   Hawk on bough !

3.

See the creature stalking
   While we speak—
Hush and hide the talking,
   Cheek on cheek !

4.

What so false as truth is,
   False to thee ?
Where the serpent's tooth is,
   Shun the tree—

5.

Where the apple reddens
    Never pry—
Lest we lose our Edens,
    Eve and I !

6.

Be a god and hold me
    With a charm—
Be a man and fold me
    With thine arm !

7.

Teach me, only teach, Love !
    As I ought
I will speak thy speech, Love,
    Think thy thought—

8.

Meet, if thou require it,
    Both demands,
Laying flesh and spirit
    In thy hands !

9.

That shall be to-morrow
    Not to-night :
I must bury sorrow
    Out of sight.

10.

—Must a little weep, Love,
    —Foolish me !
And so fall asleep, Love,
    Loved by thee.

FRA LIPPO LIPPI

———

I AM poor brother Lippo, by your leave !
You need not clap your torches to my face.
Zooks, what's to blame ? you think you see a monk !
What, it's past midnight, and you go the rounds,
And here you catch me at an alley's end
Where sportive ladies leave their doors ajar.
The Carmine's my cloister : hunt it up,
Do,—harry out, if you must show your zeal,
Whatever rat, there, haps on his wrong hole,
And nip each softling of a wee white mouse,   10
Weke, weke, that's crept to keep him company !
Aha, you know your betters ?   Then, you'll take
Your hand away that's fiddling on my throat,
And please to know me likewise.   Who am I ?
Why, one, sir, who is lodging with a friend
Three streets off—he's a certain . . . how d'ye call ?
Master—a . . . Cosimo of the Medici,
In the house that caps the corner.   Boh ! you were best !
Remember and tell me, the day you're hanged,
How you affected such a gullet's-gripe !   20

But you, sir, it concerns you that your knaves
Pick up a manner nor discredit you.
Zooks, are we pilchards, that they sweep the streets
And count fair prize what comes into their net?
He's Judas to a tittle, that man is!
Just such a face! why, sir, you make amends.
Lord, I'm not angry! Bid your hangdogs go
Drink out this quarter-florin to the health
Of the munificent House that harbours me
(And many more beside, lads! more beside!)   30
And all's come square again. I'd like his face—
His, elbowing on his comrade in the door
With the pike and lantern,—for the slave that holds
John Baptist's head a-dangle by the hair
With one hand ("look you, now," as who should say)
And his weapon in the other, yet unwiped!
It's not your chance to have a bit of chalk,
A wood-coal or the like? or you should see!
Yes, I'm the painter, since you style me so.
What, brother Lippo's doings, up and down,   40
You know them and they take you? like enough!
I saw the proper twinkle in your eye—
'Tell you I liked your looks at very first.
Let's sit and set things straight now, hip to haunch.
Here's spring come, and the nights one makes up bands
To roam the town and sing out carnival,
And I've been three weeks shut within my mew,
A-painting for the great man, saints and saints
And saints again. I could not paint all night—
Ouf! I leaned out of window for fresh air.   50
There came a hurry of feet and little feet,
A sweep of lute-strings, laughs, and whiffs of song,—

Flower o' the broom,
Take away love, and our earth is a tomb!
Flower o' the quince,
I let Lisa go, and what good's in life since?
Flower o' the thyme—and so on.   Round they went.
Scarce had they turned the corner when a titter,
Like the skipping of rabbits by moonlight,—three slim
        shapes—
And a face that looked up ... zooks, sir, flesh and blood,
That's all I'm made of!   Into shreds it went,   61
Curtain and counterpane and coverlet,
All the bed furniture—a dozen knots,
There was a ladder! down I let myself,
Hands and feet, scrambling somehow, and so dropped,
And after them.   I came up with the fun
Hard by St. Laurence, hail fellow, well met,—
Flower o' the rose,
If I've been merry, what matter who knows?
And so as I was stealing back again   70
To get to bed and have a bit of sleep
Ere I rise up to-morrow and go work
On Jerome knocking at his poor old breast
With his great round stone to subdue the flesh,
You snap me of the sudden.   Ah, I see!
Though your eye twinkles still, you shake your head—
Mine's shaved,—a monk, you say—the sting's in that!
If Master Cosimo announced himself,
Mum's the word naturally; but a monk!
Come, what am I a beast for? tell us, now!   80
I was a baby when my mother died
And father died and left me in the street.
I starved there, God knows how, a year or two

On fig-skins, melon-parings, rinds and shucks,
Refuse and rubbish.   One fine frosty day
My stomach being empty as your hat,
The wind doubled me up and down I went.
Old Aunt Lapaccia trussed me with one hand,
(Its fellow was a stinger as I knew)
And so along the wall, over the bridge,   90
By the straight cut to the convent.   Six words, there,
While I stood munching my first bread that month :
"So, boy, you're minded," quoth the good fat father
Wiping his own mouth, 'twas refection-time,—
"To quit this very miserable world ?
Will you renounce " . . .   The mouthful of bread ?
          thought I ;
By no means !   Brief, they made a monk of me ;
I did renounce the world, its pride and greed,
Palace, farm, villa, shop and banking-house,
Trash, such as these poor devils of Medici   100
Have given their hearts to—all at eight years old.
Well, sir, I found in time, you may be sure,
'Twas not for nothing—the good bellyful,
The warm serge and the rope that goes all round,
And day-long blessed idleness beside !
"Let's see what the urchin's fit for "—that came next.
Not overmuch their way, I must confess.
Such a to-do ! they tried me with their books.
Lord, they'd have taught me Latin in pure waste !
Flower o' the clove,   110
All the Latin I construe is, " amo " I love !
But, mind you, when a boy starves in the streets
Eight years together, as my fortune was,
Watching folk's faces to know who will fling

The bit of half-stripped grape-bunch he desires,
And who will curse or kick him for his pains—
Which gentleman processional and fine,
Holding a candle to the Sacrament
Will wink and let him lift a plate and catch
The droppings of the wax to sell again,   120
Or holla for the Eight and have him whipped,—
How say I ?—nay, which dog bites, which lets drop
His bone from the heap of offal in the street !
—The soul and sense of him grow sharp alike,
He learns the look of things, and none the less
For admonitions from the hunger-pinch.
I had a store of such remarks, be sure,
Which, after I found leisure, turned to use :
I drew men's faces on my copy-books,
Scrawled them within the antiphonary's marge,   130
Joined legs and arms to the long music-notes,
Found nose and eyes and chin for A.s and B.s,
And made a string of pictures of the world
Betwixt the ins and outs of verb and noun,
On the wall, the bench, the door. The monks looked
          black.
" Nay," quoth the Prior, " turn him out, d'ye say ?
In no wise.   Lose a crow and catch a lark.
What if at last we get our man of parts,
We Carmelites, like those Camaldolese
And Preaching Friars, to do our church up fine   140
And put the front on it that ought to be ! "
And hereupon they bade me daub away.
Thank you! my head being crammed, their walls a blank,
Never was such prompt disemburdening.
First, every sort of monk, the black and white,

I drew them, fat and lean : then, folks at church,
From good old gossips waiting to confess
Their cribs of barrel-droppings, candle-ends,—
To the breathless fellow at the altar-foot,
Fresh from his murder, safe and sitting there   150
With the little children round him in a row
Of admiration, half for his beard and half
For that white anger of his victim's son
Shaking a fist at him with one fierce arm,
Signing himself with the other because of Christ
(Whose sad face on the cross sees only this
After the passion of a thousand years)
Till some poor girl, her apron o'er her head
Which the intense eyes looked through, came at eve
On tip-toe, said a word, dropped in a loaf,   160
Her pair of ear-rings and a bunch of flowers
The brute took growling, prayed, and then was gone.
I painted all, then cried, " 'tis ask and have—
Choose, for more's ready ! "—laid the ladder flat,
And showed my covered bit of cloister-wall.
The monks closed in a circle and praised loud
Till checked, (taught what to see and not to see,
Being simple bodies) " that's the very man !
Look at the boy who stoops to pat the dog !
That woman's like the Prior's niece who comes   170
To care about his asthma : it's the life ! "
But there my triumph's straw-fire flared and funked—
Their betters took their turn to see and say :
The Prior and the learned pulled a face
And stopped all that in no time.   " How ? what's here ?
Quite from the mark of painting, bless us all !
Faces, arms, legs and bodies like the true

As much as pea and pea ! it's devil's-game !
Your business is not to catch men with show,
With homage to the perishable clay,   180
But lift them over it, ignore it all,
Make them forget there's such a thing as flesh.
Your business is to paint the souls of men—
Man's soul, and it's a fire, smoke . . no it's not . .
It's vapour done up like a new-born babe—
(In that shape when you die it leaves your mouth)
It's . . well, what matters talking, it's the soul !
Give us no more of body than shows soul.
Here's Giotto, with his Saint a-praising God !
That sets you praising,—why not stop with him ?   190
Why put all thoughts of praise out of our heads
With wonder at lines, colours, and what not ?
Paint the soul, never mind the legs and arms !
Rub all out, try at it a second time.
Oh, that white smallish female with the breasts,
She's just my niece . . . Herodias, I would say,—
Who went and danced and got men's heads cut off—
Have it all out ! "   Now, is this sense, I ask ?
A fine way to paint soul, by painting body
So ill, the eye can't stop there, must go further   200
And can't fare worse !   Thus, yellow does for white
When what you put for yellow's simply black,
And any sort of meaning looks intense
When all beside itself means and looks nought.
Why can't a painter lift each foot in turn,
Left foot and right foot, go a double step,
Make his flesh liker and his soul more like,
Both in their order ?   Take the prettiest face,
The Prior's niece . . . patron-saint—is it so pretty

You can't discover if it means hope, fear, 210
Sorrow or joy ? won't beauty go with these ?
Suppose I've made her eyes all right and blue,
Can't I take breath and try to add life's flash,
And then add soul and heighten them threefold ?
Or say there's beauty with no soul at all—
(I never saw it—put the case the same—)
If you get simple beauty and nought else,
You get about the best thing God invents,—
That's somewhat. And you'll find the soul you have
  missed,
Within yourself when you return Him thanks ! 220
" Rub all out ! " well, well, there's my life, in short,
And so the thing has gone on ever since.
I'm grown a man no doubt, I've broken bounds—
You should not take a fellow eight years old
And make him swear to never kiss the girls—
I'm my own master, paint now as I please—
Having a friend, you see, in the Corner-house !
Lord, it's fast holding by the rings in front—
Those great rings serve more purposes than just
To plant a flag in, or tie up a horse ! 230
And yet the old schooling sticks—the old grave eyes
Are peeping o'er my shoulder as I work,
The heads shake still—" It's Art's decline, my son !
You're not of the true painters, great and old :
Brother Angelico's the man, you'll find :
Brother Lorenzo stands his single peer.
Fag on at flesh, you'll never make the third ! "
Flower o' the pine,
You keep your mistr . . . manners, and I'll stick to mine !
I'm not the third, then : bless us, they must know ! 240

Don't you think they're the likeliest to know,
They, with their Latin ? so I swallow my rage,
Clench my teeth, suck my lips in tight, and paint
To please them—sometimes do, and sometimes don't,
For, doing most, there's pretty sure to come
A turn—some warm eve finds me at my saints—
A laugh, a cry, the business of the world—
(*Flower o' the peach,*
Death for us all, and his own life for each !)
And my whole soul revolves, the cup runs o'er,   250
The world and life's too big to pass for a dream,
And I do these wild things in sheer despite,
And play the fooleries you catch me at,
In pure rage ! the old mill-horse, out at grass
After hard years, throws up his stiff heels so,
Although the miller does not preach to him
The only good of grass is to make chaff.
What would men have ?   Do they like grass or no—
May they or mayn't they ? all I want's the thing
Settled for ever one way : as it is,   260
You tell too many lies and hurt yourself.
You don't like what you only like too much,
You do like what, if given you at your word,
You find abundantly detestable.
For me, I think I speak as I was taught—
I always see the Garden and God there
A-making man's wife—and, my lesson learned,
The value and significance of flesh,
I can't unlearn ten minutes afterward.

    You understand me : I'm a beast, I know.   270
But see, now—why, I see as certainly
As that the morning-star's about to shine,

What will hap some day.   We've a youngster here
Comes to our convent, studies what I do,
Slouches and stares and lets no atom drop—
His name is Guidi—he'll not mind the monks—
They call him Hulking Tom, he lets them talk—
He picks my practice up—he'll paint apace,
I hope so—though I never live so long,
I know what's sure to follow.   You be judge !   280
You speak no Latin more than I, belike—
However, you're my man, you've seen the world
—The beauty and the wonder and the power,
The shapes of things, their colours, lights and shades,
Changes, surprises,—and God made it all !
—For what ? do you feel thankful, ay or no,
For this fair town's face, yonder river's line,
The mountain round it and the sky above,
Much more the figures of man, woman, child,
These are the frame to ?   What's it all about ?   290
To be passed o'er, despised ? or dwelt upon,
Wondered at ? oh, this last of course, you say.
But why not do as well as say,—paint these
Just as they are, careless what comes of it ?
God's works—paint anyone, and count it crime
To let a truth slip.   Don't object, " His works
Are here already—nature is complete :
Suppose you reproduce her—(which you can't)
There's no advantage ! you must beat her, then."
For, don't you mark, we're made so that we love   300
First when we see them painted, things we have passed
Perhaps a hundred times nor cared to see ;
And so they are better, painted—better to us,
Which is the same thing.   Art was given for that—

God uses us to help each other so,
Lending our minds out.   Have you noticed, now,
Your cullion's hanging face ?   A bit of chalk,
And trust me but you should, though ! How much
      more,
If I drew higher things with the same truth !
That were to take the Prior's pulpit-place,   310
Interpret God to all of you ! oh, oh,
It makes me mad to see what men shall do
And we in our graves !   This world's no blot for us,
Nor blank—it means intensely, and means good :
To find its meaning is my meat and drink.
" Ay, but you don't so instigate to prayer "
Strikes in the Prior !   " when your meaning's plain
It does not say to folks—remember matins—
Or, mind you fast next Friday."   Why, for this
What need of art at all ?   A skull and bones,   320
Two bits of stick nailed cross-wise, or, what's best,
A bell to chime the hour with, does as well.
I painted a St. Laurence six months since
At Prato, splashed the fresco in fine style.
" How looks my painting, now the scaffold's down ? "
I ask a brother : " Hugely," he returns—
" Already not one phiz of your three slaves
That turn the Deacon off his toasted side,
But's scratched and prodded to our heart's content,
The pious people have so eased their own   330
When coming to say prayers there in a rage.
We get on fast to see the bricks beneath.
Expect another job this time next year,
For pity and religion grow i' the crowd—
Your painting serves its purpose ! "   Hang the fools !

—That is—you'll not mistake an idle word
Spoke in a huff by a poor monk, God wot,
Tasting the air this spicy night which turns
The unaccustomed head like Chianti wine !
Oh, the church knows ! don't misreport me, now ! 340
It's natural a poor monk out of bounds
Should have his apt word to excuse himself :
And hearken how I plot to make amends.
I have bethought me : I shall paint a piece
. . . There's for you ! Give me six months, then go, see
Something in Sant' Ambrogio's . . . (bless the nuns !
They want a cast of my office) I shall paint
God in the midst, Madonna and her babe,
Ringed by a bowery, flowery angel-brood,
Lilies and vestments and white faces, sweet 350
As puff on puff of grated orris-root
When ladies crowd to church at midsummer.
And then in the front, of course a saint or two—
Saint John, because he saves the Florentines,
Saint Ambrose, who puts down in black and white
The convent's friends and gives them a long day,
And Job, I must have him there past mistake,
The man of Uz, (and Us without the z,
Painters who need his patience.)   Well, all these
Secured at their devotions, up shall come 360
Out of a corner when you least expect,
As one by a dark stair into a great light
Music and talking, who but Lippo ! I !—
Mazed, motionless and moon-struck—I'm the man !
Back I shrink—what is this I see and hear ?
I, caught up with my monk's things by mistake,
My old serge gown and rope that goes all round,

I, in this presence, this pure company !
Where's a hole, where's a corner for escape ?
Then steps a sweet angelic slip of a thing   370
Forward, puts out a soft palm—" Not so fast ! "
—Addresses the celestial presence, " nay—
He made you and devised you, after all,
Though he's none of you ! Could Saint John there,
      draw—
His camel-hair make up a painting-brush ?
We come to brother Lippo for all that,
Iste perfecit opus ! "   So, all smile—
I shuffle sideways with my blushing face
Under the cover of a hundred wings
Thrown like a spread of kirtles when you're gay   380
And play hot cockles, all the doors being shut,
Till, wholly unexpected, in there pops
The hothead husband !   Thus I scuttle off
To some safe bench behind, not letting go
The palm of her, the little lily thing
That spoke the good word for me in the nick,
Like the Prior's niece . . . Saint Lucy, I would say.
And so all's saved for me, and for the church
A pretty picture gained.   Go, six months hence !
Your hand, sir, and good bye : no lights, no lights ! 390
The street's hushed, and I know my own way back—
Don't fear me !   There's the grey beginning.   Zooks !

A TOCCATA OF GALUPPI'S

—◆—

1.

Oᴴ, Galuppi, Baldassaro, this is very sad to find!
I can hardly misconceive you; it would prove me deaf
and blind;
But although I give you credit, 'tis with such a heavy
mind!

2.

Here you come with your old music, and here's all the
good it brings.
What, they lived once thus at Venice, where the mer-
chants were the kings,
Where St. Mark's is, where the Doges used to wed the
sea with rings?

3.

Ay, because the sea's the street there; and 'tis arched
by . . . what you call
. . . Shylock's bridge with houses on it, where they kept
the carnival!
I was never out of England—it's as if I saw it all!

4.

Did young people take their pleasure when the sea was
             warm in May ?
Balls and masks begun at midnight, burning ever to
             mid-day,
When they made up fresh adventures for the morrow,
             do you say ?

5.

Was a lady such a lady, cheeks so round and lips so
             red,—
On her neck the small face buoyant, like a bell-flower
             on its bed,
O'er the breast's superb abundance where a man might
             base his head ?

6.

Well (and it was graceful of them) they'd break talk off
             and afford
—She, to bite her mask's black velvet, he to finger on
             his sword,
While you sat and played Toccatas, stately at the clavi-
             chord ?

7.

What ? Those lesser thirds so plaintive, sixths diminished,
             sigh on sigh,
Told them something ?   Those suspensions, those solu-
             tions—" Must we die ? "
Those commiserating sevenths—" Life might last ! we
             can but try ! "

8.

" Were you happy ? "—" Yes."—" And are you still as
                    happy ? "—" Yes—And you ? "
—" Then more kisses "—" Did *I* stop them, when a
                    million seemed so few ? "
Hark—the dominant's persistence, till it must be
                    answered to !

9.

So an octave struck the answer.   Oh, they praised you,
                    I dare say !
" Brave Galuppi ! that was music ! good alike at grave
                    and gay !
I can always leave off talking, when I hear a master play."

10.

Then they left you for their pleasure : till in due time,
                    one by one,
Some with lives that came to nothing, some with deeds
                    as well undone,
Death came tacitly and took them where they never see
                    the sun.

11.

But when I sit down to reason,—think to take my stand
                    nor swerve
Till I triumph o'er a secret wrung from nature's close
                    reserve,
In you come with your cold music, till I creep thro'
                    every nerve.

12.

Yes, you, like a ghostly cricket, creaking where a house
was burned—
" Dust and ashes, dead and done with, Venice spent
what Venice earned !
The soul, doubtless, is immortal—where a soul can be
discerned.

13.

" Yours for instance, you know physics, something of
geology,
Mathematics are your pastime ; souls shall rise in their
degree ;
Butterflies may dread extinction,—you'll not die, it
cannot be !

14.

" As for Venice and its people, merely born to bloom
and drop,
Here on earth they bore their fruitage, mirth and folly
were the crop.
What of soul was left, I wonder, when the kissing had to
stop ?

15.

" Dust and ashes ! " So you creak it, and I want the
heart to scold.
Dear dead women, with such hair, too—what's become
of all the gold
Used to hang and brush their bosoms ? I feel chilly
and grown old.

BY THE FIRE-SIDE

1.

How well I know what I mean to do
   When the long dark Autumn evenings come,
And where, my soul, is thy pleasant hue ?
   With the music of all thy voices, dumb
In life's November too !

2.

I shall be found by the fire, suppose,
   O'er a great wise book as beseemeth age,
While the shutters flap as the cross-wind blows,
   And I turn the page, and I turn the page,
Not verse now, only prose !

3.

Till the young ones whisper, finger on lip,
   " There he is at it, deep in Greek—
Now or never, then, out we slip
   To cut from the hazels by the creek
A mainmast for our ship."

4.

I shall be at it indeed, my friends !
   Greek puts already on either side
Such a branch-work forth, as soon extends
   To a vista opening far and wide,
And I pass out where it ends.

5.

The outside-frame like your hazel-trees—
   But the inside-archway narrows fast,
And a rarer sort succeeds to these,
   And we slope to Italy at last
And youth, by green degrees.

6.

I follow wherever I am led,
   Knowing so well the leader's hand—
Oh, woman-country, wooed, not wed,
   Loved all the more by earth's male-lands,
Laid to their hearts instead !

7.

Look at the ruined chapel again
   Half way up in the Alpine gorge.
Is that a tower, I point you plain,
   Or is it a mill or an iron forge
Breaks solitude in vain ?

8.

A turn, and we stand in the heart of things ;
   The woods are round us, heaped and dim ;
From slab to slab how it slips and springs,
   The thread of water single and slim,
Thro' the ravage some torrent brings !

9.

Does it feed the little lake below ?
   That speck of white just on its marge
Is Pella ; see, in the evening glow
   How sharp the silver spear-heads charge
When Alp meets Heaven in snow.

10.

On our other side is the straight-up rock ;
   And a path is kept 'twixt the gorge and it
By boulder-stones where lichens mock
   The marks on a moth, and small ferns fit
Their teeth to the polished block.

11.

Oh, the sense of the yellow mountain flowers,
   And the thorny balls, each three in one,
The chestnuts throw on our path in showers,
   For the drop of the woodland fruit's begun
These early November hours—

12.

That crimson the creeper's leaf across
   Like a splash of blood, intense, abrupt,
O'er a shield, else gold from rim to boss,
   And lay it for show on the fairy-cupped
Elf-needled mat of moss,

13.

By the rose-flesh mushrooms, undivulged
   Last evening—nay, in to-day's first dew
Yon sudden coral nipple bulged
   Where a freaked, fawn-coloured, flaky crew
Of toad-stools peep indulged.

14.

And yonder, at foot of the fronting ridge
　That takes the turn to a range beyond,
Is the chapel reached by the one-arched bridge
　Where the water is stopped in a stagnant pond
Danced over by the midge.

15.

The chapel and bridge are of stone alike,
　Blackish grey and mostly wet ;
Cut hemp-stalks steep in the narrow dyke.
　See here again, how the lichens fret
And the roots of the ivy strike !

16.

Poor little place, where its one priest comes
　On a festa-day, if he comes at all,
To the dozen folk from their scattered homes,
　Gathered within that precinct small
By the dozen ways one roams

17.

To drop from the charcoal-burners' huts,
　Or climb from the hemp-dressers' low shed,
Leave the grange where the woodman stores his nuts,
　Or the wattled cote where the fowlers spread
Their gear on the rock's bare juts.

18.

It has some pretension too, this front,
　With its bit of fresco half-moon-wise
Set over the porch, art's early wont—
　'Tis John in the Desert, I surmise,
But has borne the weather's brunt—

19.

Not from the fault of the builder, though,
  For a pent-house properly projects
Where three carved beams make a certain show,
  Dating—good thought of our architect's—
'Five, six, nine, he lets you know.

20.

And all day long a bird sings there,
  And a stray sheep drinks at the pond at times :
The place is silent and aware ;
  It has had its scenes, its joys and crimes,
But that is its own affair.

21.

My perfect wife, my Leonor,
  Oh, heart my own, oh, eyes, mine too,
Whom else could I dare look backward for,
  With whom beside should I dare pursue
The path grey heads abhor ?

22.

For it leads to a crag's sheer edge with them ;
  Youth, flowery all the way, there stops—
Not they ; age threatens and they contemn,
  Till they reach the gulf wherein youth drops,
One inch from our life's safe hem !

23.

With me, youth led—I will speak now,
  No longer watch you as you sit
Reading by fire-light, that great brow
  And the spirit-small hand propping it
Mutely—my heart knows how—

24.

When, if I think but deep enough,
 You are wont to answer, prompt as rhyme ;
And you, too, find without a rebuff
 The response your soul seeks many a time
Piercing its fine flesh-stuff—

25.

My own, confirm me ! If I tread
 This path back, is it not in pride
To think how little I dreamed it led
 To an age so blest that by its side
Youth seems the waste instead !

26.

My own, see where the years conduct !
 At first, 'twas something our two souls
Should mix as mists do : each is sucked
 Into each now ; on, the new stream rolls,
Whatever rocks obstruct.

27.

Think, when our one soul understands
 The great Word which makes all things new—
When earth breaks up and Heaven expands—
 How will the change strike me and you
In the House not made with hands ?

28.

Oh, I must feel your brain prompt mine,
 Your heart anticipate my heart,
You must be just before, in fine,
 See and make me see, for your part,
New depths of the Divine !

29.

But who could have expected this,
    When we two drew together first
Just for the obvious human bliss,
    To satisfy life's daily thirst
With a thing men seldom miss ?

30.

Come back with me to the first of all,
    Let us lean and love it over again—
Let us now forget and then recall,
    Break the rosary in a pearly rain,
And gather what we let fall !

31.

What did I say ?—that a small bird sings
    All day long, save when a brown pair
Of hawks from the wood float with wide wings
    Strained to a bell : 'gainst the noon-day glare
You count the streaks and rings.

32.

But at afternoon or almost eve
    'Tis better ; then the silence grows
To that degree, you half believe
    It must get rid of what it knows,
Its bosom does so heave.

33.

Hither we walked, then, side by side,
    Arm in arm and cheek to cheek,
And still I questioned or replied,
    While my heart, convulsed to really speak,
Lay choking in its pride.

34.

Silent the crumbling bridge we cross,
　　And pity and praise the chapel sweet,
And care about the fresco's loss,
　　And wish for our souls a like retreat,
And wonder at the moss.

35.

Stoop and kneel on the settle under—
　　Look through the window's grated square :
Nothing to see ! for fear of plunder,
　　The cross is down and the altar bare,
As if thieves don't fear thunder.

36.

We stoop and look in through the grate,
　　See the little porch and rustic door,
Read duly the dead builder's date,
　　Then cross the bridge we crossed before,
Take the path again—but wait !

37.

Oh moment, one and infinite !
　　The water slips o'er stock and stone ;
The west is tender, hardly bright.
　　How grey at once is the evening grown—
One star, the chrysolite !

38.

We two stood there with never a third,
　　But each by each, as each knew well.
The sights we saw and the sounds we heard,
　　The lights and the shades made up a spell
Till the trouble grew and stirred.

39.

Oh, the little more, and how much it is !
   And the little less, and what worlds away !
How a sound shall quicken content to bliss,
   Or a breath suspend the blood's best play,
And life be a proof of this !

40.

Had she willed it, still had stood the screen
   So slight, so sure, 'twixt my love and her.
I could fix her face with a guard between,
   And find her soul as when friends confer,
Friends—lovers that might have been.

41.

For my heart had a touch of the woodland time,
   Wanting to sleep now over its best.
Shake the whole tree in the summer-prime,
   But bring to the last leaf no such test.
" Hold the last fast ! " says the rhyme.

42.

For a chance to make your little much,
   To gain a lover and lose a friend,
Venture the tree and a myriad such,
   When nothing you mar but the year can mend !
But a last leaf—fear to touch.

43.

Yet should it unfasten itself and fall
   Eddying down till it find your face
At some slight wind—(best chance of all !)
   Be your heart henceforth its dwelling-place
You trembled to forestal !

44.

Worth how well, those dark grey eyes,
  —That hair so dark and dear, how worth
That a man should strive and agonise,
  And taste a very hell on earth
For the hope of such a prize !

45.

Oh, you might have turned and tried a man,
  Set him a space to weary and wear,
And prove which suited more your plan,
  His best of hope or his worst despair,
Yet end as he began.

46.

But you spared me this, like the heart you are,
  And filled my empty heart at a word.
If you join two lives, there is oft a scar,
  They are one and one, with a shadowy third ;
One near one is too far.

47.

A moment after, and hands unseen
  Were hanging the night around us fast.
But we knew that a bar was broken between
  Life and life ; we were mixed at last
In spite of the mortal screen.

48.

The forests had done it ; there they stood—
  We caught for a second the powers at play :
They had mingled us so, for once and for good,
  Their work was done—we might go or stay,
They relapsed to their ancient mood.

49.

How the world is made for each of us !
    How all we perceive and know in it
Tends to some moment's product thus,
    When a soul declares itself—to wit,
By its fruit—the thing it does !

50.

Be Hate that fruit or Love that fruit,
    It forwards the General Deed of Man,
And each of the Many helps to recruit
    The life of the race by a general plan,
Each living his own, to boot.

51.

I am named and known by that hour's feat,
    There took my station and degree.
So grew my own small life complete
    As nature obtained her best of me—
One born to love you, sweet !

52.

And to watch you sink by the fire-side now
    Back again, as you mutely sit
Musing by fire-light, that great brow
    And the spirit-small hand propping it
Yonder, my heart knows how !

53.

So the earth has gained by one man more,
    And the gain of earth must be Heaven's gain too,
And the whole is well worth thinking o'er
    When the autumn comes : which I mean to do
One day, as I said before.

ANY WIFE TO ANY HUSBAND

—◆—

1.

My love, this is the bitterest, that thou
Who art all truth and who dost love me now
  As thine eyes say, as thy voice breaks to say—
Should'st love so truly and could'st love me still
A whole long life through, had but love its will,
  Would death that leads me from thee brook delay !

2.

I have but to be by thee, and thy hand
Would never let mine go, thy heart withstand
  The beating of my heart to reach its place.
When should I look for thee and feel thee gone ?
When cry for the old comfort and find none ?
  Never, I know ! Thy soul is in thy face.

3.

Oh, I should fade—'tis willed so ! might I save,
Gladly I would, whatever beauty gave
  Joy to thy sense, for that was precious too.
It is not to be granted. But the soul
Whence the love comes, all ravage leaves that whole ;
  Vainly the flesh fades—soul makes all things new.

4.

And 'twould not be because my eye grew dim
Thou could'st not find the love there, thanks to Him
   Who never is dishonoured in the spark
He gave us from his fire of fires, and bade
Remember whence it sprang nor be afraid
   While that burns on, though all the rest grow dark.

5.

So, how thou would'st be perfect, white and clean
Outside as inside, soul and soul's demesne
   Alike, this body given to show it by !
Oh, three-parts through the worst of life's abyss,
What plaudits from the next world after this,
   Could'st thou repeat a stroke and gain the sky !

6.

And is it not the bitterer to think
That, disengage our hands and thou wilt sink
   Although thy love was love in very deed ?
I know that nature !   Pass a festive day
Thou dost not throw its relic-flower away
   Nor bid its music's loitering echo speed.

7.

Thou let'st the stranger's glove lie where it fell ;
If old things remain old things all is well,
   For thou art grateful as becomes man best :
And hadst thou only heard me play one tune,
Or viewed me from a window, not so soon
   With thee would such things fade as with the rest.

8.

I seem to see ! we meet and part : 'tis brief :
The book I opened keeps a folded leaf,
    The very chair I sat on, breaks the rank ;
That is a portrait of me on the wall—
Three lines, my face comes at so slight a call ;
    And for all this, one little hour's to thank.

9.

But now, because the hour through years was fixed,
Because our inmost beings met and mixed,
    Because thou once hast loved me—wilt thou dare
Say to thy soul and Who may list beside,
" Therefore she is immortally my bride,
    Chance cannot change that love, nor time impair.

10.

" So, what if in the dusk of life that's left,
I, a tired traveller, of my sun bereft,
    Look from my path when, mimicking the same,
The fire-fly glimpses past me, come and gone ?
—Where was it till the sunset ? where anon
    It will be at the sunrise ! what's to blame ? "

11.

Is it so helpful to thee ? canst thou take
The mimic up, nor, for the true thing's sake,
    Put gently by such efforts at a beam ?
Is the remainder of the way so long
Thou need'st the little solace, thou the strong ?
    Watch out thy watch, let weak ones doze and dream !

12.

"—Ah, but the fresher faces !   Is it true,"
Thou'lt ask, " some eyes are beautiful and new ?
 Some hair,—how can one choose but grasp such wealth?
And if a man would press his lips to lips
Fresh as the wilding hedge-rose-cup there slips
 The dew-drop out of, must it be by stealth ?

13.

" It cannot change the love kept still for Her,
Much more than, such a picture to prefer
 Passing a day with, to a room's bare side.
The painted form takes nothing she possessed,
Yet while the Titian's Venus lies at rest
 A man looks.   Once more, what is there to chide ? "

14.

So must I see, from where I sit and watch,
My own self sell myself, my hand attach
 Its warrant to the very thefts from me—
Thy singleness of soul that made me proud,
Thy purity of heart I loved aloud,
 Thy man's truth I was bold to bid God see !

15.

Love so, then, if thou wilt !   Give all thou canst
Away to the new faces—disentranced—
 (Say it and think it) obdurate no more,
Re-issue looks and words from the old mint—
Pass them afresh, no matter whose the print
 Image and superscription once they bore !

16.

Re-coin thyself and give it them to spend,—
It all comes to the same thing at the end,
    Since mine thou wast, mine art, and mine shalt be,
Faithful or faithless, sealing up the sum
Or lavish of my treasure, thou must come
    Back to the heart's place here I keep for thee !

17.

Only, why should it be with stain at all ?
Why must I, 'twixt the leaves of coronal,
    Put any kiss of pardon on thy brow ?
Why need the other women know so much
And talk together, " Such the look and such
    The smile he used to love with, then as now ! "

18.

Might I die last and shew thee !   Should I find
Such hardship in the few years left behind,
    If free to take and light my lamp, and go
Into thy tomb, and shut the door and sit
Seeing thy face on those four sides of it
    The better that they are so blank, I know !

19.

Why, time was what I wanted, to turn o'er
Within my mind each look, get more and more
    By heart each word, too much to learn at first,
And join thee all the fitter for the pause
'Neath the low door-way's lintel.   That were cause
    For lingering, though thou calledst, if I durst !

20.

And yet thou art the nobler of us two.
What dare I dream of, that thou canst not do,
  Outstripping my ten small steps with one stride ?
I'll say then, here's a trial and a task—
Is it to bear ?—if easy, I'll not ask—
  Though love fail, I can trust on in thy pride.

21.

Pride ?—when those eyes forestal the life behind
The death I have to go through !—when I find,
  Now that I want thy help most, all of thee !
What did I fear ? Thy love shall hold me fast
Until the little minute's sleep is past
  And I wake saved.—And yet, it will not be !

AN EPISTLE

STRANGE MEDICAL EXPERIENCE OF KARSHISH, THE ARAB PHYSICIAN.

———

KARSHISH, the picker-up of learning's crumbs,
The not-incurious in God's handiwork
(This man's-flesh He hath admirably made,
Blown like a bubble, kneaded like a paste,
To coop up and keep down on earth a space
That puff of vapour from His mouth, man's soul)
—To Abib, all-sagacious in our art,
Breeder in me of what poor skill I boast,
Like me inquisitive how pricks and cracks
Befall the flesh through too much stress and strain,   10
Whereby the wily vapour fain would slip
Back and rejoin its source before the term,—
And aptest in contrivance, under God,
To baffle it by deftly stopping such :—
The vagrant Scholar to his Sage at home
Sends greeting (health and knowledge, fame with peace)
Three samples of true snake-stone—rarer still,
One of the other sort, the melon-shaped,
(But fitter, pounded fine, for charms than drugs)
And writeth now the twenty-second time.   20

My journeyings were brought to Jericho,
Thus I resume.   Who studious in our art
Shall count a little labour unrepaid ?
I have shed sweat enough, left flesh and bone
On many a flinty furlong of this land.
Also the country-side is all on fire
With rumours of a marching hitherward—
Some say Vespasian cometh, some, his son.
A black lynx snarled and pricked a tufted ear ;
Lust of my blood inflamed his yellow balls :   30
I cried and threw my staff and he was gone.
Twice have the robbers stripped and beaten me,
And once a town declared me for a spy,
But at the end, I reach Jerusalem,
Since this poor covert where I pass the night,
This Bethany, lies scarce the distance thence
A man with plague-sores at the third degree
Runs till he drops down dead.   Thou laughest here !
'Sooth, it elates me, thus reposed and safe,
To void the stuffing of my travel-scrip   40
And share with thee whatever Jewry yields.
A viscid choler is observable
In tertians, I was nearly bold to say,
And falling-sickness hath a happier cure
Than our school wots of : there's a spider here
Weaves no web, watches on the ledge of tombs,
Sprinkled with mottles on an ash-grey back ;
Take five and drop them . . . but who knows his mind,
The Syrian run-a-gate I trust this to ?
His service payeth me a sublimate   50
Blown up his nose to help the ailing eye.
Best wait : I reach Jerusalem at morn,
There set in order my experiences,

Gather what most deserves and give thee all—
Or I might add, Judea's gum-tragacanth
Scales off in purer flakes, shines clearer-grained,
Cracks 'twixt the pestle and the porphyry,
In fine exceeds our produce.   Scalp-disease
Confounds me, crossing so with leprosy—
Thou hadst admired one sort I gained at Zoar—   60
But zeal outruns discretion.   Here I end.

  Yet stay : my Syrian blinketh gratefully,
Protesteth his devotion is my price—
Suppose I write what harms not, though he steal ?
I half resolve to tell thee, yet I blush,
What set me off a-writing first of all.
An itch I had, a sting to write, a tang !
For, be it this town's barrenness—or else
The Man had something in the look of him—
His case has struck me far more than 'tis worth.   70
So, pardon if—(lest presently I lose
In the great press of novelty at hand
The care and pains this somehow stole from me)
I bid thee take the thing while fresh in mind,
Almost in sight—for, wilt thou have the truth ?
The very man is gone from me but now,
Whose ailment is the subject of discourse.
Thus then, and let thy better wit help all.

  'Tis but a case of mania—subinduced
By epilepsy, at the turning-point   80
Of trance prolonged unduly some three days,
When by the exhibition of some drug
Or spell, exorcisation, stroke of art
Unknown to me and which 'twere well to know,
The evil thing out-breaking all at once

Left the man whole and sound of body indeed,—
But, flinging, so to speak, life's gates too wide,
Making a clear house of it too suddenly,
The first conceit that entered pleased to write
Whatever it was minded on the wall   90
So plainly at that vantage, as it were,
(First come, first served) that nothing subsequent
Attaineth to erase the fancy-scrawls
Which the returned and new-established soul
Hath gotten now so thoroughly by heart
That henceforth she will read or these or none.
And first—the man's own firm conviction rests
That he was dead (in fact they buried him)
That he was dead and then restored to life
By a Nazarene physician of his tribe: 100
—'Sayeth, the same bade " Rise," and he did rise.
" Such cases are diurnal," thou wilt cry.
Not so this figment !—not, that such a fume,
Instead of giving way to time and health,
Should eat itself into the life of life,
As saffron tingeth flesh, blood, bones and all !
For see, how he takes up the after-life.
The man—it is one Lazarus a Jew,
Sanguine, proportioned, fifty years of age,
The body's habit wholly laudable,   110
As much, indeed, beyond the common health
As he were made and put aside to shew.
Think, could we penetrate by any drug
And bathe the wearied soul and worried flesh,
And bring it clear and fair, by three days sleep !
Whence has the man the balm that brightens all ?
This grown man eyes the world now like a child.
Some elders of his tribe, I should premise,

Led in their friend, obedient as a sheep,
To bear my inquisition.   While they spoke,   120
Now sharply, now with sorrow,—told the case,—
He listened not except I spoke to him,
But folded his two hands and let them talk,
Watching the flies that buzzed : and yet no fool.
And that's a sample how his years must go.
Look if a beggar, in fixed middle-life,
Should find a treasure, can he use the same
With straightened habits and with tastes starved small,
And take at once to his impoverished brain
The sudden element that changes things,   130
—That sets the undreamed-of rapture at his hand,
And puts the cheap old joy in the scorned dust ?
Is he not such an one as moves to mirth—
Warily parsimonious, when's no need,
Wasteful as drunkenness at undue times ?
All prudent counsel as to what befits
The golden mean, is lost on such an one.
The man's fantastic will is the man's law.
So here—we'll call the treasure knowledge, say—
Increased beyond the fleshly faculty—   140
Heaven opened to a soul while yet on earth,
Earth forced on a soul's use while seeing Heaven.
The man is witless of the size, the sum,
The value in proportion of all things,
Or whether it be little or be much.
Discourse to him of prodigious armaments
Assembled to besiege his city now,
And of the passing of a mule with gourds—
'Tis one !   Then take it on the other side,
Speak of some trifling fact—he will gaze rapt   150
With stupor at its very littleness—

(Far as I see) as if in that indeed
He caught prodigious import, whole results ;
And so will turn to us the bystanders
In ever the same stupor (note this point)
That we too see not with his opened eyes !
Wonder and doubt come wrongly into play,
Preposterously, at cross purposes.
Should his child sicken unto death,—why, look
For scarce abatement of his cheerfulness, 160
Or pretermission of his daily craft—
While a word, gesture, glance, from that same child
At play or in the school or laid asleep,
Will start him to an agony of fear,
Exasperation, just as like ! demand
The reason why—" 'tis but a word," object—
" A gesture "—he regards thee as our lord
Who lived there in the pyramid alone,
Looked at us, dost thou mind, when being young
We both would unadvisedly recite 170
Some charm's beginning, from that book of his,
Able to bid the sun throb wide and burst
All into stars, as suns grown old are wont.
Thou and the child have each a veil alike
Thrown o'er your heads from under which ye both
Stretch your blind hands and trifle with a match
Over a mine of Greek fire, did ye know !
He holds on firmly to some thread of life—
(It is the life to lead perforcedly)
Which runs across some vast distracting orb 180
Of glory on either side that meagre thread,
Which, conscious of, he must not enter yet—
The spiritual life around the earthly life !
The law of that is known to him as this—

His heart and brain move there, his feet stay here.
So is the man perplext with impulses
Sudden to start off crosswise, not straight on,
Proclaiming what is Right and Wrong across—
And not along—this black thread through the blaze—
" It should be " balked by " here it cannot be."   190
And oft the man's soul springs into his face
As if he saw again and heard again
His sage that bade him " Rise " and he did rise.
Something—a word, a tick of the blood within
Admonishes—then back he sinks at once
To ashes, that was very fire before,
In sedulous recurrence to his trade
Whereby he earneth him the daily bread—
And studiously the humbler for that pride,
Professedly the faultier that he knows   200
God's secret, while he holds the thread of life.
Indeed the especial marking of the man
Is prone submission to the Heavenly will—
Seeing it, what it is, and why it is.
'Sayeth, he will wait patient to the last
For that same death which will restore his being
To equilibrium, body loosening soul
Divorced even now by premature full growth :
He will live, nay, it pleaseth him to live
So long as God please, and just how God please.   210
He even seeketh not to please God more
(Which meaneth, otherwise) than as God please.
Hence I perceive not he affects to preach
The doctrine of his sect whate'er it be—
Make proselytes as madmen thirst to do.
How can he give his neighbour the real ground,
His own conviction ? ardent as he is—

Call his great truth a lie, why still the old
" Be it as God please " reassureth him.
I probed the sore as thy disciple should—   220
" How, beast," said I, " this stolid carelessness
Sufficeth thee, when Rome is on her march
To stamp out like a little spark thy town,
Thy tribe, thy crazy tale and thee at once ? "
He merely looked with his large eyes on me.
The man is apathetic, you deduce ?
Contrariwise he loves both old and young,
Able and weak—affects the very brutes
And birds—how say I ? flowers of the field—
As a wise workman recognises tools   230
In a master's workshop, loving what they make.
Thus is the man as harmless as a lamb :
Only impatient, let him do his best,
At ignorance and carelessness and sin—
An indignation which is promptly curbed.
As when in certain travels I have feigned
To be an ignoramus in our art
According to some preconceived design,
And happed to hear the land's practitioners
Steeped in conceit sublimed by ignorance,   240
Prattle fantastically on disease,
Its cause and cure—and I must hold my peace !

Thou wilt object—why have I not ere this
Sought out the sage himself, the Nazarene
Who wrought this cure, enquiring at the source,
Conferring with the frankness that befits ?
Alas ! it grieveth me, the learned leech
Perished in a tumult many years ago,
Accused,—our learning's fate,—of wizardry,

Rebellion, to the setting up a rule   250
And creed prodigious as described to me.
His death which happened when the earthquake fell
(Prefiguring, as soon appeared, the loss
To occult learning in our lord the sage
That lived there in the pyramid alone)
Was wrought by the mad people—that's their wont—
On vain recourse, as I conjecture it,
To his tried virtue, for miraculous help—
How could he stop the earthquake ?   That's their way !
The other imputations must be lies :   260
But take one—though I loathe to give it thee,
In mere respect to any good man's fame !
(And after all our patient Lazarus
Is stark mad—should we count on what he says ?
Perhaps not—though in writing to a leech
'Tis well to keep back nothing of a case.)
This man so cured regards the curer then,
As—God forgive me—who but God himself,
Creator and Sustainer of the world,
That came and dwelt in flesh on it awhile !   270
—'Sayeth that such an One was born and lived,
Taught, healed the sick, broke bread at his own house,
Then died, with Lazarus by, for aught I know,
And yet was . . . what I said nor choose repeat,
And must have so avouched himself, in fact,
In hearing of this very Lazarus
Who saith—but why all this of what he saith ?
Why write of trivial matters, things of price
Calling at every moment for remark ?
I noticed on the margin of a pool   280
Blue-flowering borage, the Aleppo sort,
Aboundeth, very nitrous.   It is strange !

Thy pardon for this long and tedious case,
Which, now that I review it, needs must seem
Unduly dwelt on, prolixly set forth.
Nor I myself discern in what is writ
Good cause for the peculiar interest
And awe indeed this man has touched me with.
Perhaps the journey's end, the weariness
Had wrought upon me first.   I met him thus—   290
I crossed a ridge of short sharp broken hills
Like an old lion's cheek-teeth.   Out there came
A moon made like a face with certain spots
Multiform, manifold, and menacing :
Then a wind rose behind me.   So we met
In this old sleepy town at unaware,
The man and I.   I send thee what is writ.
Regard it as a chance, a matter risked
To this ambiguous Syrian—he may lose,
Or steal, or give it thee with equal good.   300
Jerusalem's repose shall make amends
For time this letter wastes, thy time and mine,
Till when, once more thy pardon and farewell !

The very God ! think, Abib ; dost thou think ?
So, the All-Great, were the All-Loving too—
So, through the thunder comes a human voice
Saying, " O heart I made, a heart beats here !
Face, my hands fashioned, see it in myself.
Thou hast no power nor may'st conceive of mine,
But love I gave thee, with Myself to love,   310
And thou must love me who have died for thee ! "
The madman saith He said so : it is strange.

MESMERISM

—◆—

1.

ALL I believed is true !
    I am able yet
    All I want to get
By a method as strange as new :
Dare I trust the same to you ?

2.

If at night, when doors are shut,
    And the wood-worm picks,
    And the death-watch ticks,
And the bar has a flag of smut,
And a cat's in the water-butt—

3.

And the socket floats and flares,
    And the house-beams groan,
    And a foot unknown
Is surmised on the garret-stairs,
And the locks slip unawares—

4.

And the spider, to serve his ends,
 By a sudden thread,
  Arms and legs outspread,
On the table's midst descends,
Comes to find, God knows what friends !—

5.

If since eve drew in, I say,
 I have sate and brought
  (So to speak) my thought
To bear on the woman away,
Till I felt my hair turn grey—

6.

Till I seemed to have and hold
 In the vacancy
  'Twixt the wall and me,
From the hair-plait's chestnut-gold
To the foot in its muslin fold—

7.

Have and hold, then and there,
 Her, from head to foot,
  Breathing and mute,
Passive and yet aware,
In the grasp of my steady stare—

8.

Hold and have, there and then,
 All her body and soul
  That completes my Whole,
All that women add to men,
In the clutch of my steady ken—

9.

Having and holding, till
    I imprint her fast
    On the void at last
As the sun does whom he will
By the calotypist's skill—

10.

Then,—if my heart's strength serve,
    And through all and each
    Of the veils I reach
To her soul and never swerve,
Knitting an iron nerve—

11.

Commanding that to advance
    And inform the shape
    Which has made escape
And before my countenance
Answers me glance for glance—

12.

I, still with a gesture fit
    Of my hands that best
    Do my soul's behest,
Pointing the power from it,
While myself do steadfast sit—

13.

Steadfast and still the same
    On my object bent
    While the hands give vent
To my ardour and my aim
And break into very flame—

14.

Then, I reach, I must believe,
       Not her soul in vain,
       For to me again
It reaches, and past retrieve
Is wound in the toils I weave—

15.

And must follow as I require,
       As befits a thrall,
       Bringing flesh and all,
Essence and earth-attire,
To the source of the tractile fire—

16.

Till the house called hers, not mine,
       With a growing weight
       Seems to suffocate
If she break not its leaden line
And escape from its close confine—

17.

Out of doors into the night!
       On to the maze
       Of the wild wood-ways,
Not turning to left or right
From the pathway, blind with sight—

18.

Making thro' rain and wind
       O'er the broken shrubs,
       'Twixt the stems and stubs,
With a still composed strong mind,
Not a care for the world behind—

19.

Swifter and still more swift,
  As the crowding peace
  Doth to joy increase
In the wide blind eyes uplift,
Thro' the darkness and the drift !

20.

While I—to the shape, I too
  Feel my soul dilate
  Nor a whit abate
And relax not a gesture due
As I see my belief come true—

21.

For there ! have I drawn or no
  Life to that lip ?
  Do my fingers dip
In a flame which again they throw
On the cheek that breaks a-glow ?

22.

Ha ! was the hair so first ?
  What, unfilleted,
  Made alive, and spread
Through the void with a rich outburst,
Chestnut gold-interspersed !

23.

Like the doors of a casket-shrine,
  See, on either side,
  Her two arms divide
Till the heart betwixt makes sign,
Take me, for I am thine !

24.

Now—now—the door is heard
  Hark ! the stairs and near—
  Nearer—and here—
Now ! and at call the third
She enters without a word.

25.

On doth she march and on
  To the fancied shape—
  It is past escape
Herself, now—the dream is done
And the shadow and she are one.

26.

First I will pray. Do Thou
  That ownest the soul,
  Yet wilt grant controul
To another nor disallow
For a time, restrain me now !

27.

I admonish me while I may,
  Not to squander guilt,
  Since require Thou wilt
At my hand its price one day !
What the price is, who can say ?

A SERENADE AT THE VILLA

—◆—

1.

THAT was I, you heard last night
   When there rose no moon at all,
Nor, to pierce the strained and tight
   Tent of heaven, a planet small :
Life was dead, and so was light.

2.

Not a twinkle from the fly,
   Not a glimmer from the worm.
When the crickets stopped their cry,
   When the owls forbore a term,
You heard music ; that was I.

3.

Earth turned in her sleep with pain,
   Sultrily suspired for proof :
In at heaven and out again,
   Lightning !—where it broke the roof,
Bloodlike, some few drops of rain.

4.

What they could my words expressed,
    O my love, my all, my one !
Singing helped the verses best,
    And when singing's best was done,
To my lute I left the rest.

5.

So wore night ; the east was grey,
    White the broad-faced hemlock flowers ;
Soon would come another day ;
    Ere its first of heavy hours
Found me, I had past away.

6.

What became of all the hopes,
    Words and song and lute as well ?
Say, this struck you—" When life gropes
    Feebly for the path where fell
Light last on the evening slopes,

7.

" One friend in that path shall be
    To secure my steps from wrong ;
One to count night day for me,
    Patient through the watches long,
Serving most with none to see."

8.

Never say—as something bodes—
    " So the worst has yet a worse !
When life halts 'neath double loads,
    Better the task-master's curse
Than such music on the roads !

9.

" When no moon succeeds the sun,
  Nor can pierce the midnight's tent
Any star, the smallest one,
  While some drops, where lightning went,
Show the final storm begun—

10.

" When the fire-fly hides its spot,
  When the garden-voices fail
In the darkness thick and hot,—
  Shall another voice avail,
That shape be where those are not ?

11.

" Has some plague a longer lease
  Proffering its help uncouth ?
Can't one even die in peace ?
  As one shuts one's eyes on youth,
Is that face the last one sees ? "

12.

Oh, how dark your villa was,
  Windows fast and obdurate !
How the garden grudged me grass
  Where I stood—the iron gate
Ground its teeth to let me pass !

MY STAR

---·---

ALL that I know
   Of a certain star,
Is, it can throw
   (Like the angled spar)
Now a dart of red,
   Now a dart of blue,
Till my friends have said
   They would fain see, too,
My star that dartles the red and the blue !
Then it stops like a bird,—like a flower, hangs furled ;
  They must solace themselves with the Saturn above it.
What matter to me if their star is a world ?
  Mine has opened its soul to me ; therefore I love it.

INSTANS TYRANNUS

—•—

1.

Of the million or two, more or less,
I rule and possess,
One man, for some cause undefined,
Was least to my mind.

2.

I struck him, he grovelled of course—
For, what was his force?
I pinned him to earth with my weight
And persistence of hate—
And he lay, would not moan, would not curse,
As if lots might be worse.

3.

" Were the object less mean, would he stand
At the swing of my hand !
For obscurity helps him and blots
The hole where he squats."
So I set my five wits on the stretch
To inveigle the wretch.

All in vain ! gold and jewels I threw,
Still he couched there perdue.
I tempted his blood and his flesh,
Hid in roses my mesh,
Choicest cates and the flagon's best spilth—
Still he kept to his filth !

4.

Had he kith now or kin, were access
To his heart, if I press—
Just a son or a mother to seize—
No such booty as these !
Were it simply a friend to pursue
'Mid my million or two,
Who could pay me in person or pelf
What he owes me himself.
No ! I could not but smile through my chafe—
For the fellow lay safe
As his mates do, the midge and the nit,
—Through minuteness, to wit.

5.

Then a humor more great took its place
At the thought of his face,
The droop, the low cares of the mouth,
The trouble uncouth
'Twixt the brows, all that air one is fain
To put out of its pain—
And, no, I admonished myself,
" Is one mocked by an elf,
Is one baffled by toad or by rat ?
The gravamen's in that !

How the lion, who crouches to suit
His back to my foot,
Would admire that I stand in debate !
But the Small is the Great
If it vexes you,—that is the thing !
Toad or rat vex the King ?
Though I waste half my realm to unearth
Toad or rat, 'tis well worth ! "

6.

So I soberly laid my last plan
To extinguish the man.
Round his creep-hole,—with never a break
Ran my fires for his sake ;
Over-head, did my thunders combine
With my under-ground mine :
Till I looked from my labor content
To enjoy the event.

7.

When sudden . . . how think ye, the end ?
Did I say " without friend ? "
Say rather, from marge to blue marge
The whole sky grew his targe
With the sun's self for visible boss,
While an Arm ran across
Which the earth heaved beneath like a breast
Where the wretch was safe prest !
Do you see ? just my vengeance complete,
The man sprang to his feet,
Stood erect, caught at God's skirts, and prayed !
—So, I was afraid !

A PRETTY WOMAN

——+——

1.

THAT fawn-skin-dappled hair of hers,
    And the blue eye
    Dear and dewy,
And that infantine fresh air of hers !

2.

To think men cannot take you, Sweet,
    And enfold you,
    Ay, and hold you,
And so keep you what they make you, Sweet !

3.

You like us for a glance, you know—
    For a word's sake,
    Or a sword's sake,
All's the same, whate'er the chance, you know.

4.

And in turn we make you ours, we say—
    You and youth too,
    Eyes and mouth too,
All the face composed of flowers, we say.

5.

All's our own, to make the most of, Sweet—
    Sing and say for,
    Watch and pray for,
Keep a secret or go boast of, Sweet.

6.

But for loving, why, you would not, Sweet,
    Though we prayed you,
    Paid you, brayed you
In a mortar—for you could not, Sweet.

7.

So, we leave the sweet face fondly there—
    Be its beauty
    Its sole duty !
Let all hope of grace beyond, lie there !

8.

And while the face lies quiet there,
    Who shall wonder
    That I ponder
A conclusion ?   I will try it there.

9.

As,—why must one, for the love forgone,
    Scout mere liking ?
    Thunder-striking
Earth,—the heaven, we looked above for, gone !

10.

Why with beauty, needs there money be—
    Love with liking ?
    Crush the fly-king
In his gauze, because no honey bee ?

11.

May not liking be so simple-sweet,
        If love grew there
        'Twould undo there
All that breaks the cheek to dimples sweet ?

12.

Is the creature too imperfect, say ?
        Would you mend it
        And so end it ?
Since not all addition perfects aye !

13.

Or is it of its kind, perhaps,
        Just perfection—
        Whence, rejection
Of a grace not to its mind, perhaps ?

14.

Shall we burn up, tread that face at once
        Into tinder,
        And so hinder
Sparks from kindling all the place at once ?

15.

Or else kiss away one's soul on her ?
        Your love-fancies !—
        A sick man sees
Truer, when his hot eyes roll on her !

16.

Thus the craftsman thinks to grace the rose,—
        Plucks a mould-flower
        For his gold flower,
Uses fine things that efface the rose.

17.

Rosy rubies make its cup more rose,
    Precious metals
    Ape the petals,—
Last, some old king locks it up, morose !

18.

Then, how grace a rose ?   I know a way !
    Leave it rather.
    Must you gather ?
Smell, kiss, wear it—at last, throw away !

"CHILDE ROLAND TO THE DARK TOWER CAME"

(See Edgar's Song in " LEAR.")

—————

1.

My first thought was, he lied in every word,
   That hoary cripple, with malicious eye
   Askance to watch the working of his lie
On mine, and mouth scarce able to afford
Suppression of the glee that pursed and scored
   Its edge at one more victim gained thereby.

2.

What else should he be set for, with his staff ?
   What, save to waylay with his lies, ensnare
   All travellers that might find him posted there,
And ask the road ?   I guessed what skull-like laugh
Would break, what crutch 'gin write my epitaph
   For pastime in the dusty thoroughfare,

3.

If at his counsel I should turn aside
   Into that ominous tract which, all agree,
   Hides the Dark Tower.   Yet acquiescingly
I did turn as he pointed ; neither pride
Nor hope rekindling at the end descried,
   So much as gladness that some end should be.

4.

For, what with my whole world-wide wandering,
  What with my search drawn out thro' years, my hope
  Dwindled into a ghost not fit to cope
With that obstreperous joy success would bring,—
I hardly tried now to rebuke the spring
  My heart made, finding failure in its scope.

5.

As when a sick man very near to death
  Seems dead indeed, and feels begin and end
  The tears and takes the farewell of each friend,
And hears one bid the other go, draw breath
Freelier outside, (" since all is o'er," he saith,
  " And the blow fall'n no grieving can amend ")

6.

While some discuss if near the other graves
  Be room enough for this, and when a day
  Suits best for carrying the corpse away,
With care about the banners, scarves and staves,—
And still the man hears all, and only craves
  He may not shame such tender love and stay.

7.

Thus, I had so long suffered in this quest,
  Heard failure prophesied so oft, been writ
  So many times among " The Band "—to wit,
The knights who to the Dark Tower's search addressed
Their steps—that just to fail as they, seemed best,
  And all the doubt was now—should I be fit.

8.

So, quiet as despair, I turned from him,
  That hateful cripple, out of his highway
  Into the path he pointed. All the day

Had been a dreary one at best, and dim
Was settling to its close, yet shot one grim
   Red leer to see the plain catch its estray.

9.

For mark ! no sooner was I fairly found
   Pledged to the plain, after a pace or two,
   Than pausing to throw backward a last view
To the safe road, 'twas gone ! grey plain all round !
Nothing but plain to the horizon's bound.
   I might go on ; nought else remained to do.

10.

So on I went.   I think I never saw
   Such starved ignoble nature ; nothing throve :
   For flowers—as well expect a cedar grove !
But cockle, spurge, according to their law
Might propagate their kind, with none to awe,
   You'd think : a burr had been a treasure-trove.

11.

No ! penury, inertness, and grimace,
   In some strange sort, were the land's portion.   " See
   Or shut your eyes "—said Nature peevishly—
" It nothing skills : I cannot help my case :
The Judgment's fire alone can cure this place,
   Calcine its clods and set my prisoners free."

12.

If there pushed any ragged thistle-stalk
   Above its mates, the head was chopped—the bents
   Were jealous else.   What made those holes and rents
In the dock's harsh swarth leaves—bruised as to baulk
All hope of greenness ? 'tis a brute must walk
   Pashing their life out, with a brute's intents.

13.

As for the grass, it grew as scant as hair
    In leprosy—thin dry blades pricked the mud
    Which underneath looked kneaded up with blood.
One stiff blind horse, his every bone a-stare,
Stood stupified, however he came there—
    Thrust out past service from the devil's stud !

14.

Alive ? he might be dead for all I know,
    With that red gaunt and colloped neck a-strain,
    And shut eyes underneath the rusty mane.
Seldom went such grotesqueness with such woe :
I never saw a brute I hated so—
    He must be wicked to deserve such pain.

15.

I shut my eyes and turned them on my heart.
    As a man calls for wine before he fights,
    I asked one draught of earlier, happier sights
Ere fitly I could hope to play my part.
Think first, fight afterwards—the soldier's art :
    One taste of the old times sets all to rights !

16.

Not it ! I fancied Cuthbert's reddening face
    Beneath its garniture of curly gold,
    Dear fellow, till I almost felt him fold
An arm in mine to fix me to the place,
That way he used.   Alas ! one night's disgrace !
    Out went my heart's new fire and left it cold.

17.

Giles, then, the soul of honour—there he stands
    Frank as ten years ago when knighted first.
    What honest men should dare (he said) he durst.

Good—but the scene shifts—faugh ! what hangman's
Pin to his breast a parchment ? his own bands   [hands
   Read it.   Poor traitor, spit upon and curst !

18.

Better this present than a past like that—
   Back therefore to my darkening path again.
   No sound, no sight as far as eye could strain.
Will the night send a howlet or a bat ?
I asked : when something on the dismal flat
   Came to arrest my thoughts and change their train.

19.

A sudden little river crossed my path
   As unexpected as a serpent comes.
   No sluggish tide congenial to the glooms—
This, as it frothed by, might have been a bath
For the fiend's glowing hoof—to see the wrath
   Of its black eddy bespate with flakes and spumes.

20.

So petty yet so spiteful ! all along,
   Low scrubby alders kneeled down over it ;
   Drenched willows flung them headlong in a fit
Of mute despair, a suicidal throng :
The river which had done them all the wrong,
   Whate'er that was, rolled by, deterred no whit.

21.

Which, while I forded,—good saints, how I feared
   To set my foot upon a dead man's cheek,
   Each step, or feel the spear I thrust to seek
For hollows, tangled in his hair or beard !
—It may have been a water-rat I speared,
   But, ugh ! it sounded like a baby's shriek.

22.

Glad was I when I reached the other bank.
   Now for a better country.   Vain presage !
   Who were the strugglers, what war did they wage
Whose savage trample thus could pad the dank
Soil to a plash ? toads in a poisoned tank,
   Or wild cats in a red-hot iron cage—

23.

The fight must so have seemed in that fell cirque.
   What kept them there, with all the plain to choose ?
   No foot-print leading to that horrid mews,
None out of it : mad brewage set to work
Their brains, no doubt, like galley-slaves the Turk
   Pits for his pastime, Christians against Jews.

24.

And more than that—a furlong on—why, there !
   What bad use was that engine for, that wheel,
   Or brake, not wheel—that harrow fit to reel
Men's bodies out like silk ? with all the air
Of Tophet's tool, on earth left unaware,
   Or brought to sharpen its rusty teeth of steel.

25.

Then came a bit of stubbed ground, once a wood,
   Next a marsh, it would seem, and now mere earth
   Desperate and done with ; (so a fool finds mirth,
Makes a thing and then mars it, till his mood
Changes and off he goes !) within a rood
   Bog, clay and rubble, sand and stark black dearth.

26.

Now blotches rankling, coloured gay and grim,
   Now patches where some leanness of the soil's
   Broke into moss or substances like boils ;

Then came some palsied oak, a cleft in him
Like a distorted mouth that splits its rim
   Gaping at death, and dies while it recoils.

27.

And just as far as ever from the end !
  Nought in the distance but the evening, nought
  To point my footstep further !   At the thought,
A great black bird, Apollyon's bosom-friend,
Sailed past, nor beat his wide wing dragon-penned
  That brushed my cap—perchance the guide I sought.

28.

For looking up, aware I somehow grew,
  'Spite of the dusk, the plain had given place
  All round to mountains—with such name to grace
Mere ugly heights and heaps now stol'n in view.
How thus they had surprised me,—solve it, you !
  How to get from them was no plainer case.

29.

Yet half I seemed to recognise some trick
  Of mischief happened to me, God knows when—
  In a bad dream perhaps.   Here ended, then,
Progress this way.   When, in the very nick
Of giving up, one time more, came a click
  As when a trap shuts—you're inside the den !

30.

Burningly it came on me all at once,
  This was the place ! those two hills on the right
  Crouched like two bulls locked horn in horn in fight—
While to the left, a tall scalped mountain . . . Dunce,
Fool, to be dozing at the very nonce,
  After a life spent training for the sight !

31.

What in the midst lay but the Tower itself ?
 The round squat turret, blind as the fool's heart,
 Built of brown stone, without a counterpart
In the whole world.   The tempest's mocking elf
Points to the shipman thus the unseen shelf
 He strikes on, only when the timbers start.

32.

Not see ? because of night perhaps ?—Why, day
 Came back again for that ! before it left,
 The dying sunset kindled through a cleft :
The hills, like giants at a hunting, lay—
Chin upon hand, to see the game at bay,—
 " Now stab and end the creature—to the heft ! "

33.

Not hear ? when noise was everywhere ? it tolled
 Increasing like a bell.   Names in my ears,
 Of all the lost adventurers my peers,—
How such a one was strong, and such was bold,
And such was fortunate, yet each of old
 Lost, lost ! one moment knelled the woe of years.

34.

There they stood, ranged along the hill-sides—met
 To view the last of me, a living frame
 For one more picture ! in a sheet of flame
I saw them and I knew them all.   And yet
Dauntless the slug-horn to my lips I set
 And blew.   " *Childe Roland to the Dark Tower came.*"

RESPECTABILITY

1.

DEAR, had the world in its caprice
    Deigned to proclaim " I know you both,
    Have recognised your plighted troth,
Am sponsor for you—live in peace ! "—
How many precious months and years
    Of youth had passed, that speed so fast,
    Before we found it out at last,
The world, and what it fears ?

2.

How much of priceless life were spent
    With men that every virtue decks,
    And women models of their sex,
Society's true ornament,—
Ere we dared wander, nights like this,
    Thro' wind and rain, and watch the Seine,
    And feel the Boulevart break again
To warmth and light and bliss ?

3.

I know ! the world proscribes not love ;
    Allows my finger to caress
    Your lip's contour and downiness,
Provided it supply a glove.
The world's good word !—the Institute !
    Guizot receives Montalembert !
    Eh ? down the court three lampions flare—
Put forward your best foot !

A LIGHT WOMAN

1.

So far as our story approaches the end,
  Which do you pity the most of us three?—
My friend, or the mistress of my friend
  With her wanton eyes, or me?

2.

My friend was already too good to lose,
  And seemed in the way of improvement yet,
When she crossed his path with her hunting-noose
  And over him drew her net.

3.

When I saw him tangled in her toils,
  A shame, said I, if she adds just him
To her nine-and-ninety other spoils,
  The hundredth, for a whim!

4.

And before my friend be wholly hers,
  How easy to prove to him, I said,
An eagle's the game her pride prefers,
  Though she snaps at the wren instead!

5.

So I gave her eyes my own eyes to take,
  My hand sought hers as in earnest need,
And round she turned for my noble sake,
  And gave me herself indeed.

6.

The eagle am I, with my fame in the world,
  The wren is he, with his maiden face.
—You look away and your lip is curled ?
  Patience, a moment's space !

7.

For see—my friend goes shaking and white ;
  He eyes me as the basilisk :
I have turned, it appears, his day to night,
  Eclipsing his sun's disc.

8.

And I did it, he thinks, as a very thief :
  " Though I love her—that he comprehends—
One should master one's passions, (love, in chief)
  And be loyal to one's friends ! "

9.

And she,—she lies in my hand as tame
  As a pear hung basking over a wall ;
Just a touch to try and off it came ;
  'Tis mine,—can I let it fall ?

10.

With no mind to eat it, that's the worst
  Were it thrown in the road, would the case assist ?
'Twas quenching a dozen blue-flies' thirst
  When I gave its stalk a twist.

11.

And I,—what I seem to my friend, you see—
　　What I soon shall seem to his love, you guess.
What I seem to myself, do you ask of me ?
　　No hero, I confess.

12.

'Tis an awkward thing to play with souls,
　　And matter enough to save one's own.
Yet think of my friend, and the burning coals
　　He played with for bits of stone !

13.

One likes to show the truth for the truth ;
　　That the woman was light is very true :
But suppose she says,—never mind that youth—
　　What wrong have I done to you ?

14.

Well, any how, here the story stays,
　　So far at least as I understand ;
And, Robert Browning, you writer of plays,
　　Here's a subject made to your hand !

THE STATUE AND THE BUST

———

THERE'S a palace in Florence, the world knows well,
And a statue watches it from the square,
And this story of both do the townsmen tell.

Ages ago, a lady there,
At the farthest window facing the east
Asked, " Who rides by with the royal air ? "

The brides-maids' prattle around her ceased ;
She leaned forth, one on either hand ;
They saw how the blush of the bride increased—

They felt by its beats her heart expand—   10
As one at each ear and both in a breath
Whispered, " The Great-Duke Ferdinand."

That selfsame instant, underneath,
The Duke rode past in his idle way,
Empty and fine like a swordless sheath.

Gay he rode, with a friend as gay,
Till he threw his head back—" Who is she ? "
—" A Bride the Riccardi brings home to-day."

Hair in heaps laid heavily
Over a pale brow spirit-pure—   20
Carved like the heart of the coal-black tree,

Crisped like a war-steed's encolure—
Which vainly sought to dissemble her eyes
Of the blackest black our eyes endure.

And lo, a blade for a knight's emprise
Filled the fine empty sheath of a man,—
The Duke grew straightway brave and wise.

He looked at her, as a lover can;
She looked at him, as one who awakes,—
The past was a sleep, and her life began.   30

As love so ordered for both their sakes,
A feast was held that selfsame night
In the pile which the mighty shadow makes.

(For Via Larga is three-parts light,
But the Palace overshadows one,
Because of a crime which may God requite !

To Florence and God the wrong was done,
Through the first republic's murder there
By Cosimo and his cursed son.)

The Duke (with the statue's face in the square)   40
Turned in the midst of his multitude
At the bright approach of the bridal pair.

Face to face the lovers stood
A single minute and no more,
While the bridegroom bent as a man subdued—

Bowed till his bonnet brushed the floor—
For the Duke on the lady a kiss conferred,
As the courtly custom was of yore.

In a minute can lovers exchange a word ?
If a word did pass, which I do not think,   50
Only one out of the thousand heard.

That was the bridegroom.   At day's brink
He and his bride were alone at last
In a bed-chamber by a taper's blink.

Calmly he said that her lot was cast,
That the door she had passed was shut on her
Till the final catafalk repassed.

The world meanwhile, its noise and stir,
Through a certain window facing the east
She might watch like a convent's chronicler.   60

Since passing the door might lead to a feast,
And a feast might lead to so much beside,
He, of many evils, chose the least.

" Freely I choose too," said the bride—
" Your window and its world suffice."
So replied the tongue, while the heart replied—

" If I spend the night with that devil twice,
May his window serve as my loop of hell
Whence a damned soul looks on Paradise !

" I fly to the Duke who loves me well,   70
Sit by his side and laugh at sorrow
Ere I count another ave-bell.

" 'Tis only the coat of a page to borrow,
And tie my hair in a horse-boy's trim,
And I save my soul—but not to-morrow "—

(She checked herself and her eye grew dim)—
" My father tarries to bless my state :
I must keep it one day more for him.

" Is one day more so long to wait ?
Moreover the Duke rides past, I know—   80
We shall see each other, sure as fate."

She turned on her side and slept.   Just so !
So we resolve on a thing and sleep.
So did the lady, ages ago.

That night the Duke said, " Dear or cheap
As the cost of this cup of bliss may prove
To body or soul, I will drain it deep."

And on the morrow, bold with love,
He beckoned the bridegroom (close on call,
As his duty bade, by the Duke's alcove)   90

And smiled " 'Twas a very funeral
Your lady will think, this feast of ours,—
A shame to efface, whate'er befall !

" What if we break from the Arno bowers,
And let Petraja, cool and green,
Cure last night's fault with this morning's flowers ? "

The bridegroom, not a thought to be seen
On his steady brow and quiet mouth,
Said, " Too much favour for me so mean !

" Alas ! my lady leaves the south.   100
Each wind that comes from the Apennine
Is a menace to her tender youth.

" No way exists, the wise opine,
If she quits her palace twice this year,
To avert the flower of life's decline."

Quoth the Duke, " A sage and a kindly fear.
Moreover Petraja is cold this spring—
Be our feast to-night as usual here ! "

And then to himself—" Which night shall bring
Thy bride to her lover's embraces, fool—   110
Or I am the fool, and thou art his king !

" Yet my passion must wait a night, nor cool—
For to-night the Envoy arrives from France
Whose heart I unlock with thyself, my tool.

" I need thee still and might miss perchance.
To-day is not wholly lost, beside,
With its hope of my lady's countenance—

" For I ride—what should I do but ride ?
And passing her palace, if I list,
May glance at its window—well betide ! "   120

So said, so done : nor the lady missed
One ray that broke from the ardent brow,
Nor a curl of the lips where the spirit kissed.

Be sure that each renewed the vow,
No morrow's sun should arise and set
And leave them then as it left them now.

But next day passed, and next day yet,
With still fresh cause to wait one more
Ere each leaped over the parapet.

And still, as love's brief morning wore,   130
With a gentle start, half smile, half sigh,
They found love not as it seemed before.

They thought it would work infallibly,
But not in despite of heaven and earth—
The rose would blow when the storm passed by.

Meantime they could profit in winter's dearth
By winter's fruits that supplant the rose :
The world and its ways have a certain worth !

And to press a point while these oppose
Were a simple policy—best wait,   140
And lose no friends and gain no foes.

Meanwhile, worse fates than a lover's fate,
Who daily may ride and lean and look
Where his lady watches behind the grate !

And she—she watched the square like a book
Holding one picture and only one,
Which daily to find she undertook.

When the picture was reached the book was done,
And she turned from it all night to scheme
Of tearing it out for herself next sun.   150

Weeks grew months, years—gleam by gleam
The glory dropped from youth and love,
And both perceived they had dreamed a dream,

Which hovered as dreams do, still above,—
But who can take a dream for truth ?
Oh, hide our eyes from the next remove !

One day as the lady saw her youth
Depart, and the silver thread that streaked
Her hair, and, worn by the serpent's tooth,

The brow so puckered, the chin so peaked,—   160
And wondered who the woman was,
So hollow-eyed and haggard-cheeked,

Fronting her silent in the glass—
" Summon here," she suddenly said,
" Before the rest of my old self pass,

" Him, the Carver, a hand to aid,
Who moulds the clay no love will change,
And fixes a beauty never to fade.

" Let Robbia's craft so apt and strange
Arrest the remains of young and fair,   170
And rivet them while the seasons range.

" Make me a face on the window there
Waiting as ever, mute the while,
My love to pass below in the square !

" And let me think that it may beguile
Dreary days which the dead must spend
Down in their darkness under the aisle—

" To say,—' What matters at the end ?
I did no more while my heart was warm,
Than does that image, my pale-faced friend.'   180

" Where is the use of the lip's red charm,
The heaven of hair, the pride of the brow,
And the blood that blues the inside arm—

Unless we turn, as the soul knows how,
The earthly gift to an end divine ?
A lady of clay is as good, I trow."

But long ere Robbia's cornice, fine
With flowers and fruits which leaves enlace,
Was set where now is the empty shrine—

(With, leaning out of a bright blue space,   190
As a ghost might from a chink of sky,
The passionate pale lady's face—

Eyeing ever with earnest eye
And quick-turned neck at its breathless stretch,
Some one who ever passes by—)

The Duke sighed like the simplest wretch
In Florence, " So, my dream escapes !
Will its record stay ? "   And he bade them fetch

Some subtle fashioner of shapes—
" Can the soul, the will, die out of a man   200
Ere his body find the grave that gapes ?

" John of Douay shall work my plan,
Mould me on horseback here aloft,
Alive—(the subtle artisan !)

" In the very square I cross so oft !
That men may admire, when future suns
Shall touch the eyes to a purpose soft,

" While the mouth and the brow are brave in bronze—
Admire and say, ' When he was alive,
How he would take his pleasure once ! '   210

" And it shall go hard but I contrive
To listen meanwhile and laugh in my tomb
At indolence which aspires to strive."

———————

So ! while these wait the trump of doom,
How do their spirits pass, I wonder,
Nights and days in the narrow room ?

Still, I suppose, they sit and ponder
What a gift life was, ages ago,
Six steps out of the chapel yonder.

Surely they see not God, I know,   220
Nor all that chivalry of His,
The soldier-saints who, row on row,

Burn upward each to his point of bliss—
Since, the end of life being manifest,
He had cut his way thro' the world to this.

I hear your reproach—" But delay was best,
For their end was a crime ! "—Oh, a crime will do
As well, I reply, to serve for a test,

As a virtue golden through and through,
Sufficient to vindicate itself   230
And prove its worth at a moment's view.

Must a game be played for the sake of pelf ?
Where a button goes, 'twere an epigram
To offer the stamp of the very Guelph.

The true has no value beyond the sham.
As well the counter as coin, I submit,
When your table's a hat, and your prize, a dram.

Stake your counter as boldly every whit,
Venture as truly, use the same skill,
Do your best, whether winning or losing it,   240

If you choose to play—is my principle !
Let a man contend to the uttermost
For his life's set prize, be it what it will !

The counter our lovers staked was lost
As surely as if it were lawful coin :
And the sin I impute to each frustrate ghost

Was, the unlit lamp and the ungirt loin,
Though the end in sight was a crime, I say.
You of the virtue, (we issue join)
How strive you ?   *De te, fabula !*   250

LOVE IN A LIFE

---·---

1.

Room after room,
I hunt the house through
We inhabit together.
Heart, fear nothing, for, heart, thou shalt find her,
Next time, herself !—not the trouble behind her
Left in the curtain, the couch's perfume !
As she brushed it, the cornice-wreath blossomed anew,—
Yon looking-glass gleamed at the wave of her feather.

2.

Yet the day wears,
And door succeeds door ;
I try the fresh fortune—
Range the wide house from the wing to the centre.
Still the same chance ! she goes out as I enter.
Spend my whole day in the quest,—who cares ?
But 'tis twilight, you see,—with such suites to explore,
Such closets to search, such alcoves to importune !

LIFE IN A LOVE

———

Escape me ?
Never—
Beloved !
While I am I, and you are you,
  So long as the world contains us both,
  Me the loving and you the loth,
While the one eludes, must the other pursue.
My life is a fault at last, I fear—
  It seems too much like a fate, indeed !
  Though I do my best I shall scarce succeed—
But what if I fail of my purpose here ?
It is but to keep the nerves at strain,
  To dry one's eyes and laugh at a fall,
And baffled, get up to begin again,—
  So the chace takes up one's life, that's all.
While, look but once from your farthest bound,
  At me so deep in the dust and dark,
No sooner the old hope drops to ground
  Than a new one, straight to the self-same mark,
      I shape me—
      Ever
      Removed !

HOW IT STRIKES A CONTEMPORARY

—⊢—

I ONLY knew one poet in my life :
And this, or something like it, was his way.

   You saw go up and down Valladolid,
A man of mark, to know next time you saw.
His very serviceable suit of black
Was courtly once and conscientious still,
And many might have worn it, though none did :
The cloak that somewhat shone and shewed the threads
Had purpose, and the ruff, significance.
He walked and tapped the pavement with his cane,   10
Scenting the world, looking it full in face,
An old dog, bald and blindish, at his heels.
They turned up, now, the alley by the church,
That leads no whither ; now, they breathed themselves
On the main promenade just at the wrong time.
You'd come upon his scrutinising hat,
Making a peaked shade blacker than itself
Against the single window spared some house
Intact yet with its mouldered Moorish work,—
Or else surprise the ferrel of his stick   20
Trying the mortar's temper 'tween the chinks

Of some new shop a-building, French and fine.
He stood and watched the cobbler at his trade,
The man who slices lemons into drink,
The coffee-roaster's brazier, and the boys
That volunteer to help him turn its winch.
He glanced o'er books on stalls with half an eye,
And fly-leaf ballads on the vendor's string,
And broad-edge bold-print posters by the wall.
He took such cognisance of men and things,   30
If any beat a horse, you felt he saw ;
If any cursed a woman, he took note ;
Yet stared at nobody,—they stared at him,
And found, less to their pleasure than surprise,
He seemed to know them and expect as much.
So, next time that a neighbour's tongue was loosed,
It marked the shameful and notorious fact,
We had among us, not so much a spy,
As a recording chief-inquisitor,
The town's true master if the town but knew !   40
We merely kept a Governor for form,
While this man walked about and took account
Of all thought, said, and acted, then went home,
And wrote it fully to our Lord the King
Who has an itch to know things, He knows why,
And reads them in His bed-room of a night.
Oh, you might smile ! there wanted not a touch,
A tang of . . . well, it was not wholly ease
As back into your mind the man's look came—
Stricken in years a little,—such a brow   50
His eyes had to live under !—clear as flint
On either side the formidable nose
Curved, cut, and coloured, like an eagle's claw.

Had he to do with A.'s surprising fate ?
When altogether old B. disappeared
And young C. got his mistress,—was't our friend,
His letter to the King, that did it all ?
What paid the bloodless man for so much pains ?
Our Lord the King has favourites manifold,
And shifts his ministry some once a month ;   60
Our city gets new Governors at whiles,—
But never word or sign, that I could hear,
Notified to this man about the streets
The King's approval of those letters conned
The last thing duly at the dead of night.
Did the man love his office ? frowned our Lord,
Exhorting when none heard—" Beseech me not !
Too far above my people,—beneath Me !
I set the watch,—how should the people know ?
Forget them, keep Me all the more in mind ! "   70
Was some such understanding 'twixt the Two ?

I found no truth in one report at least—
That if you tracked him to his home, down lanes
Beyond the Jewry, and as clean to pace,
You found he ate his supper in a room
Blazing with lights, four Titians on the wall,
And twenty naked girls to change his plate !
Poor man, he lived another kind of life
In that new, stuccoed, third house by the bridge,
Fresh-painted, rather smart than otherwise !   80
The whole street might o'erlook him as he sat,
Leg crossing leg, one foot on the dog's back,
Playing a decent cribbage with his maid
(Jacynth, you're sure her name was) o'er the cheese

And fruit, three red halves of starved winter-pears,
Or treat of radishes in April ! nine—
Ten, struck the church clock, straight to bed went he.

   My father, like the man of sense he was,
Would point him out to me a dozen times ;
" St—St," he'd whisper, " the Corregidor ! "   90
I had been used to think that personage
Was one with lacquered breeches, lustrous belt,
And feathers like a forest in his hat,
Who blew a trumpet and proclaimed the news,
Announced the bull-fights, gave each church its turn,
And memorized the miracle in vogue !
He had a great observance from us boys—
I was in error ; that was not the man.

   I'd like now, yet had haply been afraid,
To have just looked, when this man came to die,   100
And seen who lined the clean gay garret's sides
And stood about the neat low truckle-bed,
With the heavenly manner of relieving guard.
Here had been, mark, the general-in-chief,
Thro' a whole campaign of the world's life and death,
Doing the King's work all the dim day long,
In his old coat, and up to his knees in mud,
Smoked like a herring, dining on a crust,—
And now the day was won, relieved at once !
No further show or need for that old coat,   110
You are sure, for one thing !   Bless us, all the while
How sprucely we are dressed out, you and I !
A second, and the angels alter that.
Well, I could never write a verse,—could you ?
Let's to the Prado and make the most of time.

THE LAST RIDE TOGETHER

—————

1.

I SAID—Then, dearest, since 'tis so,
Since now at length my fate I know,
Since nothing all my love avails,
Since all my life seemed meant for, fails,
  Since this was written and needs must be—
My whole heart rises up to bless
Your name in pride and thankfulness !
Take back the hope you gave,—I claim
Only a memory of the same,
—And this beside, if you will not blame,
  Your leave for one more last ride with me.

2.

My mistress bent that brow of hers,
Those deep dark eyes where pride demurs
When pity would be softening through,
Fixed me a breathing-while or two

With life or death in the balance—Right !
The blood replenished me again :
My last thought was at least not vain.
I and my mistress, side by side
Shall be together, breathe and ride,
So one day more am I deified.
    Who knows but the world may end to-night ?

3.

Hush ! if you saw some western cloud
All billowy-bosomed, over-bowed
By many benedictions—sun's
And moon's and evening-star's at once—
    And so, you, looking and loving best,
Conscious grew, your passion drew
Cloud, sunset, moonrise, star-shine too
Down on you, near and yet more near,
Till flesh must fade for heaven was here !—
Thus leant she and lingered—joy and fear !
    Thus lay she a moment on my breast.

4.

Then we began to ride.   My soul
Smoothed itself out, a long-cramped scroll
Freshening and fluttering in the wind.
Past hopes already lay behind.
    What need to strive with a life awry ?
Had I said that, had I done this,
So might I gain, so might I miss.
Might she have loved me ? just as well
She might have hated,—who can tell ?
Where had I been now if the worst befell ?
    And here we are riding, she and I.

5.

Fail I alone, in words and deeds ?
Why, all men strive and who succeeds ?
We rode ; it seemed my spirit flew,
Saw other regions, cities new,
  As the world rushed by on either side.
I thought, All labour, yet no less
Bear up beneath their unsuccess.
Look at the end of work, contrast
The petty Done the Undone vast,
This present of theirs with the hopeful past !
  I hoped she would love me. Here we ride.

6.

What hand and brain went ever paired ?
What heart alike conceived and dared ?
What act proved all its thought had been ?
What will but felt the fleshly screen ?
  We ride and I see her bosom heave.
There's many a crown for who can reach.
Ten lines, a statesman's life in each !
The flag stuck on a heap of bones,
A soldier's doing ! what atones ?
They scratch his name on the Abbey-stones.
  My riding is better, by their leave.

7.

What does it all mean, poet ? well,
Your brain's beat into rhythm—you tell
What we felt only ; you expressed
You hold things beautiful the best,

And pace them in rhyme so, side by side.
'Tis something, nay 'tis much—but then,
Have you yourself what's best for men ?
Are you—poor, sick, old ere your time—
Nearer one whit your own sublime
Than we who never have turned a rhyme ?
    Sing, riding's a joy ! For me, I ride.

8.

And you, great sculptor—so you gave
A score of years to art, her slave,
And that's your Venus—whence we turn
To yonder girl that fords the burn !
    You acquiesce and shall I repine ?
What, man of music, you, grown grey
With notes and nothing else to say,
Is this your sole praise from a friend,
" Greatly his opera's strains intend,
" But in music we know how fashions end ! "
    I gave my youth—but we ride, in fine.

9.

Who knows what's fit for us ? Had fate
Proposed bliss here should sublimate
My being ; had I signed the bond—
Still one must lead some life beyond,
   —Have a bliss to die with, dim-descried.
This foot once planted on the goal,
This glory-garland round my soul,
Could I descry such ? Try and test !
I sink back shuddering from the quest—
Earth being so good, would Heaven seem best ?
    Now, Heaven and she are beyond this ride.

10.

And yet—she has not spoke so long !
What if Heaven be, that, fair and strong
At life's best, with our eyes upturned
Whither life's flower is first discerned,
   We, fixed so, ever should so abide ?
What if we still ride on, we two,
With life for ever old yet new,
Changed not in kind but in degree,
The instant made eternity,—
And Heaven just prove that I and she
   Ride, ride together, for ever ride ?

THE PATRIOT

AN OLD STORY.

—·—

1.

It was roses, roses, all the way,
   With myrtle mixed in my path like mad.
The house-roofs seemed to heave and sway,
   The church-spires flamed, such flags they had,
A year ago on this very day!

2.

The air broke into a mist with bells,
   The old walls rocked with the crowds and cries.
Had I said, " Good folks, mere noise repels—
   But give me your sun from yonder skies!"
They had answered, " And afterward, what else?"

3.

Alack, it was I who leaped at the sun,
   To give it my loving friends to keep.
Nought man could do, have I left undone
   And you see my harvest, what I reap
This very day, now a year is run.

4.

There's nobody on the house-tops now—
   Just a palsied few at the windows set—
For the best of the sight is, all allow,
   At the Shambles' Gate—or, better yet,
By the very scaffold's foot, I trow.

5.

I go in the rain, and, more than needs,
   A rope cuts both my wrists behind,
And I think, by the feel, my forehead bleeds,
   For they fling, whoever has a mind,
Stones at me for my year's misdeeds.

6.

Thus I entered Brescia, and thus I go !
   In such triumphs, people have dropped down dead.
" Thou, paid by the World,—what dost thou owe
   Me ? " God might have questioned : but now instead
'Tis God shall requite ! I am safer so.

MASTER HUGUES OF SAXE-GOTHA

—•—

1

HIST, but a word, fair and soft!
  Forth and be judged, Master Hugues!
Answer the question I've put you so oft—
  What do you mean by your mountainous fugues?
See, we're alone in the loft,

2.

I, the poor organist here,
  Hugues, the composer of note—
Dead, though, and done with, this many a year—
  Let's have a colloquy, something to quote,
Make the world prick up its ear!

3.

See, the church empties a-pace.
  Fast they extinguish the lights—
Hallo, there, sacristan! five minutes' grace!
  Here's a crank pedal wants setting to rights,
Baulks one of holding the base.

4.

See, our huge house of the sounds
  Hushing its hundreds at once,
Bids the last loiterer back to his bounds
  —Oh, you may challenge them, not a response
Get the church saints on their rounds!

5.

(Saints go their rounds, who shall doubt ?
　—March, with the moon to admire,
Up nave, down chancel, turn transept about,
　Supervise all betwixt pavement and spire,
Put rats and mice to the rout—

6.

Aloys and Jurien and Just—
　Order things back to their place,
Have a sharp eye lest the candlesticks rust,
　Rub the church plate, darn the sacrament lace,
Clear the desk velvet of dust.)

7.

Here's your book, younger folks shelve !
　Played I not off-hand and runningly,
Just now, your masterpiece, hard number twelve ?
　Here's what should strike,—could one handle it
Help the axe, give it a helve !　　　　　[cunningly.

8.

Page after page as I played,
　Every bar's rest where one wipes
Sweat from one's brow, I looked up and surveyed
　O'er my three claviers, yon forest of pipes
Whence you still peeped in the shade.

9.

Sure you were wishful to speak,
　You, with brow ruled like a score,
Yes, and eyes buried in pits on each cheek,
　Like two great breves as they wrote them of yore
Each side that bar, your straight beak !

10.

Sure you said—" Good, the mere notes !
    Still, couldst thou take my intent,
Know what procured me our Company's votes—
    Masters being lauded and sciolists shent,
Parted the sheep from the goats ! "

11.

Well then, speak up, never flinch !
    Quick, ere my candle's a snuff
—Burnt, do you see ? to its uttermost inch—
    I believe in you, but that's not enough.
Give my conviction a clinch !

12.

First you deliver your phrase
    —Nothing propound, that I see,
Fit in itself for much blame or much praise—
    Answered no less, where no answer needs be :
Off start the Two on their ways !

13.

Straight must a Third interpose,
    Volunteer needlessly help—
In strikes a Fourth, a Fifth thrusts in his nose,
    So the cry's open, the kennel's a-yelp,
Argument's hot to the close !

14.

One disertates, he is candid—
    Two must discept,—has distinguished !
Three helps the couple, if ever yet man did :
    Four protests, Five makes a dart at the thing wished—
Back to One, goes the case bandied !

15.

One says his say with a difference—
　More of expounding, explaining !
All now is wrangle, abuse, and vociferance—
　Now there's a truce, all's subdued, self-restraining—
Five, though, stands out all the stiffer hence.

16.

One is incisive, corrosive—
　Two retorts, nettled, curt, crepitant—
Three makes rejoinder, expansive, explosive—
　Four overbears them all, strident and strepitant—
Five . . . O Danaides, O Sieve !

17.

Now, they ply axes and crowbars—
　Now, they prick pins at a tissue
Fine as a skein of the casuist Escobar's
　Worked on the bone of a lie.　To what issue ?
Where is our gain at the Two-bars ?

18.

Est fuga, volvitur rota !
　On we drift.　Where looms the dim port ?
One, Two, Three, Four, Five, contribute their quota—
　Something is gained, if one caught but the import—
Show it us, Hugues of Saxe-Gotha !

19.

What with affirming, denying,
　Holding, risposting, subjoining,
All's like . . . it's like . . . for an instance I'm trying . . .
　There !　See our roof, its gilt moulding and groining
Under those spider-webs lying !

20.

So your fugue broadens and thickens,
　　Greatens and deepens and lengthens,
Till one exclaims—" But where's music, the dickens ?
　　Blot ye the gold, while your spider-web strengthens,
Blacked to the stoutest of tickens ? "

21.

I for man's effort am zealous.
　　Prove me such censure's unfounded !
Seems it surprising a lover grows jealous—
　　Hopes 'twas for something his organ-pipes sounded,
Tiring three boys at the bellows ?

22.

Is it your moral of Life ?
　　Such a web, simple and subtle,
Weave we on earth here in impotent strife,
　　Backward and forward each throwing his shuttle,
Death ending all with a knife ?

23.

Over our heads Truth and Nature—
　　Still our life's zigzags and dodges,
Ins and outs weaving a new legislature—
　　God's gold just shining its last where that lodges,
Palled beneath Man's usurpature !

24.

So we o'ershroud stars and roses,
　　Cherub and trophy and garland.
Nothings grow something which quietly closes
　　Heaven's earnest eye,—not a glimpse of the far land
Gets through our comments and glozes.

25.

Ah, but traditions, inventions,
　　(Say we and make up a visage)

So many men with such various intentions
  Down the past ages must know more than this age !
Leave the web all its dimensions !

26.

Who thinks Hugues wrote for the deaf ?
  Proved a mere mountain in labour ?
Better submit—try again—what's the clef ?
  'Faith, it's no trifle for pipe and for tabor—
Four flats—the minor in F.

27.

Friend, your fugue taxes the finger.
  Learning it once, who would lose it ?
Yet all the while a misgiving will linger—
  Truth's golden o'er us although we refuse it—
Nature, thro' dust-clouds we fling her !

28.

Hugues ! I advise *meâ poenâ*
  (Counterpoint glares like a Gorgon)
Bid One, Two, Three, Four, Five, clear the arena !
  Say the word, straight I unstop the Full-Organ,
Blare out the *mode Palestrina*.

29.

While in the roof, if I'm right there—
  . . . Lo, you, the wick in the socket !
Hallo, you sacristan, show us a light there !
  Down it dips, gone like a rocket !
What, you want, do you, to come unawares,
Sweeping the church up for first morning-prayers,
And find a poor devil at end of his cares
At the foot of your rotten-planked rat-riddled stairs ?
  Do I carry the moon in my pocket ?

BISHOP BLOUGRAM'S APOLOGY

—◆—

No more wine ? then we'll push back chairs and talk.
A final glass for me, tho': cool, i'faith !
We ought to have our Abbey back, you see.
It's different, preaching in basilicas,
And doing duty in some masterpiece
Like this of brother Pugin's, bless his heart !
I doubt if they're half baked, those chalk rosettes,
Ciphers and stucco-twiddlings everywhere ;
It's just like breathing in a lime-kiln : eh ?
These hot long ceremonies of our church   10
Cost us a little—oh, they pay the price,
You take me—amply pay it ! Now, we'll talk.

So, you despise me, Mr. Gigadibs.
No deprecation,—nay, I beg you, sir !
Beside 'tis our engagement : don't you know,
I promised, if you'd watch a dinner out,
We'd see truth dawn together ?—truth that peeps
Over the glass's edge when dinner's done,
And body gets its sop and holds its noise
And leaves soul free a little. Now's the time—   20

'Tis break of day ! You do despise me then.
And if I say, " despise me,"—never fear—
I know you do not in a certain sense—
Not in my arm-chair for example : here,
I well imagine you respect my place
(Status, *entourage*, worldly circumstance)
Quite to its value—very much indeed
—Are up to the protesting eyes of you
In pride at being seated here for once—
You'll turn it to such capital account !   30
When somebody, through years and years to come,
Hints of the bishop,—names me—that's enough—
" Blougram ? I knew him "—(into it you slide)
" Dined with him once, a Corpus Christi Day,
All alone, we two—he's a clever man—
And after dinner,—why, the wine you know,—
Oh, there was wine, and good !—what with the wine . . .
'Faith, we began upon all sorts of talk !
He's no bad fellow, Blougram—he had seen
Something of mine he relished—some review—   40
He's quite above their humbug in his heart,
Half-said as much, indeed—the thing's his trade—
I warrant, Blougram's sceptical at times—
How otherwise ? I liked him, I confess ! "
Che ch'è, my dear sir, as we say at Rome,
Don't you protest now ! It's fair give and take ;
You have had your turn and spoken your home-truths—
The hand's mine now, and here you follow suit.

Thus much conceded, still the first fact stays—
You do despise me ; your ideal of life   50
Is not the bishop's—you would not be I—

You would like better to be Goethe, now,
Or Buonaparte—or, bless me, lower still,
Count D'Orsay,—so you did what you preferred,
Spoke as you thought, and, as you cannot help,
Believed or disbelieved, no matter what,
So long as on that point, whate'er it was,
You loosed your mind, were whole and sole yourself.
—That, my ideal never can include,
Upon that element of truth and worth   60
Never be based ! for say they make me Pope
(They can't—suppose it for our argument)
Why, there I'm at my tether's end—I've reached
My height, and not a height which pleases you.
An unbelieving Pope won't do, you say.
It's like those eerie stories nurses tell,
Of how some actor played Death on a stage
With pasteboard crown, sham orb, and tinselled dart,
And called himself the monarch of the world,
Then going in the tire-room afterward   70
Because the play was done, to shift himself,
Got touched upon the sleeve familiarly
The moment he had shut the closet door
By Death himself.   Thus God might touch a Pope
At unawares, ask what his baubles mean,
And whose part he presumed to play just now ?
Best be yourself, imperial, plain and true !

So, drawing comfortable breath again,
You weigh and find whatever more or less
I boast of my ideal realised   80
Is nothing in the balance when opposed
To your ideal, your grand simple life,

Of which you will not realise one jot.
I am much, you are nothing; you would be all,
I would be merely much—you beat me there.

No, friend, you do not beat me,—hearken why.
The common problem, yours, mine, every one's,
Is not to fancy what were fair in life
Provided it could be,—but, finding first
What may be, then find how to make it fair   90
Up to our means—a very different thing!
No abstract intellectual plan of life
Quite irrespective of life's plainest laws,
But one, a man, who is man and nothing more,
May lead within a world which (by your leave)
Is Rome or London—not Fool's-paradise.
Embellish Rome, idealise away,
Make Paradise of London if you can,
You're welcome, nay, you're wise.

                              A simile!
We mortals cross the ocean of this world   100
Each in his average cabin of a life—
The best's not big, the worst yields elbow-room.
Now for our six months' voyage—how prepare?
You come on shipboard with a landsman's list
Of things he calls convenient—so they are!
An India screen is pretty furniture,
A piano-forte is a fine resource,
All Balzac's novels occupy one shelf,
The new edition fifty volumes long;
And little Greek books with the funny type   110
They get up well at Leipsic fill the next—

Go on ! slabbed marble, what a bath it makes !
And Parma's pride, the Jerome, let us add !
'Twere pleasant could Correggio's fleeting glow
Hang full in face of one where'er one roams,
Since he more than the others brings with him
Italy's self,—the marvellous Modenese !
Yet 'twas not on your list before, perhaps.
—Alas ! friend, here's the agent . . . is't the name ?
The captain, or whoever's master here—   120
You see him screw his face up ; what's his cry
Ere you set foot on shipboard ?   " Six feet square ! "
If you won't understand what six feet mean,
Compute and purchase stores accordingly—
And if in pique because he overhauls
Your Jerome, piano and bath, you come on board
Bare—why you cut a figure at the first
While sympathetic landsmen see you off ;
Not afterwards, when, long ere half seas o'er,
You peep up from your utterly naked boards   130
Into some snug and well-appointed berth
Like mine, for instance (try the cooler jug—
Put back the other, but don't jog the ice)
And mortified you mutter " Well and good—
He sits enjoying his sea-furniture—
'Tis stout and proper, and there's store of it,
Though I've the better notion, all agree,
Of fitting rooms up ! hang the carpenter,
Neat ship-shape fixings and contrivances—
I would have brought my Jerome, frame and all ! "   140
And meantime you bring nothing : never mind—
You've proved your artist-nature : what you don't,
You might bring, so despise me, as I say.

Now come, let's backward to the starting place.
See my way : we're two college friends, suppose—
Prepare together for our voyage, then,
Each note and check the other in his work,—
Here's mine, a bishop's outfit ; criticise !
What's wrong ? why won't you be a bishop too ?

Why, first, you don't believe, you don't and can't, 150
(Not stately, that is, and fixedly
And absolutely and exclusively)
In any revelation called divine.
No dogmas nail your faith—and what remains
But say so, like the honest man you are ?
First, therefore, overhaul theology !
Nay, I too, not a fool, you please to think,
Must find believing every whit as hard,
And if I do not frankly say as much,
The ugly consequence is clear enough.   160

Now, wait, my friend : well, I do not believe—
If you'll accept no faith that is not fixed,
Absolute and exclusive, as you say.
(You're wrong—I mean to prove it in due time)
Meanwhile, I know where difficulties lie
I could not, cannot solve, nor ever shall,
So give up hope accordingly to solve—
(To you, and over the wine). Our dogmas then
With both of us, tho' in unlike degree,
Missing full credence—overboard with them !   170
I mean to meet you on your own premise—
Good, there go mine in company with yours !

And now what are we ? unbelievers both,
Calm and complete, determinately fixed
To-day, to-morrow, and for ever, pray ?
You'll guarantee me that ?   Not so, I think.
In no-wise ! all we've gained is, that belief,
As unbelief before, shakes us by fits,
Confounds us like its predecessor.   Where's
The gain ? how can we guard our unbelief,   180
Make it bear fruit to us ?—the problem here.
Just when we are safest, there's a sunset-touch,
A fancy from a flower-bell, some one's death,
A chorus-ending from Euripides,—
And that's enough for fifty hopes and fears
As old and new at once as Nature's self,
To rap and knock and enter in our soul,
Take hands and dance there, a fantastic ring,
Round the ancient idol, on his base again,—
The grand Perhaps ! we look on helplessly,—   190
There the old misgivings, crooked questions are—
This good God,—what he could do, if he would,
Would, if he could—then must have done long since :
If so, when, where, and how ? some way must be,—
Once feel about, and soon or late you hit
Some sense, in which it might be, after all.
Why not, " The Way, the Truth, the Life ? "

                                                —That way
Over the mountain, which who stands upon
Is apt to doubt if it's indeed a road ;
While if he views it from the waste itself,   200
Up goes the line there, plain from base to brow,
Not vague, mistakeable ! what's a break or two

Seen from the unbroken desert either side ?
And then (to bring in fresh philosophy)
What if the breaks themselves should prove at last
The most consummate of contrivances
To train a man's eye, teach him what is faith,—
And so we stumble at truth's very test ?
What have we gained then by our unbelief
But a life of doubt diversified by faith,   210
For one of faith diversified by doubt.
We called the chess-board white,—we call it black.

" Well," you rejoin, " the end's no worse, at least,
We've reason for both colours on the board.
Why not confess, then, where I drop the faith
And you the doubt, that I'm as right as you ? "

Because, friend, in the next place, this being so,
And both things even,—faith and unbelief
Left to a man's choice,—we'll proceed a step,
Returning to our image, which I like.   220

A man's choice, yes—but a cabin-passenger's—
The man made for the special life of the world—
Do you forget him ?   I remember though !
Consult our ship's conditions and you find
One and but one choice suitable to all,
The choice that you unluckily prefer
Turning things topsy-turvy—they or it
Going to the ground.   Belief or unbelief
Bears upon life, determines its whole course,
Begins at its beginning.   See the world   230
Such as it is,—you made it not, nor I ;

I mean to take it as it is,—and you
Not so you'll take it,—though you get nought else.
I know the special kind of life I like,
What suits the most my idiosyncrasy,
Brings out the best of me and bears me fruit
In power, peace, pleasantness, and length of days.
I find that positive belief does this
For me, and unbelief, no whit of this.
—For you, it does, however—that we'll try !   240
'Tis clear, I cannot lead my life, at least
Induce the world to let me peaceably,
Without declaring at the outset, " Friends,
I absolutely and peremptorily
Believe ! "—I say faith is my waking life.
One sleeps, indeed, and dreams at intervals,
We know, but waking's the main point with us,
And my provision's for life's waking part.
Accordingly, I use heart, head and hands
All day, I build, scheme, study and make friends ;   250
And when night overtakes me, down I lie,
Sleep, dream a little, and get done with it,
The sooner the better, to begin afresh.
What's midnight's doubt before the dayspring's faith ?
You, the philosopher, that disbelieve,
That recognise the night, give dreams their weight—
To be consistent you should keep your bed,
Abstain from healthy acts that prove you a man,
For fear you drowse perhaps at unawares !
And certainly at night you'll sleep and dream,   260
Live through the day and bustle as you please.
And so you live to sleep as I to wake,
To unbelieve as I to still believe ?

Well, and the common sense of the world calls you
Bed-ridden,—and its good things come to me.
Its estimation, which is half the fight,
That's the first cabin-comfort I secure—
The next . . . but you perceive with half an eye !
Come, come, it's best believing, if we can—
You can't but own that.

                    Next, concede again—   270
If once we choose belief, on all accounts
We can't be too decisive in our faith,
Conclusive and exclusive in its terms,
To suit the world which gives us the good things.
In every man's career are certain points
Whereon he dares not be indifferent ;
The world detects him clearly, if he is,
As baffled at the game, and losing life.
He may care little or he may care much
For riches, honour, pleasure, work, repose,   280
Since various theories of life and life's
Success are extant which might easily
Comport with either estimate of these,
And whoso chooses wealth or poverty,
Labour or quiet, is not judged a fool
Because his fellows would choose otherwise.
We let him choose upon his own account
So long as he's consistent with his choice.
But certain points, left wholly to himself,
When once a man has arbitrated on,   290
We say he must succeed there or go hang.
Thus, he should wed the woman he loves most
Or needs most, whatsoe'er the love or need—

For he can't wed twice.   Then, he must avouch
Or follow, at the least, sufficiently,
The form of faith his conscience holds the best,
Whate'er the process of conviction was.
For nothing can compensate his mistake
On such a point, the man himself being judge—
He cannot wed twice, nor twice lose his soul.   300

   Well now—there's one great form of Christian faith
I happened to be born in—which to teach
Was given me as I grew up, on all hands,
As best and readiest means of living by ;
The same on examination being proved
The most pronounced moreover, fixed, precise
And absolute form of faith in the whole world—
Accordingly, most potent of all forms
For working on the world.   Observe, my friend,
Such as you know me, I am free to say,   310
In these hard latter days which hamper one,
Myself, by no immoderate exercise
Of intellect and learning, and the tact
To let external forces work for me,
Bid the street's stones be bread and they are bread,
Bid Peter's creed, or, rather, Hildebrand's,
Exalt me o'er my fellows in the world
And make my life an ease and joy and pride,
It does so,—which for me's a great point gained,
Who have a soul and body that exact   320
A comfortable care in many ways.
There's power in me and will to dominate
Which I must exercise, they hurt me else :
In many ways I need mankind's respect,

Obedience, and the love that's born of fear :
While at the same time, there's a taste I have,
A toy of soul, a titillating thing,
Refuses to digest these dainties crude.
The naked life is gross till clothed upon :
I must take what men offer, with a grace   330
As though I would not, could I help it, take !
A uniform to wear though over-rich—
Something imposed on me, no choice of mine ;
No fancy-dress worn for pure fashion's sake
And despicable therefore ! now men kneel
And kiss my hand—of course the Church's hand.
Thus I am made, thus life is best for me,
And thus that it should be I have procured ;
And thus it could not be another way,
I venture to imagine.

                 You'll reply—   340
So far my choice, no doubt, is a success ;
But were I made of better elements,
With nobler instincts, purer tastes, like you,
I hardly would account the thing success
Though it do all for me I say.

                     But, friend,
We speak of what is—not of what might be,
And how 'twere better if 'twere otherwise.
I am the man you see here plain enough—
Grant I'm a beast, why beasts must lead beasts' lives !
Suppose I own at once to tail and claws—   350
The tailless man exceeds me ; but being tailed
I'll lash out lion-fashion, and leave apes

To dock their stump and dress their haunches up.
My business is not to remake myself,
But make the absolute best of what God made.
Or—our first simile—though you proved me doomed
To a viler berth still, to the steerage-hole,
The sheep-pen or the pig-stye, I should strive
To make what use of each were possible ;
And as this cabin gets upholstery,   360
That hutch should rustle with sufficient straw.

But, friend, I don't acknowledge quite so fast
I fail of all your manhood's lofty tastes
Enumerated so complacently,
On the mere ground that you forsooth can find
In this particular life I choose to lead
No fit provision for them.   Can you not ?
Say you, my fault is I address myself
To grosser estimators than I need,
And that's no way of holding up the soul—   370
Which, nobler, needs men's praise perhaps, yet knows
One wise man's verdict outweighs all the fools',—
Would like the two, but, forced to choose, takes that ?
I pine among my million imbeciles
(You think) aware some dozen men of sense
Eye me and know me, whether I believe
In the last winking Virgin, as I vow,
And am a fool, or disbelieve in her
And am a knave,—approve in neither case,
Withhold their voices though I look their way :   380
Like Verdi when, at his worst opera's end
(The thing they gave at Florence,—what's its name ?)
While the mad houseful's plaudits near out-bang

His orchestra of salt-box, tongs and bones,
He looks through all the roaring and the wreaths
Where sits Rossini patient in his stall.

   Nay, friend, I meet you with an answer here—
For even your prime men who appraise their kind
Are men still, catch a thing within a thing,
See more in a truth than the truth's simple self,   390
Confuse themselves.   You see lads walk the street
Sixty the minute ; what's to note in that ?
You see one lad o'erstride a chimney-stack ;
Him you must watch—he's sure to fall, yet stands !
Our interest's on the dangerous edge of things.
The honest thief, the tender murderer,
The superstitious atheist, demireps
That love and save their souls in new French books—
We watch while these in equilibrium keep
The giddy line midway : one step aside,   400
They're classed and done with.   I, then, keep the line
Before your sages,—just the men to shrink
From the gross weights, coarse scales, and labels broad
You offer their refinement.   Fool or knave ?
Why needs a bishop be a fool or knave
When there's a thousand diamond weights between ?
So I enlist them.   Your picked Twelve, you'll find,
Profess themselves indignant, scandalised
At thus being held unable to explain
How a superior man who disbelieves   410
May not believe as well : that's Schelling's way !
It's through my coming in the tail of time,
Nicking the minute with a happy tact.
Had I been born three hundred years ago

They'd say, " What's strange ?   Blougram of course
          believes ; "
And, seventy years since, " disbelieves of course."
But now, " He may believe ; and yet, and yet
How can he ? "—All eyes turn with interest.
Whereas, step off the line on either side—
You, for example, clever to a fault,   420
The rough and ready man that write apace,
Read somewhat seldomer, think perhaps even less—
You disbelieve !   Who wonders and who cares ?
Lord So-and-So—his coat bedropt with wax,
All Peter's chains about his waist, his back
Brave with the needlework of Noodledom,
Believes !   Again, who wonders and who cares ?
But I, the man of sense and learning too,
The able to think yet act, the this, the that,
I, to believe at this late time of day !   430
Enough ; you see, I need not fear contempt.

          —Except it's yours ! admire me as these may,
You don't.   But what at least do you admire ?
Present your own perfections, your ideal,
Your pattern man for a minute—oh, make haste !
Is it Napoleon you would have us grow ?
Concede the means ; allow his head and hand,
(A large concession, clever as you are)
Good !—In our common primal element
Of unbelief (we can't believe, you know—   440
We're still at that admission, recollect)
Where do you find—apart from, towering-o'er
The secondary temporary aims
Which satisfy the gross tastes you despise—

Where do you find his star ?—his crazy trust
God knows through what or in what ? it's alive
And shines and leads him and that's all we want.
Have we aught in our sober night shall point
Such ends as his were, and direct the means
Of working out our purpose straight as his,   450
Nor bring a moment's trouble on success
With after-care to justify the same ?
—Be a Napoleon and yet disbelieve !
Why, the man's mad, friend, take his light away.
What's the vague good of the world for which you'd dare
With comfort to yourself blow millions up ?
We neither of us see it ! we do see
The blown-up millions—spatter of their brains
And writhing of their bowels and so forth,
In that bewildering entanglement   460
Of horrible eventualities
Past calculation to the end of time !
Can I mistake for some clear word of God
(Which were my ample warrant for it all)
His puff of hazy instincts, idle talk,
" The state, that's I," quack-nonsense about kings,
And (when one beats the man to his last hold)
The vague idea of setting things to rights,
Policing people efficaciously,
More to their profit, most of all to his own ;   470
The whole to end that dismallest of ends
By an Austrian marriage, cant to us the church,
And resurrection of the old *régime*.
Would I, who hope to live a dozen years,
Fight Austerlitz for reasons such and such ?
No : for, concede me but the merest chance

Doubt may be wrong—there's judgment, life to come !
With just that chance, I dare not.   Doubt proves right ?
This present life is all ? you offer me
Its dozen noisy years with not a chance   480
That wedding an Arch-Duchess, wearing lace,
And getting called by divers new-coined names,
Will drive off ugly thoughts and let me dine,
Sleep, read and chat in quiet as I like !
Therefore, I will not.

                Take another case ;
Fit up the cabin yet another way.
What say you to the poet's ? shall we write
Hamlets, Othellos—make the world our own,
Without a risk to run of either sort ?
I can't !—to put the strongest reason first.   490
"But try," you urge, "the trying shall suffice :
The aim, if reached or not, makes great the life.
Try to be Shakspeare, leave the rest to fate ! "
Spare my self-knowledge—there's no fooling me !
If I prefer remaining my poor self,
I say so not in self-dispraise but praise.
If I'm a Shakspeare, let the well alone—
Why should I try to be what now I am ?
If I'm no Shakspeare, as too probable,—
His power and consciousness and self-delight   500
And all we want in common, shall I find—
Trying for ever ? while on points of taste
Wherewith, to speak it humbly, he and I
Are dowered alike—I'll ask you, I or he,
Which in our two lives realises most ?
Much, he imagined—somewhat, I possess.

He had the imagination; stick to that!
Let him say " In the face of my soul's works
Your world is worthless and I touch it not
Lest I should wrong them "—I withdraw my plea.   510
But does he say so ? look upon his life !
Himself, who only can, gives judgment there.
He leaves his towers and gorgeous palaces
To build the trimmest house in Stratford town ;
Saves money, spends it, owns the worth of things,
Giulio Romano's pictures, Dowland's lute ;
Enjoys a show, respects the puppets, too,
And none more, had he seen its entry once,
Than " Pandulph, of fair Milan cardinal."
Why then should I who play that personage,   520
The very Pandulph Shakspeare's fancy made,
Be told that had the poet chanced to start
From where I stand now (some degree like mine
Being just the goal he ran his race to reach)
He would have run the whole race back, forsooth,
And left being Pandulph, to begin write plays ?
Ah, the earth's best can be but the earth's best !
Did Shakspeare live, he could but sit at home
And get himself in dreams the Vatican,
Greek busts, Venetian paintings, Roman walls,   530
And English books, none equal to his own,
Which I read, bound in gold, (he never did).
—Terni and Naples' bay and Gothard's top—
Eh, friend ? I could not fancy one of these—
But, as I pour this claret, there they are—
I've gained them—crossed St. Gothard last July
With ten mules to the carriage and a bed
Slung inside ; is my hap the worse for that ?

We want the same things, Shakspeare and myself,
And what I want, I have : he, gifted more,   540
Could fancy he too had it when he liked,
But not so thoroughly that if fate allowed
He would not have it also in my sense.
We play one game.   I send the ball aloft
No less adroitly that of fifty strokes
Scarce five go o'er the wall so wide and high
Which sends them back to me : I wish and get.
He struck balls higher and with better skill,
But at a poor fence level with his head,
And hit—his Stratford house, a coat of arms,   550
Successful dealings in his grain and wool,—
While I receive heaven's incense in my nose
And style myself the cousin of Queen Bess.
Ask him, if this life's all, who wins the game ?

Believe—and our whole argument breaks up.
Enthusiasm's the best thing, I repeat ;
Only, we can't command it ; fire and life
Are all, dead matter's nothing, we agree :
And be it a mad dream or God's very breath,
The fact's the same,—belief's fire once in us,   560
Makes of all else mere stuff to show itself.
We penetrate our life with such a glow
As fire lends wood and iron—this turns steel,
That burns to ash—all's one, fire proves its power
For good or ill, since men call flare success.
But paint a fire, it will not therefore burn.
Light one in me, I'll find it food enough !
Why, to be Luther—that's a life to lead,
Incomparably better than my own.

He comes, reclaims God's earth for God, he says,   570
Sets up God's rule again by simple means,
Re-opens a shut book, and all is done.
He flared out in the flaring of mankind ;
Such Luther's luck was—how shall such be mine ?
If he succeeded, nothing's left to do :
And if he did not altogether—well,
Strauss is the next advance.   All Strauss should be
I might be also.   But to what result ?
He looks upon no future : Luther did.
What can I gain on the denying side ?   580
Ice makes no conflagration.   State the facts,
Read the text right, emancipate the world—
The emancipated world enjoys itself
With scarce a thank-you—Blougram told it first
It could not owe a farthing,—not to him
More than St. Paul ! 'twould press its pay, you think ?
Then add there's still that plaguey hundredth chance
Strauss may be wrong.   And so a risk is run—
For what gain ? not for Luther's, who secured
A real heaven in his heart throughout his life,   590
Supposing death a little altered things !

  " Ay, but since really I lack faith," you cry,
" I run the same risk really on all sides,
In cool indifference as bold unbelief.
As well be Strauss as swing 'twixt Paul and him.
It's not worth having, such imperfect faith,
Nor more available to do faith's work
Than unbelief like yours.   Whole faith, or none ! "

  Softly, my friend ! I must dispute that point.
Once own the use of faith, I'll find you faith.   600

We're back on Christian ground.   You call for faith :
I show you doubt, to prove that faith exists.
The more of doubt, the stronger faith, I say,
If faith o'ercomes doubt.   How I know it does ?
By life and man's free will, God gave for that !
To mould life as we choose it, shows our choice :
That's our one act, the previous work's His own.
You criticise the soil ? it reared this tree—
This broad life and whatever fruit it bears !
What matter though I doubt at every pore,   610
Head-doubts, heart-doubts, doubts at my fingers' ends,
Doubts in the trivial work of every day,
Doubts at the very bases of my soul
In the grand moments when she probes herself—
If finally I have a life to show,
The thing I did, brought out in evidence
Against the thing done to me underground
By Hell and all its brood, for aught I know ?
I say, whence sprang this ? shows it faith or doubt ?
All's doubt in me ; where's break of faith in this ?   620
It is the idea, the feeling and the love
God means mankind should strive for and show forth,
Whatever be the process to that end,—
And not historic knowledge, logic sound,
And metaphysical acumen, sure !
" What think ye of Christ," friend ? when all's done and
          said,
You like this Christianity or not ?
It may be false, but will you wish it true ?
Has it your vote to be so if it can ?
Trust you an instinct silenced long ago   630
That will break silence and enjoin you love

What mortified philosophy is hoarse,
And all in vain, with bidding you despise ?
If you desire faith—then you've faith enough.
What else seeks God—nay, what else seek ourselves ?
You form a notion of me, we'll suppose,
On hearsay ; it's a favourable one :
" But still," (you add) " there was no such good
    man,
Because of contradictions in the facts.
One proves, for instance, he was born in Rome,   640
This Blougram—yet throughout the tales of him
I see he figures as an Englishman."
Well, the two things are reconcileable.
But would I rather you discovered that,
Subjoining—" Still, what matter though they be ?
Blougram concerns me nought, born here or there."

    Pure faith indeed—you know not what you ask !
Naked belief in God the Omnipotent,
Omniscient, Omnipresent, sears too much
The sense of conscious creatures to be borne.   650
It were the seeing him, no flesh shall dare.
Some think, Creation's meant to show him forth :
I say, it's meant to hide him all it can,
And that's what all the blessed Evil's for.
Its use in time is to environ us,
Our breath, our drop of dew, with shield enough
Against that sight till we can bear its stress.
Under a vertical sun, the exposed brain
And lidless eye and disemprisoned heart
Less certainly would wither up at once   660
Than mind, confronted with the truth of Him.

But time and earth case-harden us to live ;
The feeblest sense is trusted most ; the child
Feels God a moment, ichors o'er the place,
Plays on and grows to be a man like us.
With me, faith means perpetual unbelief
Kept quiet like the snake 'neath Michael's foot
Who stands calm just because he feels it writhe.
Or, if that's too ambitious,—here's my box—
I need the excitation of a pinch   670
Threatening the torpor of the inside-nose
Nigh on the imminent sneeze that never comes.
" Leave it in peace " advise the simple folk—
Make it aware of peace by itching-fits,
Say I—let doubt occasion still more faith !

    You'll say, once all believed, man, woman, child,
In that dear middle-age these noodles praise.
How you'd exult if I could put you back
Six hundred years, blot out cosmogony,
Geology, ethnology, what not,   680
(Greek endings with the little passing-bell
That signifies some faith's about to die)
And set you square with Genesis again,—
When such a traveller told you his last news,
He saw the ark a-top of Ararat
But did not climb there since 'twas getting dusk
And robber-bands infest the mountain's foot !
How should you feel, I ask, in such an age,
How act ?   As other people felt and did ;
With soul more blank than this decanter's knob,   690
Believe—and yet lie, kill, rob, fornicate
Full in belief's face, like the beast you'd be !

No, when the fight begins within himself,
A man's worth something.   God stoops o'er his head,
Satan looks up between his feet—both tug—
He's left, himself, in the middle : the soul wakes
And grows.   Prolong that battle through his life !
Never leave growing till the life to come !
Here, we've got callous to the Virgin's winks
That used to puzzle people wholesomely—   700
Men have outgrown the shame of being fools.
What are the laws of Nature, not to bend
If the Church bid them, brother Newman asks.
Up with the Immaculate Conception, then—
On to the rack with faith—is my advice !
Will not that hurry us upon our knees
Knocking our breasts, " It can't be—yet it shall !
Who am I, the worm, to argue with my Pope ?
Low things confound the high things ! " and so forth.
That's better than acquitting God with grace   710
As some folks do.   He's tried—no case is proved,
Philosophy is lenient—He may go !

You'll say—the old system's not so obsolete
But men believe still : ay, but who and where ?
King Bomba's lazzaroni foster yet
The sacred flame, so Antonelli writes ;
But even of these, what ragamuffin-saint
Believes God watches him continually,
As he believes in fire that it will burn,
Or rain that it will drench him ?   Break fire's law, 720
Sin against rain, although the penalty
Be just a singe or soaking ?   No, he smiles ;
Those laws are laws that can enforce themselves.

The sum of all is—yes, my doubt is great,
My faith's the greater—then my faith's enough.
I have read much, thought much, experienced much,
Yet would die rather than avow my fear
The Naples' liquefaction may be false,
When set to happen by the palace-clock
According to the clouds or dinner-time.   730
I hear you recommend, I might at least
Eliminate, decrassify my faith
Since I adopt it ; keeping what I must
And leaving what I can—such points as this !
I won't—that is, I can't throw one away.
Supposing there's no truth in what I said
About the need of trials to man's faith,
Still, when you bid me purify the same,
To such a process I discern no end,
Clearing off one excrescence to see two ;   740
There's ever a next in size, now grown as big,
That meets the knife—I cut and cut again !
First cut the Liquefaction, what comes last
But Fichte's clever cut at God himself ?
Experimentalize on sacred things ?
I trust nor hand nor eye nor heart nor brain
To stop betimes : they all get drunk alike.
The first step, I am master not to take.

You'd find the cutting-process to your taste
As much as leaving growths of lies unpruned,   750
Nor see more danger in it, you retort.
Your taste's worth mine ; but my taste proves more wise
When we consider that the steadfast hold
On the extreme end of the chain of faith

Gives all the advantage, makes the difference,
With the rough purblind mass we seek to rule.
We are their lords, or they are free of us
Just as we tighten or relax that hold.
So, other matters equal, we'll revert
To the first problem—which if solved my way   760
And thrown into the balance turns the scale—
How we may lead a comfortable life,
How suit our luggage to the cabin's size.

Of course you are remarking all this time
How narrowly and grossly I view life,
Respect the creature-comforts, care to rule
The masses, and regard complacently
" The cabin," in our old phrase !   Well, I do.
I act for, talk for, live for this world now,
As this world calls for action, life and talk—   770
No prejudice to what next world may prove,
Whose new laws and requirements my best pledge
To observe then, is that I observe these now,
Doing hereafter what I do meanwhile.
Let us concede (gratuitously though)
Next life relieves the soul of body, yields
Pure spiritual enjoyments : well, my friend,
Why lose this life in the meantime, since its use
May be to make the next life more intense ?

Do you know, I have often had a dream   780
(Work it up in your next month's article)
Of man's poor spirit in its progress still
Losing true life for ever and a day
Through ever trying to be and ever being

In the evolution of successive spheres,
Before its actual sphere and place of life,
Halfway into the next, which having reached,
It shoots with corresponding foolery
Halfway into the next still, on and off !
As when a traveller, bound from north to south,   790
Scouts fur in Russia—what's its use in France ?
In France spurns flannel—where's its need in Spain ?
In Spain drops cloth—too cumbrous for Algiers !
Linen goes next, and last the skin itself,
A superfluity at Timbuctoo.
When, through his journey, was the fool at ease ?
I'm at ease now, friend—worldly in this world
I take and like its way of life ; I think
My brothers who administer the means
Live better for my comfort—that's good too ;   800
And God, if he pronounce upon it all,
Approves my service, which is better still.
If He keep silence,—why for you or me
Or that brute-beast pulled-up in to-day's " Times,"
What odds is't, save to ourselves, what life we lead ?

You meet me at this issue—you declare,
All special-pleading done with, truth is truth,
And justifies itself by undreamed ways.
You don't fear but it's better, if we doubt,
To say so, acting up to our truth perceived   810
However feebly.   Do then,—act away !
'Tis there I'm on the watch for you !   How one acts
Is, both of us agree, our chief concern :
And how you'll act is what I fain would see
If, like the candid person you appear,

You dare to make the most of your life's scheme
As I of mine, live up to its full law
Since there's no higher law that counterchecks.
Put natural religion to the test
You've just demolished the revealed with—quick,   820
Down to the root of all that checks your will,
All prohibition to lie, kill, and thieve
Or even to be an atheistic priest !
Suppose a pricking to incontinence—
Philosophers deduce you chastity
Or shame, from just the fact that at the first
Whoso embraced a woman in the plain,
Threw club down, and forewent his brains beside,
So stood a ready victim in the reach
Of any brother-savage club in hand—   830
Hence saw the use of going out of sight
In wood or cave to prosecute his loves—
I read this in a French book t'other day.
Does law so analyzed coerce you much ?
Oh, men spin clouds of fuzz where matters end,
But you who reach where the first thread begins,
You'll soon cut that !—which means you can, but
    won't
Through certain instincts, blind, unreasoned-out,
You dare not set aside, you can't tell why,
But there they are, and so you let them rule.   840
Then, friend, you seem as much a slave as I,
A liar, conscious coward and hypocrite,
Without the good the slave expects to get,
Suppose he has a master after all !
You own your instincts—why what else do I,
Who want, am made for, and must have a God

Ere I can be aught, do aught ?—no mere name
Want, but the true thing with what proves its truth,
To wit, a relation from that thing to me,
Touching from head to foot—which touch I feel,　　850
And with it take the rest, this life of ours !
I live my life here ; yours you dare not live.

Not as I state it, who (you please subjoin)
Disfigure such a life and call it names,
While, in your mind, remains another way
For simple men : knowledge and power have rights,
But ignorance and weakness have rights too.
There needs no crucial effort to find truth
If here or there or anywhere about—
We ought to turn each side, try hard and see,　　860
And if we can't, be glad we've earned at least
The right, by one laborious proof the more,
To graze in peace earth's pleasant pasturage.
Men are not gods, but, properly, are brutes.
Something we may see, all we cannot see—
What need of lying ? I say, I see all,
And swear to each detail the most minute
In what I think a man's face—you, mere cloud :
I swear I hear him speak and see him wink,
For fear, if once I drop the emphasis,　　870
Mankind may doubt if there's a cloud at all.
You take the simpler life—ready to see,
Willing to see—for no cloud's worth a face—
And leaving quiet what no strength can move,
And which, who bids you move ? who has the right ?
I bid you ; but you are God's sheep, not mine—
" *Pastor est tui Dominus.*" You find

In these the pleasant pastures of this life
Much you may eat without the least offence,
Much you don't eat because your maw objects,   880
Much you would eat but that your fellow-flock
Open great eyes at you and even butt,
And thereupon you like your friends so much
You cannot please yourself, offending them—
Though when they seem exorbitantly sheep,
You weigh your pleasure with their butts and kicks
And strike the balance.   Sometimes certain fears
Restrain you—real checks since you find them so—
Sometimes you please yourself and nothing checks ;
And thus you graze through life with not one lie,   890
And like it best.

       But do you, in truth's name ?
If so, you beat—which means—you are not I—
Who needs must make earth mine and feed my fill
Not simply unbutted at, unbickered with,
But motioned to the velvet of the sward
By those obsequious wethers' very selves.
Look at me, sir ; my age is double yours.
At yours, I knew beforehand, so enjoyed,
What now I should be—as, permit the word,
I pretty well imagine your whole range   900
And stretch of tether twenty years to come.
We both have minds and bodies much alike.
In truth's name, don't you want my bishopric,
My daily bread, my influence and my state ?
You're young, I'm old, you must be old one day ;
Will you find then, as I do hour by hour,
Women their lovers kneel to, that cut curls

From your fat lap-dog's ears to grace a brooch—
Dukes, that petition just to kiss your ring—
With much beside you know or may conceive ?   910
Suppose we die to-night : well, here am I,
Such were my gains, life bore this fruit to me,
While writing all the same my articles
On music, poetry, the fictile vase
Found at Albano, or Anacreon's Greek.
But you—the highest honour in your life,
The thing you'll crown yourself with, all your days,
Is—dining here and drinking this last glass
I pour you out in sign of amity
Before we part for ever.   Of your power   920
And social influence, worldly worth in short,
Judge what's my estimation by the fact—
I do not condescend to enjoin, beseech,
Hint secresy on one of all these words !
You're shrewd and know that should you publish it
The world would brand the lie—my enemies first,
" Who'd sneer—the bishop's an arch-hypocrite,
And knave perhaps, but not so frank a fool."
Whereas I should not dare for both my ears
Breathe one such syllable, smile one such smile,   930
Before my chaplain who reflects myself—
My shade's so much more potent than your flesh.
What's your reward, self-abnegating friend ?
Stood you confessed of those exceptional
And privileged great natures that dwarf mine—
A zealot with a mad ideal in reach,
A poet just about to print his ode,
A statesman with a scheme to stop this war,
An artist whose religion is his art,

I should have nothing to object ! such men   940
Carry the fire, all things grow warm to them,
Their drugget's worth my purple, they beat me.
But you,—you're just as little those as I—
You, Gigadibs, who, thirty years of age,
Write stately for Blackwood's Magazine,
Believe you see two points in Hamlet's soul
Unseized by the Germans yet—which view you'll print—
Meantime the best you have to show being still
That lively lightsome article we took
Almost for the true Dickens,—what's the name ?   950
" The Slum and Cellar—or Whitechapel life
Limned after dark ! " it made me laugh, I know,
And pleased a month and brought you in ten pounds.
—Success I recognise and compliment,
And therefore give you, if you please, three words
(The card and pencil-scratch is quite enough)
Which whether here, in Dublin, or New York,
Will get you, prompt as at my eyebrow's wink,
Such terms as never you aspired to get
In all our own reviews and some not ours.   960
Go write your lively sketches—be the first
" Blougram, or The Eccentric Confidence "—
Or better simply say, " The Outward-bound."
Why, men as soon would throw it in my teeth
As copy and quote the infamy chalked broad
About me on the church-door opposite.
You will not wait for that experience though,
I fancy, howsoever you decide,
To discontinue—not detesting, not
Defaming, but at least—despising me !   970

———————

Over his wine so smiled and talked his hour
Sylvester Blougram, styled *in partibus*
Episcopus, nec non—(the deuce knows what
It's changed to by our novel hierarchy)
With Gigadibs the literary man,
Who played with spoons, explored his plate's design
And ranged the olive stones about its edge,
While the great bishop rolled him out his mind.

For Blougram, he believed, say, half he spoke.
The other portion, as he shaped it thus   980
For argumentatory purposes,
He felt his foe was foolish to dispute.
Some arbitrary accidental thoughts
That crossed his mind, amusing because new,
He chose to represent as fixtures there,
Invariable convictions (such they seemed
Beside his interlocutor's loose cards
Flung daily down, and not the same way twice)
While certain hell-deep instincts, man's weak tongue
Is never bold to utter in their truth   990
Because styled hell-deep ('tis an old mistake
To place hell at the bottom of the earth)
He ignored these,—not having in readiness
Their nomenclature and philosophy :
He said true things, but called them by wrong names.
" On the whole," he thought, " I justify myself
On every point where cavillers like this
Oppugn my life : he tries one kind of fence—
I close—he's worsted, that's enough for him ;
He's on the ground ! if the ground should break away
I take my stand on, there's a firmer yet   1001

Beneath it, both of us may sink and reach.
His ground was over mine and broke the first.
So let him sit with me this many a year ! "

He did not sit five minutes.   Just a week
Sufficed his sudden healthy vehemence.
(Something had struck him in the " Outward-bound "
Another way than Blougram's purpose was)
And having bought, not cabin-furniture
But settler's-implements (enough for three)   1010
And started for Australia—there, I hope,
By this time he has tested his first plough,
And studied his last chapter of St. John.

MEMORABILIA

—◆—

1.

Ah, did you once see Shelley plain,
  And did he stop and speak to you?
And did you speak to him again?
  How strange it seems, and new!

2.

But you were living before that,
  And you are living after,
And the memory I started at—
  My starting moves your laughter!

3.

I crossed a moor with a name of its own
  And a use in the world no doubt,
Yet a hand's-breadth of it shines alone
  'Mid the blank miles round about—

4.

For there I picked up on the heather
  And there I put inside my breast
A moulted feather, an eagle-feather—
  Well, I forget the rest.

MEN AND WOMEN

BY

ROBERT BROWNING

IN TWO VOLUMES

VOL. II.

LONDON

CHAPMAN AND HALL, 193, PICCADILLY.

1855

CONTENTS

	Page
ANDREA DEL SARTO. (CALLED "THE FAULTLESS PAINTER")	167
BEFORE	176
AFTER	178
IN THREE DAYS	179
IN A YEAR	181
OLD PICTURES IN FLORENCE	185
IN A BALCONY.—FIRST PART	196
„ SECOND PART	208
„ THIRD PART	218
SAUL	231
"DE GUSTIBUS—"	252
WOMEN AND ROSES	254
PROTUS	257
HOLY-CROSS DAY. (ON WHICH THE JEWS WERE FORCED TO ATTEND AN ANNUAL CHRISTIAN SERMON IN ROME)	260

                                                          Page
THE GUARDIAN-ANGEL : A PICTURE AT FANO   .   .   .   266

CLEON   269

THE TWINS   281

POPULARITY   283

THE HERETIC'S TRAGEDY. A MIDDLE-AGE INTERLUDE   .   286

TWO IN THE CAMPAGNA   291

A GRAMMARIAN'S FUNERAL   294

ONE WAY OF LOVE   299

ANOTHER WAY OF LOVE   300

"TRANSCENDENTALISM : " A POEM IN TWELVE BOOKS   .   .   302

MISCONCEPTIONS   304

ONE WORD MORE.   TO E. B. B.   '   305

MEN AND WOMEN

ANDREA DEL SARTO

(CALLED "THE FAULTLESS PAINTER.")

But do not let us quarrel any more,
No, my Lucrezia ; bear with me for once :
Sit down and all shall happen as you wish.
You turn your face, but does it bring your heart ?
I'll work then for your friend's friend, never fear,
Treat his own subject after his own way,
Fix his own time, accept too his own price,
And shut the money into this small hand
When next it takes mine.   Will it ? tenderly ?
Oh, I'll content him,—but to-morrow, Love !   10
I often am much wearier than you think,
This evening more than usual, and it seems
As if—forgive now—should you let me sit
Here by the window with your hand in mine
And look a half hour forth on Fiesole,

Both of one mind, as married people use,
Quietly, quietly, the evening through,
I might get up to-morrow to my work
Cheerful and fresh as ever.   Let us try.
To-morrow how you shall be glad for this !   20
Your soft hand is a woman of itself,
And mine the man's bared breast she curls inside.
Don't count the time lost, either ; you must serve
For each of the five pictures we require—
It saves a model.   So ! keep looking so—
My serpentining beauty, rounds on rounds !
—How could you ever prick those perfect ears,
Even to put the pearl there ! oh, so sweet—
My face, my moon, my everybody's moon,
Which everybody looks on and calls his,   30
And, I suppose, is looked on by in turn,
While she looks—no one's : very dear, no less !
You smile ? why, there's my picture ready made.
There's what we painters call our harmony !
A common greyness silvers everything,—
All in a twilight, you and I alike
—You, at the point of your first pride in me
(That's gone you know),—but I, at every point ;
My youth, my hope, my art, being all toned down
To yonder sober pleasant Fiesole.   40
There's the bell clinking from the chapel-top ;
That length of convent-wall across the way
Holds the trees safer, huddled more inside ;
The last monk leaves the garden ; days decrease
And autumn grows, autumn in everything.
Eh ? the whole seems to fall into a shape
As if I saw alike my work and self

And all that I was born to be and do,
A twilight-piece.   Love, we are in God's hand.
How strange now, looks the life he makes us lead !   50
So free we seem, so fettered fast we are :
I feel he laid the fetter : let it lie !
This chamber for example—turn your head—
All that's behind us ! you don't understand
Nor care to understand about my art,
But you can hear at least when people speak ;
And that cartoon, the second from the door
—It is the thing, Love ! so such things should be—
Behold Madonna, I am bold to say.
I can do with my pencil what I know,   60
What I see, what at bottom of my heart
I wish for, if I ever wish so deep—
Do easily, too—when I say perfectly
I do not boast, perhaps : yourself are judge
Who listened to the Legate's talk last week,
And just as much they used to say in France.
At any rate 'tis easy, all of it,
No sketches first, no studies, that's long past—
I do what many dream of all their lives
—Dream ? strive to do, and agonise to do,   70
And fail in doing.   I could count twenty such
On twice your fingers, and not leave this town,
Who strive—you don't know how the others strive
To paint a little thing like that you smeared
Carelessly passing with your robes afloat,
Yet do much less, so much less, some one says,
(I know his name, no matter) so much less !
Well, less is more, Lucrezia ! I am judged.
There burns a truer light of God in them,

In their vexed, beating, stuffed and stopped-up brain, 80
Heart, or whate'er else, than goes on to prompt
This low-pulsed forthright craftsman's hand of mine.
Their works drop groundward, but themselves, I know,
Reach many a time a heaven that's shut to me,
Enter and take their place there sure enough,
Though they come back and cannot tell the world.
My works are nearer heaven, but I sit here.
The sudden blood of these men ! at a word—
Praise them, it boils, or blame them, it boils too.
I, painting from myself and to myself,   90
Know what I do, am unmoved by men's blame
Or their praise either.   Somebody remarks
Morello's outline there is wrongly traced,
His hue mistaken—what of that ? or else,
Rightly traced and well ordered—what of that ?
Ah, but a man's reach should exceed his grasp,
Or what's a Heaven for ? all is silver-grey
Placid and perfect with my art—the worse !
I know both what I want and what might gain—
And yet how profitless to know, to sigh   100
" Had I been two, another and myself,
Our head would have o'erlooked the world ! "   No doubt.
Yonder 's a work, now, of that famous youth
The Urbinate who died five years ago.
('Tis copied, George Vasari sent it me).
Well, I can fancy how he did it all,
Pouring his soul, with kings and popes to see,
Reaching, that Heaven might so replenish him,
Above and through his art—for it gives way ;
That arm is wrongly put—and there again—   110
A fault to pardon in the drawing's lines,

Its body, so to speak ! its soul is right,
He means right—that, a child may understand.
Still, what an arm ! and I could alter it.
But all the play, the insight and the stretch—
Out of me ! out of me !   And wherefore out ?
Had you enjoined them on me, given me soul,
We might have risen to Rafael, I and you.
Nay, Love, you did give all I asked, I think—
More than I merit, yes, by many times.   120
But had you—oh, with the same perfect brow,
And perfect eyes, and more than perfect mouth,
And the low voice my soul hears, as a bird
The fowler's pipe, and follows to the snare—
Had you, with these the same, but brought a mind !
Some women do so.   Had the mouth there urged
" God and the glory ! never care for gain.
The present by the future, what is that ?
Live for fame, side by side with Angelo—
Rafael is waiting.   Up to God all three ! "   130
I might have done it for you.   So it seems—
Perhaps not.   All is as God over-rules.
Beside, incentives come from the soul's self ;
The rest avail not.   Why do I need you ?
What wife had Rafael, or has Angelo ?
In this world, who can do a thing, will not—
And who would do it, cannot, I perceive :
Yet the will's somewhat—somewhat, too, the power—
And thus we half-men struggle.   At the end,
God, I conclude, compensates, punishes.   140
'Tis safer for me, if the award be strict,
That I am something underrated here,
Poor this long while, despised, to speak the truth.

I dared not, do you know, leave home all day,
For fear of chancing on the Paris lords.
The best is when they pass and look aside ;
But they speak sometimes ; I must bear it all.
Well may they speak ! That Francis, that first time,
And that long festal year at Fontainebleau !
I surely then could sometimes leave the ground,   150
Put on the glory, Rafael's daily wear,
In that humane great monarch's golden look,—
One finger in his beard or twisted curl
Over his mouth's good mark that made the smile,
One arm about my shoulder, round my neck,
The jingle of his gold chain in my ear,
You painting proudly with his breath on me,
All his court round him, seeing with his eyes,
Such frank French eyes, and such a fire of souls
Profuse, my hand kept plying by those hearts,—   160
And, best of all, this, this, this face beyond,
This in the back-ground, waiting on my work,
To crown the issue with a last reward !
A good time, was it not, my kingly days ?
And had you not grown restless—but I know—
'Tis done and past ; 'twas right, my instinct said ;
Too live the life grew, golden and not grey—
And I'm the weak-eyed bat no sun should tempt
Out of the grange whose four walls make his world.
How could it end in any other way ?   170
You called me, and I came home to your heart.
The triumph was to have ended there—then if
I reached it ere the triumph, what is lost ?
Let my hands frame your face in your hair's gold,
You beautiful Lucrezia that are mine !

" Rafael did this, Andrea painted that—
The Roman's is the better when you pray,
But still the other's Virgin was his wife—"
Men will excuse me.   I am glad to judge
Both pictures in your presence ; clearer grows   180
My better fortune, I resolve to think.
For, do you know, Lucrezia, as God lives,
Said one day Angelo, his very self,
To Rafael . . . I have known it all these years . . .
(When the young man was flaming out his thoughts
Upon a palace-wall for Rome to see,
Too lifted up in heart because of it)
" Friend, there's a certain sorry little scrub
Goes up and down our Florence, none cares how,
Who, were he set to plan and execute   190
As you are pricked on by your popes and kings,
Would bring the sweat into that brow of yours ! "
To Rafael's !—And indeed the arm is wrong.
I hardly dare—yet, only you to see,
Give the chalk here—quick, thus the line should go !
Ay, but the soul ! he's Rafael ! rub it out !
Still, all I care for, if he spoke the truth,
(What he ? why, who but Michael Angelo ?
Do you forget already words like those ?)
If really there was such a chance, so lost,   200
Is, whether you're—not grateful—but more pleased.
Well, let me think so.   And you smile indeed !
This hour has been an hour !   Another smile ?
If you would sit thus by me every night
I should work better, do you comprehend ?
I mean that I should earn more, give you more.
See, it is settled dusk now ; there's a star ;

Morello's gone, the watch-lights shew the wall,
The cue-owls speak the name we call them by.
Come from the window, Love,—come in, at last,   210
Inside the melancholy little house
We built to be so gay with.   God is just.
King Francis may forgive me.   Oft at nights
When I look up from painting, eyes tired out,
The walls become illumined, brick from brick
Distinct, instead of mortar fierce bright gold,
That gold of his I did cement them with !
Let us but love each other.   Must you go ?
That Cousin here again ? he waits outside ?
Must see you—you, and not with me ?   Those loans ! 220
More gaming debts to pay ? you smiled for that ?
Well, let smiles buy me ! have you more to spend ?
While hand and eye and something of a heart
Are left me, work's my ware, and what's it worth ?
I'll pay my fancy.   Only let me sit
The grey remainder of the evening out,
Idle, you call it, and muse perfectly
How I could paint were I but back in France,
One picture, just one more—the Virgin's face,
Not your's this time ! I want you at my side   230
To hear them—that is, Michael Angelo—
Judge all I do and tell you of its worth.
Will you ?   To-morrow, satisfy your friend.
I take the subjects for his corridor,
Finish the portrait out of hand—there, there,
And throw him in another thing or two
If he demurs ; the whole should prove enough
To pay for this same Cousin's freak. Beside,
What's better and what's all I care about,

Get you the thirteen scudi for the ruff.   240
Love, does that please you ?   Ah, but what does he,
The Cousin ! what does he to please you more ?

   I am grown peaceful as old age to-night.
I regret little, I would change still less.
Since there my past life lies, why alter it ?
The very wrong to Francis ! it is true
I took his coin, was tempted and complied,
And built this house and sinned, and all is said.
My father and my mother died of want.
Well, had I riches of my own ? you see   250
How one gets rich ! Let each one bear his lot.
They were born poor, lived poor, and poor they died :
And I have laboured somewhat in my time
And not been paid profusely. Some good son
Paint my two hundred pictures—let him try !
No doubt, there's something strikes a balance. Yes,
You loved me quite enough, it seems to-night.
This must suffice me here. What would one have ?
In heaven, perhaps, new chances, one more chance—
Four great walls in the New Jerusalem   260
Meted on each side by the angel's reed,
For Leonard, Rafael, Angelo and me
To cover—the three first without a wife,
While I have mine ! So—still they overcome
Because there's still Lucrezia,—as I choose.

Again the Cousin's whistle ! Go, my Love.

BEFORE

—·—

1.

LET them fight it out, friend! things have gone too far.
God must judge the couple! leave them as they are
—Whichever one's the guiltless, to his glory,
And whichever one the guilt's with, to my story.

2.

Why, you would not bid men, sunk in such a slough,
Strike no arm out further, stick and stink as now,
Leaving right and wrong to settle the embroilment,
Heaven with snaky Hell, in torture and entoilment?

3.

Which of them's the culprit, how must he conceive
God's the queen he caps to, laughing in his sleeve!
'Tis but decent to profess oneself beneath her.
Still, one must not be too much in earnest either.

4.

Better sin the whole sin, sure that God observes,
Then go live his life out! life will try his nerves,
When the sky which noticed all, makes no disclosure,
And the earth keeps up her terrible composure.

5.

Let him pace at pleasure, past the walls of rose,
Pluck their fruits when grape-trees graze him as he goes.
For he 'gins to guess the purpose of the garden,
With the sly mute thing beside there for a warden.

6.

What's the leopard-dog-thing, constant to his side,
A leer and lie in every eye on its obsequious hide ?
When will come an end of all the mock obeisance,
And the price appear that pays for the misfeasance ?

7.

So much for the culprit.   Who's the martyred man ?
Let him bear one stroke more, for be sure he can.
He that strove thus evil's lump with good to leaven,
Let him give his blood at last and get his heaven.

8.

All or nothing, stake it ! trusts he God or no ?
Thus far and no farther ? farther ? be it so.
Now, enough of your chicane of prudent pauses,
Sage provisos, sub-intents, and saving-clauses.

9.

Ah, "forgive" you bid him ? While God's champion lives,
Wrong shall be resisted : dead, why he forgives.
But you must not end my friend ere you begin him ;
Evil stands not crowned on earth, while breath is in him.

10.

Once more—Will the wronger, at this last of all,
Dare to say " I did wrong," rising in his fall ?
No ?—Let go, then—both the fighters to their places—
While I count three, step you back as many paces.

AFTER

—✦—

Take the cloak from his face, and at first
　　Let the corpse do its worst.

How he lies in his rights of a man !
　　Death has done all death can.
And absorbed in the new life he leads,
　　He recks not, he heeds
Nor his wrong nor my vengeance—both strike
　　On his senses alike,
And are lost in the solemn and strange
　　Surprise of the change.
Ha, what avails death to erase
　　His offence, my disgrace ?
I would we were boys as of old
　　In the field, by the fold—
His outrage, God's patience, man's scorn
　　Were so easily borne.

I stand here now, he lies in his place—
　　Cover the face.

IN THREE DAYS

—•—

1.

So, I shall see her in three days
And just one night, but nights are short,
Then two long hours, and that is morn.
See how I come, unchanged, unworn—
Feel, where my life broke off from thine,
How fresh the splinters keep and fine,—
Only a touch and we combine !

2.

Too long, this time of year, the days !
But nights—at least the nights are short.
As night shows where her one moon is,
A hand's-breadth of pure light and bliss,
So, life's night gives my lady birth
And my eyes hold her ! what is worth
The rest of heaven, the rest of earth ?

3.

O loaded curls, release your store
Of warmth and scent as once before

The tingling hair did, lights and darks
Out-breaking into fairy sparks
When under curl and curl I pried
After the warmth and scent inside
Thro' lights and darks how manifold—
The dark inspired, the light controlled !
As early Art embrowned the gold.

4.

What great fear—should one say, " Three days
That change the world, might change as well
Your fortune ; and if joy delays,
Be happy that no worse befell."
What small fear—if another says,
" Three days and one short night beside
May throw no shadow on your ways ;
But years must teem with change untried,
With chance not easily defied,
With an end somewhere undescried."
No fear !—or if a fear be born
This minute, it dies out in scorn.
Fear ? I shall see her in three days
And one night, now the nights are short,
Then just two hours, and that is morn.

IN A YEAR

1.

NEVER any more
  While I live,
Need I hope to see his face
  As before.
Once his love grown chill,
  Mine may strive—
Bitterly we re-embrace,
  Single still.

2.

Was it something said,
  Something done,
Vexed him ? was it touch of hand,
  Turn of head ?
Strange ! that very way
  Love begun.
I as little understand
  Love's decay.

3.

When I sewed or drew,
  I recall

How he looked as if I sang,
   —Sweetly too.
If I spoke a word,
   First of all
Up his cheek the color sprang,
   Then he heard.

4.

Sitting by my side,
   At my feet,
So he breathed the air I breathed,
   Satisfied !
I, too, at love's brim
   Touched the sweet :
I would die if death bequeathed
   Sweet to him.

5.

" Speak, I love thee best ! "
   He exclaimed.
" Let thy love my own foretell,— "
   I confessed :
" Clasp my heart on thine
   Now unblamed,
Since upon thy soul as well
   Hangeth mine ! "

6.

Was it wrong to own,
   Being truth ?
Why should all the giving prove
   His alone ?

I had wealth and ease,
   Beauty, youth—
Since my lover gave me love,
   I gave these.

7.

That was all I meant,
   —To be just,
And the passion I had raised
   To content.
Since he chose to change
   Gold for dust,
If I gave him what he praised
   Was it strange ?

8.

Would he loved me yet,
   On and on,
While I found some way undreamed
   —Paid my debt !
Gave more life and more,
   Till, all gone,
He should smile " She never seemed
   Mine before.

9.

" What—she felt the while,
   Must I think ?
Love's so different with us men,"
   He should smile.
" Dying for my sake—
   White and pink !
Can't we touch these bubbles then
   But they break ? "

10.

Dear, the pang is brief.
  Do thy part,
Have thy pleasure. How perplext
  Grows belief !
Well, this cold clay clod
  Was man's heart.
Crumble it—and what comes next ?
  Is it God ?

OLD PICTURES IN FLORENCE

1.

THE morn when first it thunders in March,
   The eel in the pond gives a leap, they say.
As I leaned and looked over the aloed arch
   Of the villa-gate, this warm March day,
No flash snapt, no dumb thunder rolled
   In the valley beneath, where, white and wide,
Washed by the morning's water-gold,
   Florence lay out on the mountain-side.

2.

River and bridge and street and square
   Lay mine, as much at my beck and call,
Through the live translucent bath of air,
   As the sights in a magic crystal ball.
And of all I saw and of all I praised,
   The most to praise and the best to see,
Was the startling bell-tower Giotto raised :
   But why did it more than startle me ?

3.

Giotto, how, with that soul of yours,
   Could you play me false who loved you so ?
Some slights if a certain heart endures
   It feels, I would have your fellows know !

'Faith—I perceive not why I should care
    To break a silence that suits them best,
But the thing grows somewhat hard to bear
    When I find a Giotto join the rest.

4.

On the arch where olives overhead
    Print the blue sky with twig and leaf,
(That sharp-curled leaf they never shed)
    'Twixt the aloes I used to lean in chief,
And mark through the winter afternoons,
    By a gift God grants me now and then,
In the mild decline of those suns like moons,
    Who walked in Florence, besides her men.

5.

They might chirp and chaffer, come and go
    For pleasure or profit, her men alive—
My business was hardly with them, I trow,
    But with empty cells of the human hive ;
—With the chapter-room, the cloister-porch,
    The church's apsis, aisle or nave,
Its crypt, one fingers along with a torch—
    Its face, set full for the sun to shave.

6.

Wherever a fresco peels and drops,
    Wherever an outline weakens and wanes
Till the latest life in the painting stops,
    Stands One whom each fainter pulse-tick pains !
One, wishful each scrap should clutch its brick,
    Each tinge not wholly escape the plaster,
—A lion who dies of an ass's kick,
    The wronged great soul of an ancient Master.

7.

For oh, this world and the wrong it does !
  They are safe in heaven with their backs to it,
The Michaels and Rafaels, you hum and buzz
  Round the works of, you of the little wit !
Do their eyes contract to the earth's old scope,
  Now that they see God face to face,
And have all attained to be poets, I hope ?
  'Tis their holiday now, in any case.

8.

Much they reck of your praise and you !
  But the wronged great souls—can they be quit
Of a world where all their work is to do,
  Where you style them, you of the little wit,
Old Master this and Early the other,
  Not dreaming that Old and New are fellows,
That a younger succeeds to an elder brother,
  Da Vincis derive in good time from Dellos.

9.

And here where your praise would yield returns
  And a handsome word or two give help,
Here, after your kind, the mastiff girns
  And the puppy pack of poodles yelp.
What, not a word for Stefano there
  —Of brow once prominent and starry,
Called Nature's ape and the world's despair
  For his peerless painting (see Vasari) ?

10.

There he stands now.   Study, my friends,
  What a man's work comes to ! so he plans it,
Performs it, perfects it, makes amends
  For the toiling and moiling, and there's its transit !

Happier the thrifty blind-folk labour,
  With upturned eye while the hand is busy,
Not sidling a glance at the coin of their neighbour !
  'Tis looking downward makes one dizzy.

11.

If you knew their work you would deal your dole.
  May I take upon me to instruct you ?
When Greek Art ran and reached the goal,
  Thus much had the world to boast *in fructu*—
The truth of Man, as by God first spoken,
  Which the actual generations garble,
Was re-uttered,—and Soul (which Limbs betoken)
  And Limbs (Soul informs) were made new in marble.

12.

So you saw yourself as you wished you were,
  As you might have been, as you cannot be ;
And bringing your own shortcomings there,
  You grew content in your poor degree
With your little power, by those statues' godhead,
  And your little scope, by their eyes' full sway,
And your little grace, by their grace embodied,
  And your little date, by their forms that stay.

13.

You would fain be kinglier, say than I am ?
  Even so, you will not sit like Theseus.
You'd fain be a model ? the Son of Priam
  Has yet the advantage in arms' and knees' use.
You're wroth—can you slay your snake like Apollo ?
  You're grieved—still Niobe's the grander !
You live—there's the Racers' frieze to follow—
  You die—there's the dying Alexander.

14.

So, testing your weakness by their strength,
    Your meagre charms by their rounded beauty,
Measured by Art in your breadth and length,
    You learn—to submit is the worsted's duty.
—When I say " you " 'tis the common soul,
    The collective, I mean—the race of Man
That receives life in parts to live in a whole,
    And grow here according to God's own plan.

15.

Growth came when, looking your last on them all,
    You turned your eyes inwardly one fine day
And cried with a start—What if we so small
    Are greater, ay, greater the while than they !
Are they perfect of lineament, perfect of stature ?
    In both, of such lower types are we
Precisely because of our wider nature ;
    For time, theirs—ours, for eternity.

16.

To-day's brief passion limits their range,
    It seethes with the morrow for us and more.
They are perfect—how else ? they shall never change :
    We are faulty—why not ? we have time in store.
The Artificer's hand is not arrested
    With us—we are rough-hewn, no-wise polished :
They stand for our copy, and, once invested
    With all they can teach, we shall see them abolished.

17.

'Tis a life-long toil till our lump be leaven—
    The better ! what's come to perfection perishes.
Things learned on earth, we shall practise in heaven.
    Works done least rapidly, Art most cherishes.

Thyself shall afford the example, Giotto !
   Thy one work, not to decrease or diminish,
Done at a stroke, was just (was it not ?) " O ! "
   Thy great Campanile is still to finish.

18.

Is it true, we are now, and shall be hereafter,
   And what—is depending on life's one minute ?
Hails heavenly cheer or infernal laughter
   Our first step out of the gulf or in it ?
And Man, this step within his endeavour,
   His face, have no more play and action
Than joy which is crystallized for ever,
   Or grief, an eternal petrifaction !

19.

On which I conclude, that the early painters,
   To cries of " Greek Art and what more wish you ? "—
Replied, " Become now self-acquainters,
   And paint man, man,—whatever the issue !
Make the hopes shine through the flesh they fray,
   New fears aggrandise the rags and tatters.
So bring the invisible full into play,
   Let the visible go to the dogs—what matters ? "

20.

Give these, I say, full honour and glory
   For daring so much, before they well did it.
The first of the new, in our race's story,
   Beats the last of the old, 'tis no idle quiddit.
The worthies began a revolution
   Which if on the earth we intend to acknowledge
Honour them now—(ends my allocution)
   Nor confer our degree when the folks leave college.

21.

There's a fancy some lean to and others hate—
   That, when this life is ended, begins
New work for the soul in another state,
   Where it strives and gets weary, loses and wins—
Where the strong and the weak, this world's congeries,
   Repeat in large what they practised in small,
Through life after life in unlimited series ;
   Only the scale's to be changed, that's all.

22.

Yet I hardly know. When a soul has seen
   By the means of Evil that Good is best, [serene,—
And through earth and its noise, what is heaven's
   When its faith in the same has stood the test—
Why, the child grown man, you burn the rod,
   The uses of labour are surely done.
There remaineth a rest for the people of God,
   And I have had troubles enough for one.

23.

But at any rate I have loved the season
   Of Art's spring-birth so dim and dewy,
My sculptor is Nicolo the Pisan ;
   My painter—who but Cimabue ?
Nor ever was man of them all indeed,
   From these to Ghiberti and Ghirlandajo,
Could say that he missed my critic-meed.
   So now to my special grievance—heigh ho !

24.

Their ghosts now stand, as I said before,
   Watching each fresco flaked and rasped,
Blocked up, knocked out, or whitewashed o'er
   —No getting again what the church has grasped

The works on the wall must take their chance,
   " Works never conceded to England's thick clime ! "
(I hope they prefer their inheritance
   Of a bucketful of Italian quick-lime.)

25.

When they go at length, with such a shaking
   Of heads o'er the old delusions, sadly
Each master his way through the black streets taking,
   Where many a lost work breathes though badly—
Why don't they bethink them of who has merited ?
   Why not reveal, while their pictures dree
Such doom, that a captive's to be out-ferreted ?
   Why do they never remember me ?

26.

Not that I expect the great Bigordi
   Nor Sandro to hear me, chivalric, bellicose ;
Nor wronged Lippino—and not a word I
   Say of a scrap of Fra Angelico's.
But are you too fine, Taddeo Gaddi,
   To grant me a taste of your intonaco—
Some Jerome that seeks the heaven with a sad eye ?
   No churlish saint, Lorenzo Monaco ?

27.

Could not the ghost with the close red cap,
   My Pollajolo, the twice a craftsman,
Save me a sample, give me the hap
   Of a muscular Christ that shows the draughtsman ?
No Virgin by him, the somewhat petty,
   Of finical touch and tempera crumbly—
Could not Alesso Baldovinetti
   Contribute so much, I ask him humbly ?

28.

Margheritone of Arezzo,
 With the grave-clothes garb and swaddling barret,
(Why purse up mouth and beak in a pet so,
 You bald, saturnine, poll-clawed parrot ?)
No poor glimmering Crucifixion,
 Where in the foreground kneels the donor ?
If such remain, as is my conviction,
 The hoarding does you but little honour.

29.

They pass : for them the panels may thrill,
 The tempera grow alive and tinglish—
Rot or are left to the mercies still
 Of dealers and stealers, Jews and the English !
Seeing mere money's worth in their prize,
 Who sell it to some one calm as Zeno
At naked Art, and in ecstacies
 Before some clay-cold, vile Carlino !

30.

No matter for these ! But Giotto, you,
 Have you allowed, as the town-tongues babble it,
Never ! it shall not be counted true—
 That a certain precious little tablet
Which Buonarroti eyed like a lover,—
 Buried so long in oblivion's womb,
Was left for another than I to discover,—
 Turns up at last, and to whom ?—to whom ?

31.

I, that have haunted the dim San Spirito,
 (Or was it rather the Ognissanti ?)
Stood on the altar-steps, patient and weary too !
 Nay, I shall have it yet, *detur amanti !*

My Koh-i-noor—or (if that's a platitude)
  Jewel of Giamschid, the Persian Sofi's eye !
So, in anticipative gratitude,
  What if I take up my hope and prophesy ?

32.

When the hour is ripe, and a certain dotard
  Pitched, no parcel that needs invoicing,
To the worse side of the Mont St. Gothard,
  Have, to begin by way of rejoicing,
None of that shooting the sky (blank cartridge),
  No civic guards, all plumes and lacquer,
Hunting Radetzky's soul like a partridge
  Over Morello with squib and cracker.

33.

We'll shoot this time better game and bag 'em hot—
  No display at the stone of Dante,
But a kind of Witan-agemot
  (" Casa Guidi," quod videas ante)
To ponder Freedom restored to Florence,
  How Art may return that departed with her.
Go, hated house, go each trace of the Loraine's !
  And bring us the days of Orgagna hither.

34.

How we shall prologuise, how we shall perorate,
  Say fit things upon art and history—
Set truth at blood-heat and the false at a zero-rate,
  Make of the want of the age no mystery !
Contrast the fructuous and sterile eras,
  Show, monarchy its uncouth cub licks
Out of the bear's shape to the chimæra's—
  Pure Art's birth being still the republic's !

35.

Then one shall propose (in a speech, curt Tuscan,
    Sober, expurgate, spare of an " *issimo*,")
Ending our half-told tale of Cambuscan,
    Turning the Bell-tower's altaltissimo.
And fine as the beak of a young beccaccia
    The Campanile, the Duomo's fit ally,
Soars up in gold its full fifty braccia,
    Completing Florence, as Florence, Italy.

36.

Shall I be alive that morning the scaffold
    Is broken away, and the long-pent fire
Like the golden hope of the world unbaffled
    Springs from its sleep, and up goes the spire—
As, " God and the People " plain for its motto,
    Thence the new tricolor flaps at the sky ?
Foreseeing the day that vindicates Giotto
    And Florence together, the first am I !

IN A BALCONY

FIRST PART

———+———

CONSTANCE *and* NORBERT

NORBERT.

Now.

CONSTANCE.

Not now.

NORBERT.

Give me them again, those hands—
Put them upon my forehead, how it throbs !
Press them before my eyes, the fire comes through.
You cruellest, you dearest in the world,
Let me ! the Queen must grant whate'er I ask—
How can I gain you and not ask the Queen ?
There she stays waiting for me, here stand you.
Some time or other this was to be asked,
Now is the one time—what I ask, I gain—
Let me ask now, Love !

CONSTANCE.

Do, and ruin us.   10

NORBERT.

Let it be now, Love !   All my soul breaks forth.
How I do love you ! give my love its way !
A man can have but one life and one death,

One heaven, one hell.   Let me fulfil my fate—
Grant me my heaven now.   Let me know you mine,
Prove you mine, write my name upon your brow,
Hold you and have you, and then die away
If God please, with completion in my soul.

CONSTANCE.

I am not yours then ? how content this man ?
I am not his, who change into himself,   20
Have passed into his heart and beat its beats,
Who give my hands to him, my eyes, my hair,
Give all that was of me away to him
So well, that now, my spirit turned his own,
Takes part with him against the woman here,
Bids him not stumble at so mere a straw
As caring that the world be cognisant
How he loves her and how she worships him.
You have this woman, not as yet that world.
Go on, I bid, nor stop to care for me   30
By saving what I cease to care about,
The courtly name and pride of circumstance—
The name you'll pick up and be cumbered with
Just for the poor parade's sake, nothing more ;
Just that the world may slip from under you—
Just that the world may cry " So much for him—
The man predestined to the heap of crowns !
There goes his chance of winning one, at least."

NORBERT.

The world !

CONSTANCE.

          You love it.   Love me quite as well,
And see if I shall pray for this in vain !   40
Why must you ponder what it knows or thinks ?

NORBERT.

You pray for—what, in vain ?

CONSTANCE.

Oh my heart's heart,

How I do love you, Norbert !—that is right !
But listen, or I take my hands away.
You say, " let it be now "—you would go now
And tell the Queen, perhaps six steps from us,
You love me—so you do, thank God !

NORBERT.

Thank God !

CONSTANCE.

Yes, Norbert,—but you fain would tell your love,
And, what succeeds the telling, ask of her
My hand.   Now take this rose and look at it,   50
Listening to me.   You are the minister,
The Queen's first favourite, nor without a cause.
To-night completes your wonderful year's-work
(This palace-feast is held to celebrate)
Made memorable by her life's success,
That junction of two crowns on her sole head
Her house had only dreamed of anciently.
That this mere dream is grown a stable truth
To-night's feast makes authentic.   Whose the praise ?
Whose genius, patience, energy, achieved   60
What turned the many heads and broke the hearts ?
You are the fate—your minute's in the heaven.
Next comes the Queen's turn.   Name your own reward !
With leave to clench the past, chain the to-come,
Put out an arm and touch and take the sun
And fix it ever full-faced on your earth,
Possess yourself supremely of her life,

You choose the single thing she will not grant—
The very declaration of which choice
Will turn the scale and neutralise your work.   70
At best she will forgive you, if she can.
You think I'll let you choose—her cousin's hand ?

NORBERT.

Wait.   First, do you retain your old belief
The Queen is generous,—nay, is just ?

CONSTANCE.

                              There, there !
So men make women love them, while they know
No more of women's hearts than . . . look you here,
You that are just and generous beside,
Make it your own case.   For example now,
I'll say—I let you kiss me and hold my hands—
Why ? do you know why ? I'll instruct you, then—   80
The kiss, because you have a name at court,
This hand and this, that you may shut in each
A jewel, if you please to pick up such.
That's horrible !   Apply it to the Queen—
Suppose, I am the Queen to whom you speak.
" I was a nameless man : you needed me :
Why did I proffer you my aid ? there stood
A certain pretty Cousin at your side.
Why did I make such common cause with you ?
Access to her had not been easy else.   90
You give my labours here abundant praise :
'Faith, labour, while she overlooked, grew play.
How shall your gratitude discharge itself ?
Give me her hand ! "

NORBERT.

                    And still I urge the same.
Is the Queen just ? just—generous or no !

CONSTANCE.

Yes, just.   You love a rose—no harm in that—
But was it for the rose's sake or mine
You put it in your bosom ? mine, you said—
Then mine you still must say or else be false.
You told the Queen you served her for herself :   100
If so, to serve her was to serve yourself
She thinks, for all your unbelieving face !
I know her.   In the hall, six steps from us,
One sees the twenty pictures—there's a life
Better than life—and yet no life at all ;
Conceive her born in such a magic dome,
Pictures all round her ! why, she sees the world,
Can recognise its given things and facts,
The fight of giants or the feast of gods,
Sages in senate, beauties at the bath,   110
Chaces and battles, the whole earth's display,
Landscape and sea-piece, down to flowers and fruit—
And who shall question that she knows them all
In better semblance than the things outside ?
Yet bring into the silent gallery
Some live thing to contrast in breath and blood,
Some lion, with the painted lion there—
You think she'll understand composedly ?
—Say, " that's his fellow in the hunting-piece
Yonder, I've turned to praise a hundred times ? "   120
Not so.   Her knowledge of our actual earth,
Its hopes and fears, concerns and sympathies,
Must be too far, too mediate, too unreal.
The real exists for us outside, not her—
How should it, with that life in these four walls,
That father and that mother, first to last

No father and no mother—friends, a heap,
Lovers, no lack—a husband in due time,
And everyone of them alike a lie !
Things painted by a Rubens out of nought   130
Into what kindness, friendship, love should be ;
All better, all more grandiose than life,
Only no life ; mere cloth and surface-paint
You feel while you admire.   How should she feel ?
And now that she has stood thus fifty years
The sole spectator in that gallery,
You think to bring this warm real struggling love
In to her of a sudden, and suppose
She'll keep her state untroubled ?   Here's the truth—
She'll apprehend its value at a glance,   140
Prefer it to the pictured loyalty !
You only have to say " so men are made,
For this they act, the thing has many names
But this the right one—and now, Queen, be just ! "
And life slips back—you lose her at the word—
You do not even for amends gain me.
He will not understand ! oh, Norbert, Norbert,
Do you not understand ?

NORBERT.
                    The Queen's the Queen,
I am myself—no picture, but alive
In every nerve and every muscle, here   150
At the palace-window or in the people's street,
As she in the gallery where the pictures glow.
The good of life is precious to us both.
She cannot love—what do I want with rule ?
When first I saw your face a year ago
I knew my life's good—my soul heard one voice

" The woman yonder, there's no use of life
But just to obtain her ! heap earth's woes in one
And bear them—make a pile of all earth's joys
And spurn them, as they help or help not here ;   160
Only, obtain her ! "—How was it to be ?
I found she was the cousin of the Queen ;
I must then serve the Queen to get to her—
No other way.   Suppose there had been one,
And I by saying prayers to some white star
With promise of my body and my soul
Might gain you,—should I pray the star or no ?
Instead, there was the Queen to serve ! I served,
And did what other servants failed to do.
Neither she sought nor I declared my end.   170
Her good is hers, my recompense be mine,
And let me name you as that recompense.
She dreamed that such a thing could never be ?
Let her wake now.   She thinks there was some cause—
The love of power, of fame, pure loyalty ?
—Perhaps she fancies men wear out their lives
Chasing such shades.   Then I've a fancy too.
I worked because I want you with my soul—
I therefore ask your hand.   Let it be now.

CONSTANCE.

Had I not loved you from the very first,   180
Were I not yours, could we not steal out thus
So wickedly, so wildly, and so well,
You might be thus impatient.   What's conceived
Of us without here, by the folks within ?
Where are you now ? immersed in cares of state—
Where am I now ?—intent on festal robes—
We two, embracing under death's spread hand !

What was this thought for, what this scruple of yours
Which broke the council up, to bring about
One minute's meeting in the corridor ?   190
And then the sudden sleights, long secresies,
The plots inscrutable, deep telegraphs,
Long-planned chance-meetings, hazards of a look,
"Does she know ? does she not know ? saved or lost ? "
A year of this compression's ecstasy
All goes for nothing ? you would give this up
For the old way, the open way, the world's,
His way who beats, and his who sells his wife ?
What tempts you ? their notorious happiness,
That you're ashamed of ours ? The best you'll get 200
Will be, the Queen grants all that you require,
Concedes the cousin, and gets rid of you
And her at once, and gives us ample leave
To live as our five hundred happy friends.
The world will show us with officious hand
Our chamber-entry and stand sentinel,
When we so oft have stolen across her traps !
Get the world's warrant, ring the falcon's foot,
And make it duty to be bold and swift,
When long ago 'twas nature.   Have it so !   210
He never hawked by rights till flung from fist ?
Oh, the man's thought !—no woman's such a fool.

NORBERT.

Yes, the man's thought and my thought, which is more—
One made to love you, let the world take note.
Have I done worthy work ? be love's the praise,
Though hampered by restrictions, barred against
By set forms, blinded by forced secresies.
Set free my love, and see what love will do

Shown in my life—what work will spring from that !
The world is used to have its business done   220
On other grounds, find great effects produced
For power's sake, fame's sake, motives you have named.
So good.   But let my low ground shame their high.
Truth is the strong thing.   Let man's life be true !
And love's the truth of mine.   Time prove the rest !
I choose to have you stamped all over me,
Your name upon my forehead and my breast,
You, from the sword's blade to the ribbon's edge,
That men may see, all over, you in me—
That pale loves may die out of their pretence   230
In face of mine, shames thrown on love fall off—
Permit this, Constance !   Love has been so long
Subdued in me, eating me through and through,
That now it's all of me and must have way.
Think of my work, that chaos of intrigues,
Those hopes and fears, surprises and delays,
That long endeavour, earnest, patient, slow
Trembling at last to its assured result—
Then think of this revulsion.   I resume
Life, after death, (it is no less than life   240
After such long unlovely labouring days)
And liberate to beauty life's great need
Of the beautiful, which, while it prompted work,
Supprest itself erewhile.   This eve's the time—
This eve intense with yon first trembling star
We seem to pant and reach ; scarce aught between
The earth that rises and the heaven that bends—
All nature self-abandoned—every tree
Flung as it will, pursuing its own thoughts
And fixed so, every flower and every weed,   250

No pride, no shame, no victory, no defeat :
All under God, each measured by itself !
These statues round us, each abrupt, distinct,
The strong in strength, the weak in weakness fixed,
The Muse for ever wedded to her lyre,
The Nymph to her fawn, the Silence to her rose,
And God's approval on his universe !
Let us do so—aspire to live as these
In harmony with truth, ourselves being true.
Take the first way, and let the second come.   260
My first is to possess myself of you ;
The music sets the march-step—forward then !
And there's the Queen, I go to claim you of,
The world to witness, wonder and applaud.
Our flower of life breaks open.   No delay !

CONSTANCE.

And so shall we be ruined, both of us.
Norbert, I know her to the skin and bone—
You do not know her, were not born to it,
To feel what she can see or cannot see.
Love, she is generous,—ay, despite your smile,   270
Generous as you are.   For, in that thin frame
Pain-twisted, punctured through and through with cares,
There lived a lavish soul until it starved
Debarred all healthy food.   Look to the soul—
Pity that, stoop to that, ere you begin
(The true man's way) on justice and your rights,
Exactions and acquittance of the past.
Begin so—see what justice she will deal !
We women hate a debt as men a gift.
Suppose her some poor keeper of a school   280
Whose business is to sit thro' summer-months

And dole out children's leave to go and play,
Herself superior to such lightness—she
In the arm-chair's state and pædagogic pomp,
To the life, the laughter, sun and youth outside—
We wonder such an one looks black on us ?
I do not bid you wake her tenderness,
—That were vain truly—none is left to wake—
But, let her think her justice is engaged
To take the shape of tenderness, and mark   290
If she'll not coldly do its warmest deed !
Does she love me, I ask you ? not a whit.
Yet, thinking that her justice was engaged
To help a kinswoman, she took me up—
Did more on that bare ground than other loves
Would do on greater argument. For me,
I have no equivalent of that cold kind
To pay her with ; my love alone to give
If I give anything. I give her love.
I feel I ought to help her, and I will.   300
So for her sake, as yours, I tell you twice
That women hate a debt as men a gift.
If I were you, I could obtain this grace—
Would lay the whole I did to love's account,
Nor yet be very false as courtiers go—
Declare that my success was recompense ;
It would be so, in fact : what were it else ?
And then, once loosed her generosity
As you will mark it—then,—were I but you
To turn it, let it seem to move itself,   310
And make it give the thing I really take,
Accepting so, in the poor cousin's hand,
All value as the next thing to the queen—

Since none loves her directly, none dares that !
A shadow of a thing, a name's mere echo
Suffices those who miss the name and thing ;
You pick up just a ribbon she has worn
To keep in proof how near her breath you came.
Say I'm so near I seem a piece of her—
Ask for me that way—(oh, you understand)   320
And find the same gift yielded with a grace,
Which if you make the least shew to extort
—You'll see ! and when you have ruined both of us,
Disertate on the Queen's ingratitude !

NORBERT.

Then, if I turn it that way, you consent ?
'Tis not my way ; I have more hope in truth.
Still if you won't have truth—why, this indeed,
Is scarcely false, I'll so express the sense.
Will you remain here ?

CONSTANCE.

        O best heart of mine,
How I have loved you ! then, you take my way ?   330
Are mine as you have been her minister,
Work out my thought, give it effect for me,
Paint plain my poor conceit and make it serve ?
I owe that withered woman everything—
Life, fortune, you, remember !   Take my part—
Help me to pay her !   Stand upon your rights ?
You, with my rose, my hands, my heart on you ?
Your rights are mine—you have no rights but mine.

NORBERT.

Remain here.   How you know me !

CONSTANCE.

               Ah, but still——

[He breaks from her : she remains.   Dance-music
from within.

SECOND PART.

Enter the QUEEN.

QUEEN.

Constance !—She is here as he said.   Speak ! quick ! 340
Is it so ? is it true—or false ?   One word !

CONSTANCE.

True.

QUEEN.

Mercifullest Mother, thanks to thee !

CONSTANCE.

Madam !

QUEEN.

I love you, Constance, from my soul.
Now say once more, with any words you will,
'Tis true—all true—as true as that I speak.

CONSTANCE.

Why should you doubt it ?

QUEEN.

Ah, why doubt ? why doubt ?
Dear, make me see it.   Do you see it so ?
None see themselves—another sees them best.
You say " why doubt it ? "—you see him and me.
It is because the Mother has such grace   350
That if we had but faith—wherein we fail—
Whate'er we yearn for would be granted us ;
Howbeit we let our whims prescribe despair,
Our very fancies thwart and cramp our will,
And so accepting life, abjure ourselves !

Constance, I had abjured the hope of love
And of being loved, as truly as yon palm
The hope of seeing Egypt from that turf.

CONSTANCE.

Heaven !

QUEEN.

But it was so, Constance, it was so.
Men say—or do men say it ? fancies say—   360
" Stop here, your life is set, you are grown old.
Too late—no love for you, too late for love—
Leave love to girls.   Be queen—let Constance love ! "
One takes the hint—half meets it like a child,
Ashamed at any feelings that oppose.
" Oh, love, true, never think of love again !
I am a queen—I rule, not love, indeed."
So it goes on ; so a face grows like this,
Hair like this hair, poor arms as lean as these,
Till,—nay, it does not end so, I thank God !   370

CONSTANCE.

I cannot understand——

QUEEN.

The happier you !
Constance, I know not how it is with men.
For women, (I am a woman now like you)
There is no good of life but love—but love !
What else looks good, is some shade flung from love—
Love gilds it, gives it worth.   Be warned by me,
Never you cheat yourself one instant.   Love,
Give love, ask only love, and leave the rest !
O Constance, how I love you !

CONSTANCE.

I love you.

QUEEN.

I do believe that all is come through you.   380
I took you to my heart to keep it warm
When the last chance of love seemed dead in me ;
I thought your fresh youth warmed my withered heart.
Oh, I am very old now, am I not ?
Not so ! it is true and it shall be true !

CONSTANCE.

Tell it me ! let me judge if true or false.

QUEEN.

Ah, but I fear you—you will look at me
And say " she's old, she's grown unlovely quite
Who ne'er was beauteous ! men want beauty still."
Well, so I feared—the curse ! so I felt sure.   390

CONSTANCE.

Be calm.   And now you feel not sure, you say ?

QUEEN.

Constance, he came, the coming was not strange—
Do not I stand and see men come and go ?
I turned a half-look from my pedestal
Where I grow marble—" one young man the more !
He will love some one,—that is nought to me—
What would he with my marble stateliness ? "
Yet this seemed somewhat worse than heretofore ;
The man more gracious, youthful, like a god,
And I still older, with less flesh to change—   400
We two those dear extremes that long to touch.
It seemed still harder when he first began
Absorbed to labour at the state-affairs
The old way for the old end, interest.
Oh, to live with a thousand beating hearts
Around you, swift eyes, serviceable hands,

Professing they've no care but for your cause,
Thought but to help you, love but for yourself,
And you the marble statue all the time
They praise and point at as preferred to life,   410
Yet leave for the first breathing woman's cheek,
First dancer's, gypsy's, or street baladine's !
Why, how I have ground my teeth to hear men's speech
Stifled for fear it should alarm my ear,
Their gait subdued lest step should startle me,
Their eyes declined, such queendom to respect,
Their hands alert, such treasure to preserve,
While not a man of these broke rank and spoke,
Or wrote me a vulgar letter all of love,
Or caught my hand and pressed it like a hand.   420
There have been moments, if the sentinel
Lowering his halbert to salute the queen,
Had flung it brutally and clasped my knees,
I would have stooped and kissed him with my soul.

CONSTANCE.

Who could have comprehended !

QUEEN.

                              Ay, who—who ?
Why, no one, Constance, but this one who did.
Not they, not you, not I.   Even now perhaps
It comes too late—would you but tell the truth.

CONSTANCE.

I wait to tell it.

QUEEN.

                Well, you see, he came,
Outfaced the others, did a work this year   430
Exceeds in value all was ever done
You know—it is not I who say it—all
Say it.   And so (a second pang and worse)

I grew aware not only of what he did,
But why so wondrously.   Oh, never work
Like his was done for work's ignoble sake—
It must have finer aims to spur it on !
I felt, I saw he loved—loved somebody.
And Constance, my dear Constance, do you know,
I did believe this while 'twas you he loved.   440

CONSTANCE.

Me, madam ?

QUEEN.

                    It did seem to me your face
Met him where'er he looked : and whom but you
Was such a man to love ? it seemed to me
You saw he loved you, and approved the love,
And that you both were in intelligence.
You could not loiter in the garden, step
Into this balcony, but I straight was stung
And forced to understand.   It seemed so true,
So right, so beautiful, so like you both
That all this work should have been done by him   450
Not for the vulgar hope of recompense,
But that at last—suppose some night like this—
Borne on to claim his due reward of me
He might say, " Give her hand and pay me so."
And I (O Constance, you shall love me now)
I thought, surmounting all the bitterness,
—" And he shall have it.   I will make her blest,
My flower of youth, my woman's self that was,
My happiest woman's self that might have been !
These two shall have their joy and leave me here."   460
Yes—yes—

CONSTANCE.

          Thanks !

QUEEN.

And the word was on my lips
When he burst in upon me.   I looked to hear
A mere calm statement of his just desire
In payment of his labour.   When, O Heaven,
How can I tell you ? cloud was on my eyes
And thunder in my ears at that first word
Which told 'twas love of me, of me, did all—
He loved me—from the first step to the last,
Loved me !

CONSTANCE.

You did not hear . . . you thought he spoke
Of love ? what if you should mistake ?

QUEEN.

No, no—   470
No mistake !   Ha, there shall be no mistake !
He had not dared to hint the love he felt—
You were my reflex—how I understood !
He said you were the ribbon I had worn,
He kissed my hand, he looked into my eyes,
And love, love was the end of every phrase.
Love is begun—this much is come to pass,
The rest is easy.   Constance, I am yours—
I will learn, I will place my life on you,
But teach me how to keep what I have won.   480
Am I so old ? this hair was early grey ;
But joy ere now has brought hair brown again,
And joy will bring the cheek's red back, I feel.
I could sing once too ; that was in my youth.
Still, when men paint me, they declare me . . . yes,
Beautiful—for the last French painter did !
I know they flatter somewhat ; you are frank—

I trust you.   How I loved you from the first !
Some queens would hardly seek a cousin out
And set her by their side to take the eye :   490
I must have felt that good would come from you.
I am not generous—like him—like you !
But he is not your lover after all—
It was not you he looked at.   Saw you him ?
You have not been mistaking words or looks ?
He said you were the reflex of myself—
And yet he is not such a paragon
To you, to younger women who may choose
Among a thousand Norberts.   Speak the truth !
You know you never named his name to me—   500
You know, I cannot give him up—ah God,
Not up now, even to you !

CONSTANCE.

                    Then calm yourself.

QUEEN.

See, I am old—look here, you happy girl,
I will not play the fool, deceive myself ;
'Tis all gone—put your cheek beside my cheek—
Ah, what a contrast does the moon behold !
But then I set my life upon one chance,
The last chance and the best—am I not left,
My soul, myself ?   All women love great men
If young or old—it is in all the tales—   510
Young beauties love old poets who can love—
Why should not he the poems in my soul,
The love, the passionate faith, the sacrifice,
The constancy ?   I throw them at his feet.
Who cares to see the fountain's very shape
And whether it be a Triton's or a Nymph's

That pours the foam, makes rainbows all around ?
You could not praise indeed the empty conch ;
But I'll pour floods of love and hide myself.
How I will love him ! cannot men love love ?   520
Who was a queen and loved a poet once
Humpbacked, a dwarf ? ah, women can do that !
Well, but men too ! at least, they tell you so.
They love so many women in their youth,
And even in age they all love whom they please ;
And yet the best of them confide to friends
That 'tis not beauty makes the lasting love—
They spend a day with such and tire the next ;
They like soul,—well then, they like phantasy,
Novelty even.   Let us confess the truth   530
Horrible though it be—that prejudice,
Prescription . . . Curses ! they will love a queen.
They will—they do.   And will not, does not—he?

CONSTANCE.

How can he ?   You are wedded—'tis a name
We know, but still a bond.   Your rank remains,
His rank remains.   How can he, nobly souled
As you believe and I incline to think,
Aspire to be your favourite, shame and all ?

QUEEN.

Hear her ! there, there now—could she love like me ?
What did I say of smooth-cheeked youth and grace ? 540
See all it does or could do ! so, youth loves !
Oh, tell him, Constance, you could never do
What I will—you, it was not born in ! I
Will drive these difficulties far and fast
As yonder mists curdling before the moon.
I'll use my light too, gloriously retrieve

My youth from its enforced calamity,
Dissolve that hateful marriage, and be his,
His own in the eyes alike of God and man.

CONSTANCE.

You will do—dare do—Pause on what you say !   550

QUEEN.

Hear her ! I thank you, Sweet, for that surprise.
You have the fair face : for the soul, see mine !
I have the strong soul : let me teach you, here.
I think I have borne enough and long enough,
And patiently enough, the world remarks,
To have my own way now, unblamed by all.
It does so happen, I rejoice for it,
This most unhoped-for issue cuts the knot.
There's not a better way of settling claims
Than this ; God sends the accident express ;   560
And were it for my subjects' good, no more,
'Twere best thus ordered.   I am thankful now,
Mute, passive, acquiescent.   I receive,
And bless God simply, or should almost fear
To walk so smoothly to my ends at last.
Why, how I baffle obstacles, spurn fate !
How strong I am ! could Norbert see me now !

CONSTANCE.

Let me consider.   It is all too strange.

QUEEN.

You, Constance, learn of me ; do you, like me.
You are young, beautiful : my own, best girl,   570
You will have many lovers, and love one—
Light hair, not hair like Norbert's, to suit yours,
And taller than he is, for you are tall.
Love him like me ! give all away to him ;
Think never of yourself ; throw by your pride,

Hope, fear,—your own good as you saw it once,
And love him simply for his very self.
Remember, I (and what am I to you ?)
Would give up all for one, leave throne, lose life,
Do all but just unlove him ! he loves me.   580

CONSTANCE.
He shall.

QUEEN.
          You, step inside my inmost heart.
Give me your own heart—let us have one heart—
I'll come to you for counsel ; " This he says,
This he does, what should this amount to, pray ?
Beseech you, change it into current coin.
Is that worth kisses ? shall I please him there ? "
And then we'll speak in turn of you—what else ?
Your love (according to your beauty's worth)
For you shall have some noble love, all gold—
Whom choose you ? we will get him at your choice. 590
—Constance, I leave you.   Just a minute since
I felt as I must die or be alone
Breathing my soul into an ear like yours.
Now, I would face the world with my new life,
With my new crown.   I'll walk around the rooms,
And then come back and tell you how it feels.
How soon a smile of God can change the world !
How we are all made for happiness—how work
Grows play, adversity a winning fight !
True, I have lost so many years.   What then ?   600
Many remain—God has been very good.
You, stay here.   'Tis as different from dreams,—
From the mind's cold calm estimate of bliss,
As these stone statues from the flesh and blood.
The comfort thou hast caused mankind, God's moon !

[*She goes out.   Dance-music from within.*

PART THIRD

———·———

NORBERT *enters.*

NORBERT.

Well ! we have but one minute and one word——

CONSTANCE.

I am yours, Norbert !

NORBERT.

Yes, mine.

CONSTANCE.

Not till now !

You were mine.   Now I give myself to you.

NORBERT.

Constance !

CONSTANCE.

Your own ! I know the thriftier way
Of giving—haply, 'tis the wiser way.   610
Meaning to give a treasure, I might dole
Coin after coin out (each, as that were all,
With a new largess still at each despair)
And force you keep in sight the deed, reserve
Exhaustless till the end my part and yours,
My giving and your taking, both our joys
Dying together.   Is it the wiser way ?
I choose the simpler ; I give all at once.
Know what you have to trust to, trade upon.
Use it, abuse it,—anything but say   620
Hereafter, " Had I known she loved me so,

And what my means, I might have thriven with it."
This is your means.   I give you all myself.

NORBERT.

I take you and thank God.

CONSTANCF.

Look on through years !
We cannot kiss a second day like this,
Else were this earth, no earth.

NORBERT.

With this day's heat
We shall go on through years of cold.

CONSTANCE.

So best.
I try to see those years—I think I see.
You walk quick and new warmth comes ; you look back
And lay all to the first glow—not sit down   630
For ever brooding on a day like this
While seeing the embers whiten and love die.
Yes, love lives best in its effect ; and mine,
Full in its own life, yearns to live in yours.

NORBERT.

Just so.   I take and know you all at once.
Your soul is disengaged so easily,
Your face is there, I know you ; give me time,
Let me be proud and think you shall know me.
My soul is slower : in a life I roll
The minute out in which you condense yours—   640
The whole slow circle round you I must move
To be just you.   I look to a long life
To decompose this minute, prove its worth.
'Tis the sparks' long succession one by one
Shall show you in the end what fire was crammed

In that mere stone you struck : you could not know,
If it lay ever unproved in your sight,
As now my heart lies ? your own warmth would hide
Its coldness, were it cold.

CONSTANCE.
                        But how prove, how ?

NORBERT.
Prove in my life, you ask ?

CONSTANCE.
                        Quick, Norbert—how ? 650

NORBERT.
That's easy told.   I count life just a stuff
To try the soul's strength on, educe the man.
Who keeps one end in view makes all things serve.
As with the body—he who hurls a lance
Or heaps up stone on stone, shews strength alike,
So I will seize and use all means to prove
And shew this soul of mine you crown as yours,
And justify us both.

CONSTANCE.
                        Could you write books,
Paint pictures ! one sits down in poverty
And writes or paints, with pity for the rich.   660

NORBERT.
And loves one's painting and one's writing too,
And not one's mistress!   All is best, believe,
And we best as no other than we are.
We live, and they experiment on life
Those poets, painters, all who stand aloof
To overlook the farther.   Let us be
The thing they look at !   I might take that face
And write of it and paint it—to what end ?

For whom ? what pale dictatress in the air
Feeds, smiling sadly, her fine ghost-like form   670
With earth's real blood and breath, the beauteous life
She makes despised for ever ?   You are mine,
Made for me, not for others in the world,
Nor yet for that which I should call my art,
That cold calm power to see how fair you look.
I come to you—I leave you not, to write
Or paint.   You are, I am.   Let Rubens there
Paint us.

CONSTANCE.

So best !

NORBERT.

I understand your soul.
You live, and rightly sympathise with life,
With action, power, success : this way is straight.   680
And days were short beside, to let me change
The craft my childhood learnt ; my craft shall serve.
Men set me here to subjugate, enclose,
Manure their barren lives and force the fruit
First for themselves, and afterward for me
In the due tithe ; the task of some one man,
By ways of work appointed by themselves.
I am not bid create, they see no star
Transfiguring my brow to warrant that—
But bind in one and carry out their wills.   690
So I began : to-night sees how I end.
What if it see, too, my first outbreak here
Amid the warmth, surprise and sympathy,
The instincts of the heart that teach the head ?
What if the people have discerned in me
The dawn of the next nature, the new man

Whose will they venture in the place of theirs,
And whom they trust to find them out new ways
To the new heights which yet he only sees ?
I felt it when you kissed me.   See this Queen,   700
This people—in our phrase, this mass of men—
See how the mass lies passive to my hand
And how my hand is plastic, and you by
To make the muscles iron !   Oh, an end
Shall crown this issue as this crowns the first.
My will be on this people ! then, the strain,
The grappling of the potter with his clay,
The long uncertain struggle,—the success
In that uprising of the spirit-work,
The vase shaped to the curl of the god's lip,   710
While rounded fair for lower men to see
The Graces in a dance they recognise
With turbulent applause and laughs of heart !
So triumph ever shall renew itself ;
Ever to end in efforts higher yet,
Ever begun——

CONSTANCE.

I ever helping ?

NORBERT.

Thus !

[*As he embraces her, enter the* QUEEN.

CONSTANCE.

Hist, madam—so I have performed my part.
You see your gratitude's true decency,
Norbert ? a little slow in seeing it !
Begun to end the sooner.   What's a kiss ?   720

NORBERT.

Constance !

CONSTANCE.

Why, must I teach it you again ?
You want a witness to your dullness, sir ?
What was I saying these ten minutes long ?
Then I repeat—when some young handsome man
Like you has acted out a part like yours,
Is pleased to fall in love with one beyond,
So very far beyond him, as he says—
So hopelessly in love, that but to speak
Would prove him mad, he thinks judiciously,
And makes some insignificant good soul   730
Like me, his friend, adviser, confidant
And very stalking-horse to cover him
In following after what he dares not face—
When his end's gained—(sir, do you understand ?)
When she, he dares not face, has loved him first,
—May I not say so, madam ?—tops his hope,
And overpasses so his wildest dream,
With glad consent of all, and most of her
The confidant who brought the same about—
Why, in the moment when such joy explodes,   740
I do say that the merest gentleman
Will not start rudely from the stalking-horse,
Dismiss it with a " There, enough of you ! "
Forget it, show his back unmannerly ;
But like a liberal heart will rather turn
And say, " A tingling time of hope was ours—
Betwixt the fears and faulterings—we two lived
A chanceful time in waiting for the prize.
The confidant, the Constance, served not ill ;
And though I shall forget her in due time,   750
Her use being answered now, as reason bids,

Nay as herself bids from her heart of hearts,
Still, she has rights, the first thanks go to her,
The first good praise goes to the prosperous tool,
And the first—which is the last—thankful kiss."

NORBERT.

—Constance ? it is a dream—ah see you smile !

CONSTANCE.

So, now his part being properly performed,
Madam, I turn to you and finish mine
As duly—I do justice in my turn.
Yes, madam, he has loved you—long and well—   760
He could not hope to tell you so—'twas I
Who served to prove your soul accessible.
I led his thoughts on, drew them to their place,
When oft they had wandered out into despair,
And kept love constant toward its natural aim.
Enough—my part is played ; you stoop half-way
And meet us royally and spare our fears—
'Tis like yourself—he thanks you, so do I.
Take him—with my full heart ! my work is praised
By what comes of it.   Be you happy, both !   770
Yourself—the only one on earth who can—
Do all for him, much more than a mere heart
Which though warm is not useful in its warmth
As the silk vesture of a queen ! fold that
Around him gently, tenderly.   For him—
For him,—he knows his own part.

NORBERT.

                              Have you done ?
I take the jest at last.   Should I speak now ?
Was yours the wager, Constance, foolish child,
Or did you but accept it ?   Well—at least,
You lose by it.

CONSTANCE.

Now madam, 'tis your turn. 780
Restrain him still from speech a little more
And make him happier and more confident !
Pity him, madam, he is timid yet.
Mark, Norbert ! do not shrink now ! Here I yield
My whole right in you to the Queen, observe !
With her go put in practice the great schemes
You teem with, follow the career else closed—
Be all you cannot be except by her !
Behold her.—Madam, say for pity's sake
Anything—frankly say you love him.   Else 790
He'll not believe it : there's more earnest in
His fear than you conceive—I know the man.

NORBERT.

I know the woman somewhat, and confess
I thought she had jested better—she begins
To overcharge her part.   I gravely wait
Your pleasure, madam : where is my reward ?

QUEEN.

Norbert, this wild girl (whom I recognise
Scarce more than you do, in her fancy-fit,
Eccentric speech and variable mirth,
Not very wise perhaps and somewhat bold 800
Yet suitable, the whole night's work being strange)
—May still be right : I may do well to speak
And make authentic what appears a dream
To even myself.   For, what she says, is true—
Yes, Norbert—what you spoke but now of love,
Devotion, stirred no novel sense in me,
But justified a warmth felt long before.
Yes, from the first—I loved you, I shall say,—

Strange ! but I do grow stronger, now 'tis said,
Your courage helps mine : you did well to speak   810
To-night, the night that crowns your twelvemonths' toil—
But still I had not waited to discern
Your heart so long, believe me !   From the first
The source of so much zeal was almost plain,
In absence even of your own words just now
Which opened out the truth.   'Tis very strange,
But takes a happy ending—in your love
Which mine meets : be it so—as you choose me.
So I choose you.

NORBERT.
                     And worthily you choose !
I will not be unworthy your esteem,   820
No, madam.   I do love you ; I will meet
Your nature, now I know it ; this was well,
I see,—you dare and you are justified :
But none had ventured such experiment,
Less versed than you in nobleness of heart,
Less confident of finding it in me.
I like that thus you test me ere you grant
The dearest, richest, beauteousest and best
Of women to my arms ! 'tis like yourself !
So—back again into my part's set words—   830
Devotion to the uttermost is yours,
But no, you cannot, madam, even you,
Create in me the love our Constance does.
Or—something truer to the tragic phrase—
Not yon magnolia-bell superb with scent
Invites a certain insect—that's myself—
But the small eye-flower nearer to the ground :
I take this lady !

CONSTANCE.

Stay—not her's, the trap—
Stay, Norbert—that mistake were worst of all.
(He is too cunning, madam!) it was I,   840
I, Norbert, who . . .

NORBERT.

You, was it, Constance?   Then,
But for the grace of this divinest hour
Which gives me you, I should not pardon here.
I am the Queen's: she only knows my brain—
She may experiment therefore on my heart
And I instruct her too by the result;
But you, sweet, you who know me, who so long
Have told my heart-beats over, held my life
In those white hands of yours,—it is not well!

CONSTANCE.

Tush! I have said it, did I not say it all?   850
The life, for her—the heart-beats, for her sake!

NORBERT.

Enough! my cheek grows red, I think.   Your test!
There's not the meanest woman in the world,
Not she I least could love in all the world,
Whom, did she love me, did love prove itself,
I dared insult as you insult me now.
Constance, I could say, if it must be said,
"Take back the soul you offer—I keep mine"
But—"Take the soul still quivering on your hand,
The soul so offered, which I cannot use,   860
And, please you, give it to some friend of mine,
For—what's the trifle he requites me with?"
I, tempt a woman, to amuse a man,
That two may mock her heart if it succumb?

No ! fearing God and standing 'neath his heaven,
I would not dare insult a woman so,
Were she the meanest woman in the world,
And he, I cared to please, ten emperors !

CONSTANCE.

Norbert !

NORBERT.

  I love once as I live but once.
What case is this to think or talk about ?   870
I love you. Would it mend the case at all
Should such a step as this kill love in me ?
Your part were done : account to God for it.
But mine—could murdered love get up again,
And kneel to whom you pleased to designate
And make you mirth ? It is too horrible.
You did not know this, Constance ? now you know
That body and soul have each one life, but one :
And here's my love, here, living, at your feet.

CONSTANCE.

See the Queen Norbert—this one more last word— 880
If thus you have taken jest for earnest—thus
Loved me in earnest . . .

NORBERT.

    Ah, no jest holds here !
Where is the laughter in which jests break up ?
And what this horror that grows palpable ?
Madam—why grasp you thus the balcony ?
Have I done ill ? Have I not spoken the truth ?
How could I other ? Was it not your test,
To try me, and what my love for Constance meant ?
Madam, your royal soul itself approves,

The first, that I should choose thus ! so one takes   890
A beggar—asks him what would buy his child,
And then approves the expected laugh of scorn
Returned as something noble from the rags.
Speak, Constance, I'm the beggar ! Ha, what's this ?
You two glare each at each like panthers now.
Constance—the world fades ; only you stand there !
You did not in to-night's wild whirl of things
Sell me—your soul of souls, for any price ?
No—no—'tis easy to believe in you.
Was it your love's mad trial to o'ertop   900
Mine by this vain self-sacrifice ? well, still—
Though I should curse, I love you.   I am love
And cannot change ! love's self is at your feet.

[QUEEN goes out.

CONSTANCE.

Feel my heart ; let it die against your own.

NORBERT.

Against my own ! explain not ; let this be.
This is life's height.

CONSTANCE.

Yours !   Yours !   Yours !

NORBERT.

You and I—

Why care by what meanders we are here
In the centre of the labyrinth ? men have died
Trying to find this place out, which we have found.

CONSTANCE.

Found, found !

NORBERT.

Sweet, never fear what she can do— 910

We are past harm now.

CONSTANCE.

On the breast of God.
I thought of men—as if you were a man.
Tempting him with a crown !

NORBERT.

This must end here—
It is too perfect !

CONSTANCE.

There's the music stopped.
What measured heavy tread ? it is one blaze
About me and within me.

NORBERT.

Oh, some death
Will run its sudden finger round this spark,
And sever us from the rest—

CONSTANCE.

And so do well.
Now the doors open—

NORBERT.

'Tis the guard comes.

CONSTANCE.

Kiss !

———————————

SAUL

1.

Said Abner, " At last thou art come ! Ere I tell, ere
      thou speak,
Kiss my cheek, wish me well ! " Then I wished it, and
      did kiss his cheek.
And he, " Since the King, O my friend, for thy counten-
      ance sent,
Neither drunken nor eaten have we ; nor until from his
      tent
Thou return with the joyful assurance the King liveth yet,
Shall our lip with the honey be bright, with the water
      be wet.
For out of the black mid-tent's silence, a space of three
      days,
Not a sound hath escaped to thy servants, of prayer·or
      of praise,
To betoken that Saul and the Spirit have ended their
      strife,
And that, faint in his triumph, the monarch sinks back
      upon life.

2.

Yet now my heart leaps, O beloved ! God's child, with
his dew

On thy gracious gold hair, and those lilies still living and
blue

Just broken to twine round thy harp-strings, as if no
wild heat

Were now raging to torture the desert ! "

3.

Then I, as was meet,

Knelt down to the God of my fathers, and rose on my
feet,

And ran o'er the sand burnt to powder. The tent was
unlooped ;

I pulled up the spear that obstructed, and under I
stooped ;

Hands and knees on the slippery grass-patch, all withered
and gone,

That extends to the second enclosure, I groped my way on

Till I felt where the foldskirts fly open. Then once
more I prayed,

And opened the foldskirts and entered, and was not
afraid,

But spoke, " Here is David, thy servant ! " And no
voice replied.

At the first I saw nought but the blackness ; but soon
I descried

A something more black than the blackness—the vast
the upright

Main prop which sustains the pavilion : and slow into
sight

Grew a figure against it, gigantic and blackest of all ;—
Then a sunbeam, that burst thro' the tent-roof,—
showed Saul.

4.

He stood as erect as that tent-prop ; both arms stretched
out wide
On the great cross-support in the centre, that goes to
each side :
He relaxed not a muscle, but hung there,—as, caught
in his pangs
And waiting his change the king-serpent all heavily
hangs,
Far away from his kind, in the pine, till deliverance come
With the spring-time,—so agonized Saul, drear and stark,
blind and dumb.

5.

Then I tuned my harp,—took off the lilies we twine
round its chords
Lest they snap 'neath the stress of the noontide—those
sunbeams like swords !
And I first played the tune all our sheep know, as, one
after one,
So docile they come to the pen-door, till folding be done.
They are white and untorn by the bushes, for lo, they
have fed
Where the long grasses stifle the water within the
stream's bed ;
And now one after one seeks its lodging, as star follows
star
Into eve and the blue far above us,—so blue and so far !

6.

—Then the tune, for which quails on the cornland will
each leave his mate
To fly after the player ; then, what makes the crickets
elate,
Till for boldness they fight one another : and then, what
has weight
To set the quick jerboa a-musing outside his sand house—
There are none such as he for a wonder, half bird and
half mouse !—
God made all the creatures and gave them our love and
our fear,
To give sign, we and they are his children, one family
here.

7.

Then I played the help-tune of our reapers, their wine-
song, when hand
Grasps at hand, eye lights eye in good friendship, and
great hearts expand
And grow one in the sense of this world's life.—And
then, the last song
When the dead man is praised on his journey—" Bear,
bear him along
With his few faults shut up like dead flowerets ! are
balm-seeds not here
To console us ? The land has none left, such as he on
the bier.
Oh, would we might keep thee, my brother ! "—And
then, the glad chaunt
Of the marriage,—first go the young maidens, next, she
whom we vaunt

As the beauty, the pride of our dwelling.—And then, the
     great march
Wherein man runs to man to assist him and buttress an
     arch
Nought can break; who shall harm them, our friends?
          —Then, the chorus intoned
As the Levites go up to the altar in glory enthroned . . .
But I stopped here—for here in the darkness, Saul
     groaned.

8.

And I paused, held my breath in such silence, and
     listened apart;
And the tent shook, for mighty Saul shuddered,—and
     sparkles 'gan dart
From the jewels that woke in his turban at once with
     a start—
All its lordly male-sapphires, and rubies courageous at
     heart.
So the head—but the body still moved not, still hung
     there erect.
And I bent once again to my playing, pursued it un-
     checked,
As I sang,—

9.

          " Oh, our manhood's prime vigour! no
          spirit feels waste,
Not a muscle is stopped in its playing, nor sinew un-
     braced.
Oh, the wild joys of living! the leaping from rock up to
     rock—
The strong rending of boughs from the fir-tree,—the
     cool silver shock

Of the plunge in a pool's living water,—the hunt of the
   bear,
And the sultriness shewing the lion is couched in his lair.
And the meal—the rich dates—yellowed over with gold
   dust divine,
And the locust's-flesh steeped in the pitcher ; the full
   draught of wine,
And the sleep in the dried river-channel where bull-
   rushes tell
That the water was wont to go warbling so softly and
   well.
How good is man's life, the mere living ! how fit to
   employ
All the heart and the soul and the senses, for ever in joy !
Hast thou loved the white locks of thy father, whose
   sword thou didst guard
When he trusted thee forth with the armies, for glorious
   reward ?
Didst thou see the thin hands of thy mother, held up as
   men sung
The low song of the nearly-departed, and heard her faint
   tongue
Joining in while it could to the witness, ' Let one more
   attest,
I have lived, seen God's hand thro' a lifetime, and all
   was for best . . . '
Then they sung thro' their tears in strong triumph, not
   much,—but the rest.
And thy brothers, the help and the contest, the working
   whence grew
Such result as from seething grape-bundles, the spirit
   strained true !

And the friends of thy boyhood—that boyhood of
wonder and hope,
Present promise, and wealth of the future beyond the
eye's scope,—
Till lo, thou art grown to a monarch ; a people is thine ;
And all gifts which the world offers singly, on one head
combine !
On one head, all the beauty and strength, love and rage,
like the throe
That, a-work in the rock, helps its labour, and lets the
gold go :
High ambition and deeds which surpass it, fame crown-
ing it,—all
Brought to blaze on the head of one creature—King
Saul ! "

10.

And lo, with that leap of my spirit, heart, hand, harp
and voice,
Each lifting Saul's name out of sorrow, each bidding
rejoice
Saul's fame in the light it was made for—as when, dare
I say,
The Lord's army in rapture of service, strains through
its array,
And upsoareth the cherubim-chariot—" Saul ! " cried
I, and stopped,
And waited the thing that should follow. Then Saul,
who hung propt
By the tent's cross-support in the centre, was struck by
his name.
Have ye seen when Spring's arrowy summons goes right
to the aim,

And some mountain, the last to withstand her, that held,
  (he alone,
While the vale laughed in freedom and flowers) on a
  broad bust of stone
A year's snow bound about for a breastplate,—leaves
  grasp of the sheet ?
Fold on fold all at once it crowds thunderously down
  to his feet,
And there fronts you, stark, black but alive yet, your
  mountain of old,
With his rents, the successive bequeathings of ages
  untold—
Yea, each harm got in fighting your battles, each furrow
  and scar
Of his head thrust 'twixt you and the tempest—all hail,
  there they are !
Now again to be softened with verdure, again hold the
  nest
Of the dove, tempt the goat and its young to the green
  on its crest
For their food in the ardours of summer ! One long
  shudder thrilled
All the tent till the very air tingled, then sank and was
  stilled,
At the King's self left standing before me, released and
  aware.
What was gone, what remained ? all to traverse 'twixt
  hope and despair—
Death was past, life not come—so he waited. Awhile
  his right hand
Held the brow, helped the eyes left too vacant forthwith
  to remand

To their place what new objects should enter : 'twas
    Saul as before.
I looked up and dared gaze at those eyes, nor was hurt
    any more
Than by slow pallid sunsets in autumn, ye watch from
    the shore
At their sad level gaze o'er the ocean—a sun's slow
    decline
Over hills which, resolved in stern silence, o'erlap and
    entwine
Base with base to knit strength more intense : so, arm
    folded in arm
O'er the chest whose slow heavings subsided.

11.

                        What spell or what charm,
(For, awhile there was trouble within me) what next
    should I urge
To sustain him where song had restored him ?—Song
    filled to the verge
His cup with the wine of this life, pressing all that it
    yields
Of mere fruitage, the strength and the beauty !   Beyond,
    on what fields,
Glean a vintage more potent and perfect to brighten the
    eye
And bring blood to the lip, and commend them the cup
    they put by ?
He saith, " It is good ; " still he drinks not—he lets me
    praise life,
Gives assent, yet would die for his own part.

12.

Then fancies grew rife
Which had come long ago on the pastures, when round
me the sheep
Fed in silence—above, the one eagle wheeled slow as in
sleep,
And I lay in my hollow, and mused on the world that
might lie
'Neath his ken, though I saw but the strip 'twixt the
hill and the sky :
And I laughed—" Since my days are ordained to be
passed with my flocks,
Let me people at least with my fancies, the plains and
the rocks,
Dream the life I am never to mix with, and image the
show
Of mankind as they live in those fashions I hardly shall
know !
Schemes of life, its best rules and right uses, the courage
that gains,
And the prudence that keeps what men strive for."
And now these old trains
Of vague thought came again ; I grew surer ; so once
more the string
Of my harp made response to my spirit, as thus—

13.

" Yea, my king,"
I began—" thou dost well in rejecting mere comforts
that spring
From the mere mortal life held in common by man and
by brute :

In our flesh grows the branch of this life, in our soul it
bears fruit.

Thou hast marked the slow rise of the tree,—how its
stem trembled first

Till it passed the kid's lip, the stag's antler ; then safely
outburst

The fan-branches all round ; and thou mindedst when
these too, in turn

Broke a-bloom and the palm-tree seemed perfect ; yet
more was to learn,

Ev'n the good that comes in with the palm-fruit. Our
dates shall we slight,

When their juice brings a cure for all sorrow ? or care
for the plight

Of the palm's self whose slow growth produced them ?
Not so ! stem and branch

Shall decay, nor be known in their place, while the palm-
wine shall staunch

Every wound of man's spirit in winter. I pour thee
such wine.

Leave the flesh to the fate it was fit for ! the spirit be thine !

By the spirit, when age shall o'ercome thee, thou still
shalt enjoy

More indeed, than at first when inconscious, the life of a boy.

Crush that life, and behold its wine running ! each deed
thou hast done

Dies, revives, goes to work in the world ; until e'en as
the sun

Looking down on the earth, though clouds spoil him,
though tempests efface,

Can find nothing his own deed produced not, must every
where trace

The results of his past summer-prime,—so, each ray of
thy will,

Every flash of thy passion and prowess, long over, shall
thrill

Thy whole people the countless, with ardour, till they
too give forth

A like cheer to their sons, who in turn, fill the south and
the north

With the radiance thy deed was the germ of. Carouse
in the past.

But the license of age has its limit; thou diest at
last.

As the lion when age dims his eye-ball, the rose at her
height,

So with man—so his power and his beauty for ever take
flight.

No! again a long draught of my soul-wine! look forth
o'er the years—

Thou hast done now with eyes for the actual; begin
with the seer's!

Is Saul dead? in the depth of the vale make his tomb
—bid arise

A grey mountain of marble heaped four-square, till built
to the skies.

Let it mark where the great First King slumbers—whose
fame would ye know?

Up above see the rock's naked face, where the record
shall go

In great characters cut by the scribe,—Such was Saul,
so he did;

With the sages directing the work, by the populace
chid,—

For not half, they'll affirm, is comprised there ! Which
fault to amend,
In the grove with his kind grows the cedar, whereon they
shall spend
(See, in tablets 'tis level before them) their praise, and
record
With the gold of the graver, Saul's story,—the states-
man's great word
Side by side with the poet's sweet comment. The
river's a-wave
With smooth paper-reeds grazing each other when
prophet winds rave :
So the pen gives unborn generations their due and their part
In thy being ! Then, first of the mighty, thank God
that thou art."

14.

And behold while I sang . . But O Thou who didst grant
me that day,
And before it not seldom hast granted, thy help to essay
Carry on and complete an adventure,—my Shield and
my Sword
In that act where my soul was thy servant, thy word
was my word,—
Still be with me, who then at the summit of human
endeavour
And scaling the highest man's thought could, gazed
hopeless as ever
On the new stretch of Heaven above me—till, Mighty
to save,
Just one lift of thy hand cleared that distance—God's
throne from man's grave !

Let me tell out my tale to its ending—my voice to my
heart,
Which can scarce dare believe in what marvels that
night I took part,
As this morning I gather the fragments, alone with my
sheep,
And still fear lest the terrible glory evanish like sleep !
For I wake in the grey dewy covert, while Hebron up-
heaves
The dawn struggling with night on his shoulder, and
Kidron retrieves
Slow the damage of yesterday's sunshine.

15.

I say then,—my song
While I sang thus, assuring the monarch, and ever more
strong
Made a proffer of good to console him—he slowly re-
sumed
His old motions and habitudes kingly. The right hand
replumed
His black locks to their wonted composure, adjusted the
swathes
Of his turban, and see—the huge sweat that his coun-
tenance bathes,
He wipes off with the robe ; and he girds now his loins
as of yore,
And feels slow for the armlets of price, with the clasp
set before.
He is Saul, ye remember in glory,—ere error had bent
The broad brow from the daily communion ; and still,
though much spent

Be the life and the bearing that front you, the same,
    God did choose,
To receive what a man may waste, desecrate, never quite
    lose.
So sank he along by the tent-prop, till, stayed by the
    pile
Of his armour and war-cloak and garments, he leaned
    there awhile,
And so sat out my singing,—one arm round the tent-
    prop, to raise
His bent head, and the other hung slack—till I touched
    on the praise
I foresaw from all men in all times, to the man patient
    there,
And thus ended, the harp falling forward. Then first
    I was 'ware
That he sat, as I say, with my head just above his vast
    knees
Which were thrust out on each side around me, like oak-
    roots which please
To encircle a lamb when it slumbers. I looked up to
    know
If the best I could do had brought solace : he spoke not,
    but slow
Lifted up the hand slack at his side, till he laid it with
    care
Soft and grave, but in mild settled will, on my brow :
    thro' my hair
The large fingers were pushed, and he bent back my
    head, with kind power—
All my face back, intent to peruse it, as men do a
    flower.

Thus held he me there with his great eyes that scruti-
nised mine—
And oh, all my heart how it loved him ! but where was
the sign ?
I yearned—" Could I help thee, my father, inventing
a bliss,
I would add to that life of the past, both the future and this.
I would give thee new life altogether, as good, ages hence,
As this moment,—had love but the warrant, love's heart
to dispense ! "

16.
Then the truth came upon me. No harp more—no
song more ! out-broke—

17.
" I have gone the whole round of Creation : I saw and
I spoke !
I, a work of God's hand for that purpose, received in my
brain
And pronounced on the rest of his handwork—returned
him again
His creation's approval or censure : I spoke as I saw.
I report, as a man may of God's work—all's love, yet
all's law !
Now I lay down the judgeship he lent me.   Each faculty
tasked
To perceive him, has gained an abyss, where a dew-
drop was asked.
Have I knowledge ? confounded it shrivels at wisdom
laid bare.
Have I forethought ? how purblind, how blank, to the
Infinite care !

Do I task any faculty highest, to image success ?
I but open my eyes,—and perfection, no more and no less,
In the kind I imagined, full-fronts me, and God is seen God
In the star, in the stone, in the flesh, in the soul and the
           clod.
And thus looking within and around me, I ever renew
(With that stoop of the soul which in bending upraises
           it too)
The submission of Man's nothing-perfect to God's All-
           Complete,
As by each new obeisance in spirit, I climb to his feet !
Yet with all this abounding experience, this Deity known,
I shall dare to discover some province, some gift of my
           own.
There's one faculty pleasant to exercise, hard to hood-
           wink,
I am fain to keep still in abeyance, (I laugh as I think)
Lest, insisting to claim and parade in it, wot ye, I worst
E'en the Giver in one gift.—Behold ! I could love if
           I durst !
But I sink the pretension as fearing a man may o'ertake
God's own speed in the one way of love : I abstain, for
           love's sake !
—What, my soul ? see thus far and no farther ? when
           doors great and small,
Nine-and-ninety flew ope at our touch, should the
           hundredth appal ?
In the least things, have faith, yet distrust in the greatest
           of all ?
Do I find love so full in my nature, God's ultimate gift,
That I doubt his own love can compete with it ? here,
           the parts shift ?

Here, the creature surpass the Creator, the end, what
        Began ?—

Would I fain in my impotent yearning do all for this man,

And dare doubt He alone shall not help him, who yet
        alone can ?

Would it ever have entered my mind, the bare will,
        much less power,

To bestow on this Saul what I sang of, the marvellous
        dower

Of the life he was gifted and filled with ? to make such
        a soul,

Such a body, and then such an earth for insphering the
        whole ?

And doth it not enter my mind (as my warm tears attest)

These good things being given, to go on, and give one
        more, the best ?

Ay, to save and redeem and restore him, maintain at
        the height

This perfection,—succeed with life's dayspring, death's
        minute of night ?

Interpose at the difficult minute, snatch Saul, the
        mistake,

Saul, the failure, the ruin he seems now,—and bid him
        awake

From the dream, the probation, the prelude, to find him-
        self set

Clear and safe in new light and new life,—a new harmony
        yet

To be run, and continued, and ended—who knows ?—or
        endure !

The man taught enough by life's dream, of the rest to
        make sure.

By the pain-throb, triumphantly winning intensified
bliss,
And the next world's reward and repose, by the struggle
in this.

18.

" I believe it ! 'tis Thou, God, that givest, 'tis I who
receive :
In the first is the last, in thy will is my power to believe.
All's one gift : thou canst grant it moreover, as prompt
to my prayer
As I breathe out this breath, as I open these arms to the
air.
From thy will, stream the worlds, life and nature, thy
dread Sabaoth :
I will ?—the mere atoms despise me ! and why am I loth
To look that, even that in the face too ? why is it I
dare
Think but lightly of such impuissance ? what stops my
despair ?
This ;—'tis not what man Does which exalts him, but
what man Would do !
See the king—I would help him but cannot, the wishes
fall through.
Could I wrestle to raise him from sorrow, grow poor to
enrich,
To fill up his life, starve my own out, I would—knowing
which,
I know that my service is perfect.—Oh, speak through
me now !
Would I suffer for him that I love ? So wilt Thou—so
wilt Thou !

So shall crown thee the topmost, ineffablest, uttermost
Crown—
And thy love fill infinitude wholly, nor leave up nor down
One spot for the creature to stand in! It is by no
breath,
Turn of eye, wave of hand, that Salvation joins issue
with death!
As thy Love is discovered almighty, almighty be proved
Thy power, that exists with and for it, of Being beloved!
He who did most, shall bear most; the strongest shall
stand the most weak.
'Tis the weakness in strength that I cry for! my flesh,
that I seek
In the Godhead! I seek and I find it. O Saul, it shall be
A Face like my face that receives thee: a Man like to me,
Thou shalt love and be loved by, for ever! a Hand like
this hand
Shall throw open the gates of new life to thee! See the
Christ stand!"

19.

I know not too well how I found my way home in the
night.
There were witnesses, cohorts about me, to left and to
right,
Angels, powers, the unuttered, unseen, the alive—the
aware—
I repressed, I got through them as hardly, as strugglingly
there,
As a runner beset by the populace famished for news—
Life or death. The whole earth was awakened, hell
loosed with her crews;

And the stars of night beat with emotion, and tingled
    and shot
Out in fire the strong pain of pent knowledge : but
    I fainted not.
For the Hand still impelled me at once and supported—
    suppressed
All the tumult, and quenched it with quiet, and holy
    behest,
Till the rapture was shut in itself, and the earth sank to rest.
Anon at the dawn, all that trouble had withered from
    earth—
Not so much, but I saw it die out in the day's tender
    birth ;
In the gathered intensity brought to the grey of the hills ;
In the shuddering forests' new awe ; in the sudden wind-
    thrills ;
In the startled wild beasts that bore off, each with eye
    sidling still
Tho' averted, in wonder and dread ; and the birds stiff
    and chill
That rose heavily, as I approached them, made stupid
    with awe !
E'en the serpent that slid away silent,—he felt the new
    Law.
The same stared in the white humid faces upturned by
    the flowers ;
The same worked in the heart of the cedar, and moved
    the vine-bowers.
And the little brooks witnessing murmured, persistent
    and low,
With their obstinate, all but hushed voices—E'en so ! it
    is so.

"DE GUSTIBUS—"

1.

YOUR ghost will walk, you lover of trees,
    (If loves remain)
    In an English lane,
By a cornfield-side a-flutter with poppies.
Hark, those two in the hazel coppice—
A boy and a girl, if the good fates please,
    Making love, say,—
    The happier they !
Draw yourself up from the light of the moon,
And let them pass, as they will too soon,
    With the beanflowers' boon,
    And the blackbird's tune,
    And May, and June !

2.

What I love best in all the world,
Is, a castle, precipice-encurled,
In a gash of the wind-grieved Apennine.
Or look for me, old fellow of mine,
(If I get my head from out the mouth

O' the grave, and loose my spirit's bands,
And come again to the land of lands)—
In a sea-side house to the farther south,
Where the baked cicalas die of drouth,
And one sharp tree ('tis a cypress) stands,
By the many hundred years red-rusted,
Rough iron-spiked, ripe fruit-o'ercrusted,
My sentinel to guard the sands
To the water's edge.   For, what expands
Without the house, but the great opaque
Blue breadth of sea, and not a break?
While, in the house, for ever crumbles
Some fragment of the frescoed walls,
From blisters where a scorpion sprawls.
A girl bare-footed brings and tumbles
Down on the pavement, green-flesh melons,
And says there's news to-day—the king
Was shot at, touched in the liver-wing,
Goes with his Bourbon arm in a sling.
—She hopes they have not caught the felons.
      Italy, my Italy!
Queen Mary's saying serves for me—
      (When fortune's malice
      Lost her, Calais.)
Open my heart and you will see
Graved inside of it, "Italy."
Such lovers old are I and she;
So it always was, so it still shall be!

WOMEN AND ROSES

—·—

1.

I DREAM of a red-rose tree.
And which of its roses three
Is the dearest rose to me ?

2.

Round and round, like a dance of snow
In a dazzling drift, as its guardians, go
Floating the women faded for ages,
Sculptured in stone, on the poet's pages.
Then follow the women fresh and gay,
Living and loving and loved to-day.
Last, in the rear, flee the multitude of maidens,
Beauties unborn.   And all, to one cadence,
They circle their rose on my rose tree.

3.

Dear rose, thy term is reached,
Thy leaf hangs loose and bleached :
Bees pass it unimpeached.

4.

Stay then, stoop, since I cannot climb,
You, great shapes of the antique time !
How shall I fix you, fire you, freeze you,
Break my heart at your feet to please you ?
Oh ! to possess, and be possessed !
Hearts that beat 'neath each pallid breast !
But once of love, the poesy, the passion,
Drink once and die !—In vain, the same fashion,
They circle their rose on my rose tree.

5.

Dear rose, thy joy's undimmed ;
Thy cup is ruby-rimmed,
Thy cup's heart nectar-brimmed.

6.

Deep as drops from a statue's plinth
The bee sucked in by the hyacinth,
So will I bury me while burning,
Quench like him at a plunge my yearning,
Eyes in your eyes, lips on your lips !
Fold me fast where the cincture slips,
Prison all my soul in eternities of pleasure !
Girdle me once ! But no—in their old measure
They circle their rose on my rose tree.

7.

Dear rose without a thorn,
Thy bud's the babe unborn :
First streak of a new morn.

8.

Wings, lend wings for the cold, the clear !
What's far conquers what is near.
Roses will bloom nor want beholders,
Sprung from the dust where our own flesh moulders.
What shall arrive with the cycle's change ?
A novel grace and a beauty strange.
I will make an Eve, be the artist that began her
Shaped her to his mind !—Alas ! in like manner
They circle their rose on my rose tree.

PROTUS

AMONG these latter busts we count by scores,
Half-emperors and quarter-emperors,
Each with his bay-leaf fillet, loose-thonged vest,
Loric and low-browed Gorgon on the breast
One loves a baby face, with violets there,
Violets instead of laurel in the hair,
As those were all the little locks could bear.

Now read here.   " Protus ends a period
Of empery beginning with a god :
Born in the porphyry chamber at Byzant ;   10
Queens by his cradle, proud and ministrant.
And if he quickened breath there, 'twould like fire
Pantingly through the dim vast realm transpire.
A fame that he was missing, spread afar—
The world, from its four corners, rose in war,
Till he was borne out on a balcony
To pacify the world when it should see.
The captains ranged before him, one, his hand
Made baby points at, gained the chief command.

And day by day more beautiful he grew   20
In shape, all said, in feature and in hue,
While young Greek sculptors gazing on the child
Were, so, with old Greek sculpture, reconciled.
Already sages laboured to condense
In easy tomes a life's experience :
And artists took grave counsel to impart
In one breath and one hand-sweep, all their art—
To make his graces prompt as blossoming
Of plentifully-watered palms in spring :
Since well beseems it, whoso mounts the throne,   30
For beauty, knowledge, strength, should stand alone,
And mortals love the letters of his name."

—Stop ! Have you turned two pages ? Still the same.
New reign, same date. The scribe goes on to say
How that same year, on such a month and day,
" John the Pannonian, groundedly believed
A blacksmith's bastard, whose hard hand reprieved
The Empire from its fate the year before,—
Came, had a mind to take the crown, and wore
The same for six years, (during which the Huns   40
Kept off their fingers from us) till his sons
Put something in his liquor "—and so forth.
Then a new reign. Stay—" Take at its just worth "
(Subjoins an annotator) " what I give
As hearsay. Some think John let Protus live
And slip away. 'Tis said, he reached man's age
At some blind northern court ; made first a page,
Then, tutor to the children—last, of use
About the hunting-stables. I deduce
He wrote the little tract ' On worming dogs,'   50

Whereof the name in sundry catalogues
Is extant yet.   A Protus of the Race
Is rumoured to have died a monk in Thrace,—
And if the same, he reached senility."

Here's John the Smith's rough-hammered head.   Great
     eye
Gross jaw and griped lips do what granite can
To give you the crown-grasper.   What a man !

HOLY-CROSS DAY

ON WHICH THE JEWS WERE FORCED TO ATTEND AN ANNUAL CHRISTIAN SERMON IN ROME.

———◆———

["Now was come about Holy-Cross Day, and now must my lord preach his first sermon to the Jews: as it was of old cared for in the merciful bowels of the Church, that, so to speak, a crumb at least from her conspicuous table here in Rome, should be, though but once yearly, cast to the famishing dogs, under-trampled and bespitten-upon beneath the feet of the guests. And a moving sight in truth, this, of so many of the besotted, blind, restive and ready-to-perish Hebrews! now paternally brought—nay, (for He saith, 'Compel them to come in') haled, as it were, by the head and hair, and against their obstinate hearts, to partake of the heavenly grace. What awakening, what striving with tears, what working of a yeasty conscience! Nor was my lord wanting to himself on so apt an occasion; witness the abundance of conversions which did incontinently reward him: though not to my lord be altogether the glory."—*Diary by the Bishop's Secretary*, 1600.]

Though what the Jews really said, on thus being driven to church, was rather to this effect:

1.

FEE, faw, fum! bubble and squeak!
Blessedest Thursday's the fat of the week.
Rumble and tumble, sleek and rough,
Stinking and savoury, smug and gruff,
Take the church-road, for the bell's due chime
Gives us the summons—'tis sermon-time.

2.

Boh, here's Barnabas ! Job, that's you ?
Up stumps Solomon—bustling too ?
Shame, man ! greedy beyond your years
To handsel the bishop's shaving-shears ?
Fair play's a jewel ! leave friends in the lurch ?
Stand on a line ere you start for the church.

3.

Higgledy piggledy, packed we lie,
Rats in a hamper, swine in a stye,
Wasps in a bottle, frogs in a sieve,
Worms in a carcase, fleas in a sleeve.
Hist ! square shoulders, settle your thumbs
And buzz for the bishop—here he comes.

4.

Bow, wow, wow—a bone for the dog !
I liken his Grace to an acorned hog.
What, a boy at his side, with the bloom of a lass,
To help and handle my lord's hour-glass !
Didst ever behold so lithe a chine ?
His cheek hath laps like a fresh-singed swine.

5.

Aaron's asleep—shove hip to haunch,
Or somebody deal him a dig in the paunch !
Look at the purse with the tassel and knob,
And the gown with the angel and thingumbob.
What's he at, quotha ? reading his text !
Now you've his curtsey—and what comes next ?

6.

See to our converts—you doomed black dozen—
No stealing away—nor cog nor cozen !
You five that were thieves, deserve it fairly ;
You seven that were beggars, will live less sparely
You took your turn and dipped in the hat,
Got fortune—and fortune gets you ; mind that !

7.

Give your first groan—compunction's at work ;
And soft ! from a Jew you mount to a Turk.
Lo, Micah,—the selfsame beard on chin
He was four times already converted in !
Here's a knife, clip quick—it's a sign of grace—
Or he ruins us all with his hanging-face.

8.

Whom now is the bishop a-leering at ?
I know a point where his text falls pat.
I'll tell him to-morrow, a word just now
Went to my heart and made me vow
I meddle no more with the worst of trades—
Let somebody else pay his serenades.

9.

Groan all together now, whee—hee—hee !
It's a-work, it's a-work, ah, woe is me !
It began, when a herd of us, picked and placed,
Were spurred through the Corso, stripped to the waist ;
Jew-brutes, with sweat and blood well spent
To usher in worthily Christian Lent.

10.

It grew, when the hangman entered our bounds,
Yelled, pricked us out to this church like hounds.
It got to a pitch, when the hand indeed
Which gutted my purse, would throttle my creed.
And it overflows, when, to even the odd,
Men I helped to their sins, help me to their God.

11.

But now, while the scapegoats leave our flock,
And the rest sit silent and count the clock,
Since forced to muse the appointed time
On these precious facts and truths sublime,—
Let us fitly employ it, under our breath,
In saying Ben Ezra's Song of Death.

12.

For Rabbi Ben Ezra, the night he died,
Called sons and sons' sons to his side,
And spoke, " This world has been harsh and strange,
Something is wrong, there needeth a change.
But what, or where ? at the last, or first ?
In one point only we sinned, at worst.

13.

" The Lord will have mercy on Jacob yet,
And again in his border see Israel set.
When Judah beholds Jerusalem,
The stranger-seed shall be joined to them :
To Jacob's House shall the Gentiles cleave.
So the Prophet saith and his sons believe.

14.

" Ay, the children of the chosen race
Shall carry and bring them to their place :
In the land of the Lord shall lead the same,
Bondsmen and handmaids.   Who shall blame,
When the slaves enslave, the oppressed ones o'er
The oppressor triumph for evermore ?

15.

" God spoke, and gave us the word to keep :
Bade never fold the hands nor sleep
'Mid a faithless world,—at watch and ward,
Till the Christ at the end relieve our guard.
By his servant Moses the watch was set :
Though near upon cock-crow—we keep it yet.

16.

" Thou ! if thou wast He, who at mid-watch came,
By the starlight naming a dubious Name !
And if we were too heavy with sleep—too rash
With fear—O Thou, if that martyr-gash
Fell on thee coming to take thine own,
And we gave the Cross, when we owed the Throne—

17.

" Thou art the Judge.   We are bruised thus.
But, the judgment over, join sides with us !
Thine too is the cause ! and not more thine
Than ours, is the work of these dogs and swine,
Whose life laughs through and spits at their creed,
Who maintain thee in word, and defy thee in deed !

18.

" We withstood Christ then ? be mindful how
At least we withstand Barabbas now !
Was our outrage sore ? but the worst we spared,
To have called these—Christians,—had we dared !
Let defiance to them, pay mistrust of thee,
And Rome make amends for Calvary !

19.

" By the torture, prolonged from age to age,
By the infamy, Israel's heritage,
By the Ghetto's plague, by the garb's disgrace,
By the badge of shame, by the felon's place,
By the branding-tool, the bloody whip,
And the summons to Christian fellowship,

20.

" We boast our proofs, that at least the Jew
Would wrest Christ's name from the Devil's crew.
Thy face took never so deep a shade
But we fought them in it, God our aid !
A trophy to bear, as we march, a band
South, east, and on to the Pleasant Land ! "

[The present Pope abolished this bad business of the
sermon.—R. B.]

THE GUARDIAN-ANGEL

A PICTURE AT FANO

———+———

1.

DEAR and great Angel, wouldst thou only leave
    That child, when thou hast done with him, for me!
Let me sit all the day here, that when eve
    Shall find performed thy special ministry
And time come for departure, thou, suspending
Thy flight, mayst see another child for tending,
    Another still, to quiet and retrieve.

2.

Then I shall feel thee step one step, no more,
    From where thou standest now, to where I gaze,
And suddenly my head be covered o'er
    With those wings, white above the child who prays
Now on that tomb—and I shall feel thee guarding
Me, out of all the world; for me, discarding
    Yon heaven thy home, that waits and opes its door!

3.

I would not look up thither past thy head
   Because the door opes, like that child, I know,
For I should have thy gracious face instead,
   Thou bird of God ! And wilt thou bend me low
Like him, and lay, like his, my hands together,
And lift them up to pray, and gently tether
   Me, as thy lamb there, with thy garment's spread ?

4.

If this was ever granted, I would rest
   My head beneath thine, while thy healing hands
Close-covered both my eyes beside thy breast,
   Pressing the brain, which too much thought expands,
Back to its proper size again, and smoothing
Distortion down till every nerve had soothing,
   And all lay quiet, happy and supprest.

5.

How soon all worldly wrong would be repaired !
   I think how I should view the earth and skies
And sea, when once again my brow was bared
   After thy healing, with such different eyes.
O, world, as God has made it ! all is beauty :
And knowing this, is love, and love is duty.
   What further may be sought for or declared ?

6.

Guercino drew this angel I saw teach
   (Alfred, dear friend)—that little child to pray,
Holding the little hands up, each to each
   Pressed gently,—with his own head turned away

Over the earth where so much lay before him
Of work to do, though heaven was opening o'er him,
   And he was left at Fano by the beach.

7.

We were at Fano, and three times we went
   To sit and see him in his chapel there,
And drink his beauty to our soul's content
   —My angel with me too : and since I care
For dear Guercino's fame, (to which in power
And glory comes this picture for a dower,
   Fraught with a pathos so magnificent)

8.

And since he did not work so earnestly
   At all times, and has else endured some wrong,—
I took one thought his picture struck from me,
   And spread it out, translating it to song.
My Love is here.   Where are you, dear old friend ?
How rolls the Wairoa at your world's far end ?
   This is Ancona, yonder is the sea.

CLEON

"As certain also of your own poets have said"—

——·——

CLEON the poet, (from the sprinkled isles,
Lily on lily, that o'erlace the sea,
And laugh their pride when the light wave lisps
    "Greece")—
To Protos in his Tryanny : much health !

  They give thy letter to me, even now :
I read and seem as if I heard thee speak.
The master of thy galley still unlades
Gift after gift ; they block my court at last
And pile themselves along its portico
Royal with sunset, like a thought of thee :   **10**
And one white she-slave from the group dispersed
Of black and white slaves, (like the chequer-work
Pavement, at once my nation's work and gift,
Now covered with this settle-down of doves)
One lyric woman, in her crocus vest
Woven of sea-wools, with her two white hands

Commends to me the strainer and the cup
Thy lip hath bettered ere it blesses mine.

    Well-counselled, king, in thy munificence !
For so shall men remark, in such an act   20
Of love for him whose song gives life its joy,
Thy recognition of the use of life ;
Nor call thy spirit barely adequate
To help on life in straight ways, broad enough
For vulgar souls, by ruling and the rest.
Thou, in the daily building of thy tower,
Whether in fierce and sudden spasms of toil,
Or through dim lulls of unapparent growth,
Or when the general work 'mid good acclaim
Climbed with the eye to cheer the architect,   30
Didst ne'er engage in work for mere work's sake—
Hadst ever in thy heart the luring hope
Of some eventual rest a-top of it,
Whence, all the tumult of the building hushed,
Thou first of men mightst look out to the east.
The vulgar saw thy tower ; thou sawest the sun.
For this, I promise on thy festival
To pour libation, looking o'er the sea,
Making this slave narrate thy fortunes, speak
Thy great words, and describe thy royal face—   40
Wishing thee wholly where Zeus lives the most
Within the eventual element of calm.

    Thy letter's first requirement meets me here.
It is as thou hast heard : in one short life
I, Cleon, have effected all those things
Thou wonderingly dost enumerate.

That epos on thy hundred plates of gold
Is mine,—and also mine the little chaunt,
So sure to rise from every fishing-bark
When, lights at prow, the seamen haul their nets.　　50
The image of the sun-god on the phare
Men turn from the sun's self to see, is mine ;
The Pœcile, o'er-storied its whole length,
As thou didst hear, with painting, is mine too.
I know the true proportions of a man
And woman also, not observed before ;
And I have written three books on the soul,
Proving absurd all written hitherto,
And putting us to ignorance again.
For music,—why, I have combined the moods,　　60
Inventing one.　In brief, all arts are mine ;
Thus much the people know and recognise,
Throughout our seventeen islands.　Marvel not.
We of these latter days, with greater mind
Than our forerunners, since more composite,
Look not so great (beside their simple way)
To a judge who only sees one way at once,
One mind-point, and no other at a time,—
Compares the small part of a man of us
With some whole man of the heroic age,　　70
Great in his way,—not ours, nor meant for ours,
And ours is greater, had we skill to know.
Yet, what we call this life of men on earth,
This sequence of the soul's achievements here,
Being, as I find much reason to conceive,
Intended to be viewed eventually
As a great whole, not analysed to parts,
But each part having reference to all,—

How shall a certain part, pronounced complete,
Endure effacement by another part ?   80
Was the thing done ?—Then what's to do again ?
See, in the chequered pavement opposite,
Suppose the artist made a perfect rhomb,
And next a lozenge, then a trapezoid—
He did not overlay them, superimpose
The new upon the old and blot it out,
But laid them on a level in his work,
Making at last a picture ; there it lies.
So, first the perfect separate forms were made,
The portions of mankind—and after, so,   90
Occurred the combination of the same.
Or where had been a progress, otherwise ?
Mankind, made up of all the single men,—
In such a synthesis the labour ends.
Now, mark me—those divine men of old time
Have reached, thou sayest well, each at one point
The outside verge that rounds our faculty ;
And where they reached, who can do more than reach ?
It takes but little water just to touch
At some one point the inside of a sphere,   100
And, as we turn the sphere, touch all the rest
In due succession : but the finer air
Which not so palpably nor obviously,
Though no less universally, can touch
The whole circumference of that emptied sphere,
Fills it more fully than the water did ;
Holds thrice the weight of water in itself
Resolved into a subtler element.
And yet the vulgar call the sphere first full
Up to the visible height—and after, void ;   110

Not knowing air's more hidden properties.
And thus our soul, misknown, cries out to Zeus
To vindicate his purpose in its life—
Why stay we on the earth unless to grow ?
Long since, I imaged, wrote the fiction out,
That he or other God, descended here
And, once for all, showed simultaneously
What, in its nature, never can be shown
Piecemeal or in succession ;—showed, I say,
The worth both absolute and relative   120
Of all His children from the birth of time,
His instruments for all appointed work.
I now go on to image,—might we hear
The judgment which should give the due to each,
Shew where the labour lay and where the ease,
And prove Zeus' self, the latent, everywhere !
This is a dream.   But no dream, let us hope,
That years and days, the summers and the springs
Follow each other with unwaning powers—
The grapes which dye thy wine, are richer far   130
Through culture, than the wild wealth of the rock ;
The suave plum than the savage-tasted drupe ;
The pastured honey-bee drops choicer sweet ;
The flowers turn double, and the leaves turn flowers ;
That young and tender crescent-moon, thy slave,
Sleeping upon her robe as if on clouds,
Refines upon the women of my youth.
What, and the soul alone deteriorates ?
I have not chanted verse like Homer's, no—
Nor swept string like Terpander, no—nor carved   140
And painted men like Phidias and his friend :
I am not great as they are, point by point :

But I have entered into sympathy
With these four, running these into one soul,
Who, separate, ignored each others' arts.
Say, is it nothing that I know them all ?
The wild flower was the larger—I have dashed
Rose-blood upon its petals, pricked its cup's
Honey with wine, and driven its seed to fruit,
And show a better flower if not so large.   150
I stand, myself.   Refer this to the gods
Whose gift alone it is ! which, shall I dare
(All pride apart) upon the absurd pretext
That such a gift by chance lay in my hand,
Discourse of lightly or depreciate ?
It might have fallen to another's hand—what then ?
I pass too surely—let at least truth stay !

    And next, of what thou followest on to ask.
This being with me as I declare, O king,
My works, in all these varicoloured kinds,   160
So done by me, accepted so by men—
Thou askest if (my soul thus in men's hearts)
I must not be accounted to attain
The very crown and proper end of life.
Inquiring thence how, now life closeth up,
I face death with success in my right hand :
Whether I fear death less than dost thyself
The fortunate of men.   " For " (writest thou)
" Thou leavest much behind, while I leave nought :
Thy life stays in the poems men shall sing,   170
The pictures men shall study ; while my life,
Complete and whole now in its power and joy,
Dies altogether with my brain and arm,

Is lost indeed ; since,—what survives myself ?
The brazen statue that o'erlooks my grave,
Set on the promontory which I named.
And that—some supple courtier of my heir
Shall use its robed and sceptred arm, perhaps,
To fix the rope to, which best drags it down.
I go, then : triumph thou, who dost not go ! "   180

    Nay, thou art worthy of hearing my whole mind.
Is this apparent, when thou turn'st to muse
Upon the scheme of earth and man in chief,
That admiration grows as knowledge grows ?
That imperfection means perfection hid,
Reserved in part, to grace the after-time ?
If, in the morning of philosophy,
Ere aught had been recorded, aught perceived,
Thou, with the light now in thee, couldst have looked
On all earth's tenantry, from worm to bird,   190
Ere man had yet appeared upon the stage—
Thou wouldst have seen them perfect, and deduced
The perfectness of others yet unseen.
Conceding which,—had Zeus then questioned thee
" Wilt thou go on a step, improve on this,
Do more for visible creatures than is done ? "
Thou wouldst have answered, " Ay, by making each
Grow conscious in himself—by that alone.
All's perfect else : the shell sucks fast the rock,
The fish strikes through the sea, the snake both swims 200
And slides ; the birds take flight, forth range the beasts,
Till life's mechanics can no further go—
And all this joy in natural life, is put,
Like fire from off Thy finger into each,

So exquisitely perfect is the same.
But 'tis pure fire—and they mere matter are ;
It has them, not they it : and so I choose,
For man, Thy last premeditated work
(If I might add a glory to this scheme)
That a third thing should stand apart from both,   210
A quality arise within the soul,
Which, intro-active, made to supervise
And feel the force it has, may view itself,
And so be happy." Man might live at first
The animal life : but is there nothing more ?
In due time, let him critically learn
How he lives ; and, the more he gets to know
Of his own life's adaptabilities,
The more joy-giving will his life become.
The man who hath this quality, is best.   220

But thou, king, hadst more reasonably said :
" Let progress end at once,—man make no step
Beyond the natural man, the better beast,
Using his senses, not the sense of sense."
In man there's failure, only since he left
The lower and inconscious forms of life.
We called it an advance, the rendering plain
A spirit might grow conscious of that life,
And, by new lore so added to the old,
Take each step higher over the brute's head.   230
This grew the only life, the pleasure-house,
Watch-tower and treasure-fortress of the soul,
Which whole surrounding flats of natural life
Seemed only fit to yield subsistence to ;
A tower that crowns a country. But alas !

The soul now climbs it just to perish there,
For thence we have discovered ('tis no dream—
We know this, which we had not else perceived)
That there's a world of capability
For joy, spread round about us, meant for us,   240
Inviting us ; and still the soul craves all,
And still the flesh replies, " Take no jot more
Than ere you climbed the tower to look abroad !
Nay, so much less, as that fatigue has brought
Deduction to it." We struggle—fain to enlarge
Our bounded physical recipiency,
Increase our power, supply fresh oil to life,
Repair the waste of age and sickness. No,
It skills not : life's inadequate to joy,
As the soul sees joy, tempting life to take.   250
They praise a fountain in my garden here
Wherein a Naiad sends the water-spurt
Thin from her tube ; she smiles to see it rise.
What if I told her, it is just a thread
From that great river which the hills shut up,
And mock her with my leave to take the same ?
The artificer has given her one small tube
Past power to widen or exchange—what boots
To know she might spout oceans if she could ?
She cannot lift beyond her first straight thread.   260
And so a man can use but a man's joy
While he sees God's. Is it, for Zeus to boast
" See, man, how happy I live, and despair—
That I may be still happier—for thy use ! "
If this were so, we could not thank our Lord,
As hearts beat on to doing : 'tis not so—
Malice it is not. Is it carelessness ?

Still, no.   If care—where is the sign, I ask—
And get no answer : and agree in sum,
O king, with thy profound discouragement,   270
Who seest the wider but to sigh the more.
Most progress is most failure ! thou sayest well.

    The last point now :—thou dost except a case—
Holding joy not impossible to one
With artist-gifts—to such a man as I—
Who leave behind me living works indeed ;
For, such a poem, such a painting lives.
What ? dost thou verily trip upon a word,
Confound the accurate view of what joy is
(Caught somewhat clearer by my eyes than thine)   280
With feeling joy ? confound the knowing how
And showing how to live (my faculty)
With actually living ?—Otherwise
Where is the artist's vantage o'er the king ?
Because in my great epos I display
How divers men young, strong, fair, wise, can act—
Is this as though I acted ? if I paint,
Carve the young Phœbus, am I therefore young ?
Methinks I'm older that I bowed myself
The many years of pain that taught me art !   290
Indeed, to know is something, and to prove
How all this beauty might be enjoyed, is more :
But, knowing nought, to enjoy is something too.
Yon rower with the moulded muscles there
Lowering the sail, is nearer it than I.
I can write love-odes—thy fair slave's an ode.
I get to sing of love, when grown too grey
For being beloved : she turns to that young man

The muscles all a-ripple on his back.
I know the joy of kingship : well—thou art king !   300

" But," sayest thou—(and I marvel, I repeat,
To find thee tripping on a mere word) " what
Thou writest, paintest, stays : that does not die :
Sappho survives, because we sing her songs,
And Æschylus, because we read his plays ! "
Why, if they live still, let them come and take
Thy slave in my despite—drink from thy cup—
Speak in my place.   Thou diest while I survive ?
Say rather that my fate is deadlier still,—
In this, that every day my sense of joy   310
Grows more acute, my soul (intensified
In power and insight) more enlarged, more keen ;
While every day my hairs fall more and more,
My hand shakes, and the heavy years increase—
The horror quickening still from year to year,
The consummation coming past escape
When I shall know most, and yet least enjoy—
When all my works wherein I prove my worth,
Being present still to mock me in men's mouths,
Alive still, in the phrase of such as thou,   320
I, I, the feeling, thinking, acting man,
The man who loved his life so over much,
Shall sleep in my urn.   It is so horrible,
I dare at times imagine to my need
Some future state revealed to us by Zeus,
Unlimited in capability
For joy, as this is in desire for joy,
To seek which, the joy-hunger forces us.
That, stung by straitness of our life, made strait

On purpose to make sweet the life at large—   330
Freed by the throbbing impulse we call death
We burst there as the worm into the fly,
Who, while a worm still, wants his wings.   But, no !
Zeus has not yet revealed it ; and, alas !
He must have done so—were it possible !

   Live long and happy, and in that thought die,
Glad for what was.   Farewell.   And for the rest,
I cannot tell thy messenger aright
Where to deliver what he bears of thine
To one called Paulus—we have heard his fame   340
Indeed, if Christus be not one with him—
I know not, nor am troubled much to know.
Thou canst not think a mere barbarian Jew,
As Paulus proves to be, one circumcised,
Hath access to a secret shut from us ?
Thou wrongest our philosophy, O king,
In stooping to inquire of such an one,
As if his answer could impose at all.
He writeth, doth he ? well, and he may write.
Oh, the Jew findeth scholars ! certain slaves   350
Who touched on this same isle, preached him and Christ ;
And (as I gathered from a bystander)
Their doctrines could be held by no sane man.

THE TWINS

"Give" and "It-shall-be-given-unto-you."

———•———

1.

GRAND rough old Martin Luther
    Bloomed fables—flowers on furze,
The better the uncouther:
    Do roses stick like burrs?

2.

A beggar asked an alms
    One day at an abbey-door,
Said Luther; but, seized with qualms,
    The Abbot replied, "We're poor!"

3.

"Poor, who had plenty once,
    "When gifts fell thick as rain:
"But they give us nought, for the nonce,
    "And how should we give again?"

4.

Then the beggar, " See your sins !
   " Of old, unless I err,
" Ye had brothers for inmates, twins,
   " Date and Dabitur."

5.

" While Date was in good case
   " Dabitur flourished too :
" For Dabitur's lenten face,
   " No wonder if Date rue."

6.

" Would ye retrieve the one ?
   " Try and make plump the other !
" When Date's penance is done,
   " Dabitur helps his brother."

7.

" Only, beware relapse ! "
The Abbot hung his head.
This beggar might be, perhaps,
   An angel, Luther said.

POPULARITY

1.

STAND still, true poet that you are,
   I know you ; let me try and draw you.
Some night you'll fail us.   When afar
   You rise, remember one man saw you,
Knew you, and named a star.

2.

My star, God's glow-worm !   Why extend
   That loving hand of His which leads you,
Yet locks you safe from end to end
   Of this dark world, unless He needs you—
Just saves your light to spend ?

3.

His clenched Hand shall unclose at last
   I know, and let out all the beauty.
My poet holds the future fast,
   Accepts the coming ages' duty,
Their present for this past.

4.

That day, the earth's feast-master's brow
  Shall clear, to God the chalice raising ;
" Others give best at first, but Thou
  For ever set'st our table praising,—
Keep'st the good wine till now."

5.

Meantime, I'll draw you as you stand,
  With few or none to watch and wonder.
I'll say—a fisher (on the sand
  By Tyre the Old) his ocean-plunder,
A netful, brought to land.

6.

Who has not heard how Tyrian shells
  Enclosed the blue, that dye of dyes
Whereof one drop worked miracles,
  And coloured like Astarte's eyes
Raw silk the merchant sells ?

7.

And each bystander of them all
  Could criticise, and quote tradition
How depths of blue sublimed some pall,
  To get which, pricked a king's ambition ;
Worth sceptre, crown and ball.

8.

Yet there's the dye,—in that rough mesh,
  The sea has only just o'er-whispered !
Live whelks, the lip's-beard dripping fresh,
  As if they still the water's lisp heard
Through foam the rock-weeds thresh.

9.

Enough to furnish Solomon
  Such hangings for his cedar-house,
That when gold-robed he took the throne
  In that abyss of blue, the Spouse
Might swear his presence shone

10.

Most like the centre-spike of gold
  Which burns deep in the blue-bell's womb,
What time, with ardours manifold,
  The bee goes singing to her groom,
Drunken and overbold.

11.

Mere conchs ! not fit for warp or woof !
  Till art comes,—comes to pound and squeeze
And clarify,—refines to proof
  The liquor filtered by degrees,
While the world stands aloof.

12.

And there's the extract, flasked and fine,
  And priced, and saleable at last !
And Hobbs, Nobbs, Stokes and Nokes combine
  To paint the future from the past,
Put blue into their line.

13.

Hobbs hints blue,—straight he turtle eats.
  Nobbs prints blue,—claret crowns his cup.
Nokes outdares Stokes in azure feats,—
  Both gorge.   Who fished the murex up ?
What porridge had John Keats ?

THE HERETIC'S TRAGEDY

A MIDDLE-AGE INTERLUDE

———✦———

(*In the original*) ROSA MUNDI ; SEU, FULCITE ME FLORIBUS. A CONCEIT
OF MASTER GYSBRECHT, CANON-REGULAR OF SAINT JODOCUS-BY-
THE-BAR, YPRES CITY. CANTUQUE, *Virgilius*. AND HATH OFTEN
BEEN SUNG AT HOCK-TIDE AND FESTIVALS. GAVISUS ERAM,
Jessides.

(It would seem to be a glimpse from the burning of Jacques du Bourg-
Molay, at Paris, A.D. 1314 ; as distorted by the refraction from Flemish
brain to brain, during the course of a couple of centuries.—R.B.)

———————

1.

PREADMONISHETH THE ABBOT DEODAET.

THE Lord, we look to once for all,
    Is the Lord we should look at, all at once :
He knows not to vary, saith St. Paul,
    Nor the shadow of turning, for the nonce.
See Him no other than as he is ;
    Give both the Infinites their due—
Infinite mercy, but, I wis,
    As infinite a justice too.

[Organ : plagal-cadence.

    As infinite a justice too.

2.

ONE SINGETH.

John, Master of the Temple of God,
　　Falling to sin the Unknown Sin,
What he bought of Emperor Aldabrod,
　　He sold it to Sultan Saladin—
Till, caught by Pope Clement, a-buzzing there,
　　Hornet-prince of the mad wasps' hive,
And clipt of his wings in Paris square,
　　They bring him now to be burned alive.
　　　　　　*[And wanteth there grace of lute or clavicithern, ye shall say
　　　　　　to confirm him who singeth—*
We bring John now to be burned alive.

3.

In the midst is a goodly gallows built ;
　　'Twixt fork and fork, a stake is stuck ;
But first they set divers tumbrils a-tilt,
　　Make a trench all round with the city muck,
Inside they pile log upon log, good store ;
　　Faggots not few, blocks great and small,
Reach a man's mid-thigh, no less, no more,—
　　For they mean he should roast in the sight of all.

CHORUS.
We mean he should roast in the sight of all.

4.

Good sappy bavins that kindle forthwith ;
　　Billets that blaze substantial and slow ;
Pine-stump split deftly, dry as pith ;
　　Larch-heart that chars to a chalk-white glow :

Then up they hoist me John in a chafe,
　　Sling him fast like a hog to scorch,
Spit in his face, then leap back safe,
　　Sing " Laudes " and bid clap-to the torch.

CHORUS.
Laus Deo—who bids clap-to the torch.

5.

John of the Temple, whose fame so bragged,
　　Is burning alive in Paris square !
How can he curse, if his mouth is gagged ?
　　Or wriggle his neck, with a collar there ?
Or heave his chest, while a band goes round ?
　　Or threat with his fist, since his arms are spliced ?
Or kick with his feet, now his legs are bound ?
　　—Thinks John—I will call upon Jesus Christ.

　　　　　　　　　　　　　　　[*Here one crosseth himself.*

6.

Jesus Christ—John had bought and sold,
　　Jesus Christ—John had eaten and drunk ;
To him, the Flesh meant silver and gold.
　　(*Salvâ reverentiâ.*)
Now it was, " Saviour, bountiful lamb,
　　I have roasted thee Turks, though men roast me.
See thy servant, the plight wherein I am !
　　Art thou a Saviour ?   Save thou me ! "

CHORUS.
'Tis John the mocker cries, Save thou me !

7.

Who maketh God's menace an idle word ?
  —Saith, it no more means what it proclaims,
Than a damsel's threat to her wanton bird ?—
  For she too prattles of ugly names.
—Saith, he knoweth but one thing,—what he knows ?
  That God is good and the rest is breath ;
Why else is the same styled, Sharon's rose ?
  Once a rose, ever a rose, he saith.

CHORUS.

  O, John shall yet find a rose, he saith !

8.

Alack, there be roses and roses, John !
  Some, honied of taste like your leman's tongue.
Some, bitter—for why ? (roast gaily on !)
  Their tree struck root in devil's dung !
When Paul once reasoned of righteousness
  And of temperance and of judgment to come,
Good Felix trembled, he could no less—
  John, snickering, crook'd his wicked thumb.

CHORUS.

  What cometh to John of the wicked thumb ?

9.

Ha ha, John plucks now at his rose
  To rid himself of a sorrow at heart !
Lo,—petal on petal, fierce rays unclose ;
  Anther on anther, sharp spikes outstart ;

And with blood for dew, the bosom boils ;
   And a gust of sulphur is all its smell ;
And lo, he is horribly in the toils
   Of a coal-black giant flower of Hell !

CHORUS.
What maketh Heaven, that maketh Hell.

10.
So, as John called now, through the fire amain,
   On the Name, he had cursed with, all his life—
To the Person, he bought and sold again—
   For the Face, with his daily buffets rife—
Feature by feature It took its place !
   And his voice like a mad dog's choking bark
At the steady Whole of the Judge's Face—
   Died.   Forth John's soul flared into the dark.

SUBJOINETH THE ABBOT DEODAET.
God help all poor souls lost in the dark !

TWO IN THE CAMPAGNA

——•——

1.

I WONDER do you feel to-day
   As I have felt, since, hand in hand,
We sat down on the grass, to stray
   In spirit better through the land,
This morn of Rome and May ?

2.

For me, I touched a thought, I know,
   Has tantalised me many times,
(Like turns of thread the spiders throw
   Mocking across our path) for rhymes
To catch at and let go.

3.

Help me to hold it : first it left
   The yellowing fennel, run to seed
There, branching from the brickwork's cleft,
   Some old tomb's ruin : yonder weed
Took up the floating weft,

4.

Where one small orange cup amassed
   Five beetles,—blind and green they grope
Among the honey-meal,—and last
   Everywhere on the grassy slope
I traced it.   Hold it fast !

5.

The champaign with its endless fleece
   Of feathery grasses everywhere !
Silence and passion, joy and peace,
   An everlasting wash of air—
Rome's ghost since her decease.

6.

Such life there, through such lengths of hours,
   Such miracles performed in play,
Such primal naked forms of flowers,
   Such letting Nature have her way
While Heaven looks from its towers.

7.

How say you ?   Let us, O my dove,
   Let us be unashamed of soul,
As earth lies bare to heaven above.
   How is it under our control
To love or not to love ?

8.

I would that you were all to me,
   You that are just so much, no more—
Nor yours, nor mine,—nor slave nor free !
   Where does the fault lie ? what the core
Of the wound, since wound must be ?

9.

I would I could adopt your will,
  See with your eyes, and set my heart
Beating by yours, and drink my fill
  At your soul's springs,—your part, my part
In life, for good and ill.

10.

No. I yearn upward—touch you close,
  Then stand away. I kiss your cheek,
Catch your soul's warmth,—I pluck the rose
  And love it more than tongue can speak—
Then the good minute goes.

11.

Already how am I so far
  Out of that minute ? Must I go
Still like the thistle-ball, no bar,
  Onward, whenever light winds blow,
Fixed by no friendly star ?

12.

Just when I seemed about to learn !
  Where is the thread now ? Off again !
The old trick ! Only I discern—
  Infinite passion and the pain
Of finite hearts that yearn.

A GRAMMARIAN'S FUNERAL

[*Time*—Shortly after the revival of learning in Europe.]

———◆———

Let us begin and carry up this corpse,
    Singing together.
Leave we the common crofts, the vulgar thorpes,
    Each in its tether
Sleeping safe on the bosom of the plain,
    Cared-for till cock-crow.
Look out if yonder's not the day again
    Rimming the rock-row !
That's the appropriate country—there, man's thought,
    Rarer, intenser,   10
Self-gathered for an outbreak, as it ought,
    Chafes in the censer !
Leave we the unlettered plain its herd and crop ;
    Seek we sepulture
On a tall mountain, citied to the top,
    Crowded with culture !
All the peaks soar, but one the rest excels ;
    Clouds overcome it ;
No, yonder sparkle is the citadel's
    Circling its summit !   20

Thither our path lies—wind we up the heights—
    Wait ye the warning ?
Our low life was the level's and the night's ;
    He's for the morning !
Step to a tune, square chests, erect the head,
    'Ware the beholders !
This is our master, famous, calm, and dead,
    Borne on our shoulders.

Sleep, crop and herd ! sleep, darkling thorpe and croft,
    Safe from the weather !   30
He, whom we convoy to his grave aloft,
    Singing together,
He was a man born with thy face and throat,
    Lyric Apollo !
Long he lived nameless : how should spring take note
    Winter would follow ?
Till lo, the little touch, and youth was gone !
    Cramped and diminished,
Moaned he, " New measures, other feet anon !
    My dance is finished ? "   40
No, that's the world's way ! (keep the mountain-side,
    Make for the city.)
He knew the signal, and stepped on with pride
    Over men's pity ;
Left play for work, and grappled with the world
    Bent on escaping :
" What's in the scroll," quoth he, " thou keepest furled ?
    Shew me their shaping,
Theirs, who most studied man, the bard and sage,—
    Give ! "—So he gowned him,   50
Straight got by heart that book to its last page :
    Learned, we found him !

Yea, but we found him bald too—eyes like lead,
 Accents uncertain :
" Time to taste life," another would have said,
 " Up with the curtain ! "
This man said rather, " Actual life comes next ?
 Patience a moment !
Grant I have mastered learning's crabbed text,
 Still, there's the comment.   60
Let me know all.   Prate not of most or least,
 Painful or easy :
Even to the crumbs I'd fain eat up the feast,
 Ay, nor feel queasy ! "
Oh, such a life as he resolved to live,
 When he had learned it,
When he had gathered all books had to give ;
 Sooner, he spurned it !
Image the whole, then execute the parts—
 Fancy the fabric   70
Quite, ere you build, ere steel strike fire from quartz,
 Ere mortar dab brick !

(Here's the town-gate reached : there's the market-place
 Gaping before us.)
Yea, this in him was the peculiar grace
 (Hearten our chorus)
Still before living he'd learn how to live—
 No end to learning.
Earn the means first—God surely will contrive
 Use for our earning.   80
Others mistrust and say—" But time escapes,—
 " Live now or never ! "
He said, " What's Time ? leave Now for dogs and apes !
 Man has For ever."

Back to his book then : deeper drooped his head ;
    Calculus racked him :
Leaden before, his eyes grew dross of lead ;
    Tussis attacked him.
" Now, Master, take a little rest ! "—not he !
    (Caution redoubled !   90
Step two a-breast, the way winds narrowly.)
    Not a whit troubled,
Back to his studies, fresher than at first,
    Fierce as a dragon
He, (soul-hydroptic with a sacred thirst)
    Sucked at the flagon.
Oh, if we draw a circle premature,
    Heedless of far gain,
Greedy for quick returns of profit, sure,
    Bad is our bargain !   100
Was it not great ? did not he throw on God,
    (He loves the burthen)—
God's task to make the heavenly period
    Perfect the earthen ?
Did not he magnify the mind, shew clear
    Just what it all meant ?
He would not discount life, as fools do here,
    Paid by instalment !
He ventured neck or nothing—heaven's success
    Found, or earth's failure :   110
" Wilt thou trust death or not ? " he answered " Yes.
    " Hence with life's pale lure ! "
That low man seeks a little thing to do,
    Sees it and does it :
This high man, with a great thing to pursue,
    Dies ere he knows it.

That low man goes on adding one to one,
    His hundred's soon hit :
This high man, aiming at a million,
    Misses an unit.   120
That, has the world here—should he need the next,
    Let the world mind him !
This, throws himself on God, and unperplext
    Seeking shall find Him.
So, with the throttling hands of Death at strife,
    Ground he at grammar ;
Still, thro' the rattle, parts of speech were rife.
    While he could stammer
He settled *Hoti's* business—let it be !—
    Properly based *Oun*—   130
Gave us the doctrine of the enclitic *De*,
    Dead from the waist down.
Well, here's the platform, here's the proper place.
    Hail to your purlieus
All ye highfliers of the feathered race,
    Swallows and curlews !
Here's the top-peak ! the multitude below
    Live, for they can there.
This man decided not to Live but Know—
    Bury this man there ?   140
Here—here's his place, where meteors shoot, clouds form,
    Lightnings are loosened,
Stars come and go ! let joy break with the storm—
    Peace let the dew send !
Lofty designs must close in like effects :
    Loftily lying,
Leave him—still loftier than the world suspects,
    Living and dying.

ONE WAY OF LOVE

—◦—

1.

ALL June I bound the rose in sheaves.
Now, rose by rose, I strip the leaves,
And strew them where Pauline may pass.
She will not turn aside ?   Alas !
Let them lie.   Suppose they die ?
The chance was they might take her eye.

2.

How many a month I strove to suit
These stubborn fingers to the lute !
To-day I venture all I know.
She will not hear my music ?   So !
Break the string—fold music's wing.
Suppose Pauline had bade me sing !

3.

My whole life long I learned to love.
This hour my utmost art I prove
And speak my passion.—Heaven or hell ?
She will not give me heaven ?   'Tis well !
Lose who may—I still can say,
Those who win heaven, blest are they.

ANOTHER WAY OF LOVE

———◆———

1.

JUNE was not over,
  Though past the full,
And the best of her roses
  Had yet to blow,
  When a man I know
(But shall not discover,
  Since ears are dull,
And time discloses)
Turned him and said with a man's true air,
Half sighing a smile in a yawn, as 'twere,—
" If I tire of your June, will she greatly care ? "

2.

Well, Dear, in-doors with you !
  True, serene deadness
Tries a man's temper.
  What's in the blossom
  June wears on her bosom ?

Can it clear scores with you ?
   Sweetness and redness,
   Eadem semper !
Go, let me care for it greatly or slightly !
If June mends her bowers now, your hand left unsightly
By plucking their roses,—my June will do rightly.

3.

And after, for pastime,
   If June be refulgent
With flowers in completeness,
   All petals, no prickles,
   Delicious as trickles
Of wine poured at mass-time,—
   And choose One indulgent
   To redness and sweetness :
Or if, with experience of man and of spider,
She use my June-lightning, the strong insect-ridder,
To stop the fresh spinning,—why, June will consider.

" TRANSCENDENTALISM "

A POEM IN TWELVE BOOKS

———◆———

Stop playing, poet! may a brother speak?
'Tis you speak, that's your error.   Song's our art:
Whereas you please to speak these naked thoughts
Instead of draping them in sights and sounds.
—True thoughts, good thoughts, thoughts fit to treasure
　　　up!
But why such long prolusion and display,
Such turning and adjustment of the harp,
And taking it upon your breast at length,
Only to speak dry words across its strings?
Stark-naked thought is in request enough—　　　　　10
Speak prose and holloa it till Europe hears!
The six-foot Swiss tube, braced about with bark,
Which helps the hunter's voice from Alp to Alp—
Exchange our harp for that,—who hinders you?

　　But here's your fault; grown men want thought, you
　　　　think;
Thought's what they mean by verse, and seek in verse:
Boys seek for images and melody,
Men must have reason—so you aim at men.
Quite otherwise!   Objects throng our youth, 'tis true,

We see and hear and do not wonder much.   20
If you could tell us what they mean, indeed !
As Swedish Bœhme never cared for plants
Until it happed, a-walking in the fields,
He noticed all at once that plants could speak,
Nay, turned with loosened tongue to talk with him.
That day the daisy had an eye indeed—
Colloquised with the cowslip on such themes !
We find them extant yet in Jacob's prose.
But by the time youth slips a stage or two
While reading prose in that tough book he wrote,   30
(Collating, and emendating the same
And settling on the sense most to our mind)
We shut the clasps and find life's summer past.
Then, who helps more, pray, to repair our loss—
Another Bœhme with a tougher book
And subtler meanings of what roses say,—
Or some stout Mage like him of Halberstadt,
John, who made things Bœhme wrote thoughts about ?
He with a " look you ! " vents a brace of rhymes,
And in there breaks the sudden rose herself,   40
Over us, under, round us every side,
Nay, in and out the tables and the chairs
And musty volumes, Bœhme's book and all,—
Buries us with a glory, young once more,
Pouring heaven into this shut house of life.

  So come, the harp back to your heart again !
You are a poem, though your poem's naught.
The best of all you did before, believe,
Was your own boy's-face o'er the finer chords
Bent, following the cherub at the top   50
That points to God with his paired half-moon wings.

MISCONCEPTIONS

—•—

1.

THIS is a spray the Bird clung to,
  Making it blossom with pleasure,
Ere the high tree-top she sprung to,
  Fit for her nest and her treasure.
  Oh, what a hope beyond measure
Was the poor spray's, which the flying feet hung to,—
So to be singled out, built in, and sung to !

2.

This is a heart the Queen leant on,
  Thrilled in a minute erratic,
Ere the true bosom she bent on,
  Meet for love's regal dalmatic.
  Oh, what a fancy ecstatic
Was the poor heart's, ere the wanderer went on—
Love to be saved for it, proffered to, spent on !

ONE WORD MORE

TO E. B. B.

1.

THERE they are, my fifty men and women
Naming me the fifty poems finished !
Take them, Love, the book and me together.
Where the heart lies, let the brain lie also.

2.

Rafael made a century of sonnets,
Made and wrote them in a certain volume
Dinted with the silver-pointed pencil
Else he only used to draw Madonnas :
These, the world might view—but One, the volume.
Who that one, you ask ?   Your heart instructs you.
Did she live and love it all her life-time ?
Did she drop, his lady of the sonnets,
Die, and let it drop beside her pillow
Where it lay in place of Rafael's glory,
Rafael's cheek so duteous and so loving—
Cheek, the world was wont to hail a painter's,
Rafael's cheek, her love had turned a poet's ?

3.

You and I would rather read that volume,
(Taken to his beating bosom by it)
Lean and list the bosom-beats of Rafael,
Would we not ? than wonder at Madonnas—
Her, San Sisto names, and Her, Foligno,
Her, that visits Florence in a vision,
Her, that's left with lilies in the Louvre—
Seen by us and all the world in circle.

4.

You and I will never read that volume.
Guido Reni, like his own eye's apple
Guarded long the treasure-book and loved it.
Guido Reni dying, all Bologna
Cried, and the world with it, " Ours—the treasure ! "
Suddenly, as rare things will, it vanished.

5.

Dante once prepared to paint an angel :
Whom to please ? You whisper " Beatrice."
While he mused and traced it and retraced it,
(Peradventure with a pen corroded
Still by drops of that hot ink he dipped for,
When, his left-hand i' the hair o' the wicked,
Back he held the brow and pricked its stigma,
Bit into the live man's flesh for parchment,
Loosed him, laughed to see the writing rankle,
Let the wretch go festering thro' Florence)—
Dante, who loved well because he hated,
Hated wickedness that hinders loving,
Dante standing, studying his angel,—

In there broke the folk of his Inferno.
Says he—" Certain people of importance "
(Such he gave his daily, dreadful line to)
Entered and would seize, forsooth, the poet.
Says the poet—" Then I stopped my painting."

6.

You and I would rather see that angel,
Painted by the tenderness of Dante,
Would we not ?—than read a fresh Inferno.

7.

You and I will never see that picture.
While he mused on love and Beatrice,
While he softened o'er his outlined angel,
In they broke, those " people of importance : "
We and Bice bear the loss forever.

8.

What of Rafael's sonnets, Dante's picture ?

9.

This : no artist lives and loves that longs not
Once, and only once, and for One only,
(Ah, the prize !) to find his love a language
Fit and fair and simple and sufficient—
Using nature that's an art to others,
Not, this one time, art that's turned his nature.
Ay, of all the artists living, loving,
None but would forego his proper dowry,—
Does he paint ? he fain would write a poem,—
Does he write ? he fain would paint a picture,
Put to proof art alien to the artist's,
Once, and only once, and for One only,

So to be the man and leave the artist,
Save the man's joy, miss the artist's sorrow.

10.

Wherefore ?   Heaven's gift takes earth's abatement !
He who smites the rock and spreads the water,
Bidding drink and live a crowd beneath him,
Even he, the minute makes immortal,
Proves, perchance, his mortal in the minute,
Desecrates, belike, the deed in doing.
While he smites, how can he but remember,
So he smote before, in such a peril,
When they stood and mocked—" Shall smiting help us ? "
When they drank and sneered—" A stroke is easy ! "
When they wiped their mouths and went their journey,
Throwing him for thanks—" But drought was pleasant."
Thus old memories mar the actual triumph ;
Thus the doing savours of disrelish ;
Thus achievement lacks a gracious somewhat ;
O'er-importuned brows becloud the mandate,
Carelessness or consciousness, the gesture.
For he bears an ancient wrong about him,
Sees and knows again those phalanxed faces,
Hears, yet one time more, the 'customed prelude—
" How should'st thou, of all men, smite, and save us ? "
Guesses what is like to prove the sequel—
" Egypt's flesh-pots—nay, the drought was better."

11.

Oh, the crowd must have emphatic warrant !
Theirs, the Sinai-forehead's cloven brilliance,
Right-arm's rod-sweep, tongue's imperial fiat.
Never dares the man put off the prophet.

12.

Did he love one face from out the thousands,
(Were she Jethro's daughter, white and wifely,
Were she but the Æthiopian bondslave,)
He would envy yon dumb patient camel,
Keeping a reserve of scanty water
Meant to save his own life in the desert ;
Ready in the desert to deliver
(Kneeling down to let his breast be opened)
Hoard and life together for his mistress.

13.

I shall never, in the years remaining,
Paint you pictures, no, nor carve you statues,
Make you music that should all-express me ;
So it seems : I stand on my attainment.
This of verse alone, one life allows me ;
Verse and nothing else have I to give you.
Other heights in other lives, God willing—
All the gifts from all the heights, your own, Love !

14.

Yet a semblance of resource avails us—
Shade so finely touched, love's sense must seize it.
Take these lines, look lovingly and nearly,
Lines I write the first time and the last time.
He who works in fresco, steals a hair-brush,
Curbs the liberal hand, subservient proudly,
Cramps his spirit, crowds its all in little,
Makes a strange art of an art familiar,
Fills his lady's missal-marge with flowerets.
He who blows thro' bronze, may breathe thro' silver,

Fitly serenade a slumbrous princess.
He who writes, may write for once, as I do.

15.

Love, you saw me gather men and women,
Live or dead or fashioned by my fancy,
Enter each and all, and use their service,
Speak from every mouth,—the speech, a poem.
Hardly shall I tell my joys and sorrows,
Hopes and fears, belief and disbelieving :
I am mine and yours—the rest be all men's,
Karshook, Cleon, Norbert and the fifty.
Let me speak this once in my true person,
Not as Lippo, Roland or Andrea,
Though the fruit of speech be just this sentence—
Pray you, look on these my men and women,
Take and keep my fifty poems finished ;
Where my heart lies, let my brain lie also !
Poor the speech ; be how I speak, for all things.

16.

Not but that you know me ! Lo, the moon's self !
Here in London, yonder late in Florence,
Still we find her face, the thrice-transfigured.
Curving on a sky imbrued with colour,
Drifted over Fiesole by twilight,
Came she, our new crescent of a hair's-breadth.
Full she flared it, lamping Samminiato,
Rounder 'twixt the cypresses and rounder,
Perfect till the nightingales applauded.
Now, a piece of her old self, impoverished,
Hard to greet, she traverses the houseroofs,

Hurries with unhandsome thrift of silver,
Goes dispiritedly,—glad to finish.

17.

What, there's nothing in the moon note-worthy ?
Nay—for if that moon could love a mortal,
Use, to charm him (so to fit a fancy)
All her magic ('tis the old sweet mythos)
She would turn a new side to her mortal,
Side unseen of herdsman, huntsman, steersman—
Blank to Zoroaster on his terrace,
Blind to Galileo on his turret,
Dumb to Homer, dumb to Keats—him, even !
Think, the wonder of the moonstruck mortal—
When she turns round, comes again in heaven,
Opens out anew for worse or better ?
Proves she like some portent of an ice-berg
Swimming full upon the ship it founders,
Hungry with huge teeth of splintered chrystals ?
Proves she as the paved-work of a sapphire
Seen by Moses when he climbed the mountain ?
Moses, Aaron, Nadab and Abihu
Climbed and saw the very God, the Highest,
Stand upon the paved-work of a sapphire.
Like the bodied heaven in his clearness
Shone the stone, the sapphire of that paved-work,
When they ate and drank and saw God also !

18.

What were seen ?   None knows, none ever shall know.
Only this is sure—the sight were other,
Not the moon's same side, born late in Florence,

Dying now impoverished here in London.
God be thanked, the meanest of his creatures
Boasts two soul-sides, one to face the world with,
One to show a woman when he loves her.

19.

This I say of me, but think of you, Love !
This to you—yourself my moon of poets !
Ah, but that's the world's side—there's the wonder—
Thus they see you, praise you, think they know you.
There, in turn I stand with them and praise you,
Out of my own self, I dare to phrase it.
But the best is when I glide from out them,
Cross a step or two of dubious twilight,
Come out on the other side, the novel
Silent silver lights and darks undreamed of,
Where I hush and bless myself with silence.

20.

Oh, their Rafael of the dear Madonnas,
Oh, their Dante of the dread Inferno,
Wrote one song—and in my brain I sing it,
Drew one angel—borne, see, on my bosom !

THE END.

NOTES

LOVE AMONG THE RUINS, p. 5

Said to have been written in Paris, 1 Jan. 1852 (GM, p. 189); but the date remains uncertain (J. Huebenthal, VP, iv, 1966, 51–4). The scenery of the poem was probably suggested by the Roman Campagna, and by popular accounts of excavations at Babylon, Nineveh, and Thebes, e.g. A. H. Layard's *Nineveh and its Remains*, 1849 (J. Parr, PMLA, lxviii, 1953, 128–37). The alternation of long lines and faintly bathetic short ones echoes the theme: the reduction of a great imperial city to a pastoral landscape peopled by two young lovers.

p. 5, st. 2. *its prince*: that its prince.

p. 6 st. 3. *certain rills*: that certain rills.

p. 6 st. 4. *men might*: that men might.
   hundred-gated . . . Twelve abreast. Both Babylon and the Egyptian Thebes were said to have hundred-gated walls, and Nineveh to have walls on which three chariots could easily drive abreast.

p. 8 st. 14. *Oh, heart . . . in*. Just as natural vegetation has covered up the city, so the natural instinct of love is to blot out the memory of a corrupt and militaristic civilization.

A LOVERS' QUARREL, p. 9

Probably written in Florence, spring 1853. Since it mentions two subjects on which RB and EB disagreed (spiritualism and Napoleon III), the poem may be partly autobiographical.

p. 9 st. 2. *rillets*: rivulets.

p. 10 st. 5. *Times . . . gold. The Times* of 31 Jan. 1853
(pp. 4–5) criticized the extravagance that marked
Napoleon's wedding to the twenty-six-year-old Eugénie
de Montijo, saying that her dresses cost £40,000; that the
bride and bridegroom sat on thrones on an ermine car-
pet; that he presented her with 'pieces of gold'; and that
the decorations included 'festoons of evergreens' on the
procession route, and the planting of 'green trees' in the
colonnades of the Louvre. EB admired Napoleon, RB
did not.

p. 10 st. 6. *Pampas . . . green.* The train of thought from
the 'gold and green' of Paris to that of the Pampas was
possibly helped by the report in *The Times* of 18 Feb.
(p. 5) that Buenos Ayres was 'closely besieged by the
gauchos' (half-caste cowboys of the Pampas).

p. 11 st. 7. *table turn.* Cf. EB: 'We tried the table experi-
ment in this room a few days since . . . and failed; but we
were impatient, and Robert was playing Mephistopheles
. . . and there was little chance of success under the cir-
cumstances' (16 May 1853; FK, ii. 116–17). In the early
1850s a craze for spiritualism started in America and
spread to Europe. EB heard of it in Florence from the
American sculptor Hiram Powers, and, while trying to be
rational, soon came to believe in it (see her letter post-
marked 14 Dec. 1853; F. C. Thomson, VN, No. 31, 1967,
49–52). RB remained deeply sceptical.

p. 12 st. 10. *two spots . . . swan*: probably the nostrils,
which, in the Mute Swan, might appear to a casual
observer as two black spots taking up about half the
width of the orange-coloured bill.

p. 12 st. 11. *mesmeriser.* EB believed in mesmerism, which
was practised by her friend, Harriet Martineau. RB's
attitude was: . . . 'I do *not* disbelieve in Mesmerism—
I only object to insufficient evidence being put forward
as quite irrefragable.—I keep an open sense on the

subject—ready to be instructed' (27 Jan. 1846; K, i. 424).

p. 13 st. 13. *Oh, power . . . saith*: Proverbs 18: 21.

p. 13 st. 16. *Is the . . . quick?* Cannot a tiny parasitic worm cause damage to the sensitive tissues of the physical heart ?

Ear . . . curd: through the ear the slightest sound is registered by the whitish substance of the brain.

p. 14 st. 18. *minor third.* In early spring the interval between the cuckoo's notes may be as little as one tone, but it gradually increases through a minor third ($1\frac{1}{2}$ tones) and a major third (2 tones, as Beethoven imitated it in his Pastoral Symphony), to as much as a fourth (W. Pole, N, xxxvi, 1887, 344).

p. 14 st. 19. *valiant . . . fee-faw-fum!* The giant's speech is from the nursery-tale *Jack the Giant-killer*. Tom Thumb is far from 'valiant' in the nursery-tale named from him, but becomes so, and kills 'millions of Giants' in Fielding's *Tom Thumb: a Tragedy* (1730).

p. 15 st. 20. *crypt.* Cf. RB, referring to the time when he just missed meeting EB, some years before he first wrote to her: 'I feel . . . as if I had been close, so close, to some world's wonder in chapel or crypt . . . only a screen to push and I might have entered.' EB replied: '. . . BUT . . . you know . . . if you had entered the "crypt", you might have caught cold, or been tired to death' (10–11 Jan. 1845; K, i. 3–4, 5).

EVELYN HOPE, p. 16

Although RB often expresses the idea that present failure implies future success, this poem should hardly be seen as expressing 'one of his deepest convictions' (S, p. 122), but rather as a dm. presenting, non-satirically, a possible human reaction to hopeless love. There is no need to accuse the speaker of 'necrophilia' (G. O. Marshall, Jr.,

VP, iv, 1966, 34), a 'wish for a Humbert–Lolita kind of relationship' (S. G. Radner, LP, xvi, 1966, 115), or murder (C. E. Tanzy, LP, xvii, 1967, 156). His worst crime a failure to face facts.

UP AT A VILLA—DOWN IN THE CITY, p. 19

An ironic reversal of a stock satiric theme, the superiority of country to town (e.g. Horace, *Sat.* II. vi). Although RB enjoyed the Italian city-scene himself, the speaker is an object of satire.

p. 19 st. 1. *house . . . square*. From Oct. 1847 to May 1848 the Bs lived in the Piazza Pitti in Florence, just opposite the Grand Duke's Palace (TP, p. 205).

p. 19 st. 2. *by Bacchus*: a common Italian oath, especially suited to the hedonistic speaker.

p. 21 st. 6. *bubble of blood*. The unpleasant simile concisely conveys the speaker's attitude towards 'the beauties of nature'.

p. 21 st. 7. *pash*: beat the water with their hoofs (an unprecedented meaning for the word).

p. 21 st. 8. *a-tingle*: quivering, vibrating.

p. 22 st. 9. *Pulcinello*: Pulcinella, the puppet-show prototype of Punch.

liberal thieves: a phrase suggesting the speaker's indifference to the movement, with which the Bs warmly sympathized, for political reform and the liberation of Italy from the Austrians.

archbishop's . . . Duke's. When elected Pope (1846) Pius IX encouraged the liberals, but after the rebellion against Austria had been crushed at Novara (1849), he became reactionary. The Grand Duke of Tuscany, Leopold II, who had also given hopes to the liberals, was forced to leave Florence in 1848 and take refuge with the Pope at Gaeta, but returned in 1849, supported by 10,000

Austrian troops. His 'little new laws' were pro-Pope and anti-liberal (e.g. the repeal of the Tuscan constitution, 1852).

Don: the title of an Italian priest.

Dante, Boccaccio . . . Cicero: i.e. a genius in every department of literature, including poetry, prose, and oratory. Jerome figures in the list as the learned translator of the Bible into Latin (the Vulgate).

seven swords: symbolizing the Seven Sorrows of the Virgin Mary.

A WOMAN'S LAST WORD, p. 24

The title refers ironically to the saying, recently popularized by D. W. Jerrold's *Mrs Caudle's Curtain Lectures* (1845), that a woman always has the last word in an argument (R. D. Altick, VP, i. 63–4). The short lines and elliptical syntax suggest speaking through tears, and trying to use as few words as possible. The pathos of the poem depends on the fact that the speaker's desperate remedy for the quarrels caused by argument will not work. Cf. RB, 9 Apr. 1846, after a disagreement about the ethics of duelling: 'I submit, unfeignedly, to you, there as elsewhere.' EB replied: '. . . you cannot, you know— you know you cannot, dearest, "submit" to me in an opinion, any more than I could to you, if I desired it ever so anxiously' (K, ii. 608–9).

p. 24 st. 2. *Hawk on bough*: when a hawk is perched beside us, i.e. when our love is in danger of destruction.

p. 24 st. 4. *false to thee*: if it seems false to thee. Cf. TRB, xii. 848–50: '. . . but here's the plague / That all this trouble comes of telling truth, / Which truth, by when it reaches him, looks false . . .'

p. 25 st. 5. *serpent's . . . Eve and I*: arguing about right and wrong is like picking the fruit of the tree of the knowledge of good and evil (Genesis 2 : 17–24).

FRA LIPPO LIPPI, p. 26

Probably written 1853 in Florence, where RB saw the picture described in ll. 346–89, and other works of Fra Filippo Lippi (c. 1406–69). The biographical details, including the window-exit, are from V, ii. 1–8, where Lippi is also said to have seduced, and had a son by, a nun whom he was using as a model for a picture of the Virgin. RB chose this poem to read aloud in response to Tennyson's reading of *Maud* (27 Sept. 1855; D, pp. 218–19).

p. 26 l. 3. *Zooks*: a mild substitute for 'By God'.

p. 26 l. 7. *Carmine*: a Carmelite monastery in Florence.

p. 26 l. 17. *Cosimo of the Medici*: ruler of Florence and patron of the arts (1389–1464).

p. 26 l. 20. *affected*: liked.

p. 27 l. 52. *whifts of song*. The examples given are imitations of *stornelli*, three-line Tuscan folk-songs based on flower-names.

p. 28 ll. 73 f. *Jerome . . . flesh*: the subject of a surviving picture by Lippi. St. Jerome was fanatically devoted to chastity (M. W. Pepperdene, Exp., xv, 1957, item 34).

p. 30 l. 121. *the Eight*: the magistrates of Florence.

p. 30 l. 139. *Camaldolese*: a religious order founded by St. Romualdo at Camaldoli, near Florence.

p. 30 l. 140. *Preaching Friars*: Dominicans.

p. 31 l. 147. *gossips*: women 'of light and trifling character' (OED).

p. 31 l. 170. *niece*: perhaps a euphemism for mistress (B. Litzinger, NQ, viii. 1961, 344–5).

p. 31 l. 172. *funked*: went out in smoke.

p. 32 l. 189. *Giotto . . . God*: perhaps suggested by V, i. 69, which describes a fresco by Giotto di Bondone (c. 1267–

1337) of St. Francis 'glorified in heaven, surrounded by those Virtues which are required of those who wish to be perfect in the sight of God'. They include Chastity and Purity.

p. 32 l. 196. *Herodias*: the mother of Salome, who actually did the dancing (Matthew 14 : 3–11). The slip may be meant to show that the Prior does not even know his Bible; but may be merely copied from Vasari, who frequently makes this mistake, and in describing Lippi's fresco of Herod's banquet at Prato mentions the skill (i.e. in dancing) of Herodias *(la destrezza di Erodiade* in the 1846–57 edn. used by RB, iv. 124; V, ii. 5–6).

p. 33 ll. 235 f. *Angelico . . . Lorenzo*. The idea of contrasting the naturalistic art of Lippi with the formal religious art of the Dominican Fra Angelico (1387–1455) and the Camaldolese Lorenzo Monaco (*c.* 1370–*c.* 1422) probably came from an essay by the Bs' friend Mrs. Anna Jameson (J. Parr, ELN, v, 1968, 277–83).

p. 34 l. 257. *grass*. Cf. 1 Peter 1 : 24: 'all flesh is as grass . . .'

p. 35 l. 277. *Hulking Tom*: Tommaso di Giovanni (1401–28), called Masaccio (hulking, clumsy Thomas) because of his personal carelessness (V, i. 264). RB turns him from Lippi's master into his pupil, through misunderstanding a footnote in the 1846–57 edn. of Vasari (J. Parr, ELN, iii, 1966, 197–201).

p. 36 l. 307. *cullion*: rascal. *hanging*: drooping, gloomy (with a hint of 'being born to be hanged').

p. 36 l. 323. *St. Laurence*: a deacon of Pope Sixtus II, said, while being roasted on a gridiron (*c.* A.D. 258) to have asked his torturers to turn him over, as he was done on one side.

p. 37 l. 346. *Something . . . Ambrogio's*: the *Coronation of the Virgin*, painted as an altar-piece for the church of the Sant' Ambrogio nunnery in Florence.

p. 37 l. 347. *cast of my office*: specimen of my work.

p. 37 l. 354. *Saint John*: the Baptist, patron saint of Florence.

p. 37 l. 358. *Uz*: Job 1 : 1.

p. 38 l. 375. *camel-hair*: a joking allusion to Matthew 3 : 4.

p. 38 l. 377. *Iste . . . opus*: This man executed the work. The words *is* [he] *perfecit opus* appear beside a kneeling figure at the bottom right-hand corner of the picture, and were long believed to mean that the figure was a self-portrait of Lippi; but M. Carmichael has shown (BM, xxi, 1912, 194–200) that the portrait is not of the artist, but of the benefactor of the church, Canon Francesco Maringhi, who ordered the altar-piece in 1441.

p. 38 l. 381. *hot cockles*: an innocent country game, here used as a euphemism for what Hamlet (III. ii. 125) calls 'country matters'.

A TOCCATA OF GALUPPI'S, p. 39

RB: 'As for Galuppi, I had once in my possession two huge manuscript volumes almost exclusively made up of his "Toccata-pieces"—apparently a slighter form of the Sonata to be "touched" lightly off' (1887; H. E. Greene, PMLA, lxii, 1947, 1099). The Venetian Baldassare Galuppi (1706–85) has been called, after D. Scarlatti, the finest eighteenth-century Italian harpsichord composer (EBL, p. 23). No Toccata, properly so called, of Galuppi's has yet been found, but the Brussels Conservatoire library has three harpsichord pieces of his in MS., which are there entitled 'Toccatas', and one of them (Sonata No. 11 in D Minor) has been suggested as RB's original (F. Torre-franca, RMI, xix, 1912, 135); but the poem probably aims to describe the general character of Galuppi's harpsichord music, rather than any single piece (C. van den Borren, MT, lxiv, 1923, 314–16).

p. 39 st. 2. *Doges . . . rings*: a reference to the annual cere-mony of throwing a gold ring into the sea, to symbolize Venetian sea-power.

p. 39 st. 3. *Shylock's bridge*: the Rialto (*Merchant of Venice*, I. iii. 105).

I was . . . England. The speaker is not RB, but a common Victorian type, insular, complacent, science-orientated, earnest, and at first inclined to 'scold' (st. 15) the Venetians for their frivolity.

p. 40 st. 6. *clavichord*: an instrument that would be almost inaudible against the noise of general conversation, pro-bably chosen (rather than *harpsichord*) for the alliteration with *Toccatas*; but RB may conceivably have played a clavichord in Florence (see Introd., p. xvii).

p. 40 st. 7. *lesser thirds*: minor thirds, characteristic of a minor key.

sixths diminished: a term without precise technical meaning in the context, but apparently used for its emotive suggestions.

suspensions . . . die. A suspension is the holding on of a note in one chord into the following chord. It produces a discord, which is only resolved (a solution) when the note falls a degree to a note appropriate to the second chord. The terms aptly symbolize reluctance to die, com-bined with the realization that in the harmony of things one cannot stay, after the time has come for one to go.

sevenths: probably an allusion to the Dominant Seventh, a mild discord commonly used in the penulti-mate chord of a Perfect Cadence.

p. 41 st. 8. *dominant's . . . answered to.* In its simplest form, the Perfect Cadence consists of the chord of the Dominant (a fifth above the Tonic or Key-note) followed by that of the Tonic. In a Sonata in D Major, Galuppi keeps repeat-ing the Dominant (A) through several bars, before drop-ping to the final low D (PM, p. 5). RB makes the repeated

Dominant symbolize the recurring thought of mortality, and the final chord, death itself.

p. 41 st. 9. *an octave*: i.e. the Tonic struck in octaves, to stress its finality.

p. 42 st. 13. *you'll not die*: Galuppi's imagined statement is sarcastic. It warns the speaker that earnest Victorian intellectuals die as surely as Venetian 'butterflies'.

p. 42 st. 15. *I want the heart to scold*. From an attitude of moral disapproval the speaker has unexpectedly been brought round to one of intense sympathy.

BY THE FIRE-SIDE, p. 43

Perhaps written 1853, the scenery suggested by a trip to Prato Fiorito, near Bagni di Lucca (D, p. 222); or 1847, the scenery based on a guide-book description of Lake Orta, in Piedmont (J. S. Lindsay, SP, xxxix, 1942, 571–9). Though clearly related to RB's love for EB, the poem is a dm., not a piece of autobiography.

p. 44 st. 4. *at it indeed*: not at Greek, but at day-dreaming (G. Tillotson, SR, lxxii, 1964, 394).

Greek: a language associated in RB's mind with EB. Cf. their letters of 27 Feb., 1, 5, 11 Mar. 1845 about the *Prometheus* of Aeschylus, which she had translated (1833; K, i. 30–8). Greek starts a train of thought, pictured as a long passage overarched by trees, first the hazels mentioned by the 'young ones', then foreign trees (a rarer sort). The speaker follows the thought of his wife (the leader's hand) down the passage, and emerges at the far end (I pass out where it ends), to find himself remembering his youth in Italy.

p. 45 st. 9. *Pella*: a town on Lake Orta.

p. 47 st. 21. *Leonor*: Leonora, the devoted wife in Beethoven's opera *Fidelio, oder Die Eheliche Liebe* (or *Married Love*).

the path: the process of recalling (look backwards) and imaginatively reliving (pursue) past experience. Grey heads abhor it, because it confronts them with a sharp contrast between 'flowery' youth and their present 'waste' (st. 25) age. But the speaker dares to relive *his* life in memory because, thanks to his wife, his age seems 'flowery' and his youth (before he met her) relatively 'waste' (V. S. Seturaman, NQ, ix, 1962, 297–8).

p. 47 st. 22. *our life's safe hem*: the edge of the ground on which we can safely stand and remain alive, i.e. when youth goes, we feel that life itself is threatened.

p. 47 st. 23. *spirit-small hand*. Cf. Hawthorne, of EB: 'I have never seen a human frame which seemed so nearly a transparent veil for a celestial and immortal spirit' (J. S. Lindsay, op. cit., p. 571.

p. 48 st. 27. *The great . . . new*. Revelation 21 : 5.
House . . . hands. 2 Corinthians 5 : 1.

p. 50 st. 38. *with never a third*. In the Bs' love-letters a 'shadowy third' (st. 46) figures as an imaginary detached observer who tends to discourage RB's advances, e.g. EB: '. . . c^d *I* be . . . justified in abetting such a step,— the step of wasting . . . your best feelings . . . of emptying your water gourds into the sand ? What I thought then I think now—just what any third person, knowing you, w^d think, I think & feel' (31 Aug. 1845). 'I have my own thoughts of course . . . & you have yours, & the worst is that a third person looking down on us from some snow-capped height, & free from personal influences, would have *his* thoughts too, . . . and *he* would think that if you had been reasonable as usual you would have gone to Italy (26 Feb. 1846). The 'third person' appears in the next three letters also (K, i. 178, 494–501).

ANY WIFE TO ANY HUSBAND, p. 54

Possibly inspired by the fact that in 1852, within three years of his wife's death, RB's father was successfully sued for breach of promise by a Mrs. von Müller (D, p. 223).

p. 57 st. 13. *Titian*: Tiziano Vecelli (*c.* 1487–1576), whose *Venus of Urbino*, a nude with 'direct sensual appeal' (OA, p. 1141), RB had doubtless seen at the Uffizi Gallery in Florence.

AN EPISTLE, p. 60

Probably written 1853–4 (D, p. 224). Based on John 11: 1–44, the poem is a historical reconstruction of a contemporary attitude to the rise of Christianity, possibly suggested by Lucian's patronizing comments on Christians in *Peregrinus*, and his satirical account in *Philopseudes* of 'that Syrian in Palestine' who casts out devils (L, pp. 10–11, 205; the Bs owned Lucian's works, BC, p. 113). It is also a psychological study of conflict between desire and inability to believe in miracles, and a parable of the Victorian religion-science dilemma.

p. 60 l. 1. *Karshish*: a phonetic transcription of an Arabic word meaning: 'one who gathers' (M. Wright, TLS, 1 May 1953, p. 285). Cf. Matthew 15 : 27, where a non-Israelite woman claims help from Jesus, saying: 'yet the dogs eat of the crumbs which fall from their masters' table.' Thus the non-Christian Karshish is picking up crumbs of Christianity.

p. 60 l. 17. *snake-stone*: a substance supposed to cure snake-bites.

p. 60 l. 20. *Karshish . . . time*: an elaborate opening in the style of St. Paul's Epistle to the Romans, 1 : 1–7 (R. D. Altick, MLN, lxxii, 1957, 494; W. Irvine, VP, ii, 1964, 161).

p. 61, l. 28. *Vespasian*: Roman Emperor (A.D. 70–9). He invaded Palestine in 66.

p. 61 l. 50. *His . . . sublimate*: i.e. he is delivering my letter in return for medical treatment.

p. 62 l. 67. *tang*: sting (an early meaning of the word).

p. 62 l. 79. *subinduced*: caused as a secondary symptom.

p. 62 l. 82. *exhibition*: administration.

p. 63 l. 103. *fume*: fanciful notion.

p. 64 l. 128. *straightened*: in later editions corrected to *straitened*.

p. 65 l. 179. *It . . . perforcedly*: i.e. he leads it only because he has to.

p. 66 l. 213. *affects*: desires.

p. 67 l. 228. *affects*: feels affection for.

p. 68 l. 252. *earthquake*: Matthew 27 : 51.

p. 68 l. 281. *Blue . . . borage*: used in ancient medicine as an antidepressant.

MESMERISM, p. 70

The theme had been controversial since 1838, when Prof. J. Elliotson had been forced to resign from London University, because of his interest in mesmerism (J. M. Schneck, BMLA, xliv, 1956, 448). For RB's attitude, see p. 12 st. 11 note. The speaker's prolonged concentration is conveyed by the syntax: a single sentence from st. 2 to st. 21.

p. 72 st. 9. *calotypist's skill*: a form of photography, invented by W. Fox Talbot (1841).

p. 72 st. 13. *flame*: a reference to 'odyl', a mesmeric 'influence' alleged by a chemist, K. von Reichenbach (1845), to be present in mesmerists, and to be visible to certain sensitive people as an effluence of light (K, ii. 640).

A SERENADE AT THE VILLA, p. 76

There is no reason to think, with T. O. Mabbott (Exp., viii, 1949, Q. 6), that the speaker, for all his lively sense of humour, is dead.

My Star, p. 79

Believed to refer to EB (cf. the similar image in sect. 17–19 of 'One Word More', pp. 311–12). RB used to write out this poem when asked for an autograph, and placed it first in *Selections*, 1872 (D, p. 227).

p. 79, l. 10. *stops like a bird*: stops 'dartling', as a bird stops working its wings (G. Tillotson, SR, lxxii, 1964, 394).

p. 79 l. 11. *Saturn*: second largest planet in the solar system, and particularly bright.

Instans Tyrannus, p. 80

The title and theme are from Horace, *Odes*, iii. iii. 1–8: 'Iustum et tenacem propositi virum / . . . non vultus instantis tyranni / mente quatit solida . . . / nec fulminantis magna manus Iovis ; / si fractus inlabatur orbis, / impavidum ferient ruinae' (the righteous man, tenacious of his purpose . . . is not shaken out of his firm mind by the face of the threatening tyrant . . . nor by the great hand of Jove with his thunder and lightning ; if the circle of the sky were to be shattered and fall, its ruins would strike him unafraid). RB gives Jove's thunder and lightning to his tyrant, turns Jove into a protecting God, the circling sky into a shield, and transfers to the tyrant the fear which the 'righteous man' does not feel. The real-life model for the tyrant was perhaps Napoleon III, whose ruthless suppression of his opponents RB had witnessed in Paris, Dec. 1851.

p. 82 st. 5. *admire . . . debate*: be surprised that I give the man so much thought.

A Pretty Woman, p. 83

Perhaps written 1847, about a girl called Gerardine Bate, who irritated RB in Florence (D, p. 228).

p. 84 st. 9. *the heaven . . . gone*: because the heaven we hoped to find above it is not there.

p. 84 st. 10. *fly-king*: presumably the Purple Emperor butterfly.

'CHILDE ROLAND TO THE DARK TOWER CAME', p. 87

Said to have been written in Paris, 3 Jan. 1852 (GM, p. 189), in fulfilment of a New Year resolution to write a poem every day (D, p. 229); but the date remains uncertain (J. Huebenthal, VP, iv, 1966, 51–4). RB, 1887: 'Childe Roland came upon me as a kind of dream. I had to write it, then and there, and I finished it the same day, I believe. But it was simply that I had to do it. I did not know then what I meant beyond that, and I'm sure I don't know now. But I am very fond of it' (LW, p. 261). The words of the title are spoken by Edgar, when pretending to be mad, *King Lear*, III, iv, 186, and the setting and atmosphere of the poem seem to be largely suggested by the nightmarish scene on the heath (C. C. Clarke, MLQ, xxiii, 1962, 323–6). Edgar keeps referring to 'the foul fiend', which perhaps reminded RB of PP, p. 56, where Christian, in the Valley of Humiliation, meets the 'foul fiend' Apollyon (cf. st. 27). Further suggestions must have come from children's tales and chivalric romances (H. Golder, PMLA, xxxix, 1924, 363–78). Visual materials mentioned by RB include 'a strange solitary little tower I have come upon more than once in Massa-Carrara, in the midst of low hills' (DK, p. 173), a painting that he saw years later in Paris, and the figure of a horse in a tapestry in his own drawing-room (reproduced BC, pp. 158–9, Lot no. 1385; O, p. 274). Among other suggested sources are a landscape described in G. de Lairesse's *Art of Painting* (D2); Dante's *Inferno* (R. E. Sullivan, VP, v, 1967, 296–303, D. S. J. Parsons, UWR, iv, 1968, 24–30), and Wordsworth's *Peter Bell* (T. P. Harrison, TSL, vi, 1961, 119–23). Although RB denied any allegorical intention, allegorical interpretations

abound, and the poem has been seen as a protest against
the evils of industrial competition (D. V. Erdman, PQ,
xxxvi, 1957, 417–35); a rehandling of archetypal myths
related to vegetation rites, employing the Waste Land
and Holy Grail themes (C. R. Woodard, SHT, pp. 93–9,
V. Hoar, VN, No. 27, 1965, 26–8); and an expression of
a 'carnality-retribution' pattern in RB's unconscious
(R. E. Hughes, LP, ix, 1959, 18–19). It is perhaps best
not to attempt any detailed interpretation, but to regard
the poem as a nightmare, expressing a mood of deep
discouragement and self-distrust, plus determination to
carry on.

p. 87 title. *Childe*: a young knight who has not yet proved
his worth (J. Lindberg, VN, No. 16, 1959, 29).

p. 89 st. 8. *estray*: stray animal, i.e. the speaker, who feels
trapped on the roadless plain.

p. 89 st. 12. *pashing*: dashing, trampling.

p. 90 st. 14. *colloped*. Since the normal meaning of the
word, 'with thick folds of fat', contradicts *gaunt*, the
sense may be 'like slices of raw meat' (W, ii. 266).

p. 91 st. 19. *bespate*: spat on, bespattered (p.p. of *bespit*).

p. 92 st. 23. *mews*: apparently used for *mew* (cage, coop).
mad: i.e. maddening.

p. 93 st. 27. *dragon-penned*: with feathers like a dragon.
Apollyon (the destroyer) has 'Wings like a Dragon' (PP,
p. 56).

p. 93 st. 30. *nonce*: critical moment.

p. 94 st. 32. *heft*: hilt.

p. 94 st. 34. *slug-horn*: an incorrect form of *slughorn*, an
earlier form of *slogan* (battle-cry), but taken by Chatter-
ton, and after him by RB, to be a kind of horn. In
blowing it, the speaker clearly challenges somebody to
combat. Cf. ML, i. 203: 'And also there was fast by a

sycamore tree, and there hung an horn, the greatest that ever they saw . . . and this Knight of the Red Laundes had hanged it up there, that if there came any errant-knight, he must blow that horn, and then he will make him ready and come to him to do battle' (MLV, i. 320).

RESPECTABILITY, p. 95

Probably written soon after 5 Feb. 1852, when RB attended the ceremony at which the royalist François Guizot (1787–1874) delivered a *discours de réception* welcoming his hated political opponent, the liberal Charles Montalembert (1810–70), into the Académie Française, since 1795 a branch of the Institut de France. In 1880 RB confessed to a 'thorough dislike' of Guizot, quoting other examples of his insincerity (LL, pp. 92–5).

p. 95 st. 2. *Boulevart*: an earlier spelling of *boulevard*.

p. 95 st. 3. *the Institute*! The speaker has just sighted the Institut de France, the courtyard of which is decorated with coloured glass lamps, in honour of the *réception*. Guizot's pretence of friendship is used to epitomize the falseness of social decorum, compared with the truth of unconventional love. The speaker hurries his companion past this symbol of 'respectability'.

A LIGHT WOMAN, p. 96

Presumably the interest of this story for RB (like that of the next poem) was its moral ambiguity (a cruel action done for an apparently good motive).

p. 98 st. 14. *writer of plays*: rueful self-ridicule, since his stage-plays had failed, and after 1846 he wrote no others.

THE STATUE AND THE BUST, p. 99

Date of composition unknown, but clearly after the Bs' arrival in Florence (Apr. 1847). The rhyme-scheme, though not the metre, is that of *terza rima*, used by the

Florentine poet Dante. For RB the story probably symbolized what might have happened if he and EB had not had the courage to elope in 1846, and perhaps what had happened to J. S. Mill and Mrs. Harriet Taylor, who had been strictly platonic lovers for over twenty years, until Mr. Taylor died, and they could get married (1851; M, pp. 48–9). The apparent moral of the poem, that cowardice may be worse than adultery, 'has been much disputed by Browning students' (BE, p. 519), in spite of the precedent of Luther's 'Pecca fortiter' (sin boldly), and the Gospel identification of contemplated with committed adultery (Matthew 5 : 28; WR, p. 215).

p. 99 l. 1. *a palace*: now the Palazzo Antinori, built by the Medici family, but at the time of the story owned by the Riccardi (D, p. 234).

p. 99 l. 2. *a statue*: an equestrian statue of the Grand Duke Ferdinand di Medici (1549–1608) by Giovanni da Bologna (Giambologna or John of Douai, where he was born, 1529–1628), in the Piazza della Annunziata.

p. 100 l. 21. *coal-black tree*: i.e. one of the trees from which ebony comes.

p. 100 l. 22. *encolure*: French for 'neck of an animal', here used for 'mane'.

p. 100 l. 23. *dissemble*: 'simulate by imitation' (OED), i.e. her hair tried in vain to be as black as her eyes.

p. 100 l. 35. *the Palace*: the Duke's palace, built for Cosimo dei Medici the Elder in 1444–59, and lived in by the Medici until 1540, but sold to the Riccardi 1659, and now known as the Palazzo Riccardi. Its shadow is made symbolic of the Medici domination of Florence.

p. 100 l. 39. *Cosimo . . . son.* Cosimo the Elder (1389–1464) made himself virtually dictator of Florence, but retained the forms of the Republic, and assumed no unconstitutional title. His son, Piero, hardly deserved the epithet 'cursed'. RB was probably thinking of Cosimo I (1519–74), who won power by mass executions, called himself Duke (1537), and was given the title of Grand Duke of Tuscany by the Pope (1569). His son Francesco (1541–87), who became his lieutenant (1564) and successor (1574), was 'cursed' enough, in view of his private vices, his neglect of government, and the bloodshed that he caused. He did, however, patronize Giambologna, hence perhaps Francesco's brother Ferdinand's choice of sculptor (l. 202).

p. 101 l. 72. *ave-bell*: rung every morning and evening.

p. 102 l. 94. *Arno*: the river on which Florence stands.

p. 102 l. 95. *Petraja*: a place on the southern slopes of Mount Morello, where Ferdinand had a villa.

p. 103 l. 113. *Envoy . . . France*. Ferdinand was seeking good relations with France, in order to counteract Spanish influence in Italy.

p. 105 l. 159. *serpent's tooth*. From its original context (*King Lear*, I. iv. 297–8) the phrase should imply 'a thankless child'; but the probable meaning is: 'temptation to eat forbidden fruit' (Genesis 3 : 1–15; cf. 'A Woman's Last Word', l. 15).

p. 105 l. 169. *Robbia*. Luca della Robbia (1400–82), inventor of Robbia ware (enamelled terracotta relief), which continued to be made after the last great sculptor of his family died, long before Ferdinand became Grand Duke (1587). The bust was RB's invention (FH, p. 199, PN, p. 248), but there is an empty shrine under the window (D, p. 234), and when the poem was written, specimens of Robbia ware still appeared on the outer cornice of the palace (O, p. 206).

p. 107 l. 225. *He had cut*: the Duke would have cut, if he had had the courage of a 'soldier-saint'. RB does not say that adultery would have qualified Ferdinand to 'see

God', but that his failure to pass the 'test' of courage certainly disqualified him.

p. 107 l. 234. *Where . . . Guelph*: when a game can be played with any sort of counter, it would be a cynical joke (implying the worthlessness of a monarch's stamp) to play it with real English coins (the English royal family are descended from the Guelphs).

p. 108 l. 247. *unlit . . . loin.* Luke 12 : 35. Cf. Matthew 25 : 1–12.

p. 108 ll. 249 f. *You of . . . strive you?* Do you 'virtuous' people act on your beliefs any more vigorously than this 'criminal' pair acted on theirs?

p. 108 l. 250. *De te fabula: mutato nomine de te / fabula narratur* (change the name, and the story is told about you. Horace, *Satires*, I. i. 69–70).

LOVE IN A LIFE, p. 109; LIFE IN A LOVE, p. 110

Allegories, perhaps, of the pursuit of the unattainable, but apparently connected with the fantasies of unsatisfactory love which RB had contrasted with his happy relationship with EB. Cf. 'Oh, how different it all *might* be! In this House of Life—where I go, you go—where I ascend, you run before—where I descend, it is after you. Now, one might have a *piece* of Ba . . . and make it up into a Lady and a Mistress, and find her a room to her mind . . . and . . . visit her there . . . and then,—after a time, leave her there and go . . . whither one liked— after, to me, the most melancholy fashion in the world. How different with us! If it were *not*, indeed—what a mad folly would marriage be!' (5 Apr. 1846, K, ii. 591; W, ii. 270). The 'house' imagery echoes RB's reaction to the news that EB had for the first time walked, instead of being carried, downstairs: 'I fancy myself meeting you "on the stairs"—stairs and passages generally, and galleries . . . I would come upon you unaware on a

landing-place in my next dream!' (19 Jan. 1846, K, i.
402–4; PR, p. 17).

HOW IT STRIKES A CONTEMPORARY, p. 111

Probably written soon after 1851, when RB described,
in his essay on Shelley, the 'objective poet' who sees
'external objects more clearly, widely, and deeply, than
is possible to the average mind', and the 'subjective poet'
who, 'gifted like the objective poet with the fuller per-
ception of nature and man, is impelled to embody the
thing he perceives, not so much with reference to the
many below as to the one above him, the supreme
Intelligence which apprehends all things in their absolute
truth' (SH, p. 1; TV, p. 115). The 'God's spy' image is
perhaps from *King Lear*, v. iii. 17 (D, p. 237). The setting
at Valladolid (in Spain), the Corregidor (l. 90) and
Jacynth (l. 84) seem to come from Lesage's *Gil Blas*, on
which RB worked in 1835 (M, pp. 20–1).

p. 111 l. 12. *an old . . . blindish*: a fair description of EB's
spaniel, Flush, in 1852 (M, p. 176).

p. 112 ll. 45–6, p. 113 ll. 68–70. *He . . . His . . . Me . . .
Me*. The capitals were omitted in later editions, doubtless
to make the allegory less obtrusive.

p. 113 ll. 68–70. *Too far . . . mind!* Perhaps RB was
thinking of his own lack of public recognition. Cf. his
letter to Ruskin, defending his 'obscurity': 'Do you think
poetry was ever generally understood—or can be ? Is the
business of it to tell people what they know already . . . ?
It is all teaching, on the contrary, and the people hate
to be taught . . . A poet's affair is with God, to whom he
is accountable, and of whom is his reward: look elsewhere,
and you find misery enough' (RW, p. 201; D, p. 237).

p. 113 l. 76. *Titians*. See p. 57 st. 13 note.

p. 113 l. 80. *new . . . otherwise*: exactly the sort of house that RB was to live in, 1862–87, at 19 Warwick Crescent, London, W. (M, p. 221).

p. 114 l. 90. *St—St*: Sh!

Corregidor: chief magistrate of a Spanish town.

p. 114 l. 103. *heavenly . . . guard*: i.e. angels might come to relieve him after his spell of duty on earth.

p. 114 l. 15. *Prado*: a fashionable parade (from the name of the public park in Madrid). The worldly speaker has been slipping into a rather other-worldly view of the poet, but now recalls himself, with a touch of embarrassment, to his normal view that time is more real than eternity.

THE LAST RIDE TOGETHER, p. 115

Thought by many nineteenth-century critics 'the noblest of all RB's love poems' (BE, p. 252); more recently interpreted as an allegory of his relations with his Muse (I. Orenstein, BBI, No. 18, 1961). The word *ride* has been given a range of symbolic meanings, including 'the fulfillment of God's purpose for man in the simple process of living' (R. D. Altick, VP, i, 1963, 64), and even, incredibly, sexual intercourse (R. M. Goldfarb, VP, iii, 1965, 255–61). Those who fail to enjoy the poem, in spite of its admirable philosophy, may enjoy J. K. Stephen's parody (P, pp. 129–31).

p. 117 st. 6. *each*: i.e. each ten-line obituary notice.

Abbey: Westminster Abbey, where RB himself was to be buried.

THE PATRIOT, p. 120

Probably written 1849 and suggested by the collapse of the Italian liberation movement after Novara (see p. 22 st. 9 note). The sub-title implies a reference, not to a particular event, but to a common type of event in political history (cf. *Julius Caesar*, i. i. 35–55).

p. 120 st. 1. *roses, roses*. When, after tea and muffins with the Browning Society at Newnham College, Cambridge, RB was crowned with roses and asked to read some of his poems, he caught sight of himself in a mirror, half-way through 'A serenade at the Villa', burst out laughing, and said: 'Shall I not read the "Patriot" instead ?' (AW, pp. 123–4).

p. 121 st. 6. *Brescia*: omitted in later editions, to contradict the suggestion that the Patriot was Arnold of Brescia, an Italian revolutionary, executed 1155 (D, p. 239).

MASTER HUGUES OF SAXE-GOTHA, p. 122

Probably written 1853 in Florence (D, p. 239). The imaginary composer's name was doubtless chosen to rhyme with *fugues*. The great organ-fugue composer J. S. Bach (1685–1750) was born at Eisenach in Saxe-Weimar, adjoining Saxe-Gothe. RB said he was thinking, however, not of 'the glorious Bach', but of 'one of the dry-as-dust imitators who would elaborate [an uninteresting five-note phrase] for a dozen pages together' (1887; H. E. Greene, PMLA, lxii, 1947, 1098). The speaker is not RB, though he could play the organ (GM, p. 161), but a church organist who has just played the voluntary after evening service. RB said (1886) 'that he had no allegorical intent in his head when he wrote the poem; that it was composed in an organ loft and was merely the expression of a fugue—the construction of which he understood . . . because he had composed fugues himself: it was an involved labyrinth of entanglement *leading to nothing*— the only allegory in it was its possible reflection of the labyrinth of human life. That was all . . .' (CC, p. 79); but it may also symbolize the superiority of intuition to intellect in perceiving religious truth (R. D. Altick, VP, iii, 1965, 1–7). The five-line stanza reflects the five-voiced fugue, and the more fantastic rhymes, while supporting the humorous tone, also represent the ingenuity displayed in fugue composition.

p. 122 st. 3. *holding the base*: playing the bass part.

p. 122 st. 4. *house of the sounds*: the organ.

Bids . . . rounds: orders the last lingering sound back into the instrument from which it came. The answer even to a church saint's 'Who goes there?' will be dead silence.

p. 123 st. 6. *Aloys . . . Just*: the names of the church saints.

p. 123 st. 7. *Help . . . helve*: help me to grasp the idea ('intent', st. 10) of your music, so that I can play it properly.

p. 123 st. 8. *claviers*: manuals or keyboards.

p. 123 st. 9. *brow . . . score*: forehead furrowed as if by the horizontal lines of a musical score.

breves: originally the short notes of music, but now the longest, and very rarely used; at first written as horizontal rectangles—an even more grotesque way of seeing eyes than the nearly horizontal ovals (flanked by double vertical lines) of modern notation.

bar: the vertical line marking the end of a bar.

p. 124 st. 10. *what . . . shent*: why I won the competition organized by the local authority for appointment as 'Town Musician', when expert candidates were praised, and those with merely superficial knowledge disgraced (W, ii. 274).

p. 124 st. 12. *phrase*: the 'subject' of the fugue, which is 'answered' by the second 'voice', usually in the Dominant key.

p. 124 st. 14. *discept*: express a difference of opinion. The development of the fugue is described as a noisy argument between five people.

p. 125 st. 16. *crepitant*: crackling, rattling.

strepitant: noisy.

Danaides, O Sieve. For murdering their husbands, the daughters of Danaus were condemned in Hades to keep trying to fill water-jars with perforated bottoms, i.e. the fugue represents infinite labour with no result.

p. 125 st. 17. *Escobar*: Escobar y Mendoza (1589–1669), a writer on casuistry and moral theology, whose name came to be used as a term for a person adroit at making rules of morality harmonize with his own interests.

Two-bars: the double bar marking the end of a section, or of a whole piece.

p. 125 st. 18. *Est . . . rota*: There is a flight (the literal meaning of *fugue*), the wheel turns (perhaps the eternally revolving wheel on which Ixion was bound in Hades (cf. Virgil, *Georgics*, iv. 484).

p. 125 st. 19. *risposting*: retorting, riposting. The spelling is probably meant to suggest *risposta*, the Italian technical term for the 'answer' in a fugue.

instance: i.e. a simile.

p. 126 st. 20. *where's music . . . gold*: possibly a reminiscence of the complaints from critics of RB's own obscurity and lack of music (W. S. Johnson, JA, xxii, 1963, 205). Cf. 'Mr. B seems . . . to be totally indifferent to pleasing our imagination and fancy by the music of verse and of thought . . .' 'The song of the bard falls dull and muffled on the ear, as from a fog . . .' '. . . We have now and then glimpses of sentiment and description, like momentary sunbeams darting out between rifted clouds; but straightway the clouds close, and we are left to plod on in deeper twilight' (CH, pp. 65, 62).

tickens: stout cotton or linen materials (ticking).

p. 126 st. 21. *I for . . . zealous*: I am anxious that human effort should not be wasted.

a lover . . . jealous: a lover of humanity is quick to suspect injury to his beloved.

p. 126 st. 23. *just . . . lodges*: just disappearing from sight where the cobwebs of human thought have settled on it.

p. 126 st. 25. *comments . . . inventions*: perhaps a reference to the complexities of theological theory and controversy.

p. 127 st. 26. *mountain in labour*. Horace, *Ars Poetica*, 139 (Teubner edition): 'Parturiunt montes, nascetur ridiculus mus' (the mountains are in labour—they will give birth to a ridiculous mouse).

clef: i.e. key.

p. 127 st. 28. *mea poena*: at the risk of being punished for it.

Palestrina: Giovanni Perluigi da Palestrina (*c.* 1525–94), organist of Palestrina cathedral at the age of about eighteen, but famous chiefly for his unaccompanied choral works. When, after the Council of Trent's censure of existing church-music (1562), it was proposed to forbid the use of all music but 'unisonous and unaccompanied plain-chant', Palestrina was commissioned, as an alternative, to produce an acceptable specimen of a mass. He submitted three (1565) of which one (*Missa Papae Marcelli*) was considered perfect. RB explained (1887): 'The "mode Palestrina" has no reference to organ-playing; it was the name given by old Italian writers on composition to a certain simple and severe style like that of the Master; just as, according to Byron, 'the word Miltonic means sublime' (H. E. Greene, PMLA, lxii, 1947, 1098–9).

BISHOP BLOUGRAM'S APOLOGY, p. 128

Probably written 1850–4 (D, pp. 240–1). The subject was topical: J. H. Newman had become an RC in 1845, and in 1850 an outcry against 'Papal Aggression' had been caused by the re-establishment of the RC hierarchy in England, with the appointment of N. P. S. Wiseman

(1802–65) as Cardinal and first Archbishop of West-
minster (R. E. Palmer, Jr., MP, lviii, 1960, 108–18).
Apology here means 'defence, vindication', like Newman's
later *Apologia pro Vita Sua* (1864). Blougram's character
was suggested by the popular conception of Wiseman,
with some features drawn from Newman. RB said (1865)
that the Bishop 'was certainly intended for the English
Cardinal, but he was not treated ungenerously' (GD,
ii. 261). The pleasant story that Wiseman himself
reviewed the poem has unfortunately been disproved
(E. R. Houghton, VN, No. 33, 1968, p. 46). Blougram
has been variously interpreted: as 'meagre swindler'
(GC, p. 202); a sincerely religious man, whose arguments
are determined by the nature of Gigadibs's criticisms
(F. E. L. Priestley, UTQ, xv, 1946, 139–47); a conform-
ing sceptic whose arguments are sound when attack-
ing Gigadibs, fallacious when justifying himself (PD,
pp. 124–43); and as a morally ambiguous figure, ironically
presented to suggest that religious faith is still possible
in Victorian England, and can be justified even by a man
who may be either a scoundrel or a saint (R. E. Palmer,
op. cit.). The thin facility of his style and imagery may
be intended to suggest the inadequate quality of his
religious belief (IA, p. 117). The philosophical scheme of
the poem was possibly suggested by Emerson's 'Mon-
taigne; or The Skeptic' in *Representative Men*, 1850
(C. E. Tanzy, VS, i, 1958, 255–66).

p. 128 l. 3. *our Abbey*: Westminster Abbey, originally the
church of a Benedictine monastery, which was dissolved
by Henry VIII (1540).

p. 128 l. 4. *basilicas*: a name particularly applied to
certain churches in Rome.

p. 128 l. 6. *Pugin*: A. W. N. Pugin (1812–52), ecclesiastical
architect, chief inspirer of the 'Gothic Revival', and an
RC convert.

p. 128 l. 13. *Gigadibs*. The name may be meant to suggest a man who will turn his hand to anything for money (*gig* = whipping-top, fool; *dibs* = money).

p. 129 l. 34. *Corpus Christi Day*: the festival in honour of the Eucharist. An ironic contrast may be intended between the bread and wine of the Last Supper, and the good food and wine of Blougram's dinner (H, p. 147).

p. 129 l. 45. *che ch'é*: corrected in later editions to *che che* (what ? what ?), an Italian exclamation expressing impatient dismissal or denial of what has just been said.

p. 130 l. 52. *Goethe*: Johann Wolfgang von Goethe (1749–1832), poet, dramatist, critic, and all-round 'literary man' (cf. l. 975).

p. 130 l. 54. *Count D'Orsay*: French wit, dandy, and artist (1801–52).

p. 130 l. 70. *tire-room*: dressing-room.

p. 131 l. 109. *new edition*: probably the *Œuvres complètes* of Balzac (1799–1800) in 55 vols. which began to come out in 1856, and of which the Bs, who wanted to buy a complete set of Balzac's novels, might have seen an advance advertisement (C. R. Tracy, TLS, xxxiv, 1935, 48).

p. 131 l. 111. *little Greek . . . Leipsic*: presumably volumes in the Teubner series of classical texts, which started in 1849.

p. 132 l. 114. *Correggio*: Antonio Allegri (*c.* 1489–1534), called Correggio from the small town where he was born (in the territory of Modena). V calls him 'a marvellous artist', and mentions 'a St. Jerome' of his (now in the Gallery at Parma) 'of such marvellous and stupendous colouring that painters admire it for this character, seeing that it is not possible to paint better' (ii. 172–4).

p. 132 l. 125. *overhauls*: hauls overboard. The 'sea-furniture' image was perhaps suggested by memories of arranging transport to Italy; cf. RB's letter of 16 Sept. 1846, urging EB to take the minimum of luggage (K, ii. 1079–80).

p. 134 l. 184. a *chorus* . . . *Euripides*: probably the lines that conclude the *Helen*, *Bacchae*, *Andromache*, *Medea* (with a few words changed), and *Alcestis* (which RB adapted in *Balaustion's Adventure*, 1871) of Euripides (*c*. 480–406 B.C.): 'Divine things take many forms, and the gods bring many surprising things to pass. What was expected is not accomplished: what was not expected, is somehow contrived by God.'

p. 134 l. 190. *The grand Perhaps*: possibly an allusion to the deathbed remark ascribed to Rabelais: 'Je vais quérir un grand Peut-Être' (I am going to look for a great May-Be) (R. D. Altick, VP, i, 1963, 64–5).

p. 134, l. 197. *The Way* . . . *Life*. John 14 : 6.

p. 135 ll. 226–8. *The choice* . . . *ground*: whereas your choice, disbelief, overturns all the things that matter in life, so that either they or it (disbelief) must be thrown down. (The participles *turning*, *going* are in the absolute construction).

p. 136 ll. 257–9. *To be* . . . *unawares*. To choose total disbelief, just because you occasionally have doubts, is like choosing to spend your life asleep in bed, and giving up all normal daytime activities, just because you may occasionally feel sleepy. The argument follows quite reasonably from a question-begging premiss: the identification of doubts with dreams.

p. 138 l. 294. *can't wed twice*. Until 1857 divorce was impossible except by a private Act of Parliament.

p. 138 ll. 309–15. *Observe* . . . *bread*. As repunctuated in later editions, this tangled sentence may be translated:

'Look, my friend. I myself, the ordinary sort of person
that you know me to be—I don't mind telling you that
I myself, even in the modern anti-religious world, can,
with a little intelligence and tact, perform the miracle
of creating bread for myself out of this urban wilder-
ness.' Blougram alludes to Matthew 4 : 1–3, but seems
unaware of the implication: that he, unlike Jesus, has
yielded to a temptation of the Devil.

p. 138 l. 316. *Hildebrand*: Pope Gregory VII (*c.* 1021–85).
He increased the temporal power of the Papacy, and
asserted its authority over kings.

p. 140 l. 377. *winking Virgin.* Newman had recently been
quoted (*Morning Chronicle*, 21 Oct. 1851) as saying:
'I think it is impossible to withstand the evidence which
is brought for the liquefaction of the blood of St. Janu-
arius at Naples, and for the motion of the eyes of the
pictures of the Madonna in the Roman States . . .' (C. R.
Tracy, MLR, xxxiv, 1939, 423).

p. 140 l. 381. *his worst opera. Macbeth*, an early opera of
Verdi (1813–1901), was first produced in Florence 1847.

p. 141 l. 386. *Rossini*: composer of thirty-six operas
(1792–1868). In 1847 the Bs planned to visit him in
Bologna (LH, p. 14).

p. 141 l. 406. *diamond weights*: i.e. grains of Troy weight,
used for measuring gold, silver, and jewels.

p. 141 l. 411. *Schelling*: F. W. J. von Schelling (1775–
1854), an idealist philosopher of constantly changing
views, who began as a pantheist, then envisaged a pur-
poseful but unconscious Nature, and finally (from 1809)
tried to reconcile this doctrine with Christianity (OC,
p. 1222).

p. 142 l. 424. *bedropt . . . wax*: i.e. from lighting holy
candles.

p. 142 l. 425. *all Peter's chains*: i.e. numerous holy relics (cf. Acts 12 : 6–7). Similar satire on RC converts had appeared in *Blackwood's*, Mar. 1851 (R. C. Schweik, MLN, lxxi, 1956, 417–18).

p. 143 l. 454. *take his light away*: a traditional treatment for madness (cf. *Twelfth Night*, IV. ii).

p. 143 l. 466. *'The state, that's I'*: 'L'état, c'est moi', said, not by Napoleon, but by Louis XIV (1655).

p. 143 l. 472. *Austrian marriage*: to Marie Louise, daughter of the Austrian Emperor (1810).

p. 143 l. 475. *Austerlitz*: where Napoleon defeated the combined forces of Russia and Austria (1805).

p. 145 l. 513. *towers . . . palaces*: *Tempest*, IV. i. 152.

p. 145 l. 516. *Giulio Romano*: architect and painter (*c.* 1499–1546). See *Winter's Tale*, v. ii. 101.

Dowland: John Dowland (1563 ?–1626), lutanist and composer, praised in *The Passionate Pilgrim* (1599), a collection of poems originally attributed to Shakespeare.

p. 145 l. 519. *Pandulph . . . cardinal*: from *King John* (III. i. 64), where Pandulph, as papal legate, excommunicates John, and so forces the French King to break his alliance with England: a fair specimen of papal power.

p. 145 l. 533. *Terni*: probably mentioned, not only as a beauty-spot, but as a town which was under papal government.

p. 146 l. 553. *cousin . . . Bess*: i.e. in Shakespeare's day Blougram, as representative of the Pope, would have been entitled to employ towards Queen Elizabeth the form of address ('cousin') then usual between sovereigns.

p. 146 l. 568. *Luther*: Martin Luther (1483–1546), leader of the Reformation in Germany.

p. 147 l. 577. *Strauss*: D. F. Strauss (1808–74), author of *Leben Jesu* (translated into English by George Eliot in

1846), which denied that the supernatural elements in the Gospels had any historical basis.

p. 147 l. 591. *supposing . . . things*: i.e. even supposing that he ended up in hell.

p. 148 l. 626. '*What . . . Christ?*': Matthew 22 : 42.

p. 149 l. 642. *born . . . Englishman.* Wiseman was born in Seville, the son of Anglo-Irish parents, and was Rector of the English College at Rome (1828–40).

p. 150 l. 663. *The feeblest . . . most.* The child, though his senses are weaker than the adult's, is entrusted with the clearest vision of God. Cf. Wordsworth's 'Heaven lies about us in our infancy' ('Ode: Intimations of Immortality', l. 67).

p. 150 l. 667. *Michael*: the archangel, usually represented in pictures standing over, or fighting with a dragon (Revelation 12 : 7–9).

p. 150 l. 677. *that dear . . . praise*: e.g. as RB's friend Carlyle had praised it in *Past and Present* (1843).

p. 150 ll. 679–83. *cosmogony . . . again.* One of the greatest religious problems of the period was the contradiction between the account of the Creation in Genesis 1–2 and the findings of geology and ethnology, widely publicized in *Vestiges of the Natural History of Creation* (1844). Cf.: '. . . there is nothing in the whole series of operations displayed in inorganic geology, which may not be accounted for by the agency of the ordinary forces of nature'. '. . . Certainly, as such [ethnological and philological] researches advance, the idea of a single origin for the [human] species is always appearing less tenable . . .' (VC, pp. 111, 268–9).

p. 150 l. 685. *Ararat*: Genesis 8 : 4.

p. 151 l. 703. *Newman.* See p. 140 l. 377 note.

p. 151 l. 704. *Immaculate Conception*: the doctrine, made an article of faith of the RC Church by Pope Pius IX (1854), that from the first moment of her conception the Virgin Mary was kept free from all stain of original sin; but since the context requires something conflicting with 'the laws of Nature' (not merely of theology), RB may have confused this doctrine with that of Virgin Birth (conception without sex; J. Britton, Exp., xvii, 1959, Item 50).

p. 151 l. 715. *Bomba's lazzaroni*: the beggars (rogues, vagabonds) of King Ferdinand II of Naples, a treacherous tyrant called Bomba because of his bombardment of Messina (1848), whose reign was described by Gladstone as 'the negation of God erected into a system of government' (PD, p. 135).

p. 151 l. 716. *Antonelli*: Cardinal G. Antonelli (1806–76). He arranged Pius IX's flight from Rome, to become Bomba's guest at Gaeta (1848), and as Secretary of State from 1850 was largely responsible for the Pope's reactionary policy. See p. 22 st. 9 note.

p. 152 l. 728. *Naples' liquefaction*. The blood of St. Januarius, kept in a small glass phial at Naples, was said to become liquid and bubble some eighteen times a year. Newman had called this miracle 'unsatisfactory', and possibly attributable to natural causes (1825–6, NM, pp. 60, 63), but had later accepted it (see p. 140 l. 377 note).

p. 152 l. 732. *decrassify*: make less gross or material.

p. 152 l. 744. *Fichte*: J. G. Fichte (1762–1814), German philosopher, who regarded God as 'the living operative moral order' but not as a personal deity (OC, p. 502). Blougram's argument is like Newman's in 1842: 'I came to the conclusion that there was no medium, in true philosophy, between Atheism and Catholicity' (NA, p. 179; C. R. Tracy, MLR, xxxiv, 1939, 424).

p. 153 l. 782. *man's . . . progress*. The idea of evolution
had been popularized by VC, which ended by observing
'a progression resembling development . . . in human
nature', and suggesting 'the possible development of
higher types of humanity' (pp. 321–2).

p. 155 l. 833. *French book*: variously identified, most
plausibly as Balzac's *Physiologie du Mariage*, Meditation
xvii, BZ, xxxii. 202 f.; R. E. N. Dodge, TLS, xxxiv,
1935, 176).

p. 156 l. 868. *man's . . . cloud*. Cf. NM, p. 63: '. . . no stress
can be laid on accounts of human shadows in the clouds
. . .' The speaker of *Christmas-Eve* has a vision of Christ's
face, not in the sky, as he anticipated, but on the earth
(sect. vi–ix).

p. 156 l. 877. *Pastor . . . Dominus*: the Lord is your
shepherd (adapted from Psalms 33 : 1. The Latin is
neither from the Vulgate nor from the 'Old Italian'
version, so may be RB's translation of the AV).

p. 158 l. 913. *my articles*. Wiseman published articles on
art and literature, was a distinguished Oriental scholar,
and wrote a novel, *Fabiola, or The Church of the Cata-
combs* (1854).

p. 158 l. 915. *Albano*: the site of some famous catacombs.
   Anacreon: a poet (sixth century B.C.) who wrote
drinking-songs and love-lyrics. RB 'was wont . . . to
soothe his little boy to sleep by humming to him an ode
of Anacreon' (OL, p. 12), and EB translated a few lines
from him in 1845 (FK, i, 263).

p. 158 l. 938. *this war*: the Crimean War, which began
Mar. 1854.

p. 159 l. 947. *the Germans*: critics like Gervinus, who
published a four-volume commentary on Shakespeare
(1840–50).

p. 159 l. 951. *Slum and Cellar*. The last two novels of Dickens (*Bleak House*, 1852–3; *Hard Times*, 1854) had been largely concerned with the condition of the poor.

p. 159 l. 957. *Dublin*. Wiseman founded an RC quarterly, *The Dublin Review* (1836).

p. 160 ll. 972–3. *Sylvester . . . nec non*. Sylvester was the name of a famous Pope, Gerbert of Aquitaine (999–1003), inventor, mathematician, and scholar. Wiseman's original title (1840) was 'Bishop of Melipotamus *in partibus infidelium* (in the lands of the unbelievers, i.e. Protestants). *nec non*: and also.

p. 160 l. 978. *his mind*. Here RB later added the line: 'Long crumpled, till creased consciousness lay smooth'.

p. 160 ll. 991–2. *mistake . . . earth*: i.e. Blougram's deepest instincts are good, not bad, the 'true things' of l. 995, the valid reasons for religious belief.

p. 161 l. 1006. *sudden . . . vehemence*. Apparently he is not convinced by Blougram's arguments, but so disgusted by his verbal sophistry that it seems imperative to escape from 'words and wind' (TRB, xii. 836) into a real life of physical action. The sceptical student-hero of Clough's *The Bothie of Toper-na-Fuosich* (1848) reacts similarly against intellectualism, and goes off with an uneducated Highland girl, a Bible, and a plough to New Zealand (sect. ix).

p. 161 l. 1013. *last chapter of St. John*. This contains a rather different after-dinner talk from Blougram's: 'So when they had dined, Jesus saith to Simon Peter, . . . Feed my lambs . . . Feed my sheep . . . Feed my sheep' (John 21 : 15–17). RB seems to imply that whereas Blougram's sermon was entirely addressed to self-interest, just as his miracle was designed to feed himself (ll. 315–18), the miraculous draught of fishes (John 21: 3–13) was designed to feed others, and real Christianity is essentially altruistic. Gigadibs may also be meant to recognize himself in the previous chapter as Doubting Thomas, who will not believe without physical proof, and is told: 'Blessed are they that have not seen, and yet have believed' (John 20 : 24–9).

MEMORABILIA, p. 162

Probably written about Dec. 1851, when RB finished his essay on Shelley, and suggested by a meeting with a man in a bookshop, who happened to mention something that Shelley had said to him. RB, who had once hero-worshipped Shelley (cf. *Pauline*, ll. 151–229), stared at the man until he burst out laughing. 'I still vividly remember', said RB, 'how strangely the presence of a man who had seen and spoken with Shelley affected me' (W. G. Kingsland, BBI, 2nd Series, 1931, p. 33; D, p. 244). The eagle-feather image was perhaps suggested by Shelley's *Revolt of Islam*, ll. 221–2.

ANDREA DEL SARTO, p. 167

Probably written 1852–3. John Kenyon, EB's cousin and friend of both the Bs, had asked for a photograph of a painting in the Pitti Palace at Florence, ascribed perhaps wrongly (PR, p. 205), to Andrea del Sarto, and entitled 'The painter and his wife'. No photograph being available, RB wrote and sent the poem instead (D, p. 245). The man in the picture, with one arm round the woman's shoulders, and a sad expression on his face, seems to be pleading with her, but she looks coldly away from him. In her hand is a letter, apparently the source of their disagreement. The poem is also based on V's life of Andrea (ii. 303–25), especially the comment: . . .'had his spirit been as bold as his judgment was profound, he would doubtless have been unequalled. But a timidity of spirit and a yielding simple nature prevented him from exhibiting a burning ardour and dash that, joined to his other qualities, would have made him divine' (ii. 303); also perhaps on Alfred de Musset's play, *André de Sarto* (1833), which the Bs might have seen performed in Paris 1851, and which contains a prototype for the 'cousin' (l. 219; B. Melchiori, VP, iv, 1966, 132–6). Andrea d'Agnolo di Francesca di Luca (1486–1531) was called 'del Sarto' because his father was a tailor, and 'Il Pittore senza Errori' (the faultless painter) because of his superb technique (v. ii. 154). V's account of Andrea's wife Lucrezia is clearly not objective, since he mentions (ii. 324) having been ill treated by her when he was Andrea's pupil. By ignoring some of V's statements, e.g. that Andrea 'improved steadily until his forty-second and last year' and 'he was one of the greatest masters who have lived hitherto' (ii. 323), RB has still further distorted the historical facts (D. B. Maceachern, VP, viii, 1970, 61–4); but the resulting dm. is possibly his best.

p. 167 l. 15. *Fiesole*: a small town about three miles NE. of Florence.

p. 168 l. 25. *It . . . model.* Cf. V, ii. 312: '. . . He never painted a woman without using her as his model, and owing to this habit all the women's heads which he did are alike.'

p. 168 l. 29. *everybody's moon.* V says (ii. 309) that Andrea was 'tormented by jealousy', but RB's character has become resigned to the situation.

p. 168 l. 35. *common . . . everything.* The effects of aging, fading, restoring, or long exposure to the open air were mistaken in RB's day for characteristics of Andrea's art, although he was reported to have experimented with a wide range of colours (P. A. Cundiff, TSL, xiii, 1968, 34), and RB uses his supposed 'greyness' to symbolize his character, expressing the same quality in the verse by unusually smooth and muted rhythms and sound-effects (H, pp. 247–8).

p. 168 ll. 42–3. *convent . . . safer*. The view of the convent
becomes an image of the security that Andrea feels in
restriction (cf. ll. 168–9), and also, perhaps, of his sexual
frustration.

p. 170 l. 93. *Morello*: a mountain near Florence.

p. 170 l. 105. *Urbinate . . . ago*. Raphael (Raffaello
Sanzio, 1483–1520) was born at Urbino. The reference
dates the dm. 1525, when the historical Andrea, far from
being in an 'autumnal' phase, painted the *Madonna del
Sacco*, sometimes thought his greatest classical success
(P. A. Cundiff, op. cit., p. 34).

p. 171 l. 135. *What wife . . . Angelo?* Raphael 'was very
amorous, and fond of women', and on one occasion failed
to complete some painting until his current mistress was
brought to live in the part of the house where he was at
work (V, ii. 241). He did eventually marry, but only
reluctantly (ii. 247). Michelangelo (Michelagnolo Buonar-
roti, 1475–1564), when a friend said, 'It is a pity you
have not married, as you might have had several children',
replied: 'I have a wife too many already, namely this art,
which harries me incessantly, and my works are my
children . . .'(V, iv. 177).

p. 172 l. 145. *fear . . . lords*. In 1518 Andrea went to
France, to work at the court of François I, but a letter
from Lucrezia made him return to Florence, promising
to come back in a few months with 'valuable paintings
and sculptures', for which the King gave him money. He
spent it all on 'building and pleasures' and stayed in
Florence, much to the King's annoyance (V, ii. 313). The
truth of this story of embezzlement has been questioned
(D, pp. 247–8).

p. 172 l. 149. *Fontainebleau*: the site of a royal palace,
thirty-seven miles SE. of Paris.

p. 172 l. 154. *mouth's . . . smile*: over the smiling mouth
that signified approval of my work.

p. 172 l. 157. *You*: corrected in later editions to *I*.

p. 172 l. 159. *frank French*: possibly a subdued pun, since it was from the Franks that France received its name.

p. 172 l. 167. *golden . . . grey*. The colour symbolism (cf. ll. 213–17) may have been partly suggested by the fact that Andrea started as a goldsmith, but gave it up for painting, 'the art for which Nature had formed him' (V, ii. 304).

p. 173 l. 177. *Roman*: Raphael, who had been working in Rome since 1509.

p. 173 ll. 183–92. *Said . . . yours*. The story is from F. Bocchi's *Le Bellezze della Città di Fiorenza*, 1591, p. 232.

p. 174 l. 209. *cue-owls*: scops owls, named in Italy from the sound of their cry: '*chiu*' (pronounced *cue*).

p. 174 l. 219. *Cousin*: a Renaissance euphemism for a married woman's lover (W. F. McNeir, NQ, cci, 1956, 500).

p. 175 l. 249. *my father . . . want*. V1, p. 744 says that Andrea abandoned his old and poor parents, and adopted the father and sisters of his wife: possibly a normal consequence of marriage for one in his social class (P. A. Cundiff, op. cit., p. 29).

p. 175 l. 260. *New Jerusalem*. See Revelation 21 : 10–16.

p. 175 l. 262. *Leonard*: Leonardo da Vinci (1452–1519).

p. 175 l. 265. *as I choose*. The tragic effect of the poem springs largely from the speaker's lack of self-deception: he cannot, finally, blame anyone but himself (R. D. Altick, BMA, pp. 18–19).

BEFORE, p. 176, AFTER, p. 178

In 1846 the Bs had an argument about the ethics of duelling (K, ii. 595–609). 'Before' (spoken by a second) roughly expresses RB's original attitude. 'After' (spoken

by the injured party, after killing his opponent) expresses
EB's view, later adopted by RB.

p. 176 st. 1. *to my story*: leave him to endure the disgrace
that will follow my report of the facts.

p. 176 st. 2. *slough*: the dishonourable situation in which
their quarrel has landed them. Cf. RB, 8 Apr.: '. . . you
know very well it is a *fact* that by his refusing to accept
a challenge, or send one, on conventionally sufficient
ground, he will be infallibly excluded from a certain class
of society thenceforth and forever' (K, ii. 601).

    entoilment: entanglement, as in a snare. The un-
settled argument between culprit and victim is a con-
fusion of right with wrong, Heaven with Hell.

p. 176 st. 3. *God's . . . to*: his reverence for God is no more
sincere than his respect for the Queen, when he takes off
his cap to her in a purely conventional gesture.

p. 177 st. 6. *Let him . . . misfeasance*: Let him enjoy the
good things of life (roses, grapes) until he gradually
realizes that he is 'dogged' by a sense of guilt (a leopard,
because the opposite of 'spotless', innocent), which at
first seems quite harmless, but will one day pounce on
him and inflict the torment of self-hatred that is the final
penalty for his crime.

p. 177 st. 7. *Who's . . . man*: i.e. what about his victim,
supposing he loses the duel ?

p. 177 st. 8. *sub-intents*: secondary intentions. The quasi-
legal term appears in no legal dictionary.

p. 177 st. 9. *While . . . resisted*. Cf. RB, 8 Apr.: 'I must
confess that I can conceive of "combinations of circum-
stances" in which I see two things only . . . or a Third:
a miscreant to be put out of the world, my own arm and
best will to do it; and, perhaps, God to excuse; which is,
approve. Mr. Ba, what is Evil, in its unmistakable shape,
but a thing to suppress at any price ?' (K, ii. 604).

end . . . begin him. Stop him before he has begun to show his true nature.

p. 177 st. 10. *rising . . . fall*: increasing in moral stature by abasing himself and admitting his fault.

p. 178 l. 3. *his rights of a man*: i.e. in asserting his 'right' to avenge himself, the speaker has violated a more fundamental human right, the right to live.

IN THREE DAYS, p. 179

Perhaps written July 1852, when the Bs were separated for the longest period in their married lives (M, p. 170).

p. 180, st. 3. *early Art*: early painters, though the 'embrownment' was probably due, not to them, but to the action of time on their varnish (GT, p. 98).

IN A YEAR, p. 181

p. 184 st. 10. *Is it God?* The man's unbelievable heartlessness has shaken the woman's faith even in a God, to be met after death.

OLD PICTURES IN FLORENCE, p. 185

Probably written in Florence, spring 1853 (GM, p. 189). Although the Bs were not living in a villa overlooking Florence, the poem seems to refer to RB's discovery, 'in a corn shop a mile from Florence' of 'five pictures among heaps of trash; and one of the best judges in Florence . . . throws out such names for them as Cimabue, Ghirlandaio, Giottino, a crucifixion . . . Giottesque, if not Giotto . . .' (EB, 4 May 1850; FK, i. 448). The rollicking rhythms and outrageous rhymes help to create a tone of light-hearted, informal chatter, rather in the style of Byron's *Don Juan*. D. G. Rossetti wrote of this poem: 'What a jolly thing! . . . It seems all the pictures desired by the poet are in his possession, in fact' (8 Jan. 1856; CH, p. 184).

p. 185 st. 2. *Giotto*: Giotto di Bondone (*c.* 1267–1337). His unfinished campanile by the Duomo was called by Ruskin 'unique in the world for its combination of power and beauty' (R, viii. 187).

p. 186 st. 4. *in chief*: i.e. it was my favourite place to lean.

p. 186 st. 5. *apsis*: apse.

p. 186 st. 6. *One*: the speaker.

p. 187 st. 8. *Dellos*: painters as obscure as Dello di Niccolo Delli (*c.* 1404–71), a Florentine artist who specialized in painting furniture, but anticipated Leonardo da Vinci in making accurate drawings of muscles (V, i. 219–21; ii. 163).

p. 187 st. 9. *girns*: bares its teeth, snarls.

Stefano: Florentine painter (1301–50). Cf. V, i. 94–7: 'Stefano . . . pupil of Giotto, was so excellent that, not only did he surpass all the artists who had studied the arts before him, but he so far surpassed his master himself that he was deservedly considered the best of the painters up to that time . . . [He] began to recognize and had partially overcome the difficulties which stand in the way of the highest excellence, the mastery of which by his successors . . . has rendered their works so remarkable. For this cause the artists nicknamed him the Ape of Nature . . . as the first investigator of these difficulties he deserves a much higher place than those who follow after the path has been made plain for them.'

p. 187 st. 10. *there's its transit*: corrected in later editions to *then, sic transit* (sc. *gloria*): so passes its glory, from 'sic transit gloria mundi' (of the world; Thomas à Kempis, *Imitatio Christi*, ch. iii, sect. 6).

p. 188 st. 11. *in fructu*: by way of profit.

p. 188 st. 13. *Theseus*: legendary King of Athens, described by Virgil (*Aen*. vi. 617–18) as sitting eternally in Hades, and represented sitting (or half-reclining) on the E. pediment of the Parthenon (GR, p. 550, fig. 622).

son of Priam: Hector, whose 'nimble knees' are mentioned in *Iliad*, xxii. 204, when he is running away from Achilles. The N. and S. pediments of the Parthenon are said to have included scenes from the Trojan War.

Apollo: the god who killed the Python at Delphi, before establishing his oracle there. Pliny (NH, ix. xxxiv. 59, 70) mentions a sculpture, by Pythagoras of Rhegium, of Apollo killing the serpent, and one by Praxiteles of a boy Apollo killing a lizard, of which copies survive (GR, p. 570, figs. 673–5).

Niobe: the mother of seven sons and seven daughters, who were killed by Apollo and Artemis. She and her children are represented in a sculpture (*c*. 440 B.C.) in the Uffizi Gallery, Florence.

Racers' frieze: presumably the Procession of Horsemen (looking almost as if racing) on the Parthenon frieze (GR, p. 506, fig. 486).

Alexander: probably Alexander the Great, of whom many portraits survive. Perhaps RB had heard of the Alexander Sarcophagus (*c*. 300 B.C.; GR, p. 598, fig. 748).

p. 189 st. 14. *the worsted*: the one who has been surpassed. *race . . . plan*. Cf. 'By the Fire-side', st. 50.

p. 189 st. 17. *lump . . . leaven*. Cf. Matthew 13 : 33, Galatians 5 : 9.

p. 190 st. 17. '*O*'. When an envoy of Pope Benedict IX asked Giotto for a drawing as evidence of his powers, Giotto 'took a sheet of paper and a red pencil, pressed his arm to his side to make a compass of it, and then, with a turn of his hand, produced a circle so perfect in every particular that it was a marvel to see' (V, i. 71–2). The idea of using this circle to symbolize the relative worthlessness of perfection was probably suggested by the

saying that V goes on to quote: 'You are more *tondo*
[= *round* and also *stupid*] than Giotto's O.'

p. 190 st. 18. *And Man . . . His face*: corrected in later
editions to *Shall Man . . . Man's face*.

p. 190 st. 20. *quiddit*: quibble, play on words.

the worthies: the older Christian painters.

p. 191 st. 21. *a fancy*: the doctrine of metempsychosis
(transmigration of souls), first associated with Orphism
(sixth century B.C.) and with Pythagoras (b. about
580 B.C.).

p. 191 st. 22. *There . . . God*: Hebrews 4 : 9.

p. 191 st. 23. *Nicolo the Pisan*: Niccola Pisano (1205 ?–78),
sculptor and architect, presumably mentioned here
because V (i. 40) described his work as an original depar-
ture from Byzantine (Greek) tradition.

Cimabue: Cenni di Peppi (*c.* 1240–1302), said by V
(i. 21) to have 'shed the first light on the art of painting',
but as only one known specimen of his work survives,
V's statement cannot be confirmed. Cimabue figures in
the poem's argument as one who started a movement
towards realism, and who 'imitated the Greeks [but]
introduced many improvements in the art and . . .
emancipated himself from their stiff manner' (V, i. 22).

Ghiberti: Lorenzo Ghiberti (1378–1455), Florentine
sculptor and painter, famous for his bronze doors for the
Baptistery of Florence, considered by Michelangelo 'so
fine that they would grace the entrance of Paradise'
(V, i. 252).

Ghirlandajo: Domenico Bigordi (*c.* 1448–94), known
as Ghirlandaio because he invented head-ornaments
called garlands (*ghirlande*). His frescoes probably
attracted RB by the lifelike portraits of contemporaries
that they contained (V, ii. 68, 73).

p. 192 st. 26. *Sandro*: Alessandro di Mariano Filipepi,
called Sandro di Botticello (Botticelli, 1445–1510). His

selling of a pupil's picture for him (V, ii. 87–8) might perhaps be thought 'chivalrous', and his contrivance to smash the house of his next-door neighbour with a large stone (V, ii. 88) was certainly 'bellicose'.

Lippino: Filippino Lippi (*c.* 1457–1504), son of Fra Lippo Lippi and Lucrezia Buti, 'wronged' perhaps because he was illegitimate (see p. 318, introductory note to 'Fra Lippo Lippi'), but according to O, p. 210, because 'others were credited with some of his best work'.

Fra Angelico: see p. 33 ll. 235 f. note.

Taddeo Gaddi: Florentine painter (1300–66), 'fine' because he 'acquired so much money that, by steadily saving, he founded the wealth and nobility of his family . . . In [Florence] he did a St. Jerome dressed as a cardinal. He held that saint in reverence, choosing him as the protector of his house, and after Taddeo's death his son Agnolo made a tomb for his descendants covered with a marble slab adorned with the arms of the Gaddi under this picture' (V, i. 139–41).

intonaco (accented, like *Monaco* on the *on*): plaster for fresco painting.

Lorenzo Monaco. See p. 33 ll. 235 f. note.

p. 192 st. 27. *Pollajolo*: Antonio Pollaiuolo (*c.* 1432–98), portrayed (in black and white) in V2 (i. 465) in a close cap rather like a fez (from which the 'red' may come, if not from the 'red cap' in which Ghirlandaio portrayed Baldovinetti (V, ii. 73). He started as a goldsmith, but then learned the art of painting (V, ii. 80–1). He 'dissected many bodies to examine their anatomy, being the first to show how the muscles must be looked for to take their proper place in figures' (V, ii. 82). See reproduction of his *Battle of the Naked Men*, OA, p. 886.

Alesso Baldovinetti: Florentine painter (1427–99). 'He was most diligent, striving to imitate all the small details . . . representing the Nativity with such pains . . . that it would be possible to count the straws of the roof, and the knots in them' (V, i. 360). He made a special tempera which he hoped 'would protect his paintings from the damp, but such was its strength that in many places where it was laid on too thickly it became *scrostata* ['crumbly', peeling, flaking off], and thus he was mistaken in thinking that he had lighted upon a valuable discovery' (V, i. 359).

p. 193 st. 28. *Margheritone*: Margarito of Arezzo (*fl. c.* 1262), portrayed in V2 (i. 115) as a white-bearded, hook-nosed, sour-looking old man, wearing a turbanlike head-dress with a flap hanging down one side, and a garment resembling a night-shirt. Its transformation into a shroud was doubtless encouraged by V, i. 65: 'Margaritone died at the age of seventy-seven, *infastidito* (disgusted), it is said, that he had lived long enough to see the changes of the age and the honours accorded to the new artists. 'He was buried in the old Duomo . . . in a tomb of travertine, which has perished in our own time by the demolition of that church.'

Crucifixion. V mentions a crucifix by Margarito at Assisi, and another large one at Arezzo, where 'he made many such crucifixes' (i. 62–5).

p. 193 st. 29. *They*: the 'ghosts' of st. 24, including the painters just mentioned, who have *not* allowed RB to find any of their work.

tinglish: tingling, quivering.

Rot or are: corrected in later editions to *Their pictures are*.

Seeing . . . Who sell: corrected to *Who, seeing . . . Will sell*.

Zeno: founder (*fl. c.* 300 B.C.) of the Stoic school of philosophy, which aimed at complete freedom from emotion.

Carlino: Cesare Carlino (1843–88), a painter of scenes from family life which RB probably found sentimental.

p. 193 st. 30. *certain . . . tablet*. Cf. V, i. 79: '. . . the screen of [the Ognissanti at Florence] contained a small panel painted in tempera by Giotto, representing the Death of our Lady . . . The work has been much praised by artists, and especially by Michelangelo Buonarotti, who declared . . . that it was not possible to represent this scene in a more realistic manner. This picture . . . has been carried away . . .' It has been tentatively identified with a panel now in the Staatliches Museen, Berlin, which reappeared in Cardinal Fesch's collection some time before 1841, passed into English ownership (when RB probably heard about it), and was exhibited by the British Institute 1857 (G, plates 218–20; F. M. Perkins, RA, xiv, 1914, 193–200, 243–5).

p. 193 st. 31. *San Spirito*: a basilica at Florence, not far from the Ognissanti (All Saints).

detur amanti: let it be given to the one who loves it.

p. 194 st. 31. *Giamschid*: legendary king of Persia. His fabulous ruby is used as a simile for an eye in Byron's *The Giaour* (l. 479). *Sofi*: Sophy, the former title of the supreme ruler of Persia. *eye*: i.e. most precious possession (cf. Greek *ophthalmos*, Latin *oculus, ocellus*).

p. 194 st. 32. *certain dotard*: Count Radetzky (1766–1858), commander of the Austrian forces in Italy.

worse side: the Swiss side.

Morello. See p. 170 l. 93 note.

p. 194 st. 33. *Dante*: who, as a member of the Bianchi faction, had resisted the power of the Pope over Florence.

Witan-agemot: a meeting of wise men, the Anglo-Saxon national council.

quod videas ante: which see before, i.e. refer back to EB's *Casa Guidi Windows*, 1851 (EBP, iv. 104, for 'a parliament of lovers of . . . Italy'; iv. 108, for 'Dante's stone', a stone in the pavement on which Dante used to sit.

Loraine: the Grand Duchy of Tuscany was first

assigned to the Duke of Lorraine in 1737, and had been continuously in the possession of the Lorraine family since 1815.

Orgagna: Andrea di Cione, nicknamed Orcagna (archangel), painter, sculptor, architect, poet and administrator (*c.* 1308–68). Cf. V, i, 'In the days of the Orcagna there were many who were skilful in sculpture and architecture whose names are unknown, but their works show that they are worthy of high praise and commendation.'

p. 194 st. 34. *set . . . zero-rate*: bring truth back to life and kill off falsehood.

Monarchy . . . chimaera's. Bears were traditionally supposed to lick their cubs into shape; but monarchy produces monstrosities instead of true works of art.

p. 195 st. 35. *expurgate . . . issimo*: purified, free from rhetorical superlatives.

half-told . . . Cambuscan. Cf. Milton, 'Il Penseroso', ll. 109–10: '. . . him that left half told / The story of *Cambuscan* bold' (a reference to the unfinished Squire's Tale in Chaucer's *Canterbury Tales*).

altaltissimo: corrected in later editions to *alt to altissimo*, i.e. high to highest.

beccaccia: woodcock.

full . . . braccia. Cf. V, i. 80: 'According to Giotto's model, the campanile should have received a pointed top or quadrangular pyramid over the existing structure, 50 braccia [nearly 100 feet] in height, but . . . modern architects have always discountenanced its construction, considering the building to be better as it is.'

p. 195 st. 36. *God and the People*: the motto of Mazzini, a republican who worked for the liberation of Italy (GH, p. 343).

IN A BALCONY, p. 196

Probably written 1853 at Bagni di Lucca. The well-reviewed production of *Colombe's Birthday* (pub. 1844) at the Haymarket Theatre, London (Apr. 1853) possibly encouraged RB to use the dramatic form. The opening argument about whether to tell the Queen the truth seems to echo the Bs' disagreement (1846, e.g. K, i. 419–23) on whether RB should ask Mr. Barrett for his daughter's hand (D, pp. 252–3). P. G. Mudford (VP, vii, 1969, 39–40) suggests an association in RB's unconscious between the Queen and his 'authoritarian mother'; but it is easier to connect ll. 106–39 with EB's life in Wimpole Street, before the appearance of RB's 'warm real struggling love'. Constance (whose name seems ironically chosen) has been much disliked. F. J. Furnivall wanted to 'shake [her] well and smack her' (WP, p. 20); but E. E. Stoll finds her 'genuinely human', and thinks her improbable behaviour a fair price to pay for the 'superbly ironical *contretemps*' of ll. 340–590 (MLQ, iii, 1942, 407–17). TV (pp. 104–5) interprets the theme as the 'conflict between the wisdom of the intuitions and the usages of society'. The poem, though not written for the stage, was given a stage-production (Nov. 1884), which was described by Alfred Domett as 'a great success', though the *Saturday Review* critic decided that the work was 'a very beautiful and an exceedingly powerful poem' but 'not a play' (WP, p. 159).

p. 196 l. 2. *Put . . . throbs*. When he first met EB, RB suffered from headaches, which he said her presence dispelled (M, p. 14). Later, when he 'could not get sleep for the pain' of a sore throat, 'my wife took my head in her two little hands, in broad daylight, and I went to sleep at once, and woke better' (JW, p. 102).

p. 198, l. 62. *You . . . heaven*: you are the embodiment of destiny; this supreme moment in your life is among the great events that heaven ordains.

p. 199 l. 92. '*Faith*: by my faith (a quasi-oath).

p. 201 l. 130. *Rubens*: Sir Peter Paul Rubens (1577–1640),

Flemish artist, probably mentioned as a highly successful court painter, especially distinguished by the 'reality of' his 'creations, the vitality he could impart to the world of myth' (OA, p. 1023).

p. 203 l. 195. *compression's ecstasy*: joy made more intense by its compression into a few snatched moments.

p. 203 l. 210. *The world . . . nature*: cf. 'Respectability'.

p. 204 l. 223. *my low ground*: my humble motive for action (love).

p. 208 l. 342. *Mother*: the Virgin Mary.

p. 210 l. 400. *change*: give in exchange.

p. 211 l. 412. *baladine*: dancing girl.

p. 217 l. 585. *change . . . coin*: translate it into ordinary words.

p. 217 l. 605. *God's moon*: love, which reflects God, as the moon reflects the sun (PN, p. 260). The image, like the 'smile of God', may come from Shelley's *Adonais*, st. 54.

p. 218 ll. 609–10. *thriftier . . . way*: cf. 'In a Year', st. 6–8.

p. 220 l. 669. *dictatress*: the Muse, like Milton's 'Celestial Patroness' who 'dictates' his poetry (PL, ix. 21–3). She uses real human life as raw material for creating 'Forms more real than living man, / Nurslings of immortality' (Shelley, PU, i. 748–9).

p. 221 l. 696. *new man*. See p. 153 l. 782 note.

p. 222 l. 718. *your . . . decency*: how fitting it is that you should show your gratitude (by kissing me). Constance is trying to excuse the embrace to the Queen, and simultaneously to warn Norbert that he must stick to his untrue story that he loves the Queen.

p. 224 l. 765. *constant*: the climax of the irony implicit in Constance's name.

p. 224 l. 778. *wager*. He can only imagine that Constance's last speech was meant to settle a bet about his reactions, if given a chance to marry the Queen instead.

p. 225 l. 795. *overcharge her part*: overact.

p. 230 l. 915. *What . . . tread?* Norbert and Constance clearly assume, as do most readers, that the approaching footsteps mean the lovers' imminent arrest and execution; but RB's interpretation was different: 'The queen had a large and passionate temperament, which had only once been touched and brought into intense life. She would have died, as by a knife in her heart. The guard would have come to carry away her dead body.' He even thought it might be advisable to 'put in the stage directions, and have it seen that they were carrying her across the back of the stage' (K. de K. Bronson, CM, xii, 1902, 159; D, p. 253).

SAUL, p. 231

The first nine sections were written 1845, and published 6 Nov. in DRL. The complete poem, with sect. 10–19 added, and a revised sect. 9, was published in MW. The theme (from 1 Samuel 16 : 14–23) was probably suggested by Christopher Smart's 'Song to David' (1763), which RB had known since 1827, and reread 1845; and from Smart's preface to his 'Ode to Music on Saint Cecilia's Day', which mentioned 'David's playing to King Saul when he was troubled with the evil spirit' as 'a fine subject' for such an ode (D, pp. 254–6). The main structure of the poem, and certain ideas and images may come from Sir Thomas Wyatt's 'Penitential Psalms' (1536 ?, 1541 ?; J. A. S. McPeek, JEGP, xliv, 1945, 360–6). By helping him to sort out his religious ideas, EB may have helped RB to finish the poem (D, pp. 256–7); but the argument for a future life (sect. 15–18) was possibly suggested by a letter of Wordsworth's, published 1851

(M. M. Bevington, VN, No. 28, 1961, 19–21). When asked in 1885 for 'Four Poems, of moderate length, which represent their writer fairly', RB chose 'Saul' as one of two specimens of lyric (T, p. 235).

p. 231 st. 1. *Abner*: 'the captain of [Saul's] host' (1 Samuel 26 : 5).

p. 232 st. 2. *blue*. RB: 'Lilies are of all colours in Palestine . . . the water lily, lotos, which I think I meant, is *blue* altogether' (16 Mar. 1846, K, i. 539; PR, p. 50).

p. 233 st. 4. *He . . . hung there*: a hint of crucifixion that serves to prepare for the prophecy of Christ (sect. 18).
his change: i.e. when he sloughs his skin.

p. 234 st. 6. *jerboa*: a rat-size rodent with long back legs and a talent for jumping.

p. 234 st. 7. *balm-seeds*: grains of comfort, i.e. the fact that death makes us forget his faults.

p. 235 st. 7. *an arch*: apparently a battle-formation like the Roman *testudo* (tortoise) in which besieging troops clustered together with their shields held over their heads.

p. 235 st. 8. *male*: used of precious stones to indicate depth, brilliance, or other special quality of colour. The metaphor is repeated in 'rubies courageous at heart', where deep red (fire, blood) is identified with a 'male' virtue, thus easing the transition to 'manhood's prime vigour'.

p. 236 st. 9. *I have . . . best*: cf. Psalms 37 : 25.

p. 237 st. 9. *throe . . . gold go*: the earthquake that splits the rock, helping it to give birth to the gold inside it.

pp. 238–9 st. 10. *too vacant . . . enter*: not yet able to register what they see, and file away each visual impression in the appropriate compartment of consciousness.

p. 243 st. 13. *paper-reeds*: papyrus, from which the ancient Egyptians, Greeks, and Romans made a writing-material.

prophet-winds: prophetic, apparently because it makes one reed pass the movement on to another, just as one written account of Saul's deeds will pass the story on to the next.

p. 244 st. 14. *Hebron*: a mountain SW. of Jerusalem.

Kidron: a valley or gorge E. of Jerusalem, called in John 18 : 1 'the brook Cedron'. It is dry in summer, and often in winter also (GH, p. 344).

retrieves . . . sunshine: gradually recovers from the dew the water lost by evaporation during the heat of the previous day.

p. 244 st. 15. *He is . . . communion*: he is again the glorious Saul that you remember from the days before his psychological trouble made him avoid ordinary human intercourse.

p. 247 st. 17. *Do I task . . . success*: if I strain any faculty to its utmost capacity in the effort to imagine an ideal.

one faculty: love.

hoodwink: i.e. to keep quiet, as hawks were kept quiet by hooding them.

p. 249 st. 18. *and why . . . loth*: changed in later editions to *Why am I not loth?* But the original text makes good sense, and perhaps better suggests the oscillating process of David's thought; the later text implies that he has already overcome his reluctance to contemplate his own 'impuissance'; the original, that he suddenly realizes that reluctance is unnecessary.

p. 250 st. 18. *to stand in*: i.e. to claim superiority in love. Cf. Romans 8 : 38–9.

It is . . . death: mankind is saved from death, not by a simple act of divine power, but by God's sufferings, in the weakness of human flesh. Thus David's willingness to give Saul eternal life, and to suffer for him, becomes evidence in advance for the Incarnation.

p. 250 st. 19. *witnesses*: cf. Hebrews 12 : 1.
repressed: pushed them aside.

p. 251 st. 19. *stars . . . knowledge*. He 'projects' on to his physical environment his own sense of excitement and impatience to reveal the newly learned secret.
sidling: glancing sideways.

'DE GUSTIBUS—', p. 252

'De gustibus non disputandum' (Latin proverb: There is no arguing about tastes). RB first went to Italy in 1838, and before he met EB '. . . I shall only say I was scheming how to get done . . . and go to my heart in Italy' (16 Nov. 1845, K, i. 271; W, ii. 304).

p. 253 st. 2. *the king*: Ferdinand II of Naples (see p. 151 l. 715 note), who came from the Spanish branch of the Bourbon family (GH, p. 344). Several attempts were made to kill him, and there had been an attempted rebellion against him in 1843, just before RB visited Naples (HM, p. 199).
liver-wing: the right wing of a fowl, which, when prepared for cooking, has the liver tucked under it (OED).
Queen . . . saying: 'when I am dead and opened, you shall find Calais lying in my heart' (HC, iv. 137; HM, p. 199). She died the year that Calais was captured by the French (1558).

WOMEN AND ROSES, p. 254

Said to have been written in Paris, 2 Jan. 1852 (GM, p. 189), but the exact date is uncertain (J. Huebenthal, VP, iv, 1966, 51–4). RB mentioned it as a product of a New Year resolution to write a poem every day: 'Well, the first day I wrote about some roses, suggested by a magnificent basket that some one had sent my wife'

(LW, p. 261; D, p. 229). It has been variously interpreted, as expressing RB's 'baffled desire to escape out of time (or history) into passion' (D. V. Erdman, PQ, xxxvi, 1957, 426); his 'desire to identify himself mystically with woman herself, the *ewigweiblich*' (HD, p. 79) even, through the 'bee-honey-gold' cluster of images, 'the pleasure of the sexual act itself' (PR, pp. 50–1). The rose symbol for love is at least as old as the thirteenth-century *Le Roman de la Rose*. RB's version presents three roses, symbolizing love for women of the past (in art and literature), of the present, and of the future. The quasi-refrain ('In vain . . . But no . . . Alas! . . .) seems to imply that for RB all three forms of love, including that for real live women, are equally frustrating.

p. 254 st. 3. *unimpeached*: without getting entangled, like the bee in sect. 6. The primary meaning of *impeach* is derived from Latin *impedicare* (fetter, entangle).

p. 255 st. 6. *where . . . slips*: a delicate circumlocution apparently suggested by the Homeric phrase for love-making: 'loosening a maiden's girdle' (e.g. *Odyssey*, xi. 245).

p. 256 st. 8. *Wings . . . clear*: i.e. 'viewless wings of Poesy' (Keats) for a flight into the abstract, but vivid regions of the imagination.

PROTUS, p. 257

Probably written during or soon after the Bs' stay in Rome, Dec. 1853–May 1854 (D, pp. 259–60). No historical Protus is known, but the name was clearly chosen as the Greek equivalent of the Latin *Princeps* (first man), the title adopted by Augustus and later Roman emperors. The poem is an ironical comment on the rapidity and violence with which Roman Emperors succeeded one another, as in Gibbon's equally ironical *Decline and Fall of the Roman Empire* (1776–88).

p. 257 l. 2. *Half-emperors and quarter-emperors*. There were two emperors 285–93, and four (Diocletian, Maximian, Constantius, and Galerius) 293–305. After 395 the Empire was never again ruled for any significant length of time by a single emperor.

p. 257 l. 4. *Loric*: leather cuirass worn by Roman soldiers.

Gorgon: the *Gorgoneion*, or Gorgon's head worn as a protective emblem on armour (owing to popular belief in the Gorgon's petrifying powers). The brow is 'low' because partly concealed by snake-hair.

p. 257 l. 9. *a god*: Augustus, deified on his death (A.D. 14).

p. 257 l. 10. *Byzant*: Byzantium, which became the seat of the Empire in A.D. 330, and was renamed Constantinople (now Istanbul).

p. 258 l. 23. *so . . . reconciled*: i.e. he was so beautiful that classical Greek sculpture no longer seemed absurdly idealized (cf. 'Old Pictures in Florence', st. 12).

p. 258 l. 36. *Pannonian*: from a Roman province between the Danube and the Alps. The irony is that this Emperor, like Augustulus, the last Emperor of the West, belongs to a semi-barbarous race which in the early days of the Empire revolted against Rome and was with difficulty subdued (A.D. 7–9).

p. 258 ll. 49–50. *hunting-stables . . . dogs*. Pannonia was famous for its breed of hunting-dogs, so perhaps that is where Protus found refuge (D, p. 260).

p. 259 l. 55. *Here's John*: possibly suggested by the Emperor John the Handsome, so called ironically because of his 'swarthy complexion and harsh features' (EG, ix. 86).

HOLY-CROSS DAY, p. 260

Probably written 1854, in Rome or Florence (D, p. 261). Holy-Cross Day (14 Sept.) commemorates the alleged

appearance to Constantine of the Cross in the sky at mid-
day. A papal bull of 1584 compelled Jews to hear sermons
in the church of S. Angelo in Pescheria. RB probably
never attended one of these services, but doubtless heard
of them when in Rome, or read of them in his friend G. S.
Hillard's *Six Months in Italy* (1853, ii. 51), or in John
Evelyn's diary for 7 Jan. 1645 (JE, i. 203; D, pp. 260–1),
which perhaps suggested the 'Diary by the Bishop's
Secretary'. Although RB was sympathetically interested
in Jews, and (wrongly) believed to be of Jewish descent
(OL, p. 1), the poem may express not so much pro-
Semitism as Protestant anti-Catholicism (MI, p. 40).

p. 260 *epigraph* ll. 3–5. *crumb . . . dogs.* Cf. Matthew 15:
22–7, where the 'table' is meant for the Jews, and the
'dogs' are the non-Jews. The Biblical quotations used by
the Bishop's secretary are often taken from contexts
which actually teach the supremacy and final triumph of
the Jewish race (MI, p. 22).

p. 260 *epigraph* l. 8. *'Compel . . . in'*: from Luke 14 : 23.

p. 260 *epigraph* ll. 13–14. *though . . . glory.* Cf. 1 Corin-
thians 10 : 31: 'whatsoever ye do, do all to the glory of
God'; but there seems to be a further ironical allusion to
the previous chapter, verses 16–20: 'For though I preach
the gospel, I have nothing to glory of . . . And unto the
Jews I become as a Jew, that I might gain the Jews'
(MI, p. 27).

p. 260 st. 1. *Fee, faw, fum!* See p. 14, st. 19 note. One ver-
sion of the giant's speech ends: 'I smell the blood of
a Christian man' (MI, p. 29).

Blessedest Thursday: perhaps aimed at Christian glut-
tony on *giovedì grasso* (fat Thursday), the last Thursday
before Lent.

smug and gruff: smart and unkempt.

p. 261 st. 2. *shaving-shears*. To be shaved was evidence
of conversion (W, ii. 305).

p. 261 st. 3. *settle your thumbs*: get ready to bite your thumbs at him (an insulting gesture, cf. *Romeo and Juliet*, I. i).

Buzz: i.e. say 'Buzz!', an exclamation of impatience or contempt at a well-known story (cf. *Hamlet*, II. ii. 418).

p. 262 st. 6. *cog . . . cozen*: cheat . . . deceive.

p. 262 st. 7. *from . . . Turk*: i.e. Christians will still hate you, but not quite so much.

   hanging. See p. 36 l. 307 note.

p. 262 st. 8. *Whom . . . serenades*. The Bishop has evidently been preaching against fornication. The speaker, a money-lender (in the Christian view 'the worst of trades'), has been lending him money, which he spends on his love-affairs.

p. 262 st. 9. *spurred . . . Corso*. RB may have heard reports that Jews had been substituted for horses in the Corsa dei Berberi, or race of Barbary horses, spurred but riderless, along the main street of Rome (MI, p. 33).

p. 263 st. 12. *Ben Ezra*: Abraham Ibn Ezra (1092–1167), a Jewish scholar who wrote commentaries on the Old Testament. Much of his work is in the Vatican library, where RB might theoretically have read the 'Song of Death'; but there is no evidence that such a poem ever existed. RB probably invented it, using Ben Ezra as a mouthpiece for his own thoughts, as in his later 'Rabbi Ben Ezra' (1864; MI, p. 20).

p. 263 st. 13. *The Lord . . . saith*: Isaiah 14 : 1 (MI, p. 35).

p. 264 st. 15. *God spoke . . . cockcrow*: almost a paraphrase of Mark 13 : 32–7 (MI, p. 36).

p. 265 st. 18. *Barabbas*: the murderer whom the Jews asked Pilate to release in preference to Jesus (Mark 15 : 6–14).

p. 265 st. 20. *Thy face . . . in it*: however much the character of Christ was obscured by the wickedness of so-called Christians, the Jews never ceased to resist them.

Pleasant Land: cf. Jeremiah 3 : 18–19.

p. 265 *postscript. The Present Pope*: corrected in later editions to *Pope Gregory XVI*. He abolished it in 1846 (D, p. 260).

THE GUARDIAN-ANGEL, p. 266

Written at Ancona, July 1848, the only poem RB is known to have written during the first three years of his marriage (M, p. 145). The Bs had just spent three days at Fano, further up the Adriatic coast. There, in the church of San Agostino, they found *L'Angelo Custode* of Gian-Francesco Barbieri (1591–1666, called Guercino because of his squint), 'a divine picture . . . worth going all that way to see' (EB, 24 Aug. 1848, FK, i. 380). RB went to look at it three days running, but admitted in 1883, when sent a print of it: 'I probably saw the original picture in a favourable *darkness*; it was blackened by taper smoke, and one fancied the angel all but surrounded with cloud—only a light on the face' (T, p. 213; D, pp. 261–3). Possibly it reminded him of another *Child with his Guardian Angel*, not by Guercino, which he had seen with Alfred Domett in his childhood at Dulwich Gallery (No. 312, 1926 Catalogue) (F. Davies, TLS, xxxii, 1933, 692). Domett (1811–87), the original of 'Waring' (1842), had gone to New Zealand, where he became Prime Minister (1862). Guercino's angel stands with wings outspread over a child half-kneeling on a tomb, his left arm round the child's shoulders, and his right hand on the child's left forearm, as if showing him how to raise his hands in prayer. Both child and angel (whose face is turned away from the child) are looking upwards. On a cloud above them are three cherubs.

p. 267 st. 3. *Bird of God*: from Dante, *Purgatorio*, ii. 38; iv. 29.

p. 267 st. 4. *healing . . . supprest.* See p. 196 l. 2 note.

p. 267 st. 6. *Guercino . . . angel.* If RB refers to another angel that he saw with Domett, the stress is on *this*; but perhaps it is on *Guercino*, and the reference is to other pictures by Guercino that the friends had seen at Dulwich.

p. 268 st. 7. *my angel*: EB.

p. 268 st. 8. *endured some wrong.* Cf. EB to Mrs. Jameson, 2 Apr. 1850: 'We both cry aloud at what you say of Guercino's angels, and never would have said if you had been to Fano and seen his divine picture . . . which affects me every time I think of it' (FK, i. 441).

Wairoa: a river in New Zealand.

CLEON, p. 269

Probably written 1854 (D, p. 263), and possibly suggested by Matthew Arnold's *Empedocles on Etna* (1852), omitted from *Poems* (1853), and reprinted at RB's request (1867; A. W. Crawford, JEGP, xxvi, 1927, 485–90). Empedocles, like Cleon, is a despairing Greek intellectual, but unlike him, he has no chance of a Christian solution to his problems. 'Cleon' is an attempt to reconstruct a contemporary view of early Christianity (see p. 324 introductory note to 'An Epistle'), with implicit reference to the religious difficulties of Victorian intellectuals. It may be meant to show that even a pagan philosopher is driven by the human condition towards a kind of spirituality akin to Christianity (Y. G. Lee, VP, vii, 1969, 57). It possibly hints at the inadequacy of Positivism, the 'Religion of Humanity' of A. Comte (1798–1857), which regarded humanity itself as the only Supreme Being, and rejected the idea of a conscious after-life (E. C. McAleer, CL, viii, 1956, 142–5). But the poem can be read without special reference to religion or philosophy, simply as a psychological study of intellectual arrogance and blindness (H, p. 134).

p. 269 *epigraph*. '*As . . . said*': from Acts 17 : 28, where
St. Paul, preaching at Athens, quotes the Greek poet
Aratus (born *c.* 315 B.C.): 'For we are also his offspring'
(*Phainomena*, l. 5). The epigraph serves to prepare for
Cleon's quasi-Christian speculations, and to imply that
he, like the Athenians, 'ignorantly worships an unknown
God' whom St. Paul, contemptuously dismissed in
ll. 340–5, could in fact 'declare' (make known) to him
(Acts 17 : 23).

p. 269 l. 1. *Cleon*. No historical figure of this name
(etymologically connected with *fame, glory*) has a charac-
ter relevant to the poem ; but the letter-writer's versatility
may have been suggested by the fact that Lemprière's
Classical Dictionary (first published 1788) lists Cleons of
many professions, including a general, a sculptor, an
orator, a commentator, and a tyrant.

p. 269 l. 2. *lily*: an emblem of whiteness and beauty,
appropriate to the metaphor of 'the sprinkled isles' (the
Sporades, from *speiro* = scatter seed, the Greek islands
off the W. coast of Asia Minor, now Turkey).

p. 269 l. 4. *Protos*: the Greek spelling of Protus (see
p. 367, introductory note to 'Protus').

p. 269 l. 10. *royal*: i.e. *porphureos*, the colour traditionally
worn by kings, purple or, as here, crimson.

p. 269 l. 16. *sea-wools*: wools dyed with sea-purple (Greek
haliporphuros, from the murex).

p. 270 l. 26. *thy tower*: suggestive of the Tower of Babel
(Genesis 11), and hinting at one theme of the poem, the
failure of purely human efforts to reach heaven.

p. 270 ll. 41–2. *Zeus . . . calm*. Even Zeus has his worries
in Homer, but the gods are generally considered 'free
from care' (*Iliad*, xxiv. 526), a point stressed by the
Epicurean Lucretius (*c.* 99–55 B.C.; DRN, v. 82).

p. 270 l. 43. *requirement*: inquiry.

p. 271 l. 51. *phare*: lighthouse.

p. 271 l. 53. *Poecile*: the *Stoa Poikile* (painted colonnade) at Athens, adorned with frescoes by famous artists, including Polygnotus (*c.* 475–445 B.C.).

p. 271 l. 60. *moods*: modes (Dorian, Phrygian, Lydian, etc.), types of scale in ancient Greek music, differing according to the order of succession of intervals.

p. 271 ll. 76–8. *Intended . . . all*: cf. 'By the Fire-side', st. 50.

p. 272 ll. 99–111. *It takes . . . properties*: the simpler minds of the ancients, like water, could reach the outer limits of human power only at one point at a time; the complex modern mind can reach them at a much greater number of points simultaneously, thus approaching the condition of air. But, like air, it is invisible, and so 'misknown'.

p. 273 l. 115. *the fiction*. The idea of a divine revelation is first suggested as a method of demonstrating the aggregate value of humanity, and assessing the relative contribution of each individual; then as a means of showing the omnipresence of Zeus in human life, by revealing what work was done with 'ease', i.e. divine inspiration. The 'fiction' resembles the Christian Incarnation, in that a god is to 'descend' in order to show the true perfection of humanity; but the idea of a god *becoming* a man is not envisaged.

p. 273 l. 140. *Terpander*: musician of Lesbos (*fl.* seventh century B.C.), said to have invented the seven-string lyre.

p. 273 l. 141. *Phidias*: Athenian sculptor and painter (died 432 B.C.). His only famous 'friend' was the statesman Pericles (*c.* 500–429 B.C.), who employed him in his plan for embellishing Athens (perhaps on the sculptures of the Parthenon) but was not himself an artist. The context seems to imply that the 'friend' was a painter, but the only possible candidate is Polygnotus, and he was about twenty-five years older than Phidias. The reference is probably to Pericles, here regarded as a sculptor and painter by proxy.

p. 274 ll. 148–9. *pricked . . . wine*: varied its sweetness with the piquant flavour of wine (W, ii. 312).

p. 276 ll. 231–2. *pleasure-house . . . soul*. For the development of the Babel-Tower image, cf. FB, iii. 294, where wrong conceptions of the 'last or furthest end of knowledge' include 'a terrace, for a wandering and variable mind to walk up and down with a fair prospect', 'a tower of state', and 'a fort'; and the right one is 'a rich store-house, for the glory of the Creator and the relief of man's estate.' If the echo of Bacon's images was deliberate, it would imply that Cleon's attitude to knowledge is insufficiently religious and humanitarian.

p. 279 l. 304. *Sappho*: poetess of Lesbos (probably mid-seventh century B.C.), who wrote nine books of odes, epithalamia, elegies, and hymns.

p. 279 l. 305. *Aeschylus*: Athenian tragic poet (525–456 B.C.).

p. 279 l. 324. *I . . . imagine*: Cleon's second quasi-Christian 'fiction'.

p. 280 ll. 332–3. *as the worm . . . wings*. The image is adapted from Dante, *Purgatorio*, x. 124–9 (C. B. Beall, MLN, lxxi, 1956, 492–3).

p. 280 l. 341. *one with him*: i.e. the same person.

THE TWINS, p. 281

Written in Rome soon after 4 Mar. 1854 (LH, p. 203) and published Apr. or May, with EB's poem, 'A Plea for the Ragged Schools of London', in a sixpenny pamphlet for sale at a bazaar organized by EB's sister Arabel, in aid of a 'Refuge for young destitute girls' which she was establishing. The story is older than Luther (1483–1546),

but RB evidently read it in Luther's *Table-Talk*, tr.
W. Hazlitt, 1848, p. 151 (D, pp. 265–6). Later (p. 246)
Luther says that angels perform 'offices and works that
one poor miserable mendicant' (the word used before for
the beggar) 'would be ashamed to do for another'. 'Date'
and 'Dabitur' are from the Vulgate, Luke 6 : 38: 'Date,
et dabitur vobis' (give, and it shall be given to you).

POPULARITY, p. 283

Probably written shortly after the publication of JK
(1848), which contained a sonnet (i. 254) sent to Keats
by a reader of *Endymion*, with a £25 note. It begins 'Star
of high promise! Not to this dark age / Do thy mild light
and loveliness belong . . . / Yet thy clear beam shall shine
through ages strong, / To ripest times a light and heritage';
and ends: 'And there is one whose hand will never scant /
From his poor store of fruit, all thou canst want' (R. D.
Altick, VP, i. 1963, 65–6). So the 'true poet' is probably
Keats (who was far from popular until after 1848, and
whom RB was the first major Victorian poet to ap-
preciate), used as a prime example of an unrecognized
poetic genius; but R. D. Altick (op. cit.) sees him as a
projection of RB himself, and W (ii. 313) and PD
(pp. 85–6) as Alfred Domett.

p. 284 st. 4. *That day . . . now*: adapted from John 2 : 9–10.
The context (the miracle of the water turned into wine)
supports the notion that the poet's work is of divine
origin.

p. 284 st. 6. *Tyrian shells*. The shellfish murex and purpura
secrete a colourless liquid which turns purple on exposure
to the atmosphere, and was used by the ancients as a dye,
produced especially at Tyre (see p. 269 ll. 10 and 16
notes).

    blue: substituted for *purple*, perhaps for reasons of
rhythm, perhaps because of Keats's sonnet to blue eyes,
beginning: 'Blue! 'Tis the life of heaven . . .' (D, p. 267).

Astarte: Ashtaroth or Ishtar, the Eastern equivalent of the Greek goddess Aphrodite.

p. 285 st. 9. *cedar-house*. See 1 Kings 7 : 2–3. The 'blue hangings' seem to come from the palace of Ahasuerus (Esther 1: 6; HM, p. 199).

Spouse: Pharaoh's daughter, whom Solomon married, and for whom he made another cedar-house (1 Kings 7: 8).

p. 285 st. 10. *groom*: bridegroom. For the imagery, see p. 367, introductory note to 'Women and Roses'.

p. 285 st. 11. *not fit . . . woof*: not yet processed for application to textiles.

proof: a special standard of strength or purity.

p. 285 st. 12. *Hobbs . . . Nokes*: poets who make a commercial success by imitating a type of poetry which the 'true poet' worked and suffered to create; possibly poets of the 'Spasmodic' school, such as A. Smith, P. J. Bailey, S. Dobell, and J. S. Biggs, who imitated Keats's imagery, and were said by critics to produce 'colour without form', but were remarkably successful. If so, the poem would have been written after Apr. 1853, when Smith's *A Life Drama* came out (J. Thale, JEGP, liv, 1955, 348–54). Reviewers of MW classed RB himself as a 'Spasmodic' (C. C. Watkins, JEGP, lvii, 1958, 57–9).

p. 285 st. 13. *What . . . Keats?* The inventor of this new line in poetry made no money out of it.

The Heretic's Tragedy, p. 286

Probably written while the Bs were in Paris (Oct. 1851 to July 1852; D, p. 268). This satire on medieval religion (and perhaps indirectly on Roman Catholicism) may owe its title to Tourneur's *The Atheist's Tragedy* (1611), but takes the form of an interlude: a dramatic piece, usually comic, introduced between the acts of a long mystery or morality play.

p. 286 *epigraph* l. 1. *Rosa . . . floribus*: The Rose of the World; or, Lay me on a Bed of Flowers.

p. 286 *epigraph* l. 3. *Cantuque, Virgilius*: and in song a Virgil, i.e. a great poet.

p. 286 *epigraph* ll. 4–5. *Gavisus eram, Jessides*: I had rejoiced, The son of Jesse (David, once believed to be the author of the Psalms). The scribe evidently intends to quote Psalms 122: 1 : 'I was glad when they said unto me, Let us go into the house of the Lord', but the Latin words come neither from the Vulgate, nor from the 'Old Italian' Latin version of the Bible, and the tense of the verb is wrong anyhow. Perhaps RB meant to suggest the canon's ignorance, not only of Christian feeling, but also of the Bible and Latin grammar.

p. 286 *epigraph* l. 6. *Jacques du Bourg-Molay*: the last Grand Master of the Knights Templar, an order founded about 1118, to safeguard pilgrims to Jerusalem, and to defend the Holy Lands against the Saracens. They became so rich and powerful that the Pope and, in France Philippe IV decided to suppress them. They were accused of blasphemy, sorcery, and various other crimes, many of which were confessed under torture ; and Jacques (mis-named 'John' in the poem, a 'distortion' of Flemish brains) was burnt alive, although he retracted his con-fession of simony at the stake.

p. 286 st. 1. *St. Paul*: another 'distortion'. The quotation is from James 1 : 17.

plagal-cadence: also known as Church Cadence and Amen Cadence (the chord of the Subdominant followed by that of the Tonic).

p. 287 st. 2. *Temple*. The Templars took their name from occupying a building on or near the site of Solomon's Temple at Jerusalem.

What . . . Saladin: a vague reference to the alleged 'simony'. Aldabrod seems never to have existed, and

Sultan Saladin (1137–93) died before Jacques was born (*c.* 1243).

and . . . grace: if you do not have the extra attraction.

clavicithern: an early keyboard instrument, like an upright spinet.

p. 287 st. 4. *bavins*: bundles of brushwood.

p. 288 st. 4. *Laudes*: praises.

Laus Deo: praise (be) to God.

p. 288 st. 6. *Salva reverentia*: (if I may say so) without violating reverence.

the mocker: an allusion to Mark 15 : 29–31, and to one charge against the Templars, that they spat and trampled on crucifixes.

p. 289 st. 7. *Sharon's Rose*: Song of Solomon, 2 : 1.

p. 289 st. 8. *When Paul . . . trembled*: Acts 24 : 25.

Two in the Campagna, p. 291

Probably written May 1854, when the Bs were in Rome, and spent 'some exquisite hours on the Campagna' (the plain surrounding Rome, dotted with the ruins of ancient Latian cities; FK, ii. 165, D, p. 269). The poem has been called 'purely dramatic' (OL, p. 199), and also considered autobiographical, expressing alienation from EB, through loss of faith in her judgement about Napoleon III, spiritualism, bringing up their son, etc. (M, pp. 182–3). It is best regarded as a dm. suggested by, but not necessarily describing, a mood experienced by RB.

p. 291 st. 2. *I touched . . . go*. The poet-speaker's difficulty in identifying and expressing an elusive thought is conveyed through the image of a floating gossamer-thread. Each point on the thread's route (tomb, weed, grassy slope) represents an element in the thought.

p. 291 st. 3. *fennel . . . ruin*. The ideas hinted at seem to be death, decay, disillusion (cf. *Hamlet*, i. ii. 133–7: 'How weary, stale, flat and unprofitable / Seem to me all the uses of this world! . . . 'tis an unweeded garden, / That grows to seed; things rank and gross in nature Possess it merely').

p. 292 st. 4. *one small . . . honey-meal*: perhaps hinting at blind instinctive behaviour, and the minuteness of individuals in comparison with the world at large.

p. 292 sts. 5–7. *champaign . . . love*: though something important has died, life is a vast natural process, supervised by Providence, in which the individual has no say. Loving and ceasing to love are beyond the individual's control, so one need not be ashamed to confess that one has partly fallen out of love. The rest of the poem completes this confession.

p. 292 st. 8. *Nor yours, nor mine.* Although the subject was *you* in the line above, it now seems to be *I*. The speaker feels neither entirely his own master (mine, free) nor totally possessed and dominated (yours, slave).

p. 293 st. 9. *I would . . . eyes.* See p. 317. introductory note to 'A Woman's Last Word'.

A GRAMMARIAN'S FUNERAL, p. 294

Perhaps written 1854 at Florence (D, p. 270). The physical setting resembles Bertinoro, between Ravenna and Rimini, on a route that the Bs travelled Aug. 1848 (MG, p. 127; GM, p. 165). The Grammarian is probably a generalized type, but has been identified as I. Casaubon (1559–1614; G. Reese, NQ, cxcii, 1947, 470–2); T. Linacre (1460 ?–1524; 'B.R.', NQ, cxciv, 1949, 284); D. Erasmus (1466–1536; M. Praz, TLS, lvi, 1957, 739).

R. L. Kelly (VP, v, 1967, 105–12) considers the poem a dm. showing a 'discrepancy between the students' extravagant pretensions to nobility and their self-revealed vulgarity'; but most critics assume that the Grammarian himself is the centre of interest, either as a serious embodiment of RB's 'philosophy of the imperfect' (D, p. 271), or as an object of satire (R. D. Altick, SEL, iii, 1963, 449–60). The most accurate account of the poem is that of C. C. Clarke (MLQ, xxiii, 1962, 324), who sees the Grammarian as 'a kind of simpleton' whose 'monomania is *both noble and absurd* . . . we are not . . . allowed to make a conventional distinction between the ludicrous and the sublime. And the verse technique is appropriate to the theme.' The ambiguity is inseparable from the subject, since minute linguistic research, ridiculous as an end in itself, was a necessary means to the immense intellectual revolution of the Renaissance.

p. 294 l. 12. *chafes*: grows warm and impatient. Thought requires concentration, when it is enclosed in the brain, like incense in a censer; but as it takes fire, it must break out (be expressed) in words which permeate the intellectual atmosphere.

p. 295 l. 22. *Wait . . . warning*: are you ready for the starting-signal?

p. 295 l. 34. *lyric*: i.e. god of the lyre (and symbol of 'lyrical' beauty).

p. 296 l. 55. *life*: i.e. serious adult life, since he has tasted plenty of pleasurable life already ('dance', 'play'; M. J. Svaglic, VP, v, 1967, 99).

p. 297 ll. 86–8. *Calculus . . . Tussis*. The use of Latin names for his ailments (stone, cough) is appropriate to a classicist, and to the language of medicine at that period; but *tussis* has a special relevance to a grammarian, since it is an irregular noun, one of the very few ending *-is* which take *-im* in the accusative singular (J. M. Ariail, PMLA, xlviii, 1933, 954–6).

p. 297 l. 95. *hydroptic*: with an insatiable thirst, a symptom of dropsy.

p. 297 l. 103. *period*: used in the sense of Greek *periodos*, a going round in a circle. A 'circle premature' is one

drawn entirely on earth, i.e. expecting a 'quick return'
for one's efforts in this life. It is better to start drawing
a larger circle, which cannot be completed before death.
The 'heavenly period' is the arc of this larger circle which
has to be drawn in heaven, after death.

p. 298 l. 122. *Let . . . mind him*: let this world look after
him.

p. 298 l. 132. *He settled . . . down. Hoti* is Greek for 'that',
'because'; *Oun* for 'therefore'; the enclitic *De* (δε,
which throws its accent on to the previous word, and
forms a suffix of it) can emphasize a demonstrative, or
indicate motion towards. The surface meaning is that the
dying Grammarian kept working at small points of Greek
grammar. Cf. RB to Tennyson, 2 July 1863: 'There are
Tritons among minnows, even—and so I wanted the
grammarian "dead from the waist down"—(or "feeling
middling", as you said last night)—to spend his last
breath on the biggest of the littlenesses: such an one is
the *"enclitic* δε" . . . just because it may be confounded
with δὲ, *"but"*, which keeps its accent.' After giving
examples of the demonstrative and the motion-towards
uses, he continues: 'See Buttmann on these points. It
was just this pin-point of a puzzle that gave "δε" its
worth rather than the heaps of obvious rhymes to *"be"*
. . . to which I beg you to add, in a guffaw, "he-he-he"!
Only, you *would* have it' (C. Ricks, TLS, lxiv, 1965, 464;
M. J. Svaglic, VP, v, 1967, 103–4). This gives little sup-
port to the idea (G. Monteiro, VP, iii, 1965, 268, and
Svaglic, op. cit.) that the Greek words mentioned in the
poem have symbolic meaning (e.g. motion-towards
heaven). RB's inclusion of 'towards hell' and 'towards
heaven' among his examples in the letter proves only
that he was copying P. Buttmann's (larger) *Greek Gram-
mar*, tr. E. Robinson, 1833, p. 313).

p. 298 l. 136. *swallows and curlews*: 'obviously migrating'

(R. L. Kelly, op. cit., p. 109). If so, they hint that
the Grammarian, too, is taking off for a better place.
Cf. Virgil's comparison of the dead to migrating birds
(*Aen.* vi. 309–12).

ONE WAY OF LOVE, p. 299; ANOTHER WAY OF
LOVE, p. 300

These contrasting poems, like 'Women and Roses', use
traditional imagery, but end on a realistic rather than
traditional note.

p. 299 st. 1. *leaves*: petals.

p. 300 st. 1. *June*: a word which seems to have three
meanings in the poem, first the prime of the woman-
speaker's life, then her beauty, then virtually her name.
 ears . . . discloses: i.e. actions speak louder than words.

p. 300 st. 2. *indoors with you!*: i.e. get out of my rose-
garden, leave me alone.

p. 301 st. 2. *clear scores*: settle accounts, i.e. is my beauty
enough to satisfy you ?
 Eadem semper: eadem sunt omnia semper (everything
is always the same), from Lucretius, DRN, iii. 945, where
Nature tells a man that she can invent nothing more to
please him, so he might as well die.
 mends: improves, i.e. becomes even more beautiful.
 your hand . . . unsightly: having scratched you (perhaps
a threat to withdraw into 'a hard bitter frigidity' HD,
pp. 107–8).

p. 301 st. 3. *man and . . . spider*: a savage hendiadys for
the man-spider with whom she is at present involved.
 consider: i.e. whether to take a new lover, or do some-
thing violent to the old one.

TRANSCENDENTALISM, p. 302

Conceivably suggested by Wordsworth's *Prelude* (1850),
a poem in fourteen books which contains some rather

prosaic philosophizing (PD, p. 44). If so, ll. 48–51 might refer to the passage beginning: 'There was a Boy . . .', first published 1800, incorporated in *Prelude* (1805) v. 389 f.; but R. D. Altick (JEGP, lviii, 1959, 24–8) thinks the poem expresses RB's criticisms of his own work before 1850. The 'entirely unintelligible' *Sordello* (1840) had been subtitled 'A Poem in Six Books', and reviewers, complaining of his obscurity, had accused him of 'transcendentalism', meaning not a specific philosophical creed but a certain nebulous quality of thought. The poem may therefore be virtually a manifesto of a new poetic policy: a shift of emphasis from abstract thought to realistic presentation of life.

p. 302 l. 4. *draping . . . sounds.* Cf. RB, 24 Feb. 1853 (GM, p. 189): 'I am writing—a first step towards popularity for me—lyrics with more music and painting then before, so as to get people to hear and see . . .'

p. 302 l. 6. *prolusion*: a display introductory to a performance.

p. 302 l. 11. *Speak prose*: advice which Carlyle had given to RB, but had taken back in 1852 (C, pp. 293, 299).

p. 303 l. 22. *Boehme*: Jacob Boehme or Behmen (1575–1624), a peasant shoemaker of Goerlitz in Germany, and a mystic. It was probably in W. Law's translation of Boehme's *Works*, 1764 (I. xiii; I. 90) that RB read of Boehme's 'communion with the Herbs and Grass of the field', when 'in his inward Light he saw into their Essences, Use and Properties' (D, p. 274). The mistake of calling him Swedish (perhaps by association with Swedenborg, 1688–1772, who had a similar revelation, and in whom EB believed) was the result of being interrupted by 'a strange accident' during the composition of the poem (T, pp. 103–4, 352).

p. 303 l. 26. *had an eye. Daisy* means 'day's eye' (cf. Chaucer, *Legend of Good Women*, l. 184).

p. 303 l. 27. *Colloquised*: conversed.

p. 303 l. 37. *him of Halberstadt*. Johannes Teutonicus, a canon of Halberstadt in Germany, who, 'having by art Magicke performed many strange prestigious feats, almost incredible; in one day . . . was transported by the Diuell in the shape of a blacke horse, and seene and heard to say Masse the same day, in Halbersted, in Mentz, and in Cullein' (Mainz and Cologne; TH, p. 253). He is not reported to have produced flowers in winter, but other medieval magicians are (O, p. 213).

p. 303 l. 47. *You are a poem*. Cf. Milton, *Apol. for Smec-tymnuus*, introduction to sect. 1: 'He who would not be frustrate of his hope to write well hereafter in laudable things ought himself to be a true poem.'

p. 303 l. 49. *finer chords*. The strings for the highest notes of the harp, which come nearest to the player's head, are thinner than the others.

MISCONCEPTIONS, p. 304

A glimpse of disappointed love, doubtless placed here as a foil to the final poem of love fulfilled.

p. 304 st. 2. *dalmatic*: a robe worn by kings at coronation.

ONE WORD MORE, p. 305

Written Sept. 1855, after the rest of the volume had gone to press. The original manuscript, signed and dated 'London, September 22, 1855, R.B.', is in the Morgan Library, New York. The poem was composed as a dedication for MW, and as a public expression of RB's love for EB, comparable to her *Sonnets from the Portuguese* (1850), which expressed her love for him. The title in the manuscript is 'A Last Word: to E.B.B.' (D, p. 275); but the association with argument (cf. 'A Woman's Last Word') doubtless seemed inappropriate. The published title probably has a private reference to EB's discouragement of RB's love ten years before: 'Therefore we must leave this subject—& I must trust you to leave it without one word more . . .' (31 Aug. 1845, K, i. 179; W, ii. 319; cf. R. D. Altick, VP, i, 1963, 66–7).

p. 305 st. 2. *Raphael . . . sonnets.* Cf. BA, iv. 26: 'There disappeared' at the time of Guido Reni's death (1642) '. . . the famous book of a hundred sonnets from the hand of Raphael, which Guido had bought in Rome not without a suggestion . . . that the whole lot had been stolen by one of his servants' (F. Page, TLS, xxxix, 1940, 255).

lady . . . sonnets. V, ii. 237 mentions 'one of his mistresses whom Raphael loved until his death. He made a beautiful life-like portrait of her which is now in Florence . . .' She may be the original of *La Fornarina*, a picture in the Palazzo Barberini, Rome, said to represent one Margherita, a baker's daughter.

p. 306 st. 3. *Her, San Sisto . . . Louvre*: the *Sistine Madonna* (Dresden Gallery), the *Madonna di Foligno* (Vatican), the *Madonna del Granduca* (Pitti, Florence), *La Belle Jardinière*. RB had probably seen all but the first (D, p. 277).

p. 306 st. 5. *Dante . . . angel.* Cf. *Vita Nuova*, ch. 35, where Dante describes how, on the first anniversary of Beatrice's death (9 June 1290), he was thinking of her and drawing an angel, when he was interrupted by 'people to whom it is proper to pay respect' (OD, p. 228; D, p. 277). RB identifies them with the political opponents whom Dante placed in his *Inferno*, though this was probably not begun before 1300. Beatrice, the central figure of the *Vita Nuova* and of the *Divina Commedia*, is commonly identified as Beatrice Portinari (familiar name: Bice).

left-hand . . . wicked. Cf. *Inferno*, Canto xxxii. 97–104.

p. 307 st. 5. *and would seize . . . poet*: RB's invention.

p. 308 st. 9. *artist's sorrow*. RB was doubtless afraid of associating EB with one more unsuccessful publication.

p. 308 st. 10. *Heaven's . . . abatement*: the artist's inspiration is diminished by human reactions to it.

He who . . . water. Cf. Exodus 17 : 1–7, where the 'chiding' of the people before the miracle supplies a hint for their ungrateful mockery after it.

his mortal: his mortal character.

Desecrates . . . doing: i.e. his awareness of a hostile audience interferes with his art, causing anxiety (o'er-importuned brows) which prevents the free expression of his inspiration (mandate), and makes his manner (gesture) either self-conscious or careless (from feeling: 'What's the use of trying ?'). RB must be thinking of how his own work has been spoilt by hostile criticism.

Egypt's flesh-pots: perhaps the more conventional poetry to which RB's audience was accustomed. Cf. Exodus 16 : 3.

p. 308 st. 11. *Oh, the crowd . . . brilliance*. To convince the people of his divine authority, Moses asked to see God, which he was allowed to do from 'a clift of the rock' on the brow of Mount Sinai. As a result, his face was still shining when he came down with the Ten Commandments (Exodus 33 : 16–35 : 29).

Never . . . prophet. RB hesitates to speak, not as a poet, but as a human being.

p. 309 st. 12. *Jethro's daughter*: Zipporah, whom Moses married (Exodus 2 : 21, 3 : 1).

Aethiopian bondslave: the Ethiopian woman whom he also married (Numbers 12 : 1).

p. 309 st. 14. *Lines . . . time*. Unable to express his love in a totally different medium (painting, sculpture, music) he will at least use a metre (trochaic pentameter) which he has never used before and never will again.

p. 310 st. 15. *Karshook*: corrected in later editions to *Karshish*. RB had written (Apr. 1854) a poem called 'Ben Karshook's Wisdom', published 1856 (D, pp. 276, 557–8).

Let . . . person. See Introduction, p. xxiii.

p. 310 st. 16. *thrice transfigured*: i.e. seen new, waxing, and waning (O, p. 220).

Samminiato: San Miniato al Monte, a conspicuous church on a hill SE. of Florence.

p. 311 st. 17. *mythos*: the Greek myth of Endymion, a shepherd on Mount Latmos who was loved by the Moon (the subject of Keats's *Endymion*, 1818).

side unseen . . . steersman: but not (unfortunately for the fine image) of astronaut.

Zoroaster: the Persian founder of the Magian religion (perhaps sixth century B.C.), regarded by the ancients as the originator of Chaldaean astronomy and astrology.

Galileo: Galileo Galilei (1564–1642), Italian astronomer who made important discoveries with his telescope, including the libration of the moon.

Homer. The so-called *Homeric Hymns* (translated by Shelley) include one to the moon.

him even: because of his *Endymion*, especially his invocation to the moon (iii. 40–71).

Moses . . . bodied heaven: Exodus 24 : 9.

p. 312 st. 19. *out of my own self*: i.e. as a mere member of the reading public.

SELECT BIBLIOGRAPHY

1. General Introduction

   J. M. Cohen, *Robert Browning*, 1952 (198 pp.).
   P. Drew, *The Poetry of Browning. A Critical Introduction*, 1970 (471 pp.).

2. Texts

   Browning, *Poetical Works 1833–64*, ed. I. Jack, 1970.
   The Ring and the Book (Everyman edn.) ed. J. Bryson, 1962.

3. Commentary

   W. C. DeVane, *A Browning Handbook*, 1955.

4. Biography

   William Irvine and Park Honan, *The Book, the Ring, and the Poet: A New Biography of Robert Browning*, 1972.
   W. H. Griffin and H. C. Minchin, *The Life of Robert Browning*, 1938.
   B. Miller, *Robert Browning: A Portrait*, 1952.

5. Letters

   The Letters of RB, ed. T. L. Hood, 1933.
   The Letters of RB and EB 1845–6, ed. E. Kintner 1969 (2 vols.).
   Selected *Love-Letters of RB and EB*, ed. V. E. Stack, 1969 (230 pp.).

6. Criticism

   R. Langbaum, *The Poetry of Experience: The Dramatic Monologue in Modern Literary Tradition*, 1957.

Park Honan, *Browning's Characters: A Study in Poetic Technique*, 1961.

RB : A Collection of Critical Essays, ed. P. Drew, 1966.

The Browning Critics, ed. B. Litzinger and K. L. Knickerbocker (paperback edn.), 1967.

INDEX OF FIRST LINES

Ah, did you once see Shelley plain   162
All I believed is true!   70
All June I bound the rose in sheaves   299
All that I know   79
Among these latter busts we count by scores   257

Beautiful Evelyn Hope is dead   16
But do not let us quarrel any more   167

Cleon the poet, (from the sprinkled isles   269

Dear and great Angel, wouldst thou only leave   266
Dear, had the world in its caprice   95

Escape me?   110

Fee, faw, fum! bubble and squeak!   260

Grand rough old Martin Luther   281

Had I but plenty of money, money enough and to spare   19
Hist, but a word, fair and soft!   122
How well I know what I mean to do   43

I am poor brother Lippo, by your leave!   26
I dream of a red-rose tree   254
I only knew one poet in my life   111
I said—Then, dearest, since 'tis so   115
I wonder do you feel to-day   291
It was roses, roses, all the way   120

June was not over   300

Karshish, the picker-up of learning's crumbs   60

Let them fight it out, friend! things have gone too far   176
Let us begin and carry up this corpse   294
Let's contend no more, Love   24

My first thought was, he lied in every word 87
My love, this is the bitterest, that thou 54

Never any more 181
No more wine ? then we'll push back chairs and talk 128

Of the million or two, more or less 80
Oh, Galuppi, Baldassaro, this is very sad to find! 39
Oh, what a dawn of day! 9

Room after room 109

Said Abner, 'At last thou art come! Ere I tell, ere thou
    speak 231
So far as our story approaches the end 96
So, I shall see her in three days 179
Stand still, true poet that you are 283
Stop playing, poet! may a brother speak ? 302

Take the cloak from his face, and at first 178
That fawn-skin-dappled hair of hers 83
That was I, you heard last night 76
The Lord, we look to once for all 286
The morn when first it thunders in March 185
There's a palace in Florence, the world knows well 99
There they are, my fifty men and women 305
This is a spray the Bird clung to 304

Where the quiet-coloured end of evening smiles 5

Your ghost will walk, you lover of trees 252

INDEX OF TITLES

After, 178.

Andrea del Sarto (called 'The Faultless Painter'), 167.

Another Way of Love, 300.

Any Wife to any Husband, 54.

Before, 176.

Bishop Blougram's Apology, 128.

By the Fire-side, 43.

'Child Roland to the Dark Tower came,' 87.

Cleon, 269.

'De Gustibus——,' 252.

Epistle containing the Strange Medical Experiences of Karshish, the Arab Physician, 60.

Evelyn Hope, 16.

Fra Lippo Lippi, 26.

Grammarian's Funeral, A, 294.

Guardian Angel, The: a Picture at Fano, 266.

Heretic's Tragedy, The. A Middle-age Interlude, 286.

Holy Cross Day (on which the Jews were forced to attend an annual Christian sermon in Rome), 260.

How it strikes a Contemporary, 111.

In a Balcony, 196.

In a Year, 181.

In Three Days, 179.

Instans Tyrannus, 80.

Last Ride Together, The, 115.

Life in a Love, 110.

Light Woman, A, 96.

Love among the Ruins, 5.

Love in a Life, 109.

Lover's Quarrel, A, 9.

Master Hugues of Saxe-Gotha, 122.

Memorabilia, 162.

Mesmerism, 70.

Misconceptions, 304.

My Star, 79.

Old Pictures in Florence, 185.

One Way of Love, 299.

One Word More. To E. B. B., 305.

Patriot, The—An Old Story, 120.

Popularity, 283.

Pretty Woman, A, 83.

Protus, 257.

Respectability, 95.

Saul, 231.
Serenade at the Villa, A, 76.
Statue and the Bust, The, 99.

Toccata of Galuppi's, A, 39.
'Transcendentalism:' a
Poem in Twelve Books,
302.

Twins, The, 281.
Two in the Campagna, 291.

Up at a Villa—Down in the
City. (As distinguished by
an Italian person of
quality), 19.

Woman's Last Word, A, 24.
Women and Roses, 254.